W9-CLZ-340

THE CAGED QUEEN

WITHDRAWN

Also by Kristen Ciccarelli
The Last Namsara
The Sky Weaver

WITHDRAWN

THE CAGED QUEEN

Book 2 of the Iskari series

KRISTEN CICCARELLI

An Imprint of HarperCollinsPublishers

HarperTeen is an imprint of HarperCollins Publishers.

The Caged Queen

Copyright © 2018 by Kristen Ciccarelli

All rights reserved. Printed in the United States of America.

No part of this book may be used or reproduced in any manner whatsoever without

written permission except in the case of brief quotations embodied in critical articles

and reviews. For information address HarperCollins Children's Books, a division of

HarperCollins Publishers, 195 Broadway, New York, NY 10007.

www.epicreads.com

ISBN 978-0-06-256802-1

Typography by Michelle Taormina

19 20 21 22 23   PC/LSCH   10 9 8 7 6 5 4 3 2 1

❖

First paperback edition, 2019

For Ferra'ol, Baldhina, and Grace: three bright sparks of hope.

Rules for Relinquishing

Snuff out the lights.

Bolt the doors.

If you must weep, find a source of rushing water to drown out the sound.

Scorch your bread. Let your wine sour. Switch your sugar and salt.

Don't travel after sunset.

Mask your face so you won't be recognized.

Though you may be frightened, let go.

The Skyweaver's Knife

Once there lived a man named Sunder who loved everything about his life. He rose every day with the dawn and walked out into his fields. He marveled at the rain that nourished his crops and the sun that made them grow. He cherished the strength of his own two hands—hands that planted and threshed and built his house. Hands that rocked his child to sleep.

He loved his life so much that when Death came for him, Sunder hid.

Death searched Sunder's house and did not find him.

Death called out over his fields, but Sunder did not come.

So, giving up, Death took someone else instead.

When Sunder came out of his hiding place, he smiled at his own cleverness. He strode down the dirt roads toward home, whistling happily. But as he approached the door of his house, a sound made him pause.

Someone was wailing.

Sunder opened the door and found his wife kneeling on the kitchen floor, clutching their child to her breast. When Sunder fell to his knees beside her, he found his small daughter's eyes lifeless. Her body cold.

Sunder cursed his cleverness. He wept and gnashed his teeth.

After that day, Sunder no longer rose with the dawn. No longer marveled at the rain or the sun. And when he looked around the house he built, he saw only what he'd lost.

He begged Death to give his daughter back. But Death could do no such thing. Her soul was with the Skyweaver.

So Sunder set out to make it right.

He found the goddess of souls at her loom. Skyweaver's warp was fashioned from the dreams of the living, her weft from the memories of the dead. At the sound of Sunder's intrusion, her shuttle stopped. She put down her threads.

Sunder fell at her feet and he begged.

"There is a price for what you're asking," she said.

"Whatever it is, I'll pay it."

Skyweaver rose from her loom. "It's your soul that is owed. Your death that was cheated."

Sunder closed his eyes, thinking of the rain that nourished his crops and the sun that made them grow and the strength of his own two hands.

"I can give back your daughter's soul. I can restore her life." Skyweaver picked up her weaving knife. "But only you can pay the price."

On his knees, Sunder looked up at the faceless god and said, "Take it, then."

So Skyweaver lifted her knife . . .

and cut his soul loose from its mooring.

One

Her sister said it would take a year to raise an army, bring down a tyrant, and marry a king.

Roa had done it in just three months.

And now here she sat, at the carved acacia table polished to a sheen, in the smallest pavilion of her father's house. It smelled smoky-sweet from the heart-fire, and Essie perched on her shoulder, her talons clenching and unclenching, while Roa's bare feet tapped the woven rug impatiently.

Five days of negotiating peace terms was starting to get to the both of them.

The ceremonial weapons of every man and woman present were piled in the middle of the table—long and short knives, elegantly carved maces, gleaming scythes—laid out of reach as a show of trust. Only three chairs sat empty. They belonged to representatives from the House of Sky, and they'd been empty all week—a fact no one was talking about. Least of all Roa.

She stared at the empty chair on the left, imagining the

young man who normally sat there. Strong shoulders. Wheat-gold eyes. Dark-brown hair pulled back from his handsome face.

Theo, heir to the House of Sky.

Roa's former betrothed.

He's always been stubborn. Essie's thoughts flooded Roa's mind as her claws dug into Roa's skin. *But never* this *stubborn.*

Roa traced the delicate wing bone of the white hawk on her shoulder. The bond they shared—something Essie called *the hum*—glowed bright and warm between them.

I betrayed him, thought Roa. *I won't be surprised if he never speaks to me again.*

Their silent conversation was suddenly interrupted by the sound of someone snoring.

The new queen and her hawk looked sharply away from Theo's chair to the young man seated beside her. The warm afternoon sunlight pooled in through the windows, alighting on his unruly brown curls. His elbow was propped on the table, his cheek rested on his fist, and those long black lashes fluttered softly against his cheeks.

This was the dragon king. Asleep in an important treaty meeting.

This . . . *waste* . . . was the person for whom Roa had given up everything.

She bristled at the sound of his snores and glanced up to the dozen men and women gathered around the table, all of them representatives of Great Houses in the scrublands.

She prayed they didn't notice the snoring.

It was a useless prayer. Of course they noticed. Dax had been falling asleep in treaty meetings all week, revealing the truth to everyone: he didn't care that his father's sanctions hadn't been lifted or that Roa's people were still going hungry.

These were not the kinds of things Dax cared about.

Which was why Roa was here. She'd insisted on traveling across the sand sea and drawing up an official treaty document herself. With a signed treaty, Dax couldn't continue to break his promises. Not without consequences.

It was why they were all here, in Roa's childhood home, with their heads bowed over a scroll.

Roa looked past the sleeping king, past the pile of weapons, to find her father studying her. A man of almost fifty, his curly black hair was speckled with gray now, and he looked thinner and more tired than she remembered. Was that possible? In just the two months she'd been gone? He wore a cotton tunic, split at the throat, with the pattern of Song fading around the collar. It matched Roa's own garment.

A proper dragon queen would have worn a brightly colored kaftan, finely stitched slippers, and a gold circlet on her head. But Roa was a scrublander first and foremost. She wore an undyed linen dress sewn by her mother and a necklace of pale blue beryl beads.

Her father's eyes held Roa's, then glanced to the young man snoring beside her. The look on his face was unmistakable.

He pitied her.

Roa's stomach tightened like a fist.

She would *not* be pitied. Certainly not by her own father.

Beneath the table Roa elbowed her new husband hard in the ribs. Surprised by the movement, Essie flexed her wings to stay balanced on her shoulder. Dax jolted awake, eyes widening as he let out a soft *oof!* But instead of sitting up and paying attention, instead of showing any sign of remorse, he yawned loudly, then stretched—drawing full attention to the fact that he'd fallen asleep.

As if he wanted everyone to know how little he cared.

More men and women around the table glanced at Roa. When she looked from one face to the next, each and every one of them averted their gaze. As if humiliated on Roa's behalf.

These were the same people who'd put their trust in her when she asked for an army to help Dax dethrone his father. And here they were, watching her now with shame in their eyes.

Daughter of Song, she could hear them all thinking, *what have you done?*

Their stares scorched her. Roa's fists clenched in her linen dress. She desperately wanted this meeting to be over. But the treaty scroll was still collecting signatures.

Roa looked to Dax, who was yawning again.

"Do we bore you, my king?" She didn't even try to keep the bitterness out of her voice.

"Not at all," he drawled, his attention snagging on something across the table. "I didn't sleep much last night."

Essie shifted restlessly from claw to claw as Roa looked where Dax did: to the young woman who'd just entered the pavilion. It was Roa's cousin, Sara, a tray balanced on her hip.

Her brown curls were tucked in a bun and held in place with an ivory comb. On her wrists were three bracelets made of shiny white nerita shells.

As Sara collected cups of cold tea from the table, she smiled brightly beneath the king's gaze.

Roa reluctantly remembered the night previous. After a round of drinking games with her brother and cousins, Dax had openly flirted with the women of her household, Sara among them. It was something she'd had to get used to: Dax's flirting.

Roa was pretty sure he'd flirt with a dragon if he were drunk enough.

She looked away from the king and her cousin. She didn't want to see the smiles passing between them. Didn't want to know how far the game had gone.

But there were only two other places to look: the embarrassed faces of the house representatives or that empty chair.

It was an unbearable choice.

In the end, Roa chose the consequence of her broken promise. She stared at Theo's chair as if he were in it, staring back at her.

Sometimes she let herself wonder what her life would be like if she'd kept her promise to him. There would certainly be no king in her father's house flirting with Roa's cousins and humiliating her in front of the people she loved most.

And there would be no one keeping the scrublands safe. Essie's voice rang through her mind. Those talons squeezed Roa's shoulder affectionately. *Dax's father would have bled us dry.*

Essie was right, of course.

You did what you needed to do, Essie told her, brushing the top of her feathered head against Roa's cheek. *They all know that.*

Truly, Roa had done it for every scrublander, Theo included. She would not allow another Firgaardian king to take whatever he wanted from them. He'd already taken enough.

Roa looked to Dax as she stroked Essie's soft feathers. When the scroll came to the king, he signed it, then took a pinch of sand from the bowl in front of them and sprinkled it across the wet ink. After it dried, he blew off the sand, rolled up the scroll, and gave it to Roa.

The relief in the room was palpable. The king was now bound to his promises. They would finally be free of Firgaard's tyranny.

Voices rose, talking and laughing easily now that it was done.

When a jug of wine was brought in, Roa frowned. It had been years since her father served wine to his guests. Few people in the scrublands could afford it anymore. She wondered what her family would give up this month in order to compensate for the indulgence.

Oblivious, Dax poured the wine into two red clay cups, then looped his arm lazily around the back of Roa's chair. Startled at his closeness, Essie flew off Roa's shoulder.

Roa, who was more used to the weight of her sister's imprisoned form than the absence of it—whose shoulders bore eight years of tiny scars from Essie's claws—went immediately cold at the loss of her.

Dax bent toward Roa, holding out a full cup.

"To peace," he said softly, the peppermint smell of him enveloping her.

Roa didn't dare look at him. She knew the kinds of spells those warm brown eyes cast. The kinds of things that curve of a mouth promised. She'd seen enough girls fall for Dax's charms to know she needed to protect herself against them.

Staring at his throat instead, she watched the steady beat of his pulse. Taking the cup from him, she said, "To kings who keep their promises."

Her gaze flickered to his. For the briefest of heartbeats, she thought she saw amusement in his eyes. But then it was gone, hidden behind a smooth smile.

She hated that smile. Hated the effect it had on her.

Roa set down the cup and quickly rose.

"If we're finished," she said, catching her father's gaze as she reached across the table toward the pile of earned weapons, "then you must excuse me. There's somewhere I need to be."

Taking her scythe from the top of the pile, Roa didn't wait for her father's answer. Just turned away from the table, left through the open door, and didn't look back.

Essie followed her out.

Roa rode hard across the border of Song. Poppy's hooves pummeled the hot, cracked earth, putting distance between her and her father's house. Between her and the boy-king.

It was as if the wide-open world Roa once knew—as open as the sunset sky above—had become a prison. She might have walked willingly into it, but her bonds still chafed.

Halfway to her destination, Roa felt a familiar hum flare

up inside her. Instinctively, she looked to find a white hawk soaring above.

Essie.

Even with so much distance between them, Roa could sense her sister's uneasiness.

Where are you going? her sister called. *You'll miss the Gleaning.*

Poppy slowed to a trot as Roa leaned back in the saddle. She'd forgotten that tonight was the Gleaning.

Once a week, the House of Song made dinner for those who were hardest hit by Firgaard's sanctions. On Gleaning nights, it was normal for the house to be full to the brim. The very poorest would eat—and take home anything extra that could be spared.

You should be there, said Essie, still trying to catch up. *You give them hope, Roa.*

But going back to the House of Song meant facing Dax. It meant watching him drink her father's wine while he flirted with every girl in her home.

Roa gritted her teeth.

I sat obediently next to him for days now. Her thoughts burned into her twin's mind. *If I have to stand by his side one more moment, I'll . . .* Her grip tightened on the reins. *I'll take it all back.*

She *could* take it back. The marriage was unconsummated. Which meant it could still be annulled.

And who will protect us if you do? came Essie's reply.

That was just it. This was the decision she'd made. It was up to Roa to keep her people safe.

She'd thought it would be easier, trading in her freedom for the protection of the scrublands. She hadn't realized it would cost her so much more than freedom.

Her sister's voice had gone soft and quiet in her mind: *You should be more careful. People are starting to notice your absences.*

Roa had been absent every night since they'd arrived home six days ago.

Let them notice, she thought, urging Poppy into a gallop.

In the distance, the red-brown earth shifted into a smudge of green forest. Roa headed straight for the hidden path through the acacias. They were entering the shadow precinct, where the fifth Great House had once stood proud . . . and then fallen into ruin.

A sharp jab of her sister's frustration shot through her. Roa ignored it.

Roa. Essie's voice flickered into her mind as she struggled to keep up. Her elegant white wings fought with a wind that kept battering her back. *You can't just run away!*

I'm queen, she thought. *I can do as I wish.*

You're not acting like a queen. Essie's thoughts were getting fainter. *You're acting like a . . . scared . . . selfish . . . child.*

That stung.

In answer, Roa sent a stab of cold at her sister's hawk form. Essie sent her version of the same feeling back—only sharper.

Just before Poppy halted and stepped into the trees, the white hawk screeched. Roa felt a painful tug and stopped them both, frowning hard. She looked over her shoulder to see Essie—a speck of white in a carnelian sky—still battling the wind, trying to get to her.

A second, sharper tug came. Roa sucked in a pained breath. She squeezed Poppy's reins in her fists and sent her thoughts into her sister's mind: *If you're trying to hurt me, it's working.*

Essie didn't respond.

Roa had thought Essie would understand. Essie knew better than anyone what it was like to be trapped. But just like Roa's friend, Lirabel, Essie seemed to side with Dax more and more these days. As if his ridiculous charms were working on them, too.

A little angrily, Roa turned away from her sister. She didn't wait for Essie to catch up, just retreated into the trees without her.

Essie would find her. She always did. The bond hummed between them, bright and strong, keeping them linked. Roa could always sense her sister—could feel the shape of her soul. Even if a desert lay between them.

Jacarandas bloomed here. Their purple flowers carpeted the ground, more beautiful than any palace rug. Roa breathed in the sweet smell of them as Poppy rode up to the entrance of the House of Shade.

Corrupted, people called this place. A man had died here, a long time ago now, and his loved ones hadn't performed the proper rites. They hadn't broken the bonds between the living and the dead. So, on the Relinquishing—the longest night of the year—the man's soul became corrupted and he slaughtered his entire household.

Or so the story went.

Corrupted spirits were dangerous things. It was why the rules for relinquishing needed to be upheld.

But even if the story was true, the man's spirit had long since moved on.

After dismounting and tying Poppy to a branch outside, Roa stepped through the crumbled entrance of the ruined house. As she walked through the roofless halls, Roa thought of that empty chair. It was an obvious insult. But Theo had been insulted first. Sky was the only Great House who voted *against* Roa helping Dax in the revolt. And in the scrublands, a unanimous vote was needed before anyone could march an army across the sand sea. Roa had broken scrublander law to do what she'd done.

And then she'd broken Theo's heart.

Roa checked every room in the ruined house. All were empty. She checked them again.

He didn't come, she thought, her heart sinking.

Theo hadn't wanted her to help Dax. He told her that if she left, she wouldn't come back.

You were wrong, she thought. *I did come back.*

She was here now, wasn't she? She'd been here in this ruin— their usual meeting place—waiting for him for five nights straight.

And for five nights straight, he didn't come. Because Roa married Dax. Because Roa was queen now.

It was too late for her and Theo.

As the wind rattled the canopy above, she climbed up onto the windowsill of a half-crumbled wall. Leaning back against the cool and dusty stone, she pressed her face into her hands.

You're queen now, she told herself. *Queens don't cry.*

It was something Essie would say. If Essie were here.

As she waited for her sister to arrive, Roa thought of the shame in her father's eyes. In all their eyes.

Maybe it was better this way. She wasn't sure she could bear that same look on Theo's face.

When a hundred-hundred heartbeats passed and Essie still hadn't shown herself, Roa looked up to the canopy. To the patch of darkening sky beyond it.

Instinctively, her gaze found Essie's two favorite stars. *Twin stars*, Essie liked to call them. The stories Essie most loved were ones about the Skyweaver, a goddess who spun souls into stars and wove them into the sky.

Roa thought of Skyweaver spinning Essie's soul into a star, then putting it up there, all alone, without Roa.

A cold feeling knotted her insides.

What was taking her sister so long?

Roa reached for that normally bright hum. Even before Essie's accident, the hum had always been there, warm and glowing inside them both.

This time when Roa reached for it, she found it dim and weak. Like a too-quiet pulse.

Essie?

No answer came.

Roa pushed herself down from the sill and walked back through the empty, ruined rooms.

"Essie?" she called, her voice echoing. "Where are you?"

Silence answered her.

Roa's pace quickened, thinking of the way her sister's thoughts had flickered strangely. At how distant she'd felt earlier.

Essie, if this is a joke, it isn't funny.

At the entrance, Roa untied Poppy and quickly mounted, nudging her back toward the tree line. When they got there, the sun was long gone and the sky was blue-black. She couldn't see any sign of a white bird in its depths.

Roa cupped her hands and called her sister's name.

"Essie!"

Her voice echoed and died. The wind rustled the leaves at her back.

It was something the two sisters never spoke about, as if speaking it would make it come true: an uncrossed soul couldn't exist forever in the world of the living. Eventually, the death call of the Relinquishing became too strong.

Essie had been resisting her death call for eight years now.

Looking up to the stars, Roa whispered, "Essie, where are you?"

A Tale of Two Sisters

Once there were two sisters, born on the longest night of the year.

This was not a night for celebrating new life; it was a night for letting go of the dead. That's why it was called the Relinquishing.

The midwives tried to bring the sisters early. When that failed, they tried to bring them late.

But the girls came at midnight, defiant.

Most newborns wail with their first taste of life. Most come into the world afraid, needing the comfort of their mothers.

The two sisters didn't come wailing. They came quietly, holding on to each other. As if they needed no one's comfort but the other's. As if, as long as they were together, there was nothing to be afraid of.

That wasn't the strange thing.

The strange thing came later.

It was their mother, Desta, who noticed it: how when one girl cried, the other comforted her. And when they both cried, the roses in the garden died. It was Desta who realized that when one girl threw a fit, the other calmed her. But when they threw a fit together, the windows cracked and the mirrors shattered.

As if, when they were of one mind, the world shifted and bent to their will.

When Desta asked the two sisters who broke the mirror, one or the other would tell her: "It wasn't us, Mama. It was the hum."

"The hum?" she'd ask. "What is that?"

The two girls stared at their mother.

"The warm, bright thing that links you like a string. Don't you and Papa have one?"

No. She and their father did not. But when Desta told her husband, he shrugged it off as the wild imaginations of children who spent too much time together. After all, the two sisters played together, studied together, slept together . . . there was hardly a moment when they were apart.

"It would be good for them to have other friends," he told his wife.

Desta agreed. She wrote her oldest friend, Amina, whose son, Dax, was falling further behind in his studies every year. His tutors had given up, declaring him illiterate and unteachable, and Amina was sick with worry. Desta told her friend to send him to the House of Song for the summer.

Perhaps that will cure my daughters of this hum, thought Desta, who was tired of her roses dying.

Perhaps, if they had other friends, she wouldn't need to keep buying new mirrors.

Two

No one understood the bond shared by Roa and Essie. Before the accident, people thought their connection strange—or worse, to be feared. For Roa, though, it was something that had always simply been. She didn't know how to be without it.

Essie was the one who named it the hum, because that's what it felt like: something deep and bright, almost like a song, vibrating inside them.

After the accident, the hum changed. They were no longer able to keep out each other's thoughts and feelings and—most especially—*pain*.

They were one.

For nearly eight years now, Essie had been in Roa's head, and Roa had been in Essie's.

Which was why her sister's silence felt so wrong.

Maybe she went back to Song, thought Roa as Poppy's ragged breathing filled the silence of the night.

Roa fixed her gaze on the jagged massifs in the distance,

rising out of the earth, each one a darker shade of blue than the last. Above them, a half-moon rose, flooding the plains with silvery light and making the sweat gleam on Poppy's coat.

Every now and again, shadows passed overhead.

Dragons, Roa knew.

Once, dragons had been plentiful here. Not so long ago, Dax's people rode the fierce creatures through the skies. But under his grandmother's reign, draksors and dragons turned on each other. Former allies became bitter enemies. Until Asha, Dax's sister, put an end to a corrupt regime.

The dragons had been returning ever since.

It was past midnight when they trotted into the familiar stables of Song. The soft *whuff*ing of horse sighs and the flick of tails greeted them. The stalls had been cleaned at the end of the day and smelled of dried mud and fresh hay.

Roa quickly untacked Poppy, then walked the lane up to the house. Except for the heart-fire in the central pavilion—which burned through the night—the lights of the House of Song were out.

"Essie?" she called, reaching again for that normally bright hum.

The dogs—Nola and Nin—were the only things that answered her, barking as she approached. When they realized who she was, they bounded up to her, trying to lick her to death. Roa slipped past them, through the rows of ropy warka trees, and stepped into the house.

All was dark inside. Roa followed the dusty stone walls with her hands. Stone. So different from the whitewashed plaster of the palace. Roa preferred the simplicity of her home's dirt floors and roughhewn windows to the palace's elaborately cut and mosaicked tiles. She preferred the smell of smoke and acacia to the smell of mint and lime.

It was a different world here. It was *her* world. The one she'd be leaving behind tomorrow—for the second and final time.

Again, she called for her sister.

Again, she received no answer.

Essie didn't just go off on her own without telling Roa. They were an inseparable pair. And tomorrow morning Roa would ride back across the desert with the husband she had no love for, to a city that wasn't her home. She couldn't go alone. Roa needed her sister by her side.

At the entry to her and Dax's room, she tried not to panic.

She's just angry at me for running away, she thought, trying to calm herself. Trying to convince herself that Essie would be nestled in her usual spot on Roa's pillow come morning.

Stepping inside her room, Roa pushed down her unease and closed the door behind her. The moonlight spilled in through the windows and across the bed.

A bed that lay empty.

It didn't surprise her. Roa avoided Dax's bed like a disease, and in return, Dax sought out the beds of other women.

Her family didn't know this. They didn't know the rumors whispered up and down the palace halls at Firgaard: that her husband took a different girl to bed every night.

Normally Roa wouldn't care how many beds he slept in as long as Dax stayed far away from hers. It made being married to him easier.

But tonight? Maybe it was the too-sharp absence of her sister, or maybe it was the five days of humiliation at his hands . . . the empty bed felt like an insult.

This was her *home*. Almost every girl beneath this roof was related to her.

It made Roa want to throw something—but that would wake her family, who would come asking what the matter was. So instead she moved to the wooden chest at the foot of her bed and lifted the ivory-inlaid lid—a gift from her mother.

Sliding off her linen dress, she quickly pulled a nightgown over her head. After checking that the knife she kept sheathed at her calf was still secure—*Essie's* knife, the one Roa promised to hold on to—she started doing up buttons.

Which was when she heard the voices in the hall.

The whispers were muffled and soft, but Roa could tell one voice belonged to a young man and the other a young woman. They giggled as if drunk, then hushed each other, and though Roa couldn't tell *who* the voices belonged to, she had her guesses.

They moved closer to her door.

Roa's hands fisted. Part of her *wanted* him to open that door. Wanted a reason to unsheathe her sister's knife and wait for him. But a wearier, unhappier part of her whispered, *Run.*

And that's what she did.

Pushing the window open, Roa climbed to the sill just as the voices reached her room. Before she could find out who Dax was with, Roa dropped into the garden. When the door swung open, she was already headed for Lirabel's room.

She'd been sharing her friend's bed all week. What was one more night?

It was a habit she'd fallen into after Essie's accident—climbing into Lirabel's bed. Knowing that someone was lying next to her, that there was another heart beating beside hers . . . it helped soothe Roa.

Roa knew there would be a night when Dax came to collect what she owed him. It could hardly be prevented. A king needed an heir, and Roa was his queen. It was her duty to provide him with one.

But it would not be tonight.

A People Divided

When the First Namsara brought the sacred flame out of the desert and founded Firgaard, no king ruled it. No walls caged them in. Instead, the Old One's people governed themselves. Each voice was heard and decisions were made all together. Those who owned much shared with those who owned nothing. And the sick and the weak were esteemed as much as the healthy and strong.

The Old One's people believed they belonged to one another, and therefore took care of each other.

But as the years wore on and their numbers grew, disagreements turned into division. They forgot how to see each other as equals, no matter the differences. Forgot that those who owned nothing were just as important as those who owned much. Forgot that everyone's voice mattered.

The Old One's people forgot how to take care of each other.

They wanted a king who could make laws to govern them. They wanted an army to protect them. They wanted a wall to keep others out.

This was not the Old One's way.

His people didn't care . . . except a devout few.

Decisions, these few thought, should be made the way a tree grows—from the earth up and from many roots. They didn't believe in building walls or hiring men with swords to keep their enemies out—because they did not believe in enemies.

For their beliefs, they were persecuted and derided as zealots. So, with heavy hearts, they decided to leave Firgaard.

It was not so easy.

They were under the dominion of a king now. A king who was not interested in letting them go. A king who ruled Firgaard and the land surrounding it, from the mountains, across the desert, to the sea.

"But," said the king, "I will be generous with you."

He would give them the scrublands beyond the desert and he would let them go peacefully—on one condition. For as long as they lived beyond Firgaard's walls, they would pay him a tax in exchange for his generosity: one tenth of their yearly harvests.

With no other choice, they agreed.

They crossed the sand sea together and when they came to the scrublands, they built five Great Houses, swearing to keep the old ways intact. To be hospitable and build no walls. To give according to the needs of others. To always make decisions as a whole, so that no one could be trampled upon.

And, most of all, to never forget they belonged to each other.

When people from far-off lands fled because of war or famine or flooding, when Firgaard shut its gates, the five Great Houses of the scrublands let the foreigners in. They gave them land to build new homes on and shared whatever they had. So the foreigners stayed, living and marrying among them. Defending them against the very ones they'd fled from and bringing with them new stories and gods: the Skyweaver, guardian of all souls, and her gift of the Relinquishing. These newcomers taught them the art of a well-crafted blade. They convinced them that sometimes, in times of great danger, you did need to pick up a sword to protect your kin.

As the years turned to centuries, the scrublanders looked less and less like the ones they'd left behind in Firgaard. And it is when you cannot see yourself in another that you turn them into an enemy.

In this one way, the scrublanders did not protect the old ways—by forgetting they did not believe in enemies.

Three

"What do you mean, you didn't pack my tent?"

Roa rounded on her brother, who was currently unbuckling his horse's bridle and sliding it over her head.

After their day's travel, the desert sun pulsed low in the sky and waves of heat rolled up from the golden sand. They'd stopped early due to a herd of dragons spotted nearby. Most people saw the return of the dragons as a sign the kingdom was healing. But they were still dangerous predators best avoided.

"There wasn't room," said Jas after tying his horse up with the others. A faded maroon sandskarf was wrapped loosely around her brother's head and shoulders, protecting him from the sun, and his two earned knives were sheathed at his hips, their blades engraved with the pattern of Song.

"So you left my tent behind?"

Turning to her, he lifted his hands, palms up. "I'm sorry. I had to."

"Where am I supposed to sleep?"

Jas looked away, out over the caravan. Roa followed his gaze.

She could see Dax from here, setting up his tent, shirtless and alone. The sweat gleamed across his arched back as he hammered pegs into the earth. Pegs that weren't strong enough to keep a tent tethered if a storm hit.

Roa had fought with Dax about it on the way *to* the scrublands, and he'd promised to buy new ones while staying at the House of Song.

Another broken promise, Roa thought now. He hadn't bought new tents just like he hadn't lifted the sanctions on her people or formed a more representative council.

He'd promised her both things before the revolt.

But that's what the treaty is for, she thought, trying to calm herself, *to make him keep his oaths.* When they returned, he would be bound by more than honor to make good on his promises. She would see to it that he did.

"You can sleep in Dax's tent," said Jas.

Roa's gaze snapped to her brother.

This felt like subterfuge. Like betrayal. Jas knew how Roa felt about sleeping in Dax's tent. Why would he do this?

"I don't understand what the problem is." Jas's voice was edged in frustration. Sweat beaded along his hairline dampening his black curls. "Isn't he your husband? Shouldn't you be sleeping in his tent?" And then, lowering his voice, he said, "People are beginning to talk."

She shot her brother a scathing look.

Jas ignored it and forged ahead. "You missed the Gleaning last night. Where were you?"

"It's none of your business where I was." It was hot beneath her sandskarf. Roa wiped the sweat from her forehead with her wrist.

"You're married to the king. You can't just run off to meet Theo whenever you feel like it."

Roa glanced around them, but they were far behind the others here. No one had heard him.

"If you knew where I was," she growled, "why did you ask?"

Jas didn't answer. Just fixed his gaze straight ahead, where Dax had stopped hammering tent pegs and rose as Lirabel approached him. The two of them walked away from the caravan, then stood close together, deep in conversation.

"And anyway, it's not what you think," Roa admitted. "I may have gone to meet Theo, but he didn't come to meet me."

Jas jerked his gaze from Lirabel to Roa.

"I haven't seen him in months. He won't even answer my letters."

"Well, I can't say I blame him. You broke his heart."

Roa looked away, feeling like a scolded child.

Again, Jas's gaze wandered to the girl speaking with the king. Roa looked back to Lirabel too. Her friend's bed had been empty when Roa crawled into it after midnight, and it was still empty when she'd woken at sunrise.

Roa was trying not to think about why that might be.

Now Lirabel's hair was tied up in her sky-blue sandskarf, but a few black curls peeked out, and there were dark half-moons under her eyes. She seemed . . . upset about something. More than once, Dax reached to touch her. As if to comfort her.

Roa kept quiet, watching her brother watch Lirabel. Thinking back over the past week, she realized she hadn't once seen Jas and Lirabel in the same room together. In fact, just a few days ago at dinner, when Jas entered the room, Lirabel had abruptly left it. Roa wouldn't have thought anything of it if Lirabel hadn't done the very same thing the next morning at breakfast.

It was odd, the way they were suddenly avoiding each other. For all their lives, Jas could always be found close to Lirabel. He followed her around like a pup, and Lirabel—who'd spent years as a ward in their home and therefore felt indebted to their father—believed she had no choice but to let Jas hover.

Now, ever since the coronation, when Dax had elevated Lirabel's status from ward to royal emissary, it was Dax who Lirabel spent all her time with. Sitting next to him at meetings. Transcribing his letters. Coming whenever he called, going wherever he told her to. And it wasn't just Jas who Lirabel kept her distance from. Recently, a gulf had opened up between her and Roa too. One that seemed to get wider and wider all the time. Roa had no idea where it came from. Nor did she know how to bridge it. Because Lirabel was always with the king, or away in the scrublands. As if she were avoiding Roa.

"Theo needs time." Jas's voice brought Roa out of her thoughts and back to the present. "Maybe you should give him that. Leave him be."

Roa stopped. "Give him up, you mean."

Jas reached his arm around her shoulders, pulling her into a hug. Despite being a year younger than Roa, her little brother towered over her. "I know it isn't easy. I just don't want you getting hurt."

Roa breathed in the smell on his clothes—smoky-sweet, like the heart-fire. "Theo would never hurt me," she said.

Jas sighed again, out of exasperation this time. "I'm talking about Firgaard. They consider you an outlander queen. They already don't trust you, Roa." He squeezed her shoulder. "Your nightly absences don't go unnoticed." It was the same thing Essie told her. "If you give the court in the capital a concrete reason to believe you're disloyal . . ."

"Like the *king* is disloyal?" Roa's temper flared. "Everyone seems to be fine with Dax's *nightly absences*, but I slip away and my own brother accuses me of treason?"

"I'm not . . ." Jas's arm fell away from her shoulders. "I'm not accusing you of anything. I'm just trying to keep you safe."

Roa prickled at that. "I have never in my life needed you to keep me safe."

"Roa . . ."

She was done talking about this. Abruptly, she changed the subject. "Are you coming the whole way with us?"

Jas sighed, letting her change it, and nodded. "I promised Papa I'd see you safely to Firgaard."

"Will you stay in the capital for a while?"

"Just until the Relinquishing."

The Relinquishing was a scrublander festival celebrated on the longest night of the year, one that was only two weeks away. It was the one day of the year Roa looked forward to most—the day Essie resumed her true form.

Her conversation with Jas fell away at the thought of her sister. Roa touched her vacant shoulder, where Essie normally perched. She felt unbalanced without the weight of her there. Felt like half of her was missing.

Where are you? she thought, glancing to the empty sky.

Her sister had not been sleeping on her pillow when Roa woke that morning. Roa called for her, but she didn't answer.

Her stomach hurt at the thought of it. Essie had never been gone this long before.

She tried to force the unease down. *Wherever she is, she'll find me.*

Essie always found her.

But as Roa and Jas walked into camp, somewhere deep inside her, she felt the hum flicker. Like a candle flame struggling to stay alight.

On their way to the scrublands, Roa had been appalled at these tents. Now she didn't care that they weren't the work of practical, experienced tentmakers. Didn't care that their brightly colored panels and decorative stitching, while beautiful, were not made for the harsh conditions of the sand sea. Didn't care that it was a typical Firgaardian show of wealth and artistry, with no knowledge of the scrublands or how to survive.

Right now, the only thing she cared about was her sister's absence.

Essie had been gone for a night and day now, and Roa was starting to unravel without her.

When the sun disappeared and the moon rose silver over the

gleaming sand, the cold rose with it. This far out, the desert was like a double-edged blade. With the day came scorching heat; with the night, lethal cold. If you weren't adequately prepared, either could kill you. Which was why, once the night descended, everyone made for their tents.

Roa stayed out longer than most, shivering, as she scanned the dark skies for her sister. When the cold became unbearable and she could no longer prolong the inevitable, Roa sought out Dax's tent.

Pushing back the canvas flap, she stepped inside, sliding her feet out of her goatskin shoes.

The dragon king rustled in the bedroll, then sat up. The tent lantern lit up his face. His curls stuck out in every direction and a shadow crept across his jaw and chin, hinting that he'd gone a day without a shave. It made him look older. And a little unpredictable.

"Roa? What are you—?"

"Jas didn't pack my tent," she said quickly.

Dax studied her in the lantern light. "So you thought you'd bed down with me."

His voice was barbed. As if Roa's presence here was an intrusion. An inconvenience.

Maybe it is, she thought. *Maybe he's waiting for someone else.*

But Roa had nowhere else to go. So, lifting her chin, she said, "I'm your wife, am I not?"

Catching sight of his wool mantle folded neatly in a pile, Roa reached for it, pulling it over her head. The smell of peppermint flooded her senses.

Ever since they were children, Dax had chewed peppermint leaves when he was worried. It cleared his mind and helped him think.

After stretching out beside the bedroll, she blew out the flame in the lantern.

Darkness descended.

Dax was still sitting. She could see the shape of him looming over her.

"There's room in here for two, Roa."

Not a chance. The desert could freeze over and she *still* wouldn't climb into that bedroll with him.

"It's going to get a lot colder," he told her.

Roa turned away from him.

"Suit yourself," he said, lying back down.

Dax was right, though. Roa had grown up with this desert. She knew, far better than he, just how cold it became. Far too cold to sleep. Soon she was shivering. Then hugging her knees to her chest. When her teeth started chattering, Roa sat up, listening carefully to Dax's breathing. She waited until it was deep and even—until she was sure he was asleep. Then, very carefully, she crawled in beside him.

Dax stirred. Half-asleep, he murmured "My star, your feet are ice."

My star? It sounded like a term of endearment.

The thought made Roa freeze. *Oh no.*

He thought she was someone else. One of the other girls he let into his bed.

Panicking, Roa pushed at the stitching of the wool lining

in an attempt to put space between them. But there was no space. There was just Dax and the heat radiating off him like a crackling fire.

His arm slid around her waist, drawing her into him. "Take my warmth."

Roa went rigid, expecting him to want something in return. Waiting for him to demand the thing she owed him, the thing other women happily gave him.

But he didn't.

A hundred heartbeats passed. Deciding it was safe, Roa slowly pressed her cold feet against his warm ones. He flinched but didn't retreat. Instead, he took each of her feet between his, rubbing them one after another, trying to warm them.

Roa tried not to think about how gently his breath caressed her neck. Tried not to think about the way their bodies fit.

Most of all, she tried not to think about how, in the days leading up to the revolt, she'd glimpsed a different Dax. A king she might come to respect, even if she couldn't love him. But that king had vanished the moment a crown settled on his head, leaving Roa alone.

Or perhaps she'd only imagined that king—decisive, thoughtful, brave—in order to convince herself she could, in fact, do everything she had done: marry the enemy and leave behind everything she'd ever loved.

Either way, just for tonight, she let herself pretend it was *that* Dax at her back—the kingly one.

Just for tonight, Roa let herself fall asleep in his arms.

The White Harvest

One fateful summer, the fields of the scrublands turned white.

In the beginning, it was just one field belonging to one man. When picked, the wheat kernels crumbled into silvery-pale dust. The man's neighbors shook their heads and scratched their beards. No one had ever seen such a blight. They gave him portions from their own harvests, secretly glad their own crops hadn't been struck.

"Next year will be a better year," said the tax collectors from Firgaard, who took a portion of the wheat his neighbors gave him.

But the following year, the blight spread.

This time, it struck all the wheat fields. It was an eerie sight, all that white where there should have been gold. Like a sea of snow. Farmers who hadn't planted wheat helped those who had by giving away portions of their own harvests, secretly glad their barley and flax hadn't been hit.

"It can't stay forever," said the tax collectors as they rode off with scrublander tithes. "By next year, the blight will be over."

The following summer, it raced from field to field, all across the scrublands, indiscriminately diminishing their food source by half. Farmers tried to salvage what they could. But the small portion of grain untouched by the blight was taken by the king.

By the fourth year, most scrublanders couldn't feed themselves, never mind their families. They begged Firgaard for help, asking them to forgive their tithes.

Firgaard refused.

So the next time a tax collector came, it was his corpse that returned to the capital. Furious, the king sent his commandant and a legion of soldats to the five Great Houses, intending to punish their insubordination.

The scrublanders chased the king's army out.

"They give me no choice," he said in his official declaration.

The sanctions came down like an executioner's sword.

No one was to send the scrublands aid. No one was to give them loans. And no one was to engage with them in any form of trade—from the heart of the capital to the port city of Darmoor.

And all the while, the white harvest spread. Their stores and granaries depleted and lay empty. Before livestock could starve to death, they were slaughtered. Their meat dried and shared with those who had the least access to food. For three more years, Firgaard turned its back while scrublanders starved. Mothers, unable to feed their children, were forced to give them up. Fathers left to find work across the desert or the sea, sending what they could back home to their families.

Those who stayed behind refused to give in. They gleaned what they could of their harvests, eating the small portions of grain that weren't diseased. They fished and hunted. They took in their neighbors' children and gave what little food they had to those who needed it most.

They survived.

And their anger grew.

Four

Roa woke to a loud, persistent sound.

Clang! Clang! Clang!

She sat up in Dax's bedroll, alone. The sun was bright against the canvas tent, giving it a honey-colored glow, and the temperature was rising.

That sound—like someone banging two pots together—quickened.

Clang! Clang! Clang!

Odd, thought Roa, raising her hands to her ears. *They must be—*

A blood-chilling scream stopped her thoughts.

Scrambling out of the bedroll, Roa dashed out of the tent in her bare feet.

She saw them immediately: two dragons. One the color of brown scrubland rock, the other a pale gold the color of wheat. Each of them was twice the size of a horse, horns twisted for goring, wings spread wide as they approached the horses. Horses that were rearing and screaming, their eyes rolling in panic.

They couldn't run. Their ropes kept them tied.

On the other side of the horses stood the source of the clanging. Just outside the cook's tent, next to an open fire, stood her brother Jas. One hand held an iron pot, the other held an iron spoon. He beat that pot with all his strength, his attention fixed on the predators, trying to scare them off.

He knew as well as Roa just how badly they needed those horses.

The sound was near deafening. The dragons shook their heads, but it didn't stop them. They prowled closer. Within heartbeats, they would be within range, their knifelike talons ripping into horse flanks.

Roa couldn't let that happen.

Jas's attention wavered, catching sight of his sister. Seeing what she was about to do.

"Roa, no!"

But Roa was already drawing her sister's knife and running for the horses.

She grabbed hold of the rope and brought the knife down hard, sawing back and forth, praying to the Skyweaver—who was good at severing things—to help her.

The rope was too thick. It burned her hand and fought against her blade. And all the while, the dragons drew nearer.

Snap!

The rope broke. The horses bolted, running straight past Jas and between the tents, leaving Roa alone and unprotected.

She looked up. The dragons stood over her now, hissing and clicking, their forked tails thrashing. They spread their wings, big as sails, and Roa gaped at the translucent membranes where the sunlight glowed through.

"Roa!"

Something whistled past her head. Roa smelled the burning before she saw the streak of fire.

A flaming arrow soared toward the dragons, missing them only by a breath. Roa glanced over her shoulder to see Lirabel, now at Jas's side, lighting her next arrow in the cook's fire and drawing it back across her bow.

"Roa, run!"

Roa stumbled back, away from the dragons.

Lirabel's arrows continued to fly. But a few arrows couldn't kill a dragon. And dragons became even more aggressive when injured. So Lirabel was missing intentionally, her flaming arrows landing at their feet, trying to frighten them.

Where's Asha when you need her? Roa thought.

Dax's sister had a way with dragons.

If only Dax were half as useful . . .

But when Roa cast her gaze around the tents, Dax was nowhere to be found.

When Lirabel's fourth arrow flew, the pale gold dragon paused. Jas's clanging stopped. Roa watched it arch its serpentine neck, looking back in the direction it came from, sensing something Roa's eyes couldn't see. It clicked to its companion, and then—as if deciding this fight wasn't worth the trouble—it beat its wings, preparing to fly. The second followed its lead.

Sand billowed up, flying into Roa's face, scratching her skin. She turned away, shutting her eyes and holding her breath.

As both dragons launched themselves into the air, she felt shadows of cold creep over her. She watched the hulking forms block out the sun. Felt the power of their massive wings beating the wind into her face.

When the sand stopped scathing, she opened her eyes, looking skyward.

The silhouettes of both dragons flew east.

Good riddance, she thought, even as she stood in awe of their terrifying beauty.

But as she turned to find Lirabel, the camp before her blurred gold. The dragons were gone, but a wind had picked up, and the sand billowed once more, making it difficult to see the tents.

Roa squinted through the sand. She caught sight of Lirabel, who stood staring in the direction opposite the dragons. She lowered her bow, eyes widening. At the same time, Jas dropped his pot and spoon.

"Tie down the horses!" he yelled to the guards, his voice battling the wind. "Tie down everything!"

Roa turned. Sand whipped through the air, obscuring her vision. As the wind screamed in her ears, goose bumps erupted across her skin.

This far out in the desert, screaming winds meant only one thing.

Sandstorm.

She raised her arm to shield her eyes.

There, in the distance, a wall of red-gold sand was rumbling and rising, coming straight for the camp.

Five

With Lirabel shouting orders, Roa ran back to Dax's tent and darted inside. Sand coated her teeth. Grit burned in her eyes. Grabbing his scarlet sandskarf, she wrapped it tight around her head, pulling it snug over her nose and mouth. Next she grabbed his mantle, pulled it on, and darted out again.

Chaos greeted her. The sun glinted off the guards' steel sabers as they buzzed like bees in a disrupted nest, scrambling to secure the caravan.

But these tents weren't sturdy enough to withstand a storm. Those pegs would fly out of the ground as easily as a needle pushed free of cloth.

Why had Dax not done as he promised? And why had no one consulted her or Lirabel or Jas—the ones who intimately knew the sand sea and its dangers?

Roa was about to whistle for Essie, except Essie wasn't here. The sharp pain of it sliced Roa anew.

She would have to survive this without her sister.

"Roa!" Lirabel's frantic voice called through the wind.

Roa spun to find her friend—her skarf gone, her long black curls glittering with golden sand.

"He wouldn't listen!" She clutched her knees, breathing hard. "Oleander spooked and . . . Roa, he's gone after her!"

Roa peered through the air, growing thicker by the heartbeat. Squinting hard, she could just make out two shapes in the distance beyond the camp: Dax and a horse.

The king didn't know the first thing about surviving a sandstorm.

Rule number one? Never leave camp.

Nearby, the cook madly tried to pack up their food. Roa grabbed her arm, stopping her, then reached into one of the still-open sacks until her hand found a crisp red apple.

Snatching it up, she tucked it into the pocket of Dax's mantle, then ran to where Jas was retying the one horse he'd been able to catch. Grabbing Poppy, Roa mounted and dug her bare heels into the horse's flanks. Poppy sped off at a gallop, whipping sand into Roa's eyes.

She could barely see Dax in the distance, shirtless and heading into the storm.

Stupid, foolish boys and their stupid, foolish notions . . .

Didn't he know how deadly it was to breathe in all that sand? It would fill his lungs and suffocate him.

"Dax!" she screamed. But the wind snatched his name right out of the air.

Oleander, a russet mare, galloped away from Dax whenever he got close, taking them farther away from camp. And the farther they got from camp, the closer the wall of sand got to them.

Roa and Poppy raced harder.

"Dax!"

This time he turned, lifting his bare arm and wincing as the sand sliced his skin. His eyes met hers—the only part of her face visible beneath the sandskarf she wore. She held the apple aloft, showing him what she was about to do, then hurled it in his direction.

Miraculously, he caught it.

The red-gold swell swallowed the rising sun and the sky darkened. Poppy, sensing danger, whinnied. Hearing it, Oleander flicked her ears, then looked at the apple in Dax's hand.

Roa closed the gap.

Poppy's hooves halted. Oleander came to Dax, taking the apple in her huge teeth. The instant she did, Dax grabbed her reins and launched himself onto her back.

A crack of thunder split the sky. Poppy reared, frightened, and Roa would have slid off if Dax hadn't reached his arm across her back, his warm hand steadying her.

With both horses under control and the storm growing behind them, Roa nudged Poppy into a gallop. Dax and Oleander kept pace with them.

They raced back to camp.

As Roa glanced toward the king, Dax caught her gaze. All trace of that witless boy was gone. In his place was someone else. Someone Roa almost recognized.

The wall of sand roared at their backs. The king and queen broke their gazes, leaning into their horses, urging them *faster.*

They hit the camp, racing through the billowing tents. Roa reached for Oleander's reins, halting both their horses at the same time.

As one, they dismounted.

The wall of sand hit, drenching them in utter darkness, and the temperature plummeted.

Roa squeezed her eyes shut and breathed into the cotton sandskarf. They had two choices now. They could blindly go in search of a tent and hope they didn't miss, or stay where they were. The first choice was more dangerous—they could walk right out of the camp without knowing, get lost in the storm, and never be found.

So Roa yanked on Poppy's reins, making her get down on all fours, then did the same with Oleander. Once both horses were down, she reached for Dax, her fingers closing tightly around his bare arm. As the sand stung her face, she slid her hand down to his wrist, then his palm. Threading their fingers together, she kept her other hand on Poppy's flank, making her way to the mare's leeward side, bringing Dax with her. Using Poppy as both a shield and a heat source, Roa dropped to her knees, forcing Dax to do the same.

The sand stung her skin. Soon it would start shredding it. In the cold and the darkness, she pushed Dax against Poppy, then tugged off the mantle she wore—*his* mantle—before dropping into his lap.

"Cover yourself with this!" The sandskarf muffled her voice as she shoved the wool garment into his hands.

Dax's arm curled around her, pulling her against him as he swept the thick wool over them both, keeping them shielded from the shrieking storm. When Roa started to shiver from the cold, Dax's arms tightened around her.

With her cheek pressed to his heart, Roa closed her eyes and prayed.

She prayed this was the kind of storm that threw a single shrill tantrum and died out quickly . . . not the kind that raged for days and swallowed you alive.

What felt like both years and heartbeats later, Poppy relaxed, sighing behind them. Roa listened carefully, noticing a difference in the wind. It still screamed, just not so angrily. The sand still whipped, but it no longer hurt.

Soon enough, the wind stopped.

The sand settled.

The storm died.

As the world fell still, Roa lifted her cheek from Dax's chest. His arms loosened around her as she pushed off the heavy mantle, then crawled out of his lap.

The sand was cold beneath her palms. But when she looked up, the darkness was gone. The sun blazed above her once more. Roa closed her eyes, letting it shine on her face, thankful to be alive.

Rising, she turned to find Dax covered in a layer of gold. The sight of him, safe, brought a rush of relief—

—followed immediately by anger.

She was about to declare how utterly dangerous it was to chase a horse into a sandstorm, when the sight over his shoulder made the words die on her tongue.

Their camp was . . . gone.

Before the storm hit, there had been half a dozen brightly colored tents. Now there was nothing but sand.

Roa quickly did a head count. Jas was pulling Lirabel up from the sand. The cook was searching for her pots—which had all been flung away—and the guards and staff were all accounted for.

But the tents were gone and with them, their supplies. Water. Food. Clothing. All of it gone.

Except Poppy and Oleander, even the horses were gone.

Roa knew what it meant to be trapped in the middle of the desert without water or shelter. If they were lucky, they might last two days.

If they were unlucky, they wouldn't survive the night.

Three Months Previous

Roa was in her father's study, hiding from the son of the king.

Dax had arrived earlier that day, without any invitation or warning. As Roa paced the room, she wondered how he dared to return, after all this time, expecting a warm welcome. Wondered how he could think to fall so easily back into place here. In Roa's own house.

The last time they'd seen each other, Roa's father was dragging him into a windowless room and locking the door.

The last time they'd seen each other, he'd taken something precious from her.

The sight of him—after these eight years—was like swallowing a stone.

At dinner, Dax spoke with her brother, Jas, as if they were old friends instead of enemies. And then, afterward, he offered to help clean up.

Roa nearly spat out her tea. The son of the king, *she thought,* helping in our kitchen?

Her mother refused, as Roa knew she would.

But Dax was not dissuaded. He smiled a winsome smile. He used those warm brown eyes to melt her mother to his will. He even took the dishes out of her hands saying, "Let me carry these for you, Desta." As if Roa's mother wasn't used to hauling heavy sacks of grain in from the fields or her own weight in water from the wells of Song.

To Roa's utter disbelief, her mother gave in—but not with a smile. Instead, Desta looked at the son of the king with sorrow in her eyes.

Next, Dax stood beside Roa at the washbasin, with a cotton towel thrown over his shoulder, drying the dishes as fast as she washed them, asking after her family, asking after her.

Roa couldn't stand it. The enemy, not just in her house, but in her own kitchen, trying to win her to his side?

As if he wasn't the heir to Firgaard's throne—a throne that had taken the lifeblood of their people, sucking the meat from their bones.

As if he wasn't the boy who'd stolen Roa's sister from her.

Didn't he remember what he'd done? Who he was?

Before Roa could smash a pot over his head, Lirabel stepped in, her gaze catching Roa's. The look on her face said: Go. Run. I'll take care of this.

Roa wanted to hug her.

She fled to her father's study, on the opposite side of the house.

But not even the study was safe. As soon as everything was put away, Dax found his way into the very next room for a game of gods and monsters with her father.

As if her father wasn't the one who'd locked him in a storeroom.

As if her father wasn't still grieving the daughter he'd lost—because of Dax.

A soft rap-rap-rap on the door drew her out of her thoughts.

Roa stopped pacing and bared her teeth. Was there no escape?

But it wasn't Dax who opened the door and stepped into the study. It was Theo. The flames lit up his dark hair, pulled back in a bun, and cast shadows in the hollows of his throat and jaw. He shut the door behind him.

Relieved, Roa let her breath out in a whoosh.

"Are you all right?" he asked.

She threw him a look that said, What do you think?

Theo crossed the room to her. When they were children, Theo had been a bully and a brute who Roa found it hard to be friends with. But eight years of sanctions had turned him into something else entirely. Eight years of sanctions had forged a tight alliance between the heirs of Song and Sky.

"Did you hear him at dinner?" Theo whispered, knowing Dax was in the next room. "Talking to your uncle about the grain harvest? As if most of that harvest won't be destroyed by the blight. As if your parents won't give what's left to those who need it more than they do." Theo's voice was bitter. "And that slave . . . how does he dare bring a slave into your house?"

Roa hugged herself. "I don't know," she whispered. It was abominable, the way draksors thought they could own other human beings.

She started to pace again.

Seeing her agitation, Theo calmed himself. "It's just a fortnight and then he'll be gone." He reached for her arms, stopping her and pulling her into him. "You can handle him for a fortnight."

She nodded. That was true.

Roa looked to the door between this room and the next. The one where Dax played gods and monsters with her father.

Why have you come? *she wondered.*

Theo's voice brought her back. He squinted down at her, as if she weren't really standing in his arms but somewhere far away and he was trying to find her. Several heartbeats passed before she realized he'd been saying something.

"Roa? Where are you?"

"I'm sorry." She pressed her palms to her eyes. "I'm so . . . unfocused tonight." She let her hands fall back to her sides. "Please distract me."

He smiled his bright smile.

"Gladly." He tugged on her hand, bringing her to the windowsill, and lifted himself into it. Roa crawled up after him, then sat against the opposite casing.

Capturing her hands, he began planting kisses on each of her fingers, then both palms. Roa closed her eyes, trying to go to the place his kisses normally sent her. But even as his lips moved up the insides of her arms, Roa's thoughts were with the boy-king in the next room.

"I changed my mind," Theo murmured against her skin. "Let's not wait."

"What?" Roa asked, coming fully out of her thoughts and opening her eyes.

Theo sat back, letting go of one hand and keeping the other. He traced soft circles on her palm. Roa stared at the movement of his thumb, willing it to soothe her.

"We can go to Odessa."

Odessa was the woman who performed bindings and burnings in the territory of Sky, Theo's home.

"She can marry us in secret. Tonight."

Roa's back was pressed firmly up against the casing as she stared at him, shocked. Their binding was only a month away. Their mothers had it all planned out already. She shook her head. "Think of how furious my father would be! He'd never forgive us."

"He would. Eventually." Theo's kisses moved up her throat and along her jaw. "If you're my wife, I can take you away from here. You wouldn't ever have to see him again."

Roa turned her face to his. Theo's pale gold eyes, framed in dark lashes, now gazed intently—hungrily—into her own.

"Marry me, Roa. Tonight."

She reached with her free hand to touch his face. But a sound issued from the room beyond, like the scraping of chairs, and her attention was once again snagged.

What was Dax speaking to her father about?

"Roa?"

Through the wall, she heard Dax laugh at something her father said.

"Roa, are you even listening?"

Suddenly, the door to the study swung open, letting in the light from the hall.

Theo flinched.

Roa turned to look.

Dax stood frozen in the doorframe.

"Roa, I—" He glanced from her to Theo and back. "Oh. Forgive me. Your father said . . ."

His gaze dropped to Roa's hand, still clasped in both of Theo's.

"He said you were in here." Dax stared hard now, his eyebrows knit in confusion, as if trying to make sense of what he'd walked in on. "I didn't realize . . ."

And then, without finishing his sentence, as abruptly as he came in, Dax stepped out of the room and closed the door behind him.

The study plummeted into silence. Only the fire crackled in the hearth, spilling golden light across the carpets.

"Idiot," hissed Theo, squeezing Roa's hand.

She didn't hear him, though. She was too busy wondering: What did he ask Papa for?

Roa trusted her father. She knew he wouldn't agree to anything that wasn't in the best interest of Song. But what if this was some kind of trap?

Dax was the son of a tyrant. He couldn't be trusted.

Roa pulled her hand free. Cupping Theo's cheeks in her hands, *she kissed him quickly on the mouth. Theo reached for her, trying to deepen it.*

But Roa pulled away.

"I'll be right back," she whispered, hopping down from the sill.

"What? Why? Where are you going?"

Roa didn't answer. Just opened the door and stepped into the hall.

There was no sign of Dax in the corridor beyond. Nor any of the rooms.

No matter, *she thought, her footsteps remembering.*

She found the son of the king on the roof of the garden shed. It was the place he used to hide from the bustle of Roa's household when he'd spent summers here as a child.

As she climbed the ladder, though, a memory pricked her like a thorn. Sadness welled up and Roa lost her footing on the rung. The clatter made her wince, and when Roa glanced up, she found herself staring into Dax's face.

His eyes were just as she remembered: the color of chestnuts gleaming in the sun. And his ears still stuck out a little too far from his head. But his nose—that was different. It was no longer so straight.

Broken, *she thought.* Maybe twice.

Again, that prick of memory. She thought she saw it reflected at her in his eyes. But if he remembered, he didn't say a word. Just made space for her as she hauled herself up.

Dax lay back down, his sleeves still rolled to his elbows from washing dishes.

"I'm sorry," he said quickly. "I should have knocked."

Not for the first time, his voice startled her. Like the rest of him, it no longer belonged to a boy but to a young man.

Roa stretched out next to him. "You weren't interrupting anything."

He glanced at her, then away.

The space between them filled up with eight years of things unsaid. Eight years of thoughts she couldn't voice and memories she'd tried to bury.

How dare you set foot here, she wanted to tell him.

But Roa was a daughter of the House of Song. Her father had taught her to be gracious even when her instinct was to draw her knife.

Especially when her instinct was to draw her knife.

Roa needed to find out why he'd come. She decided to start small.

"Who won?" she asked.

"What?"

"Gods and monsters."

"Oh." He cupped his hands behind his head, relaxing a little. "I did. Of course."

Roa glanced up to find a crooked smile on his face as he stared up at the stars.

"Liar."

Dax smiled wider. In a flash, though, the smile was gone. He glanced at her and their eyes met.

Both of them looked away.

Silence grew into the space between them, like a thick and choking weed. In it, Roa remembered the locked room. The sobs slipping through the cracks. How she'd listened at the door to the sound of him crying.

"It's . . . strange being back," he said, shattering the memory. "Everything's changed."

Yes, *she thought*. My people are destitute now. Thanks to you.

"You've changed," he said softly.

Roa bristled. Her fingers curled into her palms.

"And you . . ." She tried to hold back the anger and grief welling up inside her but couldn't. It came rushing forth like a river. "You act

as if nothing has changed. Playing gods and monsters with my father? Climbing up onto this roof like—like it never happened? Like you don't remember what you did?"

He turned his head abruptly to look at her.

"You think I came here because I forget?" He sounded angry and sad all at once. "I came here because I remember, Roa. I will never stop remembering." And then, more softly: "I think about her every day."

Roa sat up sharply. What was she thinking, coming up here? She didn't want to talk to him. Not about Essie.

She moved to leave, crawling carefully to the roof's edge, then sat facing the garden with her back to Dax. She had just swung her feet over, her toes seeking the ladder rung below, when he said, so quietly, she almost missed it, "You have to live with the loss of her, and that's the worst thing. But, Roa—I have to live knowing I took her from you. That because of me . . . she's gone."

Roa paused, sitting at the edge of the roof with her bare feet on the uppermost rung of the ladder. She felt the heat of his gaze on her bare neck—like fire, burning her up.

"Maybe this is silly," he went on. "Maybe you think I don't have a right. But I talk to her sometimes. On the roof, back at home. And here, tonight. She was always so easy to talk to." His next words were barely a whisper. "You were always more difficult."

Roa didn't turn to climb down. Instead, she sat motionless, facing the night. Tears pricked her eyes.

"Why did you come here?" she whispered, staring out over the dark-drenched garden.

She heard him sit up. Finally, she looked over her shoulder. His head was tilted back to the stars, spilled across the sky above them, and *his eyes were closed. After several heartbeats, he sucked in a breath.*

"I'm here to tell you that I'm going to steal my father's throne."

This was not at all what Roa expected.

She lifted her feet from the ladder rung and turned around.

"What?" she whispered, staring into his upturned face.

Dax opened his eyes and looked down, catching her gaze with his.

"Roa, I've come to ask—will you help me?"

Six

Roa looked from the site of their vanished camp to the king who thought he could cross the sand sea without proper provisions.

Roa stood over him, trembling with anger.

Just for a moment, though, instead of the dragon king covered in a layer of golden sand, another boy flickered before her eyes. Younger and shy. Like the summer she first met him.

The memory of it glimmered like a mirage.

Roa remembered him seated across the gods and monsters board, his eyes wide and curious, his ears jutting out in a way that might have been adorable if his presence in her home wasn't such an annoying intrusion. He'd been foisted upon Roa after Essie talked her way out of entertaining him, and he'd come with one instruction: *be his friend.*

Roa shook off the memory.

This wasn't that boy. This was a man too stupid not to walk straight into a sandstorm for the sake of a horse.

"I've never met a more senseless king."

Slowly, Dax rose, pushing the hood of his mantle back from his face. His eyes fixed on her, pupils shrinking in the dazzling sunlight. "How many kings have you met, exactly?"

Roa gritted her teeth. Was this a joke to him?

"You *never* leave camp in a storm. Not *ever.*"

"Stop shouting at me."

"I'm not shouting!"

"I couldn't leave Oleander—"

"The horse doesn't matter, Dax! If a horse gets lost in the storm, we can buy another!"

"She's my sister's horse," he said. "She matters to me."

Roa stepped in close. "Horses are expendable. Kings are not."

"I said"—he held her gaze—*"she matters to me."*

His voice was a warning, daring her to challenge him again.

Roa looked to Oleander. The mare shook the sand out of her mane, oblivious.

It struck her, then.

His sister's horse . . .

Asha was on the run. Dax was unlikely to ever see her again. Oleander was the only link he had left to his sister.

Roa stepped back, her anger fizzling out. It was then that she felt the watching eyes. Looking over his shoulder, she found the soldats covered in sand. Their hands on their hilts as they watched the outlander queen belittle their king.

Swallowing, Roa lowered her voice and motioned over his shoulder. "Everything's gone."

Dax turned to look. After a moment, he said, "We'll have to make do."

Make do? thought Roa. *Is he truly so senseless?*

"We'll stay sheltered during the day. We'll ration water."

"How will we stay sheltered, Dax? We don't have any tents. Nor do we have any water to ration. *Nor do we have any horses.*"

Except Poppy and Oleander.

Dax fell silent, thinking. But Roa didn't have time for him to come up with a plan. She knew this desert. She knew the chances of surviving beneath its scorching sun without shelter or water or horses. Knew that once the sun set, the temperature would plummet, bringing the kind of cold that killed men and women in their sleep.

Their destination—his mother's abode—was still a day's ride away. Built by the former dragon king for his wife, it had been intended as a private place for her to retreat to. From there, it was another full day's ride to Firgaard.

They wouldn't make it to Dax's mother's abode on foot by tonight. They wouldn't make it there at all.

In the distance, she watched Lirabel and Jas pull a single bedroll out of the sand.

They walked all day, trying to keep a steady pace. But without water and shelter, with the sun loud and hot in the sky, they'd slowed, and then slowed again. It was dusk now. Roa's vision had long ago started to blur, and now her tongue was starting to swell—a sign of severe dehydration.

It was about to get worse, though: When the sun disappeared, they wouldn't have any way to keep warm. No tents. No blankets. Nothing to make a fire.

Roa glanced over her shoulder to make sure the caravan

wasn't falling too far behind, then turned her attention back to the darkening horizon. To the cold that was rising.

Roa cursed these useless Firgaardians. She cursed herself for having to rely on them.

Lirabel stepped up to Roa's side, scattering her curses.

The two friends looked into the distance, where the sun was sinking into the sand. Lirabel turned her eyes on Roa. "Do you think we'll make it?"

"Not if the sun sets first," said Roa, staring straight ahead at the golden orb disappearing beneath the horizon. Soon the night would drop like a curtain.

"We're making camp," Dax's voice interrupted.

Both girls spun to stare at his dark silhouette. He had Oleander's reins gathered in his fist, his face stony.

"The guards and staff all have heatstroke."

Roa knew this. Two had fainted already, and one had vomited twice.

"We need to stop and make camp," Dax pressed.

If they stopped now, with no fire or tents to keep the death chill away, they wouldn't wake in the morning.

Roa shook her head. "We need to keep moving."

"Everyone is dehydrated, Roa. They need to rest."

Roa narrowed her eyes at him. "The longer it takes us, the less likely we are to survive. We need to move quickly."

"Didn't you hear me? *They keep fainting.*"

"Then we leave them behind."

He stared at her, horrified. But Dax didn't know this desert.

"If we stop and make camp for the sake of a few, it endangers the entire caravan," Roa said. "But if we press on through the night, we gain more ground and keep warmer on the move, increasing the chances of staying alive and making it to our destination."

This was the sand sea. Ruthlessness was key to survival.

But Dax didn't think like a scrublander. Dax had lived an easy, pampered life. One bolstered by the taxes—and then the sanctions—his father imposed on Roa's people. He'd never had to make a life-or-death decision. Other people did that for him.

He loomed over her. Due to her diminished vision, he was a blurry shape in the darkening haze of dusk. "I'm not going to risk the lives under my care for the sake of your pride."

"You *are* risking—" Roa stopped herself. "My *pride?*"

Roa's grip on Poppy's reigns tightened. Sensing her mood, the horse pressed her ears flat against her head.

Lirabel moved closer to the queen, rubbing Poppy's neck to calm her. "Roa's right. It's far more dangerous if we stop."

"I don't agree," said Jas, coming up behind them, holding Lirabel's gaze. "I think we should make camp. None of these people are in a state to keep going."

Roa glared at her brother. "If we don't continue on, *we all die.*"

"I'll take my chances," said Dax, turning back.

Roa was about to say that in stopping for the night, he'd already determined what his chances would be. He would never make it to his mother's desert home. He wouldn't even make it to *morning.*

But before she could tell him so, a familiar sound pierced the encroaching night: the high-pitched screak of a hawk.

Roa's heart kicked. She spun, searching the darkening sky.

"Did you hear that?" she whispered, afraid to trust her own ears.

She reached for the hum—which was still muted inside her.

But no, it was real. Because a heartbeat later, Essie's thoughts burst into her mind.

I found you, Roa.

It was as if someone struck a match and lit a glowing fire inside her.

"Essie . . ."

Roa pulled Poppy away, scouring the skies until she saw it: a white bird speeding toward her, as if diving out of the stars.

You were in danger—Essie's voice bled through Roa's mind—*and I heard you. I had to make sure you were safe. . . .*

Where were you? Roa called to her sister, who was getting closer by the heartbeat.

In a flash of white feathers and silver eyes, Essie crashed into Roa, her sharp claws scraping her sister's skin. *I—I don't know. I couldn't find my way. I couldn't remember where home was.*

Roa drew her sister's feathered form against her chest, holding her close. Keeping her safe. A soft bundle of warmth in her arms.

And then I heard your voice, and it seemed so far away. . . . I didn't understand. How could it get so far away?

Normally Essie hated it when Roa held her, restricting her from flying. Now, she pressed herself close to Roa's breast, letting her sister hold her as she trembled. Her tiny heart drumming against her sister's ribs.

It's all right. Roa stroked Essie's feathers as the hum glowed dimly between them. *You're here now.*

When Essie stopped trembling, she squirmed out of her sister's arms and flew to her shoulder. Her claws dug in harder than usual, piercing Roa's skin. As if she could just hold on tightly enough, maybe whatever confusion had taken hold of her wouldn't be able to take her again.

And then a voice echoed in the distance.

Both of them looked to the west.

I brought help, Essie explained.

Pinpricks of light appeared on the horizon, moving ever closer. They were torches held in the hands of scrublanders—*her* people—racing on horseback toward them. And leading them all was a young man, his face obscured by a sandskarf.

Roa didn't need to see his face to know who he was.

"Theo," Dax muttered from behind her. Roa had forgotten he was there.

The moment Theo saw her, he broke away from the others, hurtling straight for her, a torch held high in his hand.

Roa kicked her own horse into a gallop, her heart thundering in unison with Poppy's hooves. Essie flew off, trailing close behind her.

Theo called her name again, and his voice was like a fire, driving out the cold.

Bringing her home.

Three Months Previous

"*This is the only map you have?*"

A soft hiss followed by a loud thunk answered her.

Roa and Lirabel looked up just as Dax lowered the longbow. Beside him, a freckled young man grinned with pleasure, his arms crossed over his chest, staring at the whorl in the tree now pierced by Dax's arrow. This boy, Roa had learned upon meeting him, was Torwin.

"*Very good,*" *said Torwin.* "*Now go fetch it.*"

Dax raised an eyebrow at him.

"*Go on.*" *Torwin motioned to the tree with his chin.* "*Part of learning how to shoot is having to retrieve your arrows.*"

"*Is that so?*" *said Dax.*

"*It is,*" *Roa said from the ground where she and Lirabel crouched.* "*Papa used to pinch our ears if we left our arrows behind for the servants to clean up.*"

Bolstered by her allegiance, Torwin laughed. "*Did you hear that? Do you want your ears pinched by her father?*"

Dax rolled his eyes, but went to fetch the arrow.

Torwin flashed Roa a half smile. Roa flashed one back. But it died on her lips at the glint of the silver band encircling his throat.

The sight of it was like a cold blade in her belly.

Unlike scrublanders, draksors kept slaves. Half a century ago, an army from the north—a group of people called the skral—came to conquer Firgaard. They failed, and instead of sending them back where they came from, the dragon queen—Dax's grandmother—enslaved them.

Torwin, Roa had learned, was one such slave, owned by the cruelest man she had ever met. It was just another reason she'd decided to help Dax bring down his father: no human being should be owned by another.

"And, yes," said Dax, jogging back after pulling the arrow from the whorl. "That's the only map we have."

Roa looked down to the parchment spread across the ground beneath her. It was tearing along the creases from being folded one too many times and whole sections were smudged out.

Then it'll have to do, she thought.

Roa tapped the city of Darmoor, then looked to Lirabel, who crouched beside her. "What about here?"

Lirabel's curls were unbound tonight, and her earned bow was resting on the ground beside her. She smelled like rosewater.

"It's smaller than Firgaard," Roa said. "And look: no walls."

Lirabel's gaze moved from the walled capital of Firgaard, over the Rift mountains, to where Roa's finger pointed: Darmoor. A port on the sea.

Lirabel smiled a slow smile. "If you're suggesting what I think you're suggesting, then I think you're brilliant."

There were too many armed soldats within the walls of Firgaard. If they wanted to pull off Dax's revolt, they needed to cut down their numbers.

"How important is Darmoor to the king?" Roa asked Dax while staring at the map.

"Very," came the reply, followed by another thunk! "Roughly half our food and supplies come from Darmoor."

"And if it came under siege?"

Roa and Lirabel looked up, waiting for his answer. Dax paused at the tree, his hand wrapped around the arrow shaft—stuck just below the whorl this time.

"My father would send his army to reclaim it."

"Then I think Roa's solved your problem," said Lirabel.

Before Roa could bask in her triumph, though, Essie's voice broke through her mind.

Roa!

Essie had been put on lookout. They were in the ruins of the House of Shade, where no one ever came. As a precaution, Essie had been sent to watch the front entrance.

He's coming!

Roa shot to her feet. Who?

Essie didn't answer. She didn't need to. Because as Roa turned toward the half-crumbled wall behind her, she saw him.

Theo stood in the moonlight, gripping one of his earned swords. The second hung from the sheath at his belt. Both had pommels carved into the shape of a leaping deer.

I'm sorry, Roa. Essie dived out of the moonlit sky and onto Roa's outstretched fist. I fell asleep and only woke as he was walking through the entrance.

"What in all the skies is he doing here?" Theo growled, pointing the tip of the blade at the son of the king.

This was Roa's fault. She'd stayed up late talking to Dax on the garden shed roof and by the time she returned to the study, Theo wasn't in the best of moods.

When she told him she was going to Firgaard with the son of the king, Theo was furious.

And the wedding? he'd demanded.

We'll postpone it, she'd told him. Until I get back.

For several heartbeats, he'd stared at her like she wasn't the same girl she'd always been. Like he didn't know her at all. Then he got to his feet and walked away.

And now she'd made things worse by bringing Dax here, to the House of Shade. Her and Theo's meeting place.

"Theo . . . ," she said, rising in front of Lirabel, who snatched up the map and folded it quickly. "I can explain."

Can you? asked Essie, eyeing the heir of Sky. *Roa could feel her sister's agitation buzzing in her own blood.* He looks like he wants to bash Dax's head in far more than he wants an explanation.

Dax stepped past her.

Roa reached to stop him.

"Theo," *said Dax, avoiding Roa's grasp,* "why don't you put down the sword."

"Or," *Theo growled,* "you can pick one up and we can finally settle this."

Oh no, *thought Essie.*

Roa and Lirabel exchanged a look.

Fire burned in Theo's eyes. "You're no different from the tyrants before you, Dax. Coming to our home under a banner of peace, expecting us to give you everything you ask for. But it's never enough, is it? You always want more."

Torwin stepped into the space between Roa and Lirabel. Under his breath, he asked, "How good is Theo with that sword?"

"Very," *Roa and Lirabel said in unison.*

In the scrublands, weapons were earned, not given. They were symbols of skill as well as belonging. Scrublander children went through years of training before receiving the honor and responsibility of bearing one. This training was as important as learning their letters and numbers.

Roa knew—from the summers he'd spent living in her house—that Dax avoided swords the way he avoided vegetables. Roa and Essie and Lirabel used to regularly beat him in the lessons they shared.

Maybe he's improved, *thought Essie.*

Hmm, *thought Roa.*

"And Dax?" *Lirabel asked, putting a voice to Essie's hope.*

Torwin kept his eyes on the king's son. "Let's just say he's better at talking his way out of problems."

Theo drew his second sword and held it out, hilt first.

Dax didn't take it. "I'm not going to fight you."

Theo threw the blade on the ground at Dax's feet, where it clattered on the cracked stone.

"Pick it up," *Theo said.*

"I don't think—"

Theo threw a punch, his fist cracking against Dax's cheek.

Lirabel and Roa sucked in a collective breath.

Torwin moved to intervene.

"No," *said Roa, grabbing his arm, holding him back. Theo wouldn't stop until Dax accepted the challenge.* "You'll do him no favors by rescuing him. Let him defend himself."

Torwin stared at her like she'd lost her mind.

But Theo had plenty of reasons to challenge the son of the king. And if Dax wanted scrublander support in this war he was plotting, he needed to prove himself the scrublander way.

"You take." *Theo shoved Dax, who staggered back.* "And you take." *He shoved again. Dax shook his head, still trying to recover from the shock of the punch.* "And you take." *The final shove made Dax nearly crash into the wall.*

"You dare come here asking our people to fight your war? Prove you know what you're doing. Prove you deserve our help."

Theo kicked the sword at him.

"Pick. It. Up."

Dax picked up the sword.

But as he turned to face his opponent, his grip on the hilt was all wrong.

Oh, Dax, thought Essie.

He held the weapon too hard and too close.

Seeing it, Theo smirked, then kicked him in the stomach, knocking the wind from him. Dax stumbled back, his arms swinging as he tried to keep his balance. Which was when Theo parried, easily disarming him.

Once more, the sword clattered to the ground.

Theo stepped in, nose to Dax's. "Pathetic as ever."

"All right," said Roa. "You've proven your point."

Theo ignored her, ramming Dax hard into the wall with both hands. Weaponless now, Dax grunted as his back hit stone. Theo pressed his blade to Dax's throat, keeping him pinned.

Roa slid Essie's knife from its sheath at her calf and advanced. Essie flew from her shoulder to Lirabel's.

"I should do us all a favor . . . ," Theo said into Dax's ear, "and kill you right here."

"Now where have I heard that before," Dax said bitterly.

Roa pressed the tip of the knife to the spot just above Theo's kidney, piercing through the shirt. Pricking his skin.

Theo went immediately still.

"Enough," she warned.

"It's all in good fun," Theo said, keeping the steel of his blade against the heir's throat. "Isn't it, Dax?"

Roa looked to Dax, who met her solemn gaze over Theo's shoulder.

"Dax doesn't appear to be having any fun. Let him go."

Theo didn't move.

"Theo," she hissed, pressing harder, "I'm not some damsel who needs you to save her."

Immediately, his hands came up.

"Drop the sword. And step away from him."

He did as she said, but glared as he did it. Roa stared him down, not breaking her gaze until he looked away first.

"Go home," she said.

Picking up both swords, Theo sheathed them. He didn't look at her again. Nor did he look at Dax. Just walked out of the ruins, shoulders hunched like a man who'd just lost everything.

"Thank you," said Dax from where he stood against the wall.

"Don't thank me," she said, watching Theo's silhouette bleed into the night. "Just . . . do better next time."

From across the ruined court, Lirabel said, "Maybe we should go home."

Roa nodded.

As the rest of them headed for the horses, though, Roa lingered behind, tracing her sister's delicate wing bone with her fingertip.

How is he going to win a revolt if he can't even wield a sword?

That's why he needs you, *said Essie.* That's why we all need you.

Seven

Their horses halted at the same time.

Sand bloomed through the air as Theo pulled Roa to him, crushing her to his chest. The beat of his heart raced to the same tempo as hers.

As his caravan thundered past them, heading for the king's, Roa breathed in his warm, familiar scent. Like honey and wheat. She looped her arms around his neck and hugged him hard.

"Essie found me," he said against her cheek. Gripping her shoulder, he pulled her away so he could look at her. "I was terrified we wouldn't reach you in time."

Roa studied her former betrothed. His strong, unyielding jaw. His dark hair pulled back. His wheat-colored eyes set into a sun-kissed face.

In her silence, Theo reached for his water skin and uncorked it, handing it to her. Roa drank deeply.

"Are you all right?" Theo asked, assessing her for injury.

Roa didn't know how to answer that question. So, after wiping her mouth on her sleeve and handing back the water skin, she said, "You never responded to my letters. You never came to the ruins."

"I'm here now," he said, still watching her.

Suddenly, the air shifted. They both looked up to find Dax coming out of the dark and into the glow of Theo's torch. He sat atop Oleander, with Essie now perched on his fist. The fire made her white wings glow almost orange.

Dax stared at Theo's hand. The one resting on Roa's hip.

Theo didn't flinch.

"Dax," he said through his teeth. In Firgaard, Theo would never get away with being so informal with the dragon king. "It's a rare man indeed who risks not just his own safety but that of his whole caravan."

Dax smiled a cold smile. His voice, though, lacked any chill. In fact, it was irritatingly warm. "You were sorely missed at the treaty negotiations. I suppose you had more important matters to attend to? Sulking, perhaps?"

Roa stared at Dax. Was this his idea of diplomacy? Insulting the one they owed their lives to?

"You think this is funny?" Theo didn't smile. "You have no provisions. No tents. No food. How did you plan on surviving till morning?" He looked down to Roa, his grip tightening on her. "You've put enough lives in danger tonight. Let my household and me take it from here."

Dax looked from Theo's protective grip to Roa's face. His eyebrow lifted slightly, asking a silent question.

Roa lifted her chin.

"We owe him our lives," she said, holding Dax's gaze.

In the distance, she heard the hammers already driving stakes into the sand. New tents were rising quickly due to the strong, deft hands of their rescue party. Theo had brought provisions. Proper ones. They'd survive until morning because of him.

"If Theo hadn't come—"

"There's no world in which I wouldn't have come, Roa."

She looked up into Theo's face to find him staring down at her.

Dax rolled his eyes as he turned Oleander around, nudging her toward the tents. "Why don't you bat your eyelashes at each other while you're at it. I'll see you both back at camp."

His horse kicked sand in their faces as he left, taking Essie with him.

Roa and Theo glowered at the retreating king.

"Best not underestimate the sand sea again!" Theo called to his back. "She's not a merciful mistress!"

Roa lifted her hands to the fire. The rest of the caravan had long since gone to sleep, but she, Lirabel, Jas, and Theo were still up. Theo's tent was open on one side so they could look out over the camp but closed on the other three sides to keep out most of the cold.

In Roa's lap, Essie slept with her head tucked beneath her wing. She'd seemed distant tonight, just like the hum. Quiet and exhausted. As if finding her way back to Roa had taken all her strength.

When she looked up from her sister's sleeping form, Roa noticed Lirabel glance toward Dax and Roa's tent—the one Theo had brought for them—which glowed warmly from the inside, throwing Dax's shadow across the canvas. Roa looked where she looked, watching the king's silhouette as he unlaced his shirt, then tugged it off.

Lirabel never once looked at Jas across the fire. And Jas, chatting with Theo, never once directed a question Lirabel's way. It was odd. Jas and Lirabel should have more to talk about than anyone else. Ever since Dax made Lirabel his emissary to the scrublands, she'd been seeing a lot of Roa's brother.

When the glow in Dax's tent dimmed into darkness, Lirabel rose from the carpet of sheepskin and drew her sandskarf tight around her shoulders. Her curls were plaited in a long braid down her back. "It's getting cold. I'm going to sleep."

Roa watched her head off in the direction of the king's tent.

Jas didn't even say good night.

In Lirabel's absence, Roa studied him. He was the contemplative sort, her little brother. But it had always been a cheerful contemplation. Lately he was . . . broody. Like a storm cloud had settled inside him, blocking the sun that normally shone out of his eyes.

Is it because Lirabel has finally put him off? Roa wondered. *Or is it because he's worried about Song's rift with the House of Sky?*

The latter was her fault. Another consequence of the decision she'd made. If she hadn't married Dax, there would be no trouble with Sky, and therefore no burden laid across her little brother's shoulders.

Not long after Lirabel left, Jas stretched and yawned, rubbing a hand over his face. "I think I'll retire, too." Rising, he caught his sister's eye. "Coming, Roa?"

Roa shook her head no.

Her brother's forehead wrinkled as he gave Roa what Essie liked to call his *cautious study.* He'd learned it from their mother, who used it whenever Roa and her siblings did something she disapproved of: pinched brow, narrowed eyes, lips pressed firmly together.

But Jas's disapproval over his sister sitting alone after dark with a young man who wasn't her husband was nothing compared to the guilt that racked Roa. She needed to make sure things were right between her and the boy she'd betrayed.

Seeing his efforts were futile, Jas sighed, then leaned over Roa and planted a kiss on the top of her head. "It's been a long day," he said, touching her shoulder. "You should go to sleep soon."

Roa caught the warning in his tone.

If you give them a reason to believe you're disloyal . . .

She shook his voice out of her head and said, "I will . . . in a moment."

"*Good night,* Jas," said Theo. Jas frowned a little, then nodded and stepped out of the tent.

As soon as Jas was out of hearing distance, Theo rose and walked to where the tent's fourth side was rolled back and secured to the corner post. He started to unfasten it. Just before he rolled it closed and tied it securely to the canvas roof—keeping the warmth in and prying eyes out—Roa looked out into the darkness, toward Dax's tent.

The lamp was out.

She couldn't stay long.

Theo came back and sat down, planting one hand behind Roa, on the sheepskins laid down on the sand. Their shoulders brushed.

If she had ridden hard, Theo had ridden harder. She could see it in the hunch of his shoulders, the droop of his head. Exhaustion carved deep shadows under his eyes, made deeper by the fire's light. But in his gaze burned a familiar longing. One that hadn't diminished in spite of everything she'd done.

Her brother's warning flashed through Roa's mind.

She looked quickly away, fixing her eyes on Essie, still curled up asleep in her lap.

Dax might be a vow breaker, but Roa wasn't.

"I'm sorry," she said. "For marrying him."

Theo stiffened, then grabbed the stick perched on the stones ringing the fire. He prodded the flames with it. "We don't need to do this. I already know what you're going to say. I knew it before you ever left."

Roa needed to say it anyway.

"I married him to bring down a tyrant." She traced her sister's wings, gently and softly, so as not to wake her. "And solidify an alliance."

His grip tightened around the stick. "Marrying *me* would have solidified an alliance. But I suppose scrublander alliances are less important than Firgaardian ones."

The fire crackled and sparked, lighting up his skin and dancing in his eyes. Those soft lips of his were set in a firm, hard line.

She looked him in the face. "Dax's father needed to be removed. He tried to kill his own son."

Theo shrugged. "I wish he had."

Roa's fingers stopped stroking Essie. "Don't say that."

"Can you blame me? Dax took *our people* and marched them across the sand sea to fight *his war.* He stole a daughter of the House of Song and made her queen so the rest of us would be compliant."

"*I* marched that army across the sand sea. And Dax didn't—"

"Remember what happened to the last scrublander girl who married a king?"

He was talking about Amina, Dax and Asha's mother. Roa's fists tightened. No one stole Amina. She'd done what she'd done, the same as Roa had: of her own free will.

"She's dead," said Theo. After rounding up the wood still left to burn, he nudged it all toward the center. The smoke curled up through the hole at the top of the tent. "Don't be upset with me for not wanting you to end up like her." Much more quietly, he said, "Don't be upset with me for not wanting him to have you."

"Nobody *has* me." She bristled. "And this isn't a contest Dax set out to win in order to humiliate you."

"Are you sure?" he said, brow darkening. He stopped prodding the flames and lowered his voice. "Dax *will* become his father. Just like his father became the monster before him. Dax's heir will do the same. This is the way it's always been, Roa. Blood is blood. You can't run from yours as much as I can't run from mine."

A chill crept across Roa's skin. Her gaze searched his shadowed face. "What are you saying?"

"I'm saying Dax's bloodline has only ever borne monstrous kings. I'm saying so long as a *draksor* sits on the throne, scrublanders will never be free of their tyranny. We will never have autonomy. We will never have peace."

He stared down at her, rigid as stone, as if daring her to contradict him.

"And?" she whispered. "What's your solution?"

"That he give up his crown—by force if necessary."

Roa's blood ran cold.

Treason. He was proposing treason.

"Please, don't say another word." She pushed up from the sheepskins, getting to her feet. Startled, Essie woke and flapped her white wings, flying up and out of the smoke hole in the roof. Her sleepy thoughts were a confused haze in Roa's mind. "I'll pretend I never heard you, because you're my friend." *Because I love you.* "But if you say it again . . ."

He looked up. "You'll what?"

She stopped and stared down at him. His eyes were cloaked in darkness and she couldn't read them.

Please don't, she thought. *Do not be so reckless as to plot against my husband.*

"You're tired," she told him instead. "You don't know what you're saying. We'll talk more in the morning, when both of us are rested."

"I know exactly what I'm—"

Roa headed for the tent entrance. She'd spent too much time alone with him in here as it was.

"Where are you going?"

"To sleep." Roa reached for the tent flap, pulling it back.

Theo rose from the carpet of sheepskin and stepped up behind her. "Don't go to him."

Roa fell still as his arms slid around her waist.

"Stay here with me," he whispered, drawing her against his chest. He smelled like honey and warm sand. "Surely, if the rumors are true, it doesn't matter where you spend the night."

Those words scorched her. The rumors of Dax's dalliances . . . if Theo had heard them, they'd probably reached every corner of the kingdom.

Does everyone in the scrublands know? Even my parents?

It was a humiliating thought.

"I miss you," he whispered. "I've missed you from the moment you left."

She closed her eyes as he kissed the base of her neck. When she didn't resist, he pulled off her sandskarf. The wide scoop of her collar allowed him to brush his mouth slowly across her bare shoulder, pressing his lips to the tiny scars crisscrossed there from years of Essie's claws digging into her skin.

"I need you, Roa . . ."

She knew it shouldn't, but it felt good to be touched and kissed and *wanted*.

But her brother's voice was in her head, spiked with warning.

If you give the court in the capital a concrete reason to believe you're disloyal . . .

"I can't," she said.

She'd given herself to him once, before all this started. But so much had changed. She was married to Dax now. And, unlike her husband, she took her vows seriously.

She couldn't give herself to Theo again.

His kisses stopped. She felt him tense against her. "How can you lie there next to him?" he demanded, his voice rough and raised. "A man who cares so little for you, he takes your dearest friend into his bed?"

What?

Roa swung to face him, taken aback.

"What did you just say?"

Theo's eyes widened a little. "You don't know. . . ."

Something hardened inside Roa. She pushed him away.

"If you're suggesting Dax is sleeping with . . ." She fumbled the words, thinking of Lirabel staring in the direction of Dax's tent. Thinking of that last night in the House of Song, of the voices giggling in the hall, of Lirabel never coming to bed . . .

"No," Roa said, shaking the doubt from her mind and hugging herself to ward off the accusation. "She would never do that."

"Are you sure?"

Roa glared at Theo, furious he would even suggest such a thing.

"Why shouldn't she take what you clearly don't want?" he said. "It elevates her status—something she desperately needs."

Roa's mouth opened to refute this, but Theo interrupted.

"She's a ward in your house, Roa. Unless someone takes pity on her the way your father has, Lirabel has nothing. No inheritance. Just three younger sisters to provide for and a debt she can never repay. Unless her circumstances change, she'll continue to be a ward of the House of Song until the day she dies."

Roa swallowed. "Her circumstances *have* changed. She's the king's emissary now."

"And what if her new status comes at a cost? What if, in exchange for her position, Dax requires . . . something extra?"

Roa's stomach clenched. The thought made her sick.

"I won't listen to this." She stepped away from him. "I know I hurt you when I rode away to help him. I know I betrayed you completely when I married him. But this is your jealousy talking."

"My *jealousy*?" He reached for her, his strong hands cupping her face as he pressed his forehead to hers. "I'm *worried* about you, Roa."

She stepped out of reach, shaking her head.

"Do you know what I was doing these past few months? While you were off fighting his war?"

Roa paused.

"I was hunting down the Skyweaver's knife," he said. "For *you.*"

Those words made her go rigid.

They hadn't spoken of the Skyweaver's knife in years. It was a weapon rumored to have the power to restore life. To bring back the dead.

After Essie's accident, convinced of its existence, Theo

79

persuaded a grief-stricken Roa to search for it with him. They'd spent years chasing down clues found in the old stories before Roa realized it was a fool's errand.

Now she knew better. The Skyweaver's knife was a myth, nothing more.

"It doesn't exist."

"I found it." He reached for her shoulders, turning her back to him. "I've seen it with my own eyes."

Roa pulled away, annoyed. "Where is it, then?"

"In transit from Darmoor. A baron in Firgaard bought it for his private collection."

She couldn't believe in magical knives. Not again. Too much hope led to heartache.

"I'm not doing this." She said it firmly. Defiantly. "*Good night*, Theo. I'll see you in the morning."

Roa walked swiftly out of the tent and into the cold sand. Essie flew after her.

Are you all right?

Her sister's voice was hazy, fading. But with sleep or something else, Roa couldn't say.

Her own thoughts were spinning.

Theo can't be plotting against the king, Roa told her sister. *And Lirabel can't be sleeping with Dax.*

Theo was just angry. And hurt. That was why he'd said those things.

And the skyweaver's knife . . .

It's a myth.

Shivering, she put the notion out of her mind. Pulling her

sandskarf up over her head, Roa moved between the darkened tents, heading for the king's.

When she stood before it, the guards looked at her warily, reminding Roa of the way their hands went to their hilts when she'd argued with Dax earlier. Reminding her of their inherent distrust.

She pushed aside the tent flaps.

The warm, golden glow of her lamp fell on an empty bed-roll.

Roa blinked.

"Where is he?" she demanded, retreating back into the cold night.

The guards exchanged nervous glances. "We were given orders to remain here."

"That wasn't my question."

They stood silent, not looking at her. Not answering.

Panic rose like a sandstorm. Wasn't it their job to keep an eye on him? Hadn't Dax walked straight out into a sandstorm that morning? He was surrounded by members of the House of Sky now—the very scrublanders who hated him most. He needed his guards more than ever.

She was about to snap at them when it suddenly became painfully obvious. There was only one circumstance in which Dax would command his soldats not to follow him.

He'd gone to someone else's tent.

How can you lie there next to him? Theo's words echoed through her mind. *A man who cares so little for you, he takes your dearest friend into his bed?*

Roa thought of all the time Dax and Lirabel spent alone together, in private meetings. She thought of the voices in the hall outside her door, the two lovers heading for her room . . .

Why shouldn't she take what you clearly don't want?

An image of them, together, flashed through her head. Roa stepped back, the storm dead inside her.

"My queen?" asked one of the soldats with peppered gray hair. "Is everything all right?"

"Yes, everything's fine," she lied, pushing back the flap once more and stepping through. She let it fall behind her, then stood very still, focusing on the breath rushing in and out of her lungs.

Don't jump to conclusions, she told herself. But her hands shook as she unraveled her sandskarf and set it on the floor of sheepskins. Sliding off her sandals, she crawled into the bedroll. The cold made her shiver. Roa pulled her knees up to her chest, hugging them hard, trying to keep warm.

A heartbeat later, she heard voices. A heartbeat after that, the flap lifted, and there was Dax, ducking inside. In the light, Roa saw his face was still unshaven.

"Roa," he said in greeting, his voice clipped.

She looked quickly away. She didn't want to see if his cheeks were flushed or his hairline damp with sweat. If his clothes were wrinkled from being taken off in a rush and carelessly tossed aside. Roa turned onto her side, listening to the sounds of those same clothes being shed now, folded, and placed next to hers.

He slid in beside her, and with him came a rush of cold air. This bedroll was larger than the last, which meant they could sleep without touching.

Dax turned down the lamp.

Roa lay awake, shivering in the darkness for a long time. His arm didn't come around her like the night before. Nor did he pull her against him, letting her take his warmth.

Instead, he turned his back to her and fell immediately asleep.

Two Months Previous

Roa walked in darkness, her footsteps cutting through the heart of the war camp. One by one she pulled the fingers of her riding gloves loose, then tugged them off. She'd ridden hard from Darmoor, the port on the sea, to New Haven, the war camp in the mountains. She'd spent the whole ride alone with her thoughts.

Thoughts that tossed and turned like an unruly sea.

Thoughts that scared her to her core.

Most of the camp slept, but now and then Roa heard stragglers whispering or laughing around dying fires. Her legs shook and her back ached from riding so long. Her stomach growled with hunger. But there was no time to waste.

She needed to do this before she changed her mind.

Roa stepped up to the meeting tent. Two scrublanders stood guard outside it. Each raised their fists over their hearts at the sight of her, and Roa returned the greeting.

Pausing at the entrance, she breathed in deeply, reaching for whatever courage she had left, then stepped into the glowing tent.

Dax was alone. He sat backward on a chair, leaning toward the rough-hewn desk so that two of the wooden chair legs were in the air. His temple rested on his fist as he stared down the map of Firgaard. There were dark smudges beneath his eyes and a deep frown between his eyebrows. A shadow of stubble stretched across his cheeks.

As soon as she stepped into view, the words tumbled out of Roa's mouth: "Marry me."

He looked up, his gaze calm on her face. As if he'd been waiting for her. As if he somehow expected this question.

"You don't even like me," he finally said, the back legs of his chair hitting the floor.

"How do you know what I like?"

He studied her with a gaze that seemed both exhausted and more awake than usual.

"I've given you an army. I've taken Darmoor for you." Roa took a step toward him. "Now you need reinforcements. Marry me, and I'll get you the men and women you need."

His eyebrows shot upward. "Reinforcements in exchange for a crown? That's a deal much further in your favor than mine."

"We both know that without the continued help of the scrublands, you'll lose this war."

He said nothing.

"Fine," Roa said. "Then we're finished here. I'll take my people and go home."

But as she turned to leave, he rose and stepped out from behind the desk, coming toward her.

"Roa." His fingers slid around her wrist. "Wait."

She went still, her heart thundering, then turned to face him.

His eyes searched hers. "Why?"

"Because if you win this war, you'll become king." She lowered her eyes, faltering.

And I don't trust you to keep my people safe, *she thought.* The only way I can ensure you do right by the scrublands is if I'm there, ruling at your side.

He frowned. But when she raised her eyes to see if this was his answer, she found him studying her mouth.

Roa's pulse quickened.

Warmth flooded her as his thumb brushed slowly across her wrist, feeling just how fast her heart beat.

When he reached for her with his other hand, before his fingertips could graze her cheek, Roa stepped back, her heart thudding like a drum in her chest.

"Do we have a deal?" she whispered.

His hand fell to his side and his face shuttered closed, like a door locking on a secret room.

"A deal. Yes," he said. "Send for reinforcements, and I'll make you queen."

Roa dipped her head to him. "It's already done."

Before he could say another word, Roa left the tent.

After the wedding, while the music played through the camp and people shouted and danced, Roa and Dax lay side by side, staring at the canvas tent ceiling. He hadn't drunk anything all evening. He'd been offered wine over and over, and each time Roa watched him refuse.

For every drink Dax rejected, Roa drank two. Trying to numb herself to what she'd done. To what she was about to do.

Her mouth tasted sour now. Her body hummed with heat.

"I won't hurt you," he whispered, breaking the silence. "I will never hurt you, Roa."

Roa knew what came next. They were bound, and the binding needed to be sealed, absolutely, with an intimate act.

She thought of Theo, sleeping on the other side of the sand sea, completely unaware that Roa had just married the boy he hated most.

Completely unaware of how deeply she'd betrayed him.

Roa fisted her hands to hide their trembling.

Taking Darmoor had been easier than this. Than lying here next to Dax.

She remembered the first and last time she'd done this. How it was over so quickly, and how it had hurt. How Theo had kissed her afterward, smiling, and she knew in that moment that he didn't realize he'd hurt her.

He hadn't meant to take and give nothing back. But he had. He'd left her aching and alone.

And here was another boy—a boy she didn't even love—who was going to do the same thing.

Roa couldn't do it again. It was too much.

She sat up, her head spinning.

Dax looked at her.

"You won't ever hurt me," she'd said more calmly than she felt, "because you won't ever touch me."

It was a command, soft but final. And with it ringing in her ears, she left him there, all alone, and stumbled to Lirabel's tent.

Her head ached from the wine, her stomach rolled, and the world tilted around her. Roa climbed in beside her friend. For several heartbeats, there was silence.

And then Lirabel reached out her hand, lacing her fingers through Roa's.

It undid her. Tears welled in her eyes. She bit down on her lip to stifle the strange sob welling up in her; and Lirabel gathered her up, pulled her in, held her while she wept.

What have I done? *she'd thought that night and so many nights since.* What have I done?

Eight

Roa woke to the smell of peppermint and the sound of a strong, steady heartbeat. The sun lit up the canvas all around her. The air was stuffy and warm. And her cheek was pressed to someone's chest.

Her whole body was pressed to someone's chest.

Peppermint.

Roa swallowed.

Dax.

She kept very still. From his breathing, he was awake. Awake and trying not to move. She felt his arm resting across her lower back, his fingers curled lightly over the curve of her hip.

Roa squeezed her eyes shut.

This was not good.

Not good. Not good.

She must have been so cold in the night, she'd climbed on top of him for warmth.

"I won't tell anyone if you won't," he said softly.

Roa pushed herself up. She glanced down at the bare-chested king whose other arm was bent behind his head. A rusted iron key hung from a cord around his neck.

She meant to look away, but her gaze snagged on the smooth shape of his shoulders. They sloped ever so slightly, curving away from his neck and down to his strong arms. Her gaze continued downward, noticing how his waist tapered. Noticing the dark, curling hairs below his belly button. The ones that trailed down and . . .

Look away, Roa!

She looked away, right into his face. Disheveled dark curls, warm brown eyes, stubbled jaw.

She had a sudden, troubling urge to run her fingertip along his cheek—just to feel the roughness.

The corner of his mouth curved, watching her look at him.

"Please," he said. "Take your time."

Panic flared through her. She slid out of the bedroll, needing to get out of this tent.

Her heart hammered in her ears as her hands searched the floor for her clothes, then pulled them on, keeping her back to Dax.

He sat up to watch her. "Since when are you so skittish?"

Roa didn't answer him. Didn't dare look his way. She was not like his other girls. She would not be lured in by his charming smile, by that silver tongue, only to be cast aside when he'd had his fill of her.

To break the silence, she said, "Watch your back today." Catching sight of her sandskarf, Roa quickly grabbed it, then started wrapping it around her shoulders. "Theo is not your ally. So long as Sky travels with us, you need to stay alert."

Dax stretched, yawning, then ran a hand through his mess of curls.

She averted her eyes, looking down at the tent floor.

"Really, Roa. I'm touched. It's almost like you care."

Roa glanced up to find that annoying smile on his face.

"Care?" she said coldly. "You think I care for a king whose intelligence begins and ends with his ability to choose a good wine—or a good bedfellow?" Something prowled in her chest, snapping and growling. "My care for you is directly proportionate to how useful you are. The moment you cease to benefit the scrublands is the moment my care runs out."

Her words sapped the warmth from his eyes.

"Why not depose me, then?"

Roa froze in the tent entrance. "What?" she whispered.

"You could rule alone," he said. "It would be incredibly convenient."

"Don't tempt me," she muttered as she pulled her sandskarf up over her head. Opening the tent flap, she stepped into the sunlight.

The moment the tent flap fell closed, a blur of white feathers almost barreled into her.

Roa! Essie flew in tight circles around her, her worry bleeding into Roa. *Come quickly.*

Roa ran after her, trying to keep up, as Essie led her to the edge of camp. There she found Lirabel retching up dinner from the night before.

"Lirabel—"

"I'm fine," said her friend, crouching low to the ground, her arms trembling a little.

"You don't look fine," whispered Roa. She ran for a water skin, then sank down next to her friend, uncorking the skin and holding it out.

Lirabel ignored her. Wiping her mouth on her wrist, she rose—a little shakily—to her feet. "I said I'm fine."

But even her voice trembled.

What's wrong? Roa asked Essie, who ruffled her feathers from her perch on her sister's shoulder.

She's been sick every day since we came to the scrublands. I thought you knew.

Together they watched Lirabel walk back into camp.

Why hadn't Roa noticed?

Dax had noticed. This was obvious as they rode through the morning. He kept casting concerned glances Lirabel's way, riding close beside her as they made their way to his mother's abode.

Roa watched them carefully, Theo's accusation ringing through her head.

What if her new status comes at a cost?

Roa wouldn't—couldn't—believe it. Dax would never use Lirabel like that. And Lirabel would never allow herself to be used.

Roa refused to indulge such an odious thought.

By early evening, their destination shimmered in the distant heat. Here the pale sand turned to packed, dry earth. To the east and west, wild yellow grasses gleamed in the setting sun. And in the midst of it all, the white walls of Amina's desert home shone like glass.

They would sleep within those walls tonight, then arrive in Firgaard by dusk tomorrow.

The house was just north of the main travel route between Firgaard and the scrublands, and off-limits to anyone but Amina, the former dragon queen. It had been built for her by her husband as a wedding gift.

Dax had inherited it upon her death; and after the coronation, he'd come here several times. It was just a day's ride from Firgaard and an easy retreat from palace life. The last two times Lirabel had accompanied him, on her way to the scrublands as emissary. Roa had never set foot here before. The only reason they were staying tonight was because Dax needed to retrieve something he'd left behind on his last visit.

A horse pulled up beside Lirabel. Both of them looked to see the king himself, staring straight ahead.

"Race you," he said.

Lirabel looked queasy at the thought and shook her head. "Not me."

So Dax leaned forward, looking around her. "Roa?"

At first she thought it was a joke. But then he smiled a strange smile. It reminded her of rainy afternoons, playing gods and monsters with him. She knew that smile. It was the one that slipped out when he thought he was about to win.

"What's the prize?" she asked, despite herself.

Dax grinned. As if her question meant he was already victorious.

"The loser has to give the winner a kiss."

Roa made a disgusted face.

His smile faded. "Fine then. If you win, what do you want?"

Roa was about to say *Nothing*, because she wasn't going to race him. Except there *was* something she wanted.

"I want you to call an Assembly as soon as we return to Firgaard."

The next scheduled Assembly—where Dax and his council made decisions, passing or overturning laws before a public audience—wasn't for three weeks. Roa didn't want to wait that long. She wanted the treaty terms imposed as soon as possible.

Dax cocked his head, studying her. "Fine," he said, turning to squint into the distance. "But if I win, you owe me a kiss."

"Fine," she agreed. After all, Oleander was a lackluster horse who did as she was told only half the time.

Roa didn't wait for him to count them down. She dug her heels into Poppy, who lurched forward. Her hooves kicked up a plume of gold dust that bloomed through the air as they galloped away from Dax and Lirabel.

Roa kept her eyes on the white walls ahead, following the path carved through yellow grass. Essie soared high above, trailing her.

Suddenly, the hooves of a second horse drummed the ground behind her, coming up on her right side.

Roa threw a look over her shoulder. The dragon king kept low to his horse, gaining ground fast, covered in a thin layer of dust.

Roa slowed long enough to ask him where the finish line was.

"The stables!" he called, as the wind whipped through his curls. "Around the back of the house!"

Roa nudged Poppy, who pulled ahead.

There was no gate in the walls, just an opening wide enough to fit a wagon. It reminded Roa of home, where doors were always open or unlocked. Where gates were unnecessary.

She rode Poppy past the walls crawling with green ivy. A hill rose before them, painted in reds and greens, sloping with gardens and jagged with rock.

Amina's house stood at the top of the hill, half-hidden by jacaranda trees.

This was the dragon queen's abode, and yet it felt nothing like the close confinements of Firgaard. It felt wild and fierce and free. Like the scrublands from which they'd come.

When the path diverged, Roa had to slow. Dax said the stables were around the other side, but which path would take her there?

Essie flew higher. *Help,* Roa pleaded. But before her sister could see the clearest path, the clatter of hooves made Roa turn. Wind rushed into her face as Dax raced past them. Looking back over his shoulder, he gave Roa a mock salute.

Follow him! Essie swooped after the king. *I'll find you a shortcut!*

Roa dug her heels into Poppy, who lurched forward.

But the path twisted and turned around thorny angular trees, then broke off—again and again—in different directions. She lost Dax. She halted Poppy twice, looking for Oleander's hoofprints, waiting for Essie's directions, before gritting her teeth and racing on.

Finally, through the trees, she saw a long white stable with a thatched roof.

When they entered, Poppy's hooves clopped on the stone floor. Their echo broke through the quiet. It was cool and dim inside. It smelled like dust and old hay.

Roa scanned the aisle of stalls for Dax, but found no sign of him.

Letting out a breath, she relaxed.

The moment she dismounted, a shape materialized out of the shadows.

"That's one pokey horse you have."

Roa spun. The dragon king leaned against the door of a stall farther down, arms crossed over his chest. The evening's lazy sunlight slanted through the narrow windows, casting him in warm, golden light.

Oleander poked her nose out of the stall, already untacked. Surely, he hadn't had *that* much time . . .

"It was an unfair race."

His eyebrow quirked upward. "Unfair how?"

"You're familiar with the grounds." She tipped her chin up. "Whereas I've never even been here."

"Two facts you were aware of before you agreed to race me," he said, taking Poppy's reins from Roa. "But I'll take pity on you." He rubbed Poppy's velvet nose. "Even though you lost, I'll still call the Assembly. I'll do it the moment we return to the palace."

He stepped in close then. So close, Roa could see the dust on his lips. It made her want to lick her own, to see if they were dusty, too.

She thought of the one and only time she'd ever kissed him. So long ago now.

The memory sliced her with sadness, and she stepped back. Her shoulder blades hit the stable wall. Swallowing, she said, "Let's get this over with before the others arrive."

Dax let go of Poppy's reins. He closed the distance between them, pressing both palms to the stone on either side of Roa's head.

Caging her in.

Roa was about to growl a warning, but before she could, the tips of their noses brushed, and that snapping, growling creature went silent and soft.

"Silly girl," he murmured, his breath warm on her lips. "I don't want to kiss you *right here*." Lifting his thumb, he slowly swept the dust from her lower lip. "I'll come to collect when it suits me."

The impertinence of it scorched her. Roa lifted her angry gaze to his. If he thought she was anything like his mistresses, if he thought she would happily receive him any time it pleased him, he was . . .

He was . . .

It was difficult to think, with Dax looking at her like that, his gaze fixed on her mouth. It made Roa wonder if he might change his mind. Might lean in and devour her right here.

But the sound of clattering hooves broke the quiet. As a dozen horses trotted into the stable, Dax stepped immediately away, linking his hands behind his neck.

Cool air rushed between them, making Roa realize just how warm she was.

Dax reached for Poppy's reins and, without a word or backward glance, led the horse into the stall next to Oleander's.

Roa's eyes lifted to Jas and Lirabel, the first two riders to come through the doors, and then behind them, to Theo.

Their gazes met. Roa looked instantly away. She felt ashamed. Then angry for *being* ashamed.

With them came Essie, who was at her shoulder now. Claws digging gently into Roa's skin. Roa turned her face into her sister's feathers, taking comfort in their softness.

What happened?

Nothing.

Then why are you trembling?

As the rest of the caravan poured into the stables, filling it with noise and commotion, Roa took her sister and left. They walked past quiet fountains and still pools. Through rows of highland roses buzzing with bees. Stopping at the edge of a hill, Roa hugged herself hard, staring out over the gardens below. Gardens that had once belonged to another outlander queen.

Slowly, Roa raised her fingers to her lower lip, where Dax had touched it.

Silly girl, he'd said.

Perhaps he was right. Perhaps that was why, just for a heartbeat, Roa had wanted him to lean in and take what she owed him.

Before

Roa was nine years old on the day of her earning. She stood with her sister in the middle of the threshing floor. The sky was storm gray and the air was misty. Beside her, Essie's unruly black curls shone with raindrops and her hands were restless: clenching and unclenching, tapping her thighs.

Essie took the responsibility of earning more seriously than Roa. She'd been in constant debate with their teachers these past few months over who had the right to earn a weapon. Several times Roa woke to find her sister pacing their room late at night. When she asked what was wrong, Essie would come back to bed and say strange things. Like "Define the term enemy," and "What came first, do you think, the weapon or the adversary?"

Most of all, Essie studied harder and practiced more than Roa. She deserved to earn her weapon today.

Now, though, as they stood on the threshing floor, Essie's jaw clenched. Her hands fiddled with the buttons down the front of her blue dress. Roa kept shooting her glances, agitated by her sister's agitation.

"Stop fidgeting," Roa hissed while keeping her eyes on their father.

The master of the House of Song towered over his daughters, gripping the head of his own earning: a staff carved by Roa's grandmother. His skin glistened with rain and his purple cotton shirt was soaked through, making it look almost black. Beyond him stood the rest of the House of Song, gathered in a circle to bear witness.

Their father motioned to Lirabel, a girl Roa and Essie's age and a ward in their house. The House of Song took in Lirabel and her sisters when the white harvest starved their family almost to death, forcing their mother to give them up.

Lirabel stepped forward now. She wore her hair in a thick braid over one shoulder, and the bow and arrows she'd earned the previous summer were strapped to her back. Inscribed into her bow's leather were the words: Earned by Lirabel, ward of the House of Song.

Roa remembered the day of her friend's earning. How Lirabel burst into tears when she read the inscription. Roa thought they were tears of gratitude, after everything the House of Song had done for her. It was only afterward that Essie corrected her.

It says ward, Essie explained. Not daughter.

But she is a ward, thought Roa at the time.

It would be years before Roa realized what it meant: that Lirabel could never be their equal. Never be their sister. Only a recipient of their charity.

You gave us a place here so easily, Lirabel told her. You could take it away with just as little effort.

Now, pelted by rain, Lirabel handed their father the first of two bundles wrapped in silk.

He unwrapped the first and presented it to Roa.

It was a scythe—a favorite weapon of Song, hearkening to their agrarian roots. The steel had been skillfully hammered by blacksmiths from Sky. The hilt was fashioned out of wood, inlaid with alabaster, and engraved with the star she and Essie had been born under, as well as an inscription: Earned by Roa, daughter of the House of Song.

She looked from her father's gentle gaze to her twin's bright ebony eyes. The hum glowed warmly between them.

Essie smiled at her. Roa beamed back.

From the second bundle, their father drew out a knife. It was the length of Essie's small forearm. The blade didn't curve like Roa's scythe, but narrowed to a needle-sharp point.

As he presented it to Essie, though, she stepped back, shaking her head.

Roa's smile slid away.

What are you doing? *she thought.*

Essie wouldn't look at her. So Roa glanced to Lirabel, as if she might hold the answer. But Lirabel's eyes only widened.

"I'm sorry," Essie said, staring at her sandaled feet—flecked with mud and chaff. She spoke loud enough for those gathered around the threshing floor to hear. "I can't accept."

Their father drew himself up, his grip tightening on the carved lion head of his staff. "Explain yourself, daughter."

Essie looked up into his face.

"The old stories say we belong to each other," she said quietly, as if she were afraid but was determined to speak the words anyway. "If that's true, then our enemies are not our enemies but our brothers." She looked to Roa. "And our sisters."

Roa stared at Essie, her forehead crumpling into a frown.

She'd been planning this for a long time, Roa now realized, remembering the debates Essie engaged in with their teachers. Remembering the nights Roa woke to find her pacing.

But why didn't she tell me? *They told each other everything.*

Their father stepped forward. Wiping the rain out of his eyes, he bent down so his face was level with Essie's. "Do you realize what this will mean?"

Essie nodded.

"You'll be thought of as weak."

Essie said nothing.

"You'll be seen as a girl who belongs nowhere and to no one."

Essie held their father's gaze. "I know where I belong," she said. "And to whom."

As if that were enough.

Their father lowered the knife, looking from Essie to Roa, his eyes pleading for her help. But one glance at Essie's face and Roa knew there would be no convincing her.

Roa reached to take the blade, staring at the hilt of her sister's earning. Earned by Essie, *the inscription read,* daughter of the House of Song. *The blades might be different, but the hilts were exactly the same. Both inlaid with alabaster. Both engraved with the same star.*

A perfect match.

"I'll hold on to it for her," said Roa. "In case she changes her mind."

Nine

After dinner, Roa and Essie set out for the former dragon queen's room.

Roa's room now.

With the sun setting, it was cooler in the east wing's halls. Roa pulled her sandskarf up over her head to keep the warmth in.

The house had been modeled after the round homes scrublanders were known for, with a terra-cotta roof and a central pavilion. But this house had too many wings for a scrublander home, and in this way it borrowed from Firgaardian architecture, too. The gardens were full of highland roses, juniper trees, jacarandas, and other plants native to both Roa's home and Dax's. It was a perfect blend of both, and a reminder that before she'd become queen, Dax's mother was a scrublander.

Amina, who'd been born into the House of Stars, was childhood friends with Roa's mother. Roa remembered the first time the queen came to visit them. She and Jas were playing gods and monsters on the floor of her father's study and Roa was about to take his skyweaver piece when the queen stepped into the room and lowered herself to her knees at Roa's side. Roa remembered the way her beautiful layers of blue silk pooled onto the dirt floor. Remembered the thin golden circlet shining above her glittering black eyes.

She was perfect. Like a painting.

Now, as Roa's bare feet padded the tile floors, she wondered what it had been like for Amina, living all the way across the sand sea. Being separated from her loved ones. Being *queen*.

Theo had compared Roa to Amina, believing they were both victims whose stories would end the same way.

I don't believe that, Essie interrupted from her perch on Roa's shoulder. Her sister had been quiet and distant all day, but the hum was back. Bright and strong, linking them both.

As Roa approached a familiar door, she looked to her sister. *Believe what?*

That Amina was a victim.

Roa wasn't so sure.

I think she knew exactly what she was walking into, said Essie. *I think she had her own reasons for marrying him.*

Maybe, Roa thought. *Or maybe she didn't realize he was a monster until too late.*

A scrublander symbol had been carved into this door: three vertical lines, confined in a circle. It was the same symbol painted above her father's study. Roa lifted her fingers, tracing the lines.

"We've passed this door three times," she said aloud, sighing heavily. "I think we're lost."

Roa's tracing fingers must have pressed too hard, because the door creaked and swung slowly in.

Her fingers paused in midair.

"Hello?"

No one answered. So she pushed the door all the way open and stepped inside.

It was a small, dim room that smelled like candle smoke and parchment. Rough-hewn shelves were built into the walls and each cubby was crammed with scrolls.

"Is anyone here?"

Silence answered her. Essie flew off to investigate while Roa stepped closer to the shelves. Most of the scrolls were yellowed and crinkled with age. But some, in a cubby at the end, were crisp and new.

Roa was reaching for one of these when a bright, startled feeling raced through her.

Roa. Essie's voice rang through her mind. *Look.*

She turned to find her sister's hawk form perched on the edge of a desk beneath the window, staring down at crisp white parchment, folded and stamped with a red wax seal. Roa stepped toward it. Impressed into the wax was the shape of an elegant, seven-petaled flower—a namsara. Roa had given this same flower to Dax's sister, Asha, the night before she escaped the city.

Roa looked to Essie.

It isn't addressed to anyone, said her sister.

So Roa broke the seal, unfolded it, and read:

> *Three days ago, a shipment from Darmoor was due to arrive at Baron Silva's stronghold. Despite the price on our heads, Torwin insisted on going, determined to intercept it. There's a weapon in the shipment which, in the wrong hands, could unleash a monster.*

We quarreled about it. He took Kozu and left in the night while I slept. I was furious at first, but he should have returned by now, and I'm worried they expected him. I'm afraid of what they'll do if they've caught him.

I can't wait here any longer.

I'm going after him.

There was no signature, but when Roa turned it over, touching the namsara flower on the seal, she knew who it was from. "Asha."

After the revolt, when the law demanded Dax's sister pay the killing price of a king, Roa had helped her and Torwin escape. They'd been on the run for over a month now, with an abundance of prices on their heads. Not everyone was pleased with the new king's reign, and Dax's enemies had only to gain by using his sister against him—*if* they could catch her.

Asha was here? said Essie. Her silver eyes scanned the shadows and corners of the study, searching for traces of her.

Roa skimmed the black handwriting once more. "Who's the intended recipient?"

Isn't it obvious? Essie took the letter in her beak, then set it down on the desk where she could examine it more closely.

It wasn't obvious to Roa.

Dax is the only one who comes here. When he does, he brings only a select few with him. They've probably been passing messages this way since Asha and Torwin escaped the city. Taking the letter in her beak once more, she lifted it up to Roa. *If they're in danger, Dax needs to know.*

✦✦✦

Dax wasn't in the dining room where Roa and Essie had left him and the others. So they checked the terrace, then the gardens, but he wasn't there either. Finally, the cook led Roa to his room and told her to wait. She'd find the king and send him to her.

There were no guards standing outside. So Roa walked right in and shut the door behind her.

The evening sunlight pooled on the dirt floor, spilled across the bed, and illuminated the tapestries hanging on the plain white walls.

With no one here to see her, Roa moved toward the first tapestry. It was of a scrublander woman with dark curls and clear black eyes. She wore a gold circlet on her head and was smiling in a way that said she knew something Roa didn't. Her two children were with her: a very young and unscarred Asha, held aloft in her mother's arms, and a slightly older Dax, standing next to them. The artist had captured the exact color of his eyes—a warm brown, wide and curious—as well as those jug-handle ears.

Beside this tapestry hung two others. By the brighter quality of the colors, she could tell both were more recently made.

The first one was of Asha, rendered in gold and red threads, with a burn scar running down her face. She held a hunting axe in one hand and a scroll in the other. Beside her was a freckle-faced young man playing a lute.

Torwin, thought Roa, touching the threads with her right hand while her left tightened around the letter.

She hoped he was safe. She hoped they both were.

The last tapestry was of Dax's cousin, Safire. The new commandant. Her keen blue eyes peered out at Roa, as if trying to decide if she was a threat.

They were images of the king's family.

But why keep them here? asked Essie, who'd been snooping around the room while Roa studied the tapestries. She came now to settle on the top of Dax's bedpost. *So far from the palace?*

Roa didn't know.

As she turned to face her sister, she found herself at the foot of Dax's bed.

Roa looked down at the silky blue sheets and gold cushions. As she reached to touch the translucent canopied veils, she wondered how many girls he'd brought here, and if they'd spent the night in this bed.

She wondered what it would be like.

Maybe you should climb in and see, said Essie from her perch on the bedpost.

Roa's face flamed. This was one of the few unfortunate consequences of their bond. Essie knew her most embarrassing thoughts.

Roa threw her a look.

What? Those silver eyes flashed.

Roa glowered at her sister, who radiated warm delight back at her.

Oh come on, Roa. I dare you.

You dare me? What are we, eight years old?

You, Essie shot back, *are obviously scared.*

Hot, sharp anger burst through Roa. She blasted her sister

with it, then pushed aside the veils.

She considered the bed. Her heart beat wildly.

Maybe Roa *was* scared. Just a little.

Sliding off her slippers, she climbed onto the sheets and sat cross-legged, staring up at the white bird at the top of the bedpost.

There. See?

Maybe you should lie down, Essie said, teeming with mischief. *Really test it out.*

Roa gritted her teeth. *Fine.* She flopped stiffly back against the pillows.

The sheets were soft and smooth. They smelled like they'd been spritzed with rosewater, perhaps by one of the staff.

Roa closed her eyes, just for a heartbeat, breathing in the sweet, floral scent.

That doesn't look so bad, Essie said. *Maybe I'll—*

A heart-stopping sound cut her off: the creak of a knob, turning. The slow groan of a door, opening.

Roa's eyes flew open.

Quick! Essie said, her voice full of laughter. *Hide!*

She flew out into the gardens. Roa rolled off the bed and onto the floor, humiliation flaring through her. She quickly slid underneath, her heart pounding so hard she felt certain it would burst right out of her chest.

"Roa?" Dax called.

His footsteps echoed across the floor, from the hall to the terrace. Roa looked to the door, but it was shut.

Worst of all? Her slippers were lying in full view. Just out of her reach.

Roa cursed her own carelessness.

To Essie, who was somewhere out in the garden, she said, *This is all your fault.*

Essie sent a golden feeling back—her version of a laugh.

As if this was funny.

Roa felt like such a fool. If she answered Dax, he would clearly see she was hiding under his bed. He would want to know why. But if he knew what she'd done just now—lying down in his sheets, breathing in the smell of his pillows—there was only one conclusion he could come to.

Roa squeezed the letter in her hand.

I need to give it to him, she thought, even as she lay frozen in place, her cheek pressed against the cool dirt floor.

Dax stood at the window now, the breeze ruffling his curls. Roa's heart pounded as she watched his fingers loosen the laces of his shirt, then roll his sleeves up to his elbows. She watched him kick off his boots and lean, barefoot, against the sill as he stared out across the sand sea.

Sighing roughly, he turned around, then sank slowly down the wall to the floor. He sat with his knees bent and his hands tangled in his hair, like he was trying to solve an unsolvable problem.

Sooner or later, he was going to see the slippers beside the bed. Then see Roa beneath it.

Better to get it over with . . .

But at the same moment Roa decided to reveal herself, someone knocked on the door.

Roa went still, pulling back as Dax rose to his feet.

Halfway to the door, though, something made him stop. He

turned back, paused, then came toward the bed.

Roa could only see his bare feet as he bent down, then his fingers as he reached for her slippers. He picked one up. All he had to do was get down on his hands and knees . . .

All he had to do was *look*.

Roa bit down hard on her lip, praying to any gods who just might happen to be listening.

The knock came again. Dax straightened.

"Who is it?"

"Just me," came a too-familiar voice. Lirabel.

The king went to answer the door, taking the slipper with him.

Roa let out a breath.

"Oh, Dax." Lirabel's strained voice echoed through the room. "We're in so much trouble."

She was pacing. Frantic. Her sandals had tracked sand in, and it scattered in her wake. "I'd hoped it was just an illness . . ."

"Lirabel—"

But whatever Dax was going to say fell away as the room plunged into a stilted silence. And even though Roa could only see her friend's legs, she could hear Lirabel's tiny punctuated gasps of breath.

She was crying.

"Today I counted," Lirabel whispered when she'd gotten control of herself. "It's been eleven weeks."

Dax stayed near the door, completely silent.

"It's been eleven weeks since the last time I *bled*."

A cold feeling spread through Roa. Like the early-morning

frost that settles over the ground in the cold season.

When Dax still didn't respond, Lirabel said: "Eleven weeks is too long, Dax!"

Roa wanted to peer out and look at them. But if she did that, she would surely be seen.

"Lirabel," Dax finally said, perfectly calm, "I don't understand what you're saying."

"I'm saying . . . ," she whispered, "that I'm pregnant."

Roa flinched.

It was quiet for several heartbeats. And then Dax whispered: "What?"

Eleven weeks. That would have been before the revolt. When Dax was visiting the scrublands, asking for Roa's help.

Had they—had *this*—been going on for that long? Right under Roa's nose?

Was this the reason for Lirabel's distance?

She suddenly saw them in her mind. Dax and Lirabel— her husband and her friend—together in the very bed she hid beneath. The bed Essie dared her to lie in.

She told herself she didn't care. That it didn't matter.

But if that were true, why did it feel like she'd just been stabbed in the ribs?

"What am I going to do?" Lirabel whispered.

Roa moved ever so slightly, trying to see, when another knock came on the door.

She watched Dax's hands clenching and unclenching. But that was the only visible sign of distress she could see in him.

Finally, he moved to answer it. Lirabel turned to the wall,

concealing her tears from whoever was interrupting.

"What is it?" Dax asked.

"I was sent to fetch you, my lord." The voice sounded like one of the staff. Out of breath. "A fight's broken out between your caravan and members of the House of Sky. We . . . we aren't sure what to do."

"Give us a moment," Dax said, shutting the door and turning to Lirabel.

"I'm sorry," he told her. "I need to deal with this."

Roa frowned. Dax had guards to deal with things like skirmishes.

Lirabel remained facing the wall.

"I'll make sure you're taken care of. As soon as we arrive back in Firgaard, I'll see what I can do for you. All right?"

A cold silence bloomed through the air. Lirabel had nothing else to say to him.

So Dax turned on his heel and left the room.

A dark anger swept through Roa. He'd make sure she was taken care of? He would see what he could do for her?

What kind of a man said these things?

The kind of man who sleeps with his wife's friend, gets her pregnant, then leaves her crying and alone.

It made Roa want to go after him, corner him, and force him to fix this. Now. Not when they got to Firgaard.

Roa clenched her fists, watching as Lirabel sank to the floor, her body shaking with sobs. The letter from Asha was all but forgotten as Roa listened to her friend weep.

What if, Theo's voice rang through her mind, *in exchange for her position, Dax requires something . . . extra?*

Roa's nails bit into her palms. She didn't want to believe such a thing. The reason Lirabel was a ward in Roa's house was because of the sanctions imposed by Dax's father. Sanctions that impoverished Lirabel's family and destroyed their farm. Sanctions that Dax still hadn't lifted, despite all his promises.

It didn't make sense that Lirabel would willingly choose such a man.

I should have protected you, she thought. *I should have paid attention.*

Roa longed to go and comfort her friend. But if Lirabel wanted Roa to know all of this, she would have told her . . . wouldn't she? Roa feared that revealing herself now would shame Lirabel and make the whole situation worse. She didn't want to drive her friend even further away.

Eventually, Lirabel fell silent. She pressed her hands to her eyes, then dried them with the hem of her riding shirt. After taking a deep shuddering breath, Lirabel got to her feet and left.

Ten

Roa couldn't get out of that room fast enough.

Her thunderous footsteps echoed through the empty hall. Her red-hot anger made the walls blur. She gripped Essie's knife tight in one hand, needing to find Dax.

She would make him fix this.

Roa thought of that moment in the stables, when he'd brushed his thumb across her lip. How she would have let him kiss her—would have *welcomed* it—if they hadn't been interrupted.

It disgusted her now.

There was a reason Dax was the enemy. How could she let herself forget it?

Roa! Essie's white body blurred as it flew past her, then turned back, cutting her off. Roa halted as her sister flapped her wings, silver eyes shining. *Are you all right?*

"Am *I* all right?" Roa said aloud. "I think it's Lirabel we need to worry about."

Essie flew in swooping circles around her.

Even Theo heard the rumors of Dax and Lirabel. Roa watched the circling white bird. *Theo, who wasn't anywhere near Firgaard these last few months.* She gritted her teeth at her own negligence. *If I had just paid attention . . .*

No, said Essie. *This is not your fault.*

Wasn't it, though?

If Roa had never married Dax, never helped him dethrone his father, Lirabel wouldn't be in this position. In fact, Roa's actions seemed to only bring unhappiness to the ones she loved—Theo, Jas, and now Lirabel.

Maybe Theo was right. Roa was no different from Amina. Just like Amina, Roa thought marrying a king would bring peace to their people.

Just like Amina, Roa hadn't realized she was marrying a monster.

Roa walked on.

Essie flew after her.

You've had a thousand other things to worry about.

Roa stopped before a wide stained-glass window. Its bright reds and blues were lit up by the sunset beyond.

Roa had given up everything for this king. The king responsible for Essie's accident. The king who didn't care that his father's sanctions on her people were starving them. The king who'd slept with Lirabel, then discarded her like worthless refuse.

The hum started deep in Roa's belly. Like lightning, it buzzed and crackled and sparked.

The hum was bright and alive within Essie, too, like a fire fusing them together.

"I hate him," Roa said bitterly.

But even as she said it, tears pricked her eyes.

Oh, Roa. Essie's voice seemed suddenly fainter. *I wish I could fix this.*

"I hate him for using her. . . ."

The hum reverberated in Roa's ears now. Rattled in her bones, making her temperature rise. Roa shook her head, clenching her teeth against the deafening roar of it.

"I hate him for making me into a fool. . . ."

Essie's eyes shone more fiercely than usual as she circled Roa, carving through the air, swooping around and around her sister. Just for a moment, Roa thought she felt her sister's soul flicker.

"I hate him most of all for what he did to you." Her fists were clenched. The air between them was white-hot and her next words came out like a sob. "I hate him for shattering us!"

The hum exploded, searing them both. As it did, a resounding crash rang out as the windows in the hallway burst.

The heat that had been rising between them vanished.

A cold emptiness rushed in.

Roa stared at the white bird before her. Those silver eyes stared back, but they seemed startled. Frightened. Confused.

Essie?

Her sister's silence pierced her.

Roa reached across their bond, only to lose it. She reached again, but her sister's spirit was like water slipping through her fingers. The hum—so bright and strong moments before—was like the heartbeat of a wounded, dying creature. Still there, but ever so faint.

It terrified her.

She watched the white bird swoop out through the broken window and up into the pomegranate sky. Roa followed it to the window. The sun was gone, but its light glowed just above the desert's horizon.

"Essie!"

But no answer came.

Before

The very first summer Dax came to stay in the scrublands, their mother made Roa and Essie take him everywhere. Essie wasn't allowed to go to the cliffs unless Dax went, too. Roa wasn't allowed to play gods and monsters unless it was Dax she played against.

Roa, who hated cliff jumping, never went to the cliffs. And Essie, who hated board games, wandered off with Lirabel, leaving Roa stranded with the king's son for entire afternoons.

They knew what their mother was doing. She was interfering, and they didn't appreciate it.

So the sisters made a pact. They would not be friends with the disruptive visitor from Firgaard. They would shun him on principle.

It was easy at first. The king's son had never played gods and monsters before. He was a boring opponent and it annoyed Roa. Eventually, if she beat him enough times, he would stop wanting to play her.

Or so she thought.

But the more ruthless she was on the board, the more eager he was to learn. The more she beat him, the more he begged to play again.

His unyielding enthusiasm made her soften, just a little. Sometimes, when he stared for long stretches of silence at the checkered stone board, thinking hard, she gave in. Helping him see things he couldn't. Telling him how to predict her moves. Giving him the knowledge her father had once given her, when she first learned to play.

He improved quickly after that, and strangely, it pleased her.

Even more strangely, he seemed to enjoy pleasing her.

When he said something that made Roa smile, he smiled twice as brightly. When he made her laugh, it was like he'd solved a puzzle he'd been working on for months. It lit him up from the inside.

The more they played, the more her pact with Essie got harder to keep and soon she didn't hate this annoying boy from Firgaard. In fact, she didn't find him annoying at all.

Traitor, whispered a voice inside her.

One day, Dax asked Roa to come with him and Essie to the cliffs. Roa never went to the cliffs. She didn't like watching her sister and their friends jump from the heights and into the water. It made her queasy, watching them fall and fall and fall.

But Dax convinced her.

It was that day at the cliffs when she realized her sister was a traitor, too.

Dax begged Roa to jump with them, but Roa kept her feet planted firmly on the ground. So they left her behind. She watched them from the grass. The way Dax made Essie laugh . . . it was just like the way he made Roa laugh. Only Essie laughed louder and freer.

Essie was like that. Uninhibited. She could tell a secret to someone she'd just met and not think twice about it.

Roa didn't know how to be like that.

If she and her sister were two books in their father's study, Essie would be the one lying open on the desk, enticing you to read it. Roa would be the one stuffed between a dozen others, high up on the shelf.

It wasn't just Essie's laugh, though. It was the sight of Essie and Dax having fun without her, teasing and splashing and racing each other up and down the rocks. It made Roa realize something she didn't want to realize.

She got up from the grass and left.

Essie came after her.

"What's wrong?" Her sister trailed her down the dirt path through the cliffs, dripping wet and shivering.

"Nothing," said Roa. "I'm bored, that's all."

Since when did she lie to her sister?

"Then come jump with us."

Roa thought of the way Essie flung herself from the cliffs. Of the way Dax flung himself after her.

Roa kept walking.

"Dax is right," Essie said to her back. "You hoard your thoughts like a dragon."

The words hurt—not because they were untrue, but because they meant Essie and Dax were talking about her when she wasn't there.

Roa turned to face her sister.

"I didn't realize you were such close friends," she said, her voice wobbly.

Essie's lips parted. Her wet curls dripped.

"Roa . . ."

She didn't finish, though. She didn't need to. Essie was that open book on the desk. Easy to read. Everything there on the surface.

In her sister's eyes, Roa saw the truth. It was like the day of their earning. Essie had been keeping another secret from her.

Essie liked Dax.

And it made Roa jealous. Not of Essie, though. Of Dax.

It had never before occurred to Roa that she could lose her sister. And as silly as it was, the thought of losing her to Dax terrified Roa.

She didn't know how to say that, though. So she fled.

It was an absurd notion. Running from her sister? Essie would find her. She always found her. It was like trying to run from her own self.

"I'm not the only one keeping secrets," said Essie, breathing hard as her bare feet padded the cracked dirt floors of Roa's hiding place.

Roa lifted her forehead from her arms, hugging her knees. Essie came and sat beside her, pressing her back to the crumbled wall of the ruined House of Shade.

"I don't keep secrets from you," Roa whispered, hooking her chin around her arms and staring straight ahead at the abandoned fire basin, half-eaten by rust and sinking into the ground.

Essie rested her head on Roa's shoulder, soaking Roa's dress with her wet hair. "This is a secret you don't realize you have."

Roa frowned at her, not understanding. She shook it away. "We made a pact," she said. "He's not allowed to come between us."

"He's not between us. Look." Essie squished herself right up against Roa's hip, until more of their bodies were touching than not. She grinned at Roa.

Roa looked away, trying to stay cross. But her sister's grin melted her anger and a smile touched her lips.

"He's not going to take me away from you," Essie whispered, knowing Roa's innermost fear. "Besides, you're the one he likes. Not me."

Roa pulled away, staring at her. "What?"

But she remembered the way Dax smiled at her lately. The way he loved to make her laugh.

Maybe it was true. But even so, who cared? Certainly not Roa.

"If he's going to take anyone away," said Essie, a little soberly, "it's going to be you."

Roa shook her head. "You're daft."

Essie bent her head toward her sister's so that their temples touched. "Just wait and see," she said, snaking an arm around Roa's waist and holding her tight.

Eleven

Roa didn't hear the footsteps crunching glass. Didn't feel someone at her side, saying her name, until he started wrapping a torn strip of his own shirt tightly around her arm.

"Are you all right?" Theo asked gently.

Roa looked down to find slivered shards of blue and red glass scattered all around her on the floor. Blown out of the window.

It was then that she felt the warm blood seeping through the cotton bandage tied around her arm. One of the shards must have cut her.

Roa looked from Theo's handiwork up into his eyes.

His gaze swept over the shattered glass, up to the empty window and the red sky beyond, then back to the bloody strip of linen tied around Roa's arm.

"What happened?"

Roa thought about that strange look in her sister's silver eyes just before she flew through the broken window. As if she didn't recognize Roa. As if she didn't know her own sister.

As if her time was running out.

Roa and Essie never spoke about what it meant, about *why* Essie was trapped in hawk form. They never spoke about why Essie's feathers had turned white after the last Relinquishing, or her eyes silver.

But they knew.

Uncrossed spirits couldn't linger among the living forever.

"I'm losing her," she whispered.

Speaking her deepest fear aloud undid something inside Roa. She remembered what it was like after the accident. The unbearable ache of loneliness. The chilling absence where her sister had always been warm and bright and *alive*.

She couldn't bear that again.

Wouldn't bear it.

Roa didn't know how to live in a world where Essie didn't exist.

After everyone else had gone to bed, Roa and Theo stayed up to snuff the lights.

It was a household routine in the scrublands, usually performed at sunset in the month leading up to the Relinquishing. Uncrossed spirits were attracted to warmth and light. So the darker you kept your house at night, the less likely an uncrossed spirit was to visit you on the longest night of the year, when they resumed their true forms and walked among the living.

Roa made an exception for Essie though.

No one knew Roa kept a candle lit for her sister on the longest night of the year.

No one knew she cherished those visits more than anything.

But if she's fading, thought Roa, *what will happen this year?*

As Roa and Theo walked the house, squeezing out candle flames and turning down lamps, Roa whispered, "I think I've made a mistake."

Theo went still in the darkness beside her. "A mistake?"

His gaze traced the silhouette of her as she walked the circular path around the garden, toward the window emitting an orange glow.

"I thought he was a fool."

The air was cool and dry out here. Roa trailed her hand along the wall—still warm from the day's heat.

"And now?" Theo prompted.

She remembered Lirabel crying on the floor, cast aside by Dax. "Now I think he's worse than that."

Theo's footsteps trailed her as she stepped up to the door of the next room. It was the study, where she'd found Asha's letter. A letter still lying beneath Dax's bed.

"What are you saying?"

"What if you're right?" Her fingers curled into her palms. She looked back over her shoulder. "What if he's no different from his father? What if he's the kind of man who takes what he wants and doesn't care who he hurts?" She looked to the twin stars in the northern sky. Essie's favorites.

She tried the latch on the door, which opened easily. Roa entered the room, scanning it to ensure it was empty, before turning down the lamps. When she stepped back outside, she found Theo waiting where she'd left him.

"So you agree with me." He took her hand in his, and she could feel the excited thrum of his pulse as they walked deeper into the garden, away from the walls of the house. Roa felt him look around, but the garden was empty and dark. "Dax must give up the throne."

Roa pulled her hand free, staring up at him. She hadn't said that. "No. I didn't mean . . ."

"I have fifty men from the House of Sky. They're ready for my command."

Roa's mouth dropped open. "You won't be able to get fifty men from Sky into Firgaard."

Theo looped his arms around her waist, drawing her against him. "I was hoping you could help with that."

A shiver coursed through Roa. With the sun gone, the temperature was dropping, but she wasn't shivering from the cold.

"I have contacts inside the city—enemies of Dax's—who are on our side." He reached for her hand again, running his thumb over her knuckles. "They want to help us."

Enemies of Dax's . . .

Roa shook her head. He had the wrong idea entirely. "There is no *us*," she whispered, pulling free. "As much as I loathe him, Dax is the king. Plotting against him is treason. I would be betraying every scrublander who ever believed in me. Every scrublander who believed that my marrying him would make a difference for our people."

Theo scowled in the dark. "And what difference *has* it made?"

Roa's heart fell.

None at all.

But that would soon change. Once they arrived back in Fir-gaard, she would use the treaty to *make* Dax uphold his promises.

"Listen to me." He took her shoulders in his hands, gripping firmly. "Every Firgaardian king is a monster. If Dax isn't one yet, he will be. We need to act swiftly. We don't have time for you to give him any more chances."

Roa shook her head and looked away, into the dark garden around them. Anyone could be out here, listening. He would get himself killed saying these things. "Theo——"

"Just . . . hear me out. It's the least you can do."

Roa gritted her teeth, relenting. "Then the least *you* can do is keep your voice down."

Theo breathed in, then let out the breath. His hands fell away from her shoulders as he scanned the garden.

"I told you I've located the Skyweaver's knife."

Not this again, thought Roa, remembering their long-ago hunts for the blade that cut far deeper than flesh. For a weapon that could trade one soul for another.

Roa was about to protest. To say once again that it was a myth. But Theo continued before she could.

"I found the former owner of it. The woman who sold it to the baron in Firgaard. She, like you, lost someone she loved."

Roa paused, then nodded for him to go on.

"Years ago, her best friend was convicted of a horrible crime: she'd poisoned her father in order to gain her inheritance. It was decided that her punishment should match her crime, and so she was sentenced to death by poison. Even though they burned her body and said the rites, she didn't pass into the world beyond this one. Her soul stayed behind."

Roa stepped closer, enrapt now.

Theo continued: "Year after year, she didn't cross. Each Relinquishing, she became less and less herself. As if her death call was getting stronger, taking part of her with it each time. As if she were fading away.

"Before she faded completely, she told her friend a secret: she *hadn't* killed her father. It was her husband who wanted the inheritance, and so he framed her for the crime. It should have been him who took the punishment. It should have been him who died. *This* was why she was trapped.

"The woman swore to avenge her friend. She knew the story of Sunder, and the knife that carved out his soul in exchange for his daughter's life. She knew if there was any chance to save her friend, she needed to find that knife.

"She tracked it down and found it in the posssession of a merchant who was happy to sell it to her. He told her how to use it, and that she needed to wait until the Relinquishing. On that night, if she plunged the knife into the one who'd eluded death, the Skyweaver would take his soul instead . . . and her friend's life would be restored."

"And?" Roa asked. She'd been leaning closer and closer as Theo spoke. She was now a mere breath away.

"And that's what she did."

"Did it work?"

The wind whispered through the garden. The night bugs chirped around them.

"Yes," he finally said. "It worked."

"And you're sure the knife is in Firgaard?"

He nodded.

Roa stepped away from him, her feet moving in time with her thoughts. Back and forth, she paced. Thinking of what it meant: *Essie, restored.* And what it would require: *killing the one responsible for her death, on the night of the Relinquishing.*

Roa stopped pacing.

Could she really kill her own husband?

Of course not. She pressed her palms to her eyes. *What am I thinking?*

Theo touched her arm. Her hands fell to her sides and she looked up into his silhouetted face. "You can save her, Roa. You can save all of us."

She looked up at him miserably. "By killing the king."

"By removing the next tyrant from the throne." He took her hands in his, warming them. "We can help each other. Help me smuggle my men into the palace, and I'll help you obtain the Skyweaver's knife and make the exchange."

She shook her head, feeling hollow. "And then what?"

Roa wanted her sister. But at what cost?

"And then you rule alone, as a just and powerful queen." He cupped her face in his hands. "Think of how much good you could do for our people, Roa. *Without him.*"

If the Skyweaver's knife existed, if it really could save her sister the way the stories claimed . . .

"No," she said, her tone final. "I'm not a murderer."

And Dax had promised to hold an Assembly as soon as they

returned. With the treaty signed, he had to uphold his oaths now. He had to lift the sanctions. Things would change for their people soon. Roa had all but ensured it.

"Well then," Theo said, stepping away from her. "Come find me if you change your mind."

I won't, she thought, and put the notion out of her head.

Before

When Roa and Essie were eleven, the son of the king came to the scrublands early. It was late spring, after the big rains, and the rivers had swelled. With the swell came thousands upon thousands of fish.

The day after his arrival, they were on the lake, mending nets while their parents helped the House of Springs bring in their catches. Roa sat with Essie, their small two-person reed boat bobbing on the water of the lake. Their heads were down, their fingers picking knots. Dax sat in a boat with Jas, and in between were other reed boats full of children untangling fishing nets.

"Tell us, Dax, have you learned to read yet?"

Roa's head shot up. She looked to Theo—the one who spoke. Except for Dax, Theo was the eldest. The boys in the other boats sniggered at his question.

Dax ignored them. But Roa saw his hand tighten on his net.

"Is that a no?"

"Stop it, Theo," Lirabel said from the boat next to theirs, her gutting knife working out a particularly nasty tangle.

Theo ignored her. "Here. Tell me what this says."

He traced the letters i-d-i-o-t in the air for all of them to see.

Roa, Essie, and Lirabel looked to Dax, who gripped the slippery net tightly between his fingers, bracing himself for whatever was to come.

"Theo," Essie snapped, lowering her own knife in her lap.

"What about this one?"

Roa also lowered her knife, watching Theo's tanned fingers spell the letters i-m-b-e-c-i-l-e.

Dax's skin darkened with a blush.

"Not that one either?" Theo shot a derisive look to the other boys. "Hmm. Do you think you inherited stupidity from your father or your mother?"

Jas stood up a split second after Dax did—only to hold him back, though. The pale-yellow reed boat rocked beneath them. If they weren't careful, they would tip, taking their nets overboard and down to the bottom of the lake.

"He's trying to upset you," Jas said. "Ignore him."

Dax glanced to Roa, who held his gaze, wordlessly agreeing with Jas.

Sit down, she thought.

Theo saw the look passing between them. Like an arrow seeking out its next target, his attention moved to Roa.

"She definitely draws the eyes. Doesn't she?"

"What?" It was Roa's turn to blush.

"That's enough," Essie warned, setting her knife down, her dark eyes flashing.

Roa felt the hum flare up between them, bright and hot.

But Theo wasn't done.

"Is that why you keep coming back, sandeater? Because you like the look of her?"

Dax's hands balled into fists.

Roa reached for her sister's hand, threading their fingers together as she narrowed her eyes at Theo. Why was he being like this? It was one thing to tease Dax—he was an outsider, and it was a favorite pastime. It was quite another thing to bring Roa into it.

"Shut up, Theo."

"Or maybe you want to do more than just look at her. Is that it?" He made a rude gesture, thrusting his hips.

Essie's grip tightened on Roa's hand.

Dax grabbed Jas's gutting knife and pulled the closest boat toward him—where two girls from the House of Springs sat talking to themselves, ignoring the fight brewing around them. He stepped into their small reed boat, which rocked and bobbed, earning him nothing more than a pause and a glance before they went back to talking. Theo's boat was only a step away now. Dax leaned across the space, his face inches from the other boy's. "Stop this. Now."

"What will you do if I don't?" Theo rose, taller and stronger than Dax. His eyes glittered, but he didn't smile. There was a gutting knife in his hand, too. "You don't like me talking about Roa that way? Why not? Everyone knows it's the truth. Everyone knows how you feel about her."

Those words hit like a punch. All the air emptied out of Roa's lungs and without realizing it, she dropped her net.

The hum buzzed in her blood. Beside her, Essie's face had gone stony.

"They're just friends," said Lirabel softly from the boat beside them.

Roa felt hot, suddenly. Like she was burning from the inside out. She looked to her sister, knowing she felt it, too. Essie glared at Theo like she wanted him to disappear.

Theo smirked. He shoved Dax, who grappled for his balance—arms swinging wildly—as the boat he stood in floated back toward Jas.

"Go back to where you came from, sandeater."

The hum rose to a roar inside Roa. Essie's eyes were slits as her gaze narrowed. Roa stared at the son of the king, willing him to fight back. To defend himself.

But Dax simply turned away and did as Theo said: he climbed back into Jas's boat.

Suddenly, Roa saw white as the hum seared through her. She squeezed Essie's hand and nearly cried out as it surged one final time.

There was a startled yelp and then a huge splash as Theo's boat capsized, throwing him overboard. For one sweet moment, the bulbous reedy hull bobbed above the surface, like the belly of a giant fish.

Silence.

And then Theo came up spluttering and thrashing.

The hum quieted within Roa. She looked to her twin, who'd just picked up her net. Essie kept her eyes on her fingers, working through a knot.

As Theo cursed and struggled to get his boat upright, Essie glanced up, catching Roa's gaze and grinning triumphantly. Just for her.

Roa looked back to her own net, grinning, too.

Twelve

Roa spent her first morning back in Firgaard searching the skies and calling her sister's name. But just like the first time, there was no sign of Essie. And when Roa called, only silence answered her.

She longed for Essie's familiar weight perched on her shoulder. For the feel of her soul, warm and close. For the normally bright hum of their bond.

What if she didn't come back?

What if they'd run out of time?

But beneath these questions, growing like a root in the darkness, was another: what if everything Theo said was true? What if the Skyweaver's knife not only existed, but really was right here in Firgaard?

Ever since their conversation in the garden, Roa couldn't stop thinking about the knife. The more days that passed, the stronger her urge was to see it. To hold it in her hands. To decide for herself if it and the stories were real.

Theo's words had unearthed something in Roa. A yearning she thought she'd buried for good, years ago. It made her realize that, more than anything—more than her people's freedom from tyranny—she wanted Essie back. Not as a bird. As her *sister.*

She wanted Essie to walk barefoot down the roads of Song again. Wanted to fight with her, and then apologize for fighting with her. Wanted to sit in the kitchen after all the dishes were put away, talking with their mother deep into the night, just like they used to do. She wanted to watch her jump from the cliffs, then watch her shake the water from her curls. Wanted her to fall in love and raise children and grow old and live a whole, full, happy life.

None of these things were possible with her soul trapped as it was. And once the Relinquishing took her for good, they would never be possible.

Which was how Roa found herself asking the question: If there really was a chance to give Essie her life back, could Roa truly say she wouldn't take it?

A few days later, Roa sat in the Assembly hall—a huge circular room with a copper-domed roof in the heart of the city. Her ornate marble chair chilled her to the bone.

Dax sat to her right, looking half-asleep in a throne that matched his queen's. His curls were a wild tangle and his jaw was still flecked with stubble. As if he'd rolled out of bed and come straight here.

On the other side sat Safire, Dax's new commandant and his

closest confidante. Her fingers drummed the arm of her chair as her blue eyes scanned and rescanned the room.

The three of them sat on a raised, semicircular dais. Before them sat the eleven members of the king's council who were already entrenched in heated debate.

Sunlight streamed in through the tall windows on the western side of the circular Assembly. The light gleamed on the lime-washed walls, reflected off the sheen of the copper dome above, then alighted on the crowd inside the room.

Roa's gaze skimmed the colorful silk tunics and intricately sewn kaftans of the wealthy spectators, here to watch the king's council make or change laws in response to their grievances.

What could your grievances possibly be? she wondered as their gold bands and jewel-encrusted rings flickered in the sunlight. Roa's mother had sold off all their gold and jewels in order to keep people fed. *How many of you became wealthy while my people suffered?*

And yet, instead of discussing those very injustices and how to right them, they were debating some law regulating *dragons*, of all things.

After the coronation, Dax outlawed dragon hunting and sanctioned the Rift mountains as grounds for studying and training the beasts.

The council, it seemed to Roa, wanted to turn the sanctuary grounds into profit centers. If the dragons could be controlled, they argued, the beasts could be sold to the highest bidder. Dax thought it exploitative and wanted no such thing.

Roa didn't care about dragons. She cared about people. *Her* people. Firgaard's sanctions were still starving them. She cared, too, that conditions for the recently freed skral—who'd been slaves in Firgaard for several decades before Dax overthrew his father—did not seem to be improving.

She wanted Dax to fulfill his treaty promises.

Once he lifted the sanctions, scrublanders would be allowed to trade openly again and receive loans for food until the blight ran its course and their crops recovered. Her people would stop going hungry. They wouldn't need to leave their homes and seek work across the sea. Families would be reunited. They could begin to thrive again.

Roa was about to interrupt the debate and turn the session to the treaty when Dax jolted to attention in his chair. Roa and Safire both glanced at him to find his gaze fixed on the councillor who'd risen from her seat. She was a tall young woman, probably close to Roa's nineteen years of age, and draped in swaths of indigo. Her hair was bound up in an embroidered skarf, and around her throat hung a gold pendant bearing Dax's emblem: a black dragon with a red heart of flame—the same pendant worn by all eleven of the king's council members.

"This matter is settled. Do you have something new to put forward, my king?" the young woman asked Dax, clearly also tired of this discussion.

She didn't once look at Roa.

"A few things, actually," said Dax who, until a few heart-beats ago, seemed on the verge of sleep.

Roa watched him motion to Lirabel, who stood with Jas along the wall. She wore a mulberry kaftan with creamy jasmine flowers embroidered up the sleeves, and her black curls were pinned up with ivory combs. Her hands gripped a scroll with acacia handles, each carved with the symbol of the House of Song.

It was the treaty they'd negotiated in the scrublands.

Roa's grip loosened as she stared at Dax. Deep down, she hadn't believed he would really do it—hadn't believed he would uphold his promises.

Lirabel handed the scroll to the young councillor, who gave the king's emissary a quick, dismissive look before taking it.

"What is this?" she asked, unrolling it.

"My treaty with the five Great Houses of the scrublands."

The councillor stopped unrolling. Roa watched her hands tighten, ever so slightly, around the handles.

"It states three things," Dax went on, leaning back in his chair. That strange sudden alertness left his body, replaced by the lazy slouch. "First, the sanctions will be lifted as of the end of this Assembly."

A sharp, startled murmur rippled through the crowd. On Dax's other side, Safire's back went sword straight and her eyes narrowed.

"Second," Dax went on, ignoring the chatter, "as of the *next* Assembly, my council will be equally representative of the kingdom to ensure it can adequately make decisions in favor of all—draksors, scrublanders, and skral alike."

The startled murmurs turned to exclamations of outrage. A restructuring of the council meant more than half the councillors—currently all draksors—would lose their positions.

But such a move was necessary if the skral, who were still vulnerable in the wake of the revolt, were to find equal footing among their former masters in Firgaard.

Roa's heart quickened. This was more than she had hoped for—

"And third," Dax continued, not bothering to raise his voice above the din, "the law against regicide will be struck down."

The crowd erupted. Safire rose to her feet, communicating wordlessly with every soldat in the room, who immediately formed a strong, steadfast line between the now-outraged spectators and the king's council.

The law against regicide was the oldest law in Firgaard. For centuries, kings rose and fell, but the law against regicide was ancient and unbreakable.

It was the reason Dax's sister, Asha, was on the run for her life.

"If you cannot control yourselves"—Safire's voice cut through the noise like a sharply honed knife—"my soldats will escort you all out."

Her eyes glittered dangerously and her fingers tapped the smooth, simple hilts of her throwing knives—Saf's weapons of choice.

The crowd fell into silence.

Roa couldn't help it. A flame of admiration flared in her heart.

And then, shattering the moment: someone laughed. It was a beautiful laugh. Like bells chiming. It echoed through the Assembly.

All the eyes in the domed room fell on the young councillor. Despite her laugh, the girl's eyes were cold and hard as Roa's marble chair.

"Surely you're joking, my king."

Dax sighed. "I'm afraid it's no joke, Councillor Silva."

Silva. Where had Roa heard that name?

She smiled sweetly. Too sweetly. "We've discussed this before, my king. Your revolt and subsequent succession has already caused this city and its people considerable strife. What you propose—the abolition of the sanctions—will weaken Firgaard's already damaged economy. It's something that needs to be done carefully and gradually. By experts."

Resting his cheek against his fist, Dax listened as Councillor Silva went on.

"As for your second motion: since the council is voted on, not appointed, that treaty promise was not for you to make. *Your people* determine the men and women who sit on your council."

The crowd murmured its assent, nodding their heads. Roa waited for Dax to cut in, to refute her. But he didn't.

"As for the law against regicide"—her smile turned piteous—"we all know why you want it struck down. And we sympathize."

The council remained quiet, their eyes on the king, thinking, Roa assumed, of Asha escaping the city on the morning before her beheading.

Everyone assumed it was Dax who helped her.

But they were wrong.

"You can't amend an ancient law purely for your own benefit." Councillor Silva lowered her voice and stepped closer to Dax. "It's no way to begin an already fragile reign."

Their gazes locked as some silent battle waged between the king and his councillor, unseen by everyone else in the room.

Roa stared at Dax, willing him to assert himself. He was *king*. And these were promises encoded in a treaty. He didn't have a choice. He needed to uphold them.

Instead, he buckled.

Looking away from his councillor, he said, "Then I expect to speak with these experts, so we can decide how the sanctions can best be dismantled."

Councillor Silva smiled a slow, victorious smile.

Roa stared at Dax, who watched his councillor return to her seat.

"What are you doing?" Roa demanded, leaning in toward him. She would not let it end like this. "Command that the sanctions be lifted."

He didn't look at her. "She's right. Reckless action will bring chaos." He said it so calmly. As if this was what he expected to happen all along. "And I can't force my will on my people."

"You can and *should*." Roa's hands shook with anger. "You're king, Dax."

He met her angry gaze. "But not a tyrant."

"There are worse things to be."

"Truly?" he asked, his full attention on her. "You would prefer a tyrant?"

"Over a puppet who dances on his council's strings? Yes."

Councillor Silva had taken her seat and an older man with hunching shoulders and white hair—a man Dax earlier referred to as Councillor Barek—was moving things along. Roa could tell by the stirring crowd that the session was coming to an end.

"You say you don't want to force your will on your people." She kept her voice low, holding his gaze. "But the will of your people has been forced on mine for decades. And if you think *this* is a democratic solution"—she gestured to the wealthy draksor council and the even wealthier draksor crowd beyond it—"you're a fool."

Dax leaned in so close, Roa could feel the warmth of him. "If I'm a fool"—his gaze hooked into hers—"what does that make the one who married me?"

Roa didn't notice the eyes of the Assembly on them. But Dax did. Something shifted then, and the tension building in him melted away, replaced by that smooth exterior. He flashed Roa that smile of his. As if she weren't his queen, but rather some silly thing to be charmed and flirted with.

Roa wanted to smack him.

She looked away, furious and humiliated. If it was true—if Dax had expected this outcome all along—then he'd intentionally deceived the Great Houses. By signing that treaty, by swearing to uphold it, he'd made false promises.

Was this truly the man she'd given up everything to marry?

Roa's anger burned within her. She was sick to death of her people's powerlessness. Of mothers giving up children they could no longer provide for, then living with the shame of it. Of fathers moving across the desert or sea in search of ways to feed their families, unable to watch their children grow. Of the sickness and weakness and purposelessness that malnourishment bred.

Roa would not abide it any longer.

Fixing her attention on Councillor Silva, she said, "What do you think will happen when my father realizes his treaty is broken?" Her voice rang out through the room, echoing off the dome above. "What do you think will happen when the Great Houses understand they've been betrayed?"

Silva's pretty brown eyes lifted to Roa's for the first time since she'd entered the room.

"*Betrayed?* That's a little . . . dramatic, don't you think?" Again, that smile lit up Councillor Silva's face—but not her eyes. "This is how things are done in Firgaard: carefully and meticulously. If you're going to be our queen, you will need to get used to our ways."

She turned back to the council, dismissing Roa.

"Your *ways* are unjust." Roa's voice rang out clear in the Assembly.

The air went cold. The room fell to silence.

Dax reached for her wrist in warning. Roa jerked away.

Councillor Silva turned back.

"It's because of draksors that my people have been slowly starving to death," Roa continued. "So forgive me if I don't quite trust the draksor *way*."

Councillor Silva looked to Dax. "Is it the scrublander way to blame everyone else for their problems?"

The crowd nodded and murmured their assent.

The statement shocked Roa. Is this how they thought of her? Of her people?

"Trust goes both ways, my queen," Councillor Silva said. "When a scrublander blackmails our king into marrying her, we'd be naïve to think she has anything but her own interests at heart." She turned back to the council. "This Assembly is finished for today."

"Actually," said Dax from beside Roa, "there is one more thing."

All the councillors now rising from their seats paused half-way to their feet.

Roa glanced at her husband, daring to hope that he'd changed his mind. That he intended to *do* something.

"This year, as a sign of our goodwill toward the scrublands, Firgaard will celebrate the Relinquishing."

A confused quiet followed these words.

Even Roa was perplexed.

The Relinquishing was a scrublander holiday. Why would Firgaard celebrate it?

"What this kingdom needs is unity," Dax went on, smiling as he did. "And what better way to bring us together than a celebration?"

A celebration of what? thought Roa bitterly. *How useless you are?*

Dax wasn't interested in goodwill toward scrublanders, nor was he invested in a unified kingdom. He'd just proven this by bending to his council's demands instead of upholding his promises.

So why celebrate the Relinquishing?

A few councillors spoke quietly amongst themselves, away from the rest of the council. Roa watched them, listening hard.

He loves to indulge in fine things, she heard one of them say. *What better way to indulge than with a celebration?*

Roa frowned, looking back to the king.

Was that what this was? Was Dax giving the scrublands a token gesture of goodwill, while simultaneously giving himself an excuse to drink expensive wine, seduce pretty women, and distract himself from the things that really mattered?

Roa didn't want to believe it. But she hadn't wanted to believe he would buckle under his council's pressure, either. And he did.

"Draksors don't celebrate the Relinquishing," Councillor Silva said, her voice cold and hard as ice, breaking up the clamor.

"We do now," Dax said, looking to Jas, who nodded from his place against the wall next to Lirabel. "I've just declared it. Invitations have been sent to all the Great Houses. The north and south gates will remain open for the next seven days to allow for safe passage into and out of the city."

Councillor Silva's gaze narrowed on the king like a dragon on its prey. She stepped away from her seat, her indigo silks swishing as she stalked toward him.

She was elegance and venom, grace and ire.

"It is one thing to take an enemy for your wife and make her *queen*." The air between the councillor and the king seemed to spark. "It's another to sabotage this city's safety to appease her."

Appease me? thought Roa. Clearly she misunderstood.

When Councillor Silva was mere steps away, Safire rose, stepping in front of her. The look in her eye said, *Take one more step. I dare you.*

"I can assure you," Safire said instead, "the safety of this city is my only concern."

Councillor Silva raised an eyebrow. "If that were true, Safire, you'd have refused the position of commandant when it was first offered to you."

It was strange, how familiar this girl seemed to be with both the king and his cousin. She challenged them so easily and rallied others against them, with no fear of any consequences.

Who was she?

"Keeping the gates open for seven days? Allowing our *enemies* to come and go as they please? Forgive me if I don't have the same faith in the abilities of a commandant who, upon being appointed, lost half her army to defection."

"Councillor, I don't care who you do or don't have faith in," Dax said, rising and stepping down from the dais. "The invitations have been sent and the orders have been given." His shoulder brushed the councillor's as he paused beside her, and Roa saw the poison in both their eyes—just for a heartbeat—as Dax leaned in. "The gates *will* remain open. Firgaard *will* celebrate the Relinquishing. I look forward to your compliance, *Bekah*."

Dax stepped past her, collected his guards, then moved toward the archway doors.

Roa stared after him, defeat settling like a heavy stone in her heart.

Despite all her efforts—the revolt, the marriage, the treaty—

the scrublands were still at the mercy of Firgaard. The skral were still considered second-class citizens. And all the while, draksors prospered.

Dax had just proven—beyond a doubt—that he didn't care. About any of it.

This was an unacceptable trait in a king, not to mention a dangerous one.

Nothing will change, she realized now. *Nothing* can *change with Dax as king.*

It was up to Roa.

But what could she do? She was an outlander queen without allies. She had no sway with her husband or his council. She was mistrusted and powerless and alone here.

She needed help.

Roa thought of her last conversation with Theo.

Think of how much good you could do for our people. His words rang through her mind. *Without him.*

If the gates of the city remained open, if scrublanders were traveling to Firgaard for the Relinquishing . . . how easy would it be for Theo's men to assemble here in the capital?

Easy as breathing.

Without knowing it, Dax had just given her the opportunity to set true change in motion.

A plan began to form in Roa's mind. It was reckless and dangerous. But the alternative was to sit by and watch Dax and his council drive her people to the brink of starvation. Dax had proven today that he wasn't the king this kingdom needed. That under his rule, Roa's people would continue to suffer.

A group of councillors approached the king on his way to

the doors. They stepped directly in Dax's path, halting his and Roa's departure from the Assembly.

Roa looked to the archway, whose doors were still shut tight. She needed to get a message to Theo and tell him her plan. But the councillors were obstructing the exit.

"My queen."

Roa straightened at that honeyed voice.

"It's nice to finally meet you in the flesh."

Roa turned to face the tall young woman beside her.

"Councillor Silva," she said in cold greeting.

"Please, just Rebekah. Silva is my father's name." The girl was even more beautiful up close, with elegant cheekbones, wide brown eyes, and long black lashes. Like a tapestry woven in the richest threads. "But where is your pet bird?"

The word *pet* made Roa stiffen.

"Essie doesn't like places where she can't see the sky." It wasn't a lie, exactly. Roa ached with her sister's absence as she looked to the domed roof above them.

"I see." Rebekah flashed that sweet smile and changed the subject. "I'm hosting a dinner tomorrow night. I'd like for you and Dax to come."

A warning bell chimed inside Roa. Rebekah had used the king's name, not his title. And she hadn't bowed to Roa, as was the custom. More than this, she'd made it perfectly clear mere moments ago that she didn't consider a lowly scrublander girl worthy of reverence—even if she was queen.

So why was she inviting Roa to dinner?

Roa tried to think of a compelling reason to refuse, when

Dax called her name. She turned to find the king walking back toward her. His dark blue tunic showed off his tall frame and broad shoulders. But the look on his face was a complicated mixture of annoyance and . . . fear?

Fear of what?

"Bekah." He nodded curtly, stepping up beside them. "Cornering my wife, I see."

Bekah. The girl before them winced at the nickname. Or possibly the words *my wife*.

Roa looked from Rebekah to Dax and back. Clearly there was history here.

But what kind?

"You haven't come to see my father in months." Rebekah's attention was on the king now. "He's beginning to take offense."

Dax slid his hand around Roa's wrist.

Her skin prickled at his touch. She twisted free.

"I've been a little . . . preoccupied." Dax's hand paused awkwardly in midair before falling to his side. "How *is* your father?" His eyes were on Rebekah, but he didn't sound interested in the answer.

"The same." She seemed almost sad about this. "Still collecting his little relics."

Dax reached for Roa's wrist *again*, this time tapping her bone with his thumb. Twice.

Roa looked down at his fingers.

What is he doing?

"You know how Father is. Spending his time on things no one else sees the value of." Rebekah looked to Dax's grip on

Roa. "In fact, a shipment arrived just a few days ago. If you came to visit, I'm sure he'd love to show you its contents."

Roa was about to twist her arm away again, when her thoughts snagged.

A shipment.

She remembered Asha's letter, still lying on the floor beneath the bed.

That was where she knew the councillor's name from. Roa could picture the black ink scrawled elegantly across the parchment: *Three days ago, a shipment from Darmoor was due to arrive at Baron Silva's stronghold.*

It was the message Roa had never delivered to Dax.

"You'll have to give Baron Silva my apologies," Dax said, gripping Roa's wrist tighter. Again, his thumb tapped. "Tell him I'll visit as soon as I'm able."

"How about tomorrow night?" Rebekah pressed. "I'm hosting a dinner at the stronghold. Father asked specifically for you—both of you—to be in attendance. He very much wants to meet the new . . . queen."

Roa's mind whirred, remembering the night in the sand sea, inside Theo's tent. He said the Skyweaver's knife was in transit from Darmoor. That a baron in Firgaard bought it for his private collection.

And then Asha's letter mentioned a shipment from the same city—Darmoor. What were the chances that shipment was the same one Theo mentioned? What were the chances the Skyweaver's knife was in the possession of Rebekah's father?

"I'm afraid we've only just returned from the scrublands,"

Dax was saying. He stepped back, taking Roa with him. "After such a tiring journey, my wife—"

"I would be honored," said Roa.

Dax looked at her sharply.

A smile slid across Rebekah's lips. "Excellent. I'll have the cooks prepare something special."

If the Skyweaver's knife was in Baron Silva's possession, Roa intended to find out. She wanted to see it with her own eyes.

"Oh, Roa? Bring your pet." Rebekah's eyes sparkled. "My father loves birds."

Before

The night after Essie capsized Theo's boat, Roa couldn't sleep. She kept thinking about what Theo said. About all the things she thought she knew and didn't.

Essie growled from beside her, half-asleep. "Roa! Stop squirming!"

Though they had two beds, they always slept in the same one.

Roa fell still, waiting for her sister to fall back asleep. Trying to fall asleep herself.

But her thoughts kept returning to the boats. And Dax. And the way he never refuted Theo's words.

Everyone knows how you feel about her, Theo said.

It was nearly the same thing Essie said, not so long ago: You're the one he likes.

Roa turned over.

Essie's pillow came down hard on her head.

"Next time I'm going to push you onto the floor."

Smiling, Roa slammed her own pillow back at her sister. Before Essie could retaliate, she escaped from under the woven blue blankets, raising her hands.

"Truce?"

Essie sat up. "Where are you going?"

"For a walk."

Maybe a walk would tire her out.

As she stepped into the hall, Essie chucked Roa's pillow through the doorway. But it was dark, and she missed by a lot.

The pillow hit the wall and fell to the floor.

Roa grinned.

Beyond their room, the House of Song was silent. Everyone had gone to bed a long time ago. But as she made her way from the bedroom to the kitchen, she noticed a glow coming from her father's study.

Which was odd. Her father was always the first one to retire.

Crossing to the door, Roa pushed it open to find someone sitting at her father's desk. Or rather, sleeping at his desk.

Dax's crooked arm cradled his head of dark curls and his fingers were stained with ink. Beside him glowed a candle nearly burned down to the base of the brass holder.

Roa crossed the room and shook him awake. "Dax."

He startled, arms flailing, nearly knocking the candle over. Roa snatched it up before that happened, spilling wax on the floor.

He squinted through the soft light. When he finally recognized her, his spine straightened.

"What are you doing in here?" she asked.

Dax looked from the rush pen to the alabaster inkwell. When his gaze fell on the scattered parchments laid out across the desktop, he immediately tried to shuffle them all into a pile.

Roa touched his shoulder and Dax stilled. Setting down the candle, she reached for the piece on top of the pile.

It was a letter.

From Roa.

She'd been sending him letters all winter as part of her lessons. It was practice, her tutors told her, for the day she became mistress of the House of Song.

She stared at her own elegant handwriting. He'd circled various words from her letter and copied them over and over all down the back of the parchment. It was an exercise one of her own tutors had given him last summer, to help with his reading and writing difficulties.

She glanced up from the page. "I thought they never reached you."

Dax stared miserably into his lap.

"Why didn't you send any back?" she demanded.

"Why do you think?" he whispered, his knee bouncing nervously.

"If I knew," she muttered, "I wouldn't have asked."

"Because I couldn't read them!"

Her lips parted. This was part of the reason he'd spent last summer in the House of Song, learning from her tutors—because his own tutors had failed to teach him.

Roa had thought he'd been getting better.

"You didn't read them? Not any of them?"

His silence confirmed it.

For some reason, this made her angry. "You're the son of the king, Dax. You could have had someone read them to you."

That blush crept into his cheeks again.

"You could have dictated a response," she continued. "People dictate letters all the time."

Dax glanced up at her now, looking even more miserable. As if she didn't understand at all.

Roa looked down to the parchment in her hands, her attention catching on her name.

He'd written it over and over in shaky black letters, all down the page.

Her pulse sped up at the sight of it.

"What if Theo's right?" he whispered, staring at the quill and the inkpot. "What if there's something wrong with me and I never learn how to do this?"

The thought of Theo and the things he'd said in the boats that morning made Roa burn with anger all over again.

"Listen." She hoisted herself up onto the desk in front of him. "First of all, Theo is a bully." Dax stared at her bare legs, swinging loose between them. "And second of all, there's nothing wrong with you."

He glanced up. "Then why can't I do something that comes so easily to everyone else?"

Roa didn't know the answer to that.

Seeing it, Dax turned his face away and pushed the chair out.

"It's late. We should go to sleep. If your father—"

Roa reached for his arm, stopping him. Dax went immediately still.

"I have an idea," she said, getting down from the desk.

He watched her build a small fire in the fire basin, then sit down on the carpet. When she told him to bring the stack of letters from the desk, he picked them up and cautiously came to sit beside her.

Roa unfolded the first one and started to read.

She read him every letter she'd written that winter. The boring ones about working in the fields. The personal ones about her fights with Essie. The serious ones about her fear of one day inheriting the House of Song. And even the one where she admitted that she missed him—or at least, missed playing gods and monsters with him.

As she read, she followed each word with her finger, so Dax could know both the shape and the sound of the words. She read until her voice grew hoarse and her eyes grew heavy. She read until her head started to droop.

They fell asleep there, on the carpet of her father's study. And when Roa woke at daybreak, the sun hadn't yet risen, but the world hummed blue-gold in anticipation. She turned to find Dax fast asleep beside her.

Roa watched his chest rise and fall. He was thirteen this summer, just two years older than her, and not only was he taller, but his shoulders were wider than she remembered. She could see the curve of muscle as his elbow cradled his head.

A startling warmth spread through Roa as she watched him sleep. Her gaze traced the arc of his throat. The line of his jaw. The soft shape of his mouth.

She felt guilty about it.

It was Essie who liked Dax, not her.

She should have risen right then and slipped silently away. That would have been the right thing to do.

But Roa didn't do the right thing.

Instead, she pushed herself up onto her elbow, studying Dax's face in the early-morning light. Again and again, her gaze moved to his mouth.

What would it be like, she wondered, to kiss the son of a king?

Roa leaned in.

As if sensing the breach, Dax stirred.

Roa tore away, heart thundering, and lay back down, pretending to sleep. She could hear Dax wake beside her. Her pulse pounded out its betrayal as she listened to him turn and stretch.

Roa opened her eyes and saw him look away, rubbing at the back of his neck, as if it were sore.

From the gardens, the roosters crowed, heralding the start of day.

"We should get out of here," he said, looking to the windows, where the smoke from several chimneys curled across the morning sky. "Before your father finds us and chases me out of his house." He half smiled, half winced at the thought.

Heat rushed up Roa's neck at the implication. He was right. They were no longer children. They couldn't be seen like this. In here. Together.

Roa rose first.

Together, they crept to the door. Roa opened it and peered out, but there was no one in the hall. Dax would have gone straight through the central pavilion, but Roa grabbed his hand, stopping him. He looked down at her and she shook her head. The servants would be lighting the fire in there, warming the room up for her father. Her fingers slid through his as she tugged him the other way, to a darkened hallway nearer the guest wing.

Their hearts hammered in unison until they arrived at his bedroom door, where Dax let go of her hand.

Before he could disappear inside, Roa reached for him, pulling him back, remembering the shape of her name in his shaky handwriting.

"Dax . . ."

He looked down at her.

Roa's cheeks burned. What was she doing?

Dax must have known. Because he touched her, his eyes searching hers, and leaned in.

Before she could think twice about it, Roa pushed up on her toes and kissed him.

It was clumsy and short—more of a bump than a kiss—but for a moment, with his lips warm and soft against hers, Roa thought she felt the hum flare up inside her.

Except . . . no.

This was something else.

When he stepped back, Dax smiled the shyest smile she'd ever seen.

A sound from down the hall made them step away from each other. But no one was there. No one had seen. Still, Roa gave him a gentle push toward his door, then turned away, leaving him behind.

She glanced back once to find him staring after her, still smiling.

Roa looked away, smiling, too.

It would be the last time either of them smiled for a very long time.

Thirteen

Meet me at moonrise.

Roa folded Theo's message—a response to the one she'd sent after the council meeting.

She held the parchment in her hand as she paced her rooms, reading the directions to the guesthouse he was staying in, then glancing out through her terrace archway. When the moon's white halo could be seen just beyond the palace rooftop, Roa opened her doors and stepped out into the hall.

"My queen?" came the voice of one of her guards, a young man named Sirin with blue eyes; straight teeth; and a tall, lean stature. "What are you doing up so late?"

"I can't sleep," she said, already trotting down the hall. "I want to go for a walk. In the city."

She wore an unadorned dress made of gray wool and her sandskarf was pulled up over her head.

Her guards followed her.

Guards. Roa hated the very concept of them. They were like armed shadows, following her everywhere, never leaving her alone.

There was no scrubland equivalent because there was no need for a scrublander to have a guard. It was why Roa hadn't taken these, from the palace, with her back home. It was why Dax's guards disarmed themselves and were given their own rooms in the House of Song—because the king knew it was an insult to bring an armed guard into the home of a scrublander. It meant you didn't trust him.

"My queen . . ."

Roa squeezed her hands into fists. Composing herself, she halted, then turned. "Yes, Sirin?"

"The palace gates are shut and locked at night. You need special permission to open them."

Roa raised an eyebrow. "Am I not queen? Do *I* need permission to come and go as I please?"

The guards exchanged nervous glances.

"They're Safire's orders," said the guard beyond Sirin—a man with light brown eyes and graying hair.

"None of you will go against Safire," muttered Roa.

The things Rebekah said in the Assembly were true: Dax *did* lose half his army by appointing his cousin commandant, because most soldats didn't trust a young woman with skral blood running through her veins to lead them.

What most people didn't know was that every soldat who questioned Safire's authority was given a choice: fight her or leave. Those Safire fought, she bested. And in besting them, won their admiration.

The army might be half as large as it once was, but it was twice as loyal.

As Roa studied all four of her guards now, standing straight in their steel morions with the king's emblem on their chests, she knew none of them would defy their commandant.

Well, maybe not *none* of them . . .

Roa turned to Sirin, who was watching her. Sirin, Roa had long ago taken note, was a little too attractive for a soldat. It made him bold and flirtatious. Even with Roa.

If she were honest, Sirin had always made her uncomfortable.

"What about you?" she said.

"Me?" Sirin asked, his eyebrows shooting upward.

"Will you also choose your commandant over your queen?"

"We have a duty to uphold the rules," he said.

"*And* a duty to keep me safe."

Sirin smiled, seeing what she was doing. "That, too."

"So if I told you I was going out into the city, you wouldn't want me to go alone, would you? That would be unsafe."

Sirin's smile widened. "Indeed, it would."

"Well, then." Roa turned back, continuing on.

"How will you convince them to open the gate?" he called after her.

Roa slowed. If the soldats at the gate were as loyal to Saf as Roa's other three guards, she wouldn't convince them.

Sirin caught up to her, the scabbard of his sword clinking against the buckles at the top of his boots. "Don't worry, my queen." He shot a look back at the other three guards, who appeared anxious as they watched their comrade break the rules. "There's a guard on duty who owes me a favor."

True to his word, Sirin got them through the gate. Roa watched him reach into the pocket of his tunic, pull something out, then show it to the guard in charge. A whispered conversation passed between them as Sirin tucked the object out of sight again.

Roa didn't know the nature of the exchange, only that the gazes of both boys slid over her in a way that made her uneasy.

She suddenly wondered if Sirin had the wrong idea about their trip into the city.

But Roa needed to see Theo. So she let Sirin think what he liked. After all, she had Essie's knife sheathed at her calf. If she needed to, she would put him in his place.

Together, Roa and her guard took the dark and desolate streets to one of the city's seedier guesthouses. It gleamed white as alabaster in the light of the rising moon, starkly contrasted against the black sky. Roa stopped at the back door—where Theo had told her to enter—pulling her sandskarf farther over her head to keep her face in shadow.

"Wait here," she told Sirin.

"And if someone recognizes you?" He shook his head. "I'll come with you."

She lifted her hand, warning him back. "No," she said. "You won't."

His eyes flashed in the darkness. But it was so fast, and the smile that replaced it so easy, Roa thought she might have mistaken it, so she let it go.

"I won't be long." Opening the door, she stepped through. It led straight into a narrow hallway smelling of roasted meat and spices. She heard the crash of pots and pans. Cooks in smeared aprons held steaming platters of food above their heads and cursed as they pushed past her into the main floor of the guesthouse.

Go past the kitchens to the stairway, Theo told her in his message. *My room is on the second floor.*

Roa found the creaking steps and took them. Then found the door to Theo's room.

He opened on the second knock.

His hair was damp and loose around his shoulders, as if he'd just bathed. He wore simple cotton trousers and a shirt, which Roa knew he'd sleep in.

She knew it, because she'd slept next to him once. The night before she rode off to fight in Dax's revolt.

Or rather, *he'd* slept. Roa had lain there, wide-awake, thinking about what they'd done.

"Roa." He drew her into a hug. Roa breathed in the soapy smell of him and soaked up the warmth of him, remembering that night.

Sometimes she wondered if she'd yielded out of guilt. As if she'd known, even then, that she wasn't coming back to him.

"I can't stay long," she said, finally pulling away and pushing her sandskarf back to fall around her shoulders. "There's a guard out front, and I don't quite trust him."

Theo frowned, but nodded, ushering her into the room. The walls were saffron yellow and the bed took up nearly two-thirds of the space. In the corner, a low-lying crimson sofa in need of reupholstering was pressed up against the wall.

On the bedside table a slender vase held a single white highland rose.

"How did the Assembly go?" Theo asked, sitting on the arm of the dilapidated sofa.

Roa sank into the cushions and told him everything, ending with Dax's proclamation about the Relinquishing.

"Is that supposed to be a peace offering?" Theo rolled his eyes. "Why can't he just do as he promised and lift the sanctions?"

"Because he's a weak king," she said, thinking of the way Dax buckled so easily under the pressure his council exerted. "And he doesn't care. But don't you see? This is your chance. The gates will be open from now until the Relinquishing. Scrublanders are free to pass into the city, unchecked, as a show of Dax's hospitality. And on the longest night of the year—six days from now—everyone will be wearing masks for the festival."

Theo went quiet, staring at her, his lips parting in surprise.

"It's the perfect opportunity," she said.

The words snapped him out of his reverie. He lowered himself down from the sofa's arm to the cushions. "You've changed your mind, then? You'll help me?"

Roa looked down into her lap, nodding. "On one condition."

He lifted his hands, palms up, like an offering. "I'll do anything for you, Roa. You know I will. Just name it."

Roa breathed in deep and said: "You can't harm him."

Theo blinked at her. Before he could counter, Roa pressed on.

"With enough armed men and a well-executed plan, we can take the palace and force him to abdicate the throne."

"Abdicate," Theo murmured. "And then what? You send him into exile and rule alone? If he's alive, he'll always be a danger to you."

Roa shrugged. "That's a risk we'll have to take."

"It's not a risk I'm willing to take," said Theo sharply. "I want *you* on that throne. For a long time."

She drew Essie's knife out of its sheath and ran her thumb along the hilt's inscription. "I barely have enough support in Firgaard as it is. If I were to kill him, I'll lose any support I might have. And more importantly: I'll be guilty of regicide. That's a death sentence."

Most importantly: Roa wasn't a murderer.

After a long pause, he said more softly: "What if I could get you the support you need? Someone who could protect you?"

She lowered the knife in her lap. "What?"

He leaned back into the cushions, linking his arms behind his head. "I have a meeting tomorrow with someone sympathetic to our cause."

"Who?"

"A powerful enemy of Dax's. They wouldn't give me their name. I think they're afraid I'll inform on them to the king. Once I determine if they can truly help us, I'll send for you, and we can decide how to proceed."

Roa rose from the sofa, sheathing Essie's knife. Her hands trembled. For several heartbeats, Theo's gaze followed her back and forth as she paced.

"You can do this, Roa."

Could she? Plot against the one she'd fought beside mere weeks ago?

"You gave up everything for him, and he's thrown it in your face. You said it yourself: Dax is not the king you thought he was. He has no interest in lifting the sanctions. Under his rule, people—and not just scrublanders—will continue to suffer."

Roa stopped pacing and pressed her hands to her face. She already knew these things.

More quietly, Theo said: "He's the reason she's dead, Roa."

Roa dropped her hands, clenching her fists as she stared him down. "Don't do that."

"Do what?" he asked from the sofa.

"Talk like I don't know exactly why she's dead."

"Ever since you left to fight a war at his side, you've forgotten those of us you left behind. Why not her too?"

Anger flickered like lightning through Roa. How *dare* he say that.

"You could have come with me!" She strode back to the sofa, standing over him now. "It could have been you fighting at my side!"

Theo rose to his feet, tipping the scales, glaring down at her. "And watch the one I love give herself to the man I hate? No, Roa. Refusing to go with you was the best decision I ever made." He looked away as he said it, his mouth thinning into a sharp line, his eyes shining with regret. "It should have been Dax who died that day, not Essie."

"You don't think I know that? I think it every time I look at him!"

He turned his face sharply back to hers, his eyes dark. "Then this is your chance to make things right—for Essie *and* for scrublanders."

It was Roa's turn to look away.

"You can save her," he said. "Don't you think that if the situation was reversed, she would do whatever it took to save *you*?"

Roa bit down hard on her lip.

"Yes," she whispered. *Of course she would.*

Roa wished Essie were here to tell her what she should do.

But Essie wasn't here. And Theo was right—about all of it. Dax was a weak king, easily manipulated by his council. He didn't care about keeping his promises or alleviating their people's suffering. He was a king who took what he wanted and didn't care who he hurt.

By refusing to act, by refusing to do what was necessary, she was no better.

Roa—who hadn't seen her sister in days, who could feel the hum fading away within her—needed to make a choice. She was losing her sister. If she didn't act, and act swiftly, Essie would soon be gone for good.

Roa couldn't let that happen.

This was her chance to be the queen her people needed. To be the sister Essie needed.

Dax was a dangerous king. Dax was the reason her sister was dead.

The exchange of souls would be just.

"All right," she said. "I'll find the Skyweaver's knife and do what needs to be done."

Theo tilted her face so that their gazes met. "And I'll get

you the support and protection you need. I won't let you come to any harm—I swear it." He cupped her face in his hands, peering down at her. "I'll send for you after my meeting tomorrow and we can make a plan."

She nodded. The ache of her sister's absence was sharper than ever. The empty space where Essie should be grew bigger every day, threatening to swallow Roa.

If I fail, she thought, *I hope it does swallow me.*

Theo moved to the bedside table, jolting Roa out of her dark thoughts. Sliding the white rose out of the vase there, he snapped off the stem and came back to her.

"What are you doing?" she asked as he tucked it behind her ear.

"Treating you as you should be treated," he said, running the backs of his fingers down her cheek.

This is not what you came for, Roa told herself.

She stepped back, putting space between them.

Theo's hand hovered in midair for a moment, then clenched as he brought it back down to his side. "Your mind plots against your husband, yet your body remains loyal to him."

She looked away, down to the carpet beneath her feet.

"I should go," she said. "Before my guard comes looking for me."

Before turning for the door, though, she remembered the letter from Asha. She'd meant to ask about the shipment Torwin was tracking.

"Do you remember the name of the wealthy Firgaardian who bought the Skyweaver's knife?"

He tilted his head at her. "His name is Baron Silva."

Roa's blood hummed in her veins. She'd been right.

"I'm having dinner at his home tomorrow night," she said.

Theo's eyes widened. "What?"

"What do you know about him?"

"Only that he's the wealthiest man in Firgaard."

"Barring the king," Roa corrected him.

"Barring no one," he said.

Roa shot him a look.

"His daughter, Rebekah, is Silva's only child. He dotes on her. He even purchased her place on the king's council."

Roa shook her head. "That's not possible. Councillors are voted on."

Theo snorted and shook his head. "Elections are held every three years, but you have to pay a fee if you want a vote."

Roa hadn't known that.

"A girl from Sky, Selina, is employed in his household. From what she says, Rebekah has half of Firgaard in her pocket," Theo said. "She sounds like a force to be reckoned with."

"Are you certain Silva has the knife in his possession?"

Theo nodded. "Selina confirmed it arrived several days ago."

Again, Roa remembered Asha's letter, still lying under that bed in Amina's house. If the Skyweaver's knife arrived, then Torwin failed to intercept it.

Worry gnawed at Roa. Perhaps Torwin and Asha were in trouble.

Or perhaps I was wrong. Perhaps it wasn't the Skyweaver's knife he was tracking at all.

She would investigate tomorrow.

"Did Selina happen to say where it's kept?" she asked Theo.

He followed her to the door. "I'll ask. If she knows, I'll send a message to the palace first thing tomorrow. Roa?"

She turned to face him, already thinking of the task that lay ahead of her. He planted his hands on the lintel, leaning over her.

"Maybe I should walk you back. These streets are unfriendly."

"Thank you," Roa said, pulling her sandskarf up over her head, careful not to damage the rose Theo tucked behind her ear. "But I led a revolt without you there to protect me. I think I'll manage."

Essie's Story

Once there was a girl who loved the sky almost as much as she loved her sister.

She climbed rooftops and cliff faces and acacia trees, just to be nearer to it. She knew the name of every type of cloud and the story behind every star. She envied the birds their wings, wanting to know what it felt like to soar through that vast expanse of blue.

One night, she lay on the highest roof of the House of Song, spread out beneath the diamond-studded sky with her friends. They'd spent the morning climbing the highland cliffs and throwing themselves into the blue-green waters of the quarry. The girl threw herself harder and farther and higher than the rest. But no matter how hard or high or far she flung herself, she always fell.

Her sister watched with worried eyes. Her sister hated being up high. She much preferred her feet on the ground.

Now the girl lifted her eyes to the stars and said, "Do you think anyone we know is up there?"

"Don't be morbid," said her sister, fingers deftly plaiting her hair.

Unlike her sister, whose hair was cropped short to her head, Essie kept her hair long enough to braid. It was the easiest way to tell the two apart.

The hum of their bond glowed warmly between them, brighter than any star. And at the edge of her vision, the girl saw their friend—the shy son of the king who spent his summers in their house—wander to the edge of the roof.

"It's not morbid," she whispered, thinking of the Skyweaver spinning the souls of the dead into stars. Thinking of her own soul, bound so tightly to her sister's. "It's beautiful." She turned her gaze on the two brightest stars in the south sky. The twin stars. "That's going to be us one day—you and me."

Suddenly, a sharp snap broke the silence. She shot up at the sound, her braid coming undone, her curls spiraling free. As one, they looked to the son of the king: arms out, body frozen, struggling to regain his balance as more and more cracks spread through the clay shingles at his feet.

He was at the edge of the roof, where no reeds or beams lay beneath the shingles. Where there was nothing to support him.

His eyes met hers and in that moment, she felt his fear. It spread through her like the cracks at his feet.

She didn't think. Just flew to the edge of the roof, grabbing his shirt and flinging him hard away from her, back to where the others sat.

The moment she did, the shingles gave out.

She fell from the highest roof of the house.

The last thing she thought was, I wish I were a bird. A bird would take flight.

The last thing she felt wasn't pain, it was the hum. She heard her sister scream her name. Felt the bond flare up inside her.

Bright and alive as a star.

Fourteen

Roa's thoughts spun as she walked through the night-drenched city. She still wasn't used to Firgaard's labyrinthine streets. This, combined with her whirling thoughts, meant she didn't notice when Sirin started taking her the wrong way.

It was only when they turned down an alley and Roa stood staring up at a green-washed wall—a dead end—that she started to pay attention.

Roa spun on her heel. Sirin stood before her, bathed in moonlight, blocking her way out. His morion glinted, the steel brim keeping his eyes in shadow.

For the second time that night, her hair rose on end.

Instinctively, she called for Essie.

Except Essie was gone. Roa was alone here, with an armed guard obviously used to taking liberties.

Roa stared him down. "What are you doing?"

"Ridding the king of his problem."

Sirin's voice had changed. It was no longer so charming. His smile was long gone, replaced by a grim stare.

"First, you blackmail him into marrying you. And now here you are, sneaking off in the night to meet with his enemies. Like a traitorous whore."

Roa bristled at the words. "I never blackmailed anyone."

But the second accusation . . . that rang too close to the truth.

"The king deserves better."

"So you're here to dispose of me?" Roa narrowed her eyes. "You'd better not fail. If you do, I'll make sure you never see another dawn."

"I've been paid too well to fail," he said.

Paid? thought Roa. *By whom?*

He drew his saber from its sheath, the steel scraping against the leather. His hands shook—just a little.

Odd, thought Roa. Was he scared of her? Or whoever had paid him?

Roa stepped back, trying to remember how far the wall was behind her. She had the knife at her calf. But a knife was no match for a saber, and she didn't want to reveal that she was armed. Not until she had to.

He wasted no time. The blade sliced through the air, coming straight for her. Roa threw herself hard to the right, narrowly dodging the blow. She felt the air rush against her skin, heard the soft hiss of torn wool. Sirin quickly doubled back, keeping himself between her and her escape.

Roa's hands were slick with cold sweat.

He drew his second saber and walked toward her, trapping her in the corner, ensuring she wouldn't be able to dodge him again.

Roa wiped her palms on the wool of her dress, her fingers itching for her sister's knife.

No. Not yet.

Sirin bared his teeth and lunged. His blades flashed in the moonlight as he bore down on her. Only this time, the furious cry of a hawk rang out.

Sirin stopped, his focus broken.

Roa's soul hummed at the sound.

They both looked up.

Essie descended out of the dark, white wings spread wide, gold talons sharp and gleaming, ready to claw out the eyes of the man who cornered her sister.

Sirin raised both sabers, ready to cut her down.

Roa drew her knife and sprang.

She grabbed the wrist of his sword arm, digging in her fingernails.

But Sirin had two arms and two swords. He raised the second and swung at Essie, trying to kill her.

Before he could, Roa plunged her knife into his throat.

She felt the sharpened tip sink into soft flesh. Hot flecks of blood splattered her wrist. Both sabers clattered to the ground as he grabbed for his neck.

Roa kicked the weapons out of reach and stepped back, wide-eyed and breathing hard.

Essie screeched and flapped her wings, wanting to claw out his eyes.

Essie, Roa called when he fell to his knees.

But Essie didn't stop. She was a flash of white feathers and gleaming talons.

"Essie!"

At the sound of Roa's voice, her sister paused. She shook her white head, as if shaking off her bloodlust, and flew to Roa's outstretched fist. Sirin's eyes had gone wide, showing the whites. Blood streamed from the smiling gash in his neck, running down over his hands.

When he crumpled to the ground, dead, Roa's body shook from the shock.

In the silence, she lifted the bloodied knife in her trembling hand.

She'd killed men during the revolt, but that was different. Those men were nameless. None of them had stood guard outside her door while she slept.

She remembered the way Sirin's hands had trembled too. As if he was afraid.

Roa forced herself to walk. To crouch down over the body of her dead guard and wipe the blood from her knife on his shirt. After sheathing it, she was about to rise when the sight of something half hidden in his pocket stopped her. Remembering Sirin's conversation with the guard at the gate, Roa reached into the pocket and pulled out a wooden seal with an image carved into the base. An image of a black dragon with a red heart of flame.

It was Dax's official seal. He sometimes gave it to Safire or certain trusted members of his staff when he needed to be in two places at once. It was a way for someone to carry out the king's orders in his stead.

As Roa stared down at her husband's seal, taken from the body of her dead guard, a sick feeling festered in her belly.

He wouldn't . . .

Or would he?

Hadn't Roa been plotting against him this very night? Wasn't she a threat to his throne?

Shakily, she rose to her feet, gripping Dax's seal hard in her hand. It was only as she walked out of the alley, heading for the palace, that she noticed her sister's silence.

"Essie? Are you all right?"

Essie didn't answer. Her mind was completely blank.

Essie's silence continued all the way back to the palace. Roa asked her where she'd gone, how she'd come back. But it was as if her thoughts weren't getting through to Essie. As if Essie's mind were shrouded in fog.

I couldn't find my way, Essie had told her that night in the sand sea. *I couldn't remember where home was.*

Roa knew what it meant. Essie was running out of time.

At the palace, the soldier whose gaze crept over her earlier was surprised to find Roa alone.

"Where's Sirin?" he asked, opening the gate for her. The huge, iron door—meticulously cast in repeating patterns of moons and namsaras—creaked as it opened.

"He needed to rid the king of a problem," she repeated numbly, stepping through and past the soldier, leaving him to draw his own conclusions.

It was midnight now, and the palace was quiet. A few guards stood at doors or paced entrances to rooms, but no servants walked. Roa's footsteps and the soft hush of her gray wool dress brushing against her legs seemed unnaturally loud in contrast.

As she made her way through long halls and lavish indoor gardens, she couldn't stop thinking about the blood streaming down Sirin's throat, the sound of him choking.

But more than these things was what Sirin said.

I've been paid too well to fail.

Roa had refused to consummate her marriage and, by doing so, refused to give Dax an heir. She'd made things difficult by insisting on the treaty with the Great Houses and then threatening his council when they refused to uphold it in the Assembly that morning.

Plenty of people in his court disliked her. Plenty wanted her gone.

But were these reasons enough for Dax to want her dead?

She was trying to puzzle it out when she ran straight into a solid chest.

Hands reached to steady her.

"Roa? What are you doing here?"

Her heart raced. Trapped. She didn't want to be trapped again.

Essie spread her wings in warning as Roa pushed the hands away and stepped abruptly back.

Dax stood before them.

He wore a white cotton shirt, unlaced at the throat. Dark circles shadowed his eyes.

"Where are your guards?" he asked, studying her and the hawk.

Her skin prickled with wariness. She squeezed his seal against her palm as she took another step back. "My guards?"

"Yes. The four men who follow you around day and night, keeping you safe?"

Those words sharpened something inside Roa.

"Sometimes," she said, "the ones closest to us are the least safe."

"Indeed," he said, his gaze taking in too much. He saw how she trembled. Saw her wrist, still splattered with flecks of blood.

Roa pulled down her sleeve to hide it.

His gaze moved over her gray wool gown. It was a practical scrublander dress that came to her ankles. She'd worn it out in the city to keep from being recognized.

He looked from the dress to the flower tucked behind her ear. A flower she'd completely forgotten about.

Roa quickly reached to touch the petals of the rose Theo gave her.

"Someone should let him know you prefer jacarandas."

Roa's fingers froze. "W-what?"

Dax stepped toward her. Roa tensed, ready to spring away at the slightest threatening movement. But all he did was pluck the rose from behind her ear. He held it in the space between them, its petals swooping elegantly into his palm.

"You love when they drop their flowers," he murmured.

She stared at him, remembering the first summer he came to Song. She and Essie had wanted to explore the ruins of Shade and their mother would only let them if they brought Dax along. Jacaranda trees grew in almost every ruined room, throwing soft purple flowers down and carpeting the dirt floors.

"That was ten years ago," she said, squeezing the seal in her hand. "A lot can change in ten years."

You most of all, she thought.

Once he was the boy who sat across the gods and monsters board, soaking up all her friendship and advice.

Now he was the boy who took every girl but her into his bed. He was the king who broke all his promises. He was the enemy who had stolen her sister from her.

And tonight . . .

Had he given the order to strike her down?

Roa lifted her hand, uncurling her fingers from around the seal, letting it rest on her palm.

"I think this belongs to you." She no longer cared if he saw the blood on her wrist. Let him see it. If it was Dax who gave the order, let him know what happened to the guard who tried to carry it out.

His eyes darkened. Reaching, he said, "Where did you . . . ?"

The moment he took it from her, Roa stepped swiftly back.

"You should be more careful next time," she said, moving around him. "Good night."

He fell silent. When she was halfway up the hall, he called after her. "Your rooms are in the opposite direction, Roa."

But she wasn't going to her rooms. There were three other guards standing outside her door. How many of them could do what Sirin had done?

"I don't want to sleep alone tonight," she said, touching Essie's feathers for comfort.

Roa stood in front of an arched doorway just beyond the royal quarters. Two soldats stood guard on either side of it.

She opened the door and stepped quietly inside.

Lirabel's room was half the size of Roa's, and so was the bed. Her friend was asleep in it, curled on her side, while the moon shone in through the windows, illuminating the soft curves of her face.

Roa stood frozen in the entranceway, watching her sleep, wondering where and when they went wrong.

She made for the bed.

Lirabel stirred as Roa pulled back the covers and climbed in. Essie hopped off her shoulder and onto the pillows, curling up near their heads.

"Roa?" Lirabel murmured, her voice raspy with sleep. "What's wrong?"

Essie's disappearing, Roa thought. *I'm involved in a treasonous plot with Theo. And I found Dax's seal on the guard who just tried to kill me.*

Instead, wrapping her arms around Lirabel, she said, "I miss you."

She didn't realize the truth of it until the words were out of her mouth.

"Oh, Roa," Lirabel whispered, pulling her close and kissing her head. "I'm right here."

But their friendship had been fraying for months now and Roa wasn't sure how to fix it. Lirabel kept moving further and further out of reach.

"Are you homesick?" Lirabel whispered as Roa clung to her. "Is that what it is?"

Homesickness was the least of Roa's problems.

"It's okay if you are," Lirabel said, rubbing Roa's back. "I'm homesick every day."

Roa held her tighter, wanting to ask a question, but too afraid of the answer.

She thought of the conversation she'd overheard from beneath Dax's bed. Thought of Lirabel crying all alone when he left her.

"You would tell me if you were in trouble, right?" Roa whispered.

She felt Lirabel frown. "What? I'm not—"

"If you needed help—any kind of help—you would come to me, wouldn't you?"

Lirabel fell silent.

"Yes," she said after a long time. "If I need help, I'll come to you."

"Do you promise?"

"Yes."

Roa's grip on her friend loosened—just a little.

"No matter what happens," she whispered, thinking of the baby in Lirabel's belly. Thinking of Theo and what they were planning to do. "I'll keep you safe." *Both of you.*

Lirabel wrapped her arms around Roa's waist, squeezing her tight.

They fell asleep like that. Holding on to each other.

Sisterless

On the night they burned her, the girl couldn't look away.

The wind howled with sorrow as she watched them wrap her sister's body in cotton and lay her on the pyre. She saw them strike the flint, again and again, until the sparks caught the tinder and the fire blazed, devouring the one she loved best.

She'd seen her sister fall. Heard the sickening crack when her body hit the ground, four stories below. Felt the hum roar in her ears, louder and fiercer than ever.

But she never felt her sister's life wink out. Instead, she felt the bond glow brighter and stronger between them.

It was glowing even now.

Maybe that was why she didn't cry. Why she turned away when the messenger came and whispered something to her father.

"Amina—the queen—is dead. Killed by the king."

The girl saw her father's wet eyes go wide. He turned back, away from the pyre, looking over the fields and down the dirt road, all the way back to the House of Song.

Where a mob was gathering.

The sight of their torches made the girl's breath catch.

The son of the king was inside that house. Alone and unprotected.

"They intend to strike at the king by striking his son," her father realized aloud.

"Perhaps you should let them," said the messenger. "That son is responsible for the death of your own daughter. How many more horrors will he be responsible for once he's grown?"

Her father was no longer listening. He was grabbing his horse. He mounted, kicked the mare, and was gone.

The girl looked back to the funeral. To the mourners who'd smeared their foreheads with ash. To her wailing mother and her weeping brother and that raging blaze.

Her sister wasn't on that pyre.

Her sister wasn't here at all.

So the girl went after her father.

When she arrived at the House of Song, the mob had reached the doors. The girl pressed her horse on, pushing her way up to the house. Men and women wept and shouted. Some wielded weapons and scythes, while others brought only their fists.

Fists they banged on the doors.

"Send him out!"

The girl ducked into the gardens and sneaked soundlessly inside.

The house was quiet. Servants gathered in dark corners, wringing their hands, looking to the east wing.

The girl didn't need to ask why. The answer was coming down the hall.

She watched her father drag a fighting, sobbing boy into the small room across from her.

"Hush. This is for your own good."

The son of the king swung his fists and dragged his feet.

"Where's my mother?" His voice trembled. Tears streamed down his cheeks. "I want to see my mother!"

His eyes caught sight of the girl.

"Help!" he cried, reaching for her. "Help me, please!"

The girl stood silent, watching as he begged. Watching as her father shoved him into the storeroom—the only room in the house without windows—and locked the door from the outside.

It shocked her.

Scrublanders didn't lock things. It was a violation.

Her father fell against the wooden door, his mouth twisting with sorrow as the boy banged from the inside, his questions getting more and more frantic, until they broke into sobs.

The girl felt nothing.

Her heart was already broken.

Her father, however, pressed one palm to the door, then covered his face with the other. His shoulders shook. The girl watched.

When he finished, when he dried his eyes, he straightened and strode to the front of the house to address the crowd. They shouted at him, demanding he hand over the son of the king.

"Go home!" said her father. "The boy has been dealt with! He's imprisoned and will be held here until my daughter is mourned. You will get your justice. I swear it."

The angry, grieving crowd dispersed. The servants returned to work. Warily, her father rode back to the funeral.

The girl remained behind, staring at the locked door.

Slowly, she approached and sat down.

With her back pressed to the wood, she listened to the sound of him crying.

"It should have been you," she whispered, thinking of her sister falling from the roof—right after she saved him. "It should have been you."

The girl hated him.

She would never stop hating him for what he'd taken from her.

And yet, she couldn't bring herself to leave him.

They intend to strike at the king by striking his son, *her father had said.*

Perhaps you should let them.

The girl stayed there all night, like a sentinel, listening to the sound of him weeping. Her father found her just after midnight, curled up outside the storeroom door, asleep.

Carefully, he unlocked it. The boy sat on the storeroom floor, his arms gripped tight around his knees. He stared up at the man before him, the salt of his tears encrusted on his cheeks.

The girl's father lifted a finger to his lips and beckoned him out.

Silently, beneath the cover of night, he took the boy to the stables. They saddled a horse, mounted up, rode out. The moon rose high and full above them, lighting their path through the blight-ridden fields of Song.

Because no one should suffer for the crimes of their fathers.

Fifteen

Roa woke the next morning to find Lirabel gone and her sister's silver hawk eyes watching her from the pillows. Roa turned onto her side, cradling her cheek on her crooked arm, and stared back.

Essie. She sent the name toward her sister's mind, like she usually did, like she'd always done. But the thought was met with silence. And the hum was weaker than ever.

The Relinquishing was only five days away now, and if Roa didn't lose her sister before then, she would certainly lose her on the longest night. Essie's soul had lingered for eight years now. Eight years was too long. She couldn't keep resisting her death call.

Roa stared at her sister.

The Skyweaver's knife was their only chance. She needed to find it tonight, in the home of her enemy. A home she'd never been to.

"Essie," she said aloud this time. The white hawk lifted her head, her gaze piercing Roa.

What if I can't do it? Her eyes prickled with tears and her vision blurred. *What if I fail?*

Suddenly, the weight on the pillows shifted. Soft feathers brushed Roa's forehead, then the tip of her nose. A solid, familiar warmth curled itself up against her chest, close to her heart.

Roa palmed the tears from her eyes and found Essie pressed against her, perfectly still, listening to the sound of her sister's heartbeat. Roa's arm came gently around her.

"I won't fail," she whispered into her feathers. "That's a promise."

When Roa opened the door to step out into the hall, Safire's grinning face greeted her.

"Finally. I was beginning to think you'd sleep all day."

The commandant didn't wear the king's crest—a dragon entwined around a sword—but a seven-petaled flower that mimicked the shape of a flame. A namsara flower.

Safire's gold tunic was fitted to her tall, strong form; while her face was measured and calm, her eyes raged like bright blue flames.

"Saf?" Roa frowned, looking beyond her to the three soldats—all young women—standing behind her. "What is this?"

"I'm officially on guard duty," said Safire. She stepped into the room, forcing Roa back, and immediately started looking around. The three soldats filed in after her, two of them taking up positions inside the door. The last one, Roa noticed, was a scrublander with bright onyx eyes. Her curls haloed her head and she lifted a fisted hand over her heart in a scrublander salute, just for Roa.

"My name is Celeste." The girl let her fist uncurl and fall back to her side. Looking to the other two soldats, she said, "This is Saba and Tati."

Though neither Saba nor Tati was a scrublander, they both followed Celeste's lead and gave Roa the same fisted salute.

Stunned, Roa returned the gesture.

"Guard duty?" she murmured, turning to Safire.

The commandant crouched down near the bed, scanning the floor.

"What are you doing?" Roa demanded.

"A member of the queen's personal guard was found dead in an alley this morning." Safire rose, her gaze fixing on the queen. "His throat was cut open. From the look of the wound, it was a small blade that did it."

Roa pulled her sleeve down to cover her wrist—still flecked with Sirin's blood.

"The soldats at the gate told me he left with you in the night." Safire's black hair was pulled into a simple bun at the nape of her neck, keeping it off her face. Those blue eyes watched Roa closely, as if measuring her reaction. "Where did you go?"

Roa forced herself to remain composed.

There were three other guards who—she was sure—had already told Safire the truth. That Roa had left with Sirin as her escort, and neither of them returned to her rooms.

"I went for a walk," she said. "I needed some air."

Safire pulled one of the throwing knives from her belt and

started examining its very sharp edge. "You needed air . . . at midnight?" Her gaze returned to Roa.

"It was only moonrise when I left."

"And Sirin escorted you out?"

Roa nodded.

"But didn't escort you back in?"

"Is this an interrogation?" On her shoulder, Essie flexed her wings in agitation.

Safire smiled, but there was no warmth in it. "If this were an interrogation, you would be in the dungeons right now."

Roa lifted her chin in defiance.

"Sirin didn't escort you back in," Safire repeated, waiting for Roa to confirm or deny it.

Roa shook her head. "He said"—she shivered at the memory—"something about *ridding the king of his problem*."

Roa's eyes held Safire's, daring her to press harder. To ask Roa what the king's problem was, exactly.

But Safire didn't. Instead, she turned and walked to one of three arched windows against the south wall of Lirabel's small room.

"Until a replacement can be found," said Safire, her back to Roa as she glanced out the window, the sunlight washing over her, "I'm the new captain of your guard."

Roa frowned. *"What?"*

The person *most* loyal to Dax, his own flesh and blood, watching her every move? It was the last thing she needed.

"And these"—Safire nodded toward the young women near the door—"are my three most trusted soldats."

Roa glanced at the armed guards, all of them staring atten-tively at their commandant. From the looks on their faces, Roa knew without a doubt their loyalty couldn't be bought. From the looks on their faces, they would cut down anyone who so much as *tried* to turn them against Safire.

"Their orders are to defend you with their lives," said Safire, walking back toward Roa. "So that's what they'll do."

"Perfect," Roa said through gritted teeth. "I hope they do a better job than Sirin."

"You can count on it," said Safire. Her throwing knife flashed as she tossed it in the air, then sheathed it next to the others in her belt.

But as inconvenient as it was, Roa found herself relaxing. In the presence of these new guards, she felt truly safe.

"Now." Safire smiled, and this time, it was a cheerful one. "Shall we escort you to your rooms? I'm sure you'd like a bath and a fresh change of clothes before Baron Silva's dinner party tonight."

The dinner party.

How was she going to find and steal the Skyweaver's knife with Safire's too-keen eyes trailing her wherever she went?

Roa followed Tati and Saba through the door. Celeste and Safire fell into step behind her.

I'll have to lose her somehow.

How Roa would manage that, she had no idea.

An Unexpected Visitor

On the first Relinquishing after her sister died, the girl helped her mother snuff all the lights while her brother bolted the doors and let in only the living.

The Relinquishing was not a time for celebration. You did not wear fancy clothes or eat lavish meals. You didn't sing or dance.

The rules for relinquishing needed to be carefully observed. Otherwise, the worst could happen.

In the girl's household, when the sun went down, her family and neighbors put on their masks, gathered in the central pavilion, and told each other stories until sunrise.

Normally, the girl and her sister loved Relinquishing nights. Loved listening to her father tell stories about the Skyweaver and the world beyond this one. Loved the way the heart-fire—the only flame allowed tonight—flickered across their masks, keeping their identities hidden. They even loved the burned bread. Loved to dip it in soured wine.

This year was different.

The girl didn't want to hear her father's stories, nor did she want to think about the Skyweaver. She didn't like the look of the wooden masks painted white, hiding the faces of her loved ones. She had no appetite for scorched bread.

It reminded her of everything she'd lost.

So the girl got up and left.

She didn't leave the house—she knew better than that. But she left the pavilion and walked the dark, silent halls to the parlor.

It was too dark. With the heart-fire burning on the other side of the house, she couldn't see a thing. So the girl lit a candle—what harm could a single candle do?—and set it on the window ledge.

The girl stepped onto the table where a gods and monsters board sat, then climbed on the windowsill and looked out. No moon glowed in the sky. Everything was black.

Except her candle, burning bright.

Like a beacon.

It wasn't long before the door creaked. The girl sucked in a breath and went very still. But the light of her candle couldn't reach that far, and the door remained in shadow.

She felt the rush of cool air from the hall.

"Who's there?" she whispered, the hair on the back of her neck rising.

A voice answered from the shadows: "It's the longest night of the year and you put a candle in the window?"

The girl's heart hammered. She grabbed the candle and held it out.

"Who are you?" she whispered, her hands shaking, the candle flickering.

She knew, though.

Of course she knew.

The thing behind the door stepped into the light. It wore her sister's face, her plaited dark hair, and the sky-blue dress she died in—a cotton one that came to her knees.

"Hello, sister."

The girl swallowed hard from behind her Relinquishing mask, knowing the danger. Knowing that what stood before her could wear the face of her sister but be a twisted version of her.

"Stay back."

The thing paused, its brow wrinkling, as if puzzled.

"You think I'm corrupted," it said, looking to where the girl's hand slid beneath her dress, to where a knife was sheathed at her calf. "A knife is no good against a corruption, silly."

The girl didn't take her hand away from her knife. "My sister died. Months and months ago. If you want me to believe you're her, and not her corrupted spirit, prove it."

The thing with her sister's face chewed its lip. Its gaze swept over their parlor and came to settle on the table just beneath the windowsill. On the gods and monsters board.

"Could a corrupted spirit beat you at gods and monsters?"

"My sister couldn't even beat me at gods and monsters."

The thing put its hands on its hips and smiled just like her sister smiled. "Is that so?"

It wasn't so. It was a test.

The thing came toward the window.

The girl drew back, afraid.

It raised its hands, then slowly reached for the black and white pieces scattered on the table, so as not to scare her again.

"Would a corrupted spirit know that this piece is your favorite?"

The thing sitting at the board lifted the ivory caged queen. The girl took it, still wary, then slid down off the sill and sat across the table.

"If I win," said the thing, setting up the board, "I want you to come cliff jumping with me."

Its fingers ran gently over the chiseled pieces, as if this was the last game it would ever play and it wanted to memorize everything.

"If you were my sister, you'd know I hate cliff jumping."

The thing looked up, and their eyes met. "But I love it. I want to do all the things I love tonight. With you."

The girl softened.

She gave in and played the game.

When the thing wasn't looking, the girl studied it. It had her sister's ebony eyes, black frizzy braids, and soft round cheeks. It even had her snaggle tooth. Every now and then, when their father's voice would float down the halls, still telling stories, the thing with her sister's face would look up and the girl would watch an unbearable sadness flicker in her eyes.

When the candle was on the verge of guttering, the thing said, "Would a corrupted spirit know the secret code?"

The girl looked up, surprised. Back when their mother suffered from debilitating headaches, on her very bad days, their father instituted a no-talking-in-the-house rule. So the girl and her sister made up a series of complex gestures. They didn't remember most of them. The fun was in making them up.

One, however, had stuck.

The thing smiled. Very slowly, it reached across the table and touched the girl's wrist. The girl shivered, even though its hand was warm, its fingers soft. When it found the girl's wrist bone, it tapped twice.

Pay attention, it meant. I'm about to win the game.

The girl looked to the board and saw, indeed, the game was over. She turned to the grinning face of her sister, who laughed a golden laugh. It was so familiar, that laugh. It was her favorite sound in the world.

"I believe you," she whispered. "But if you aren't corrupted, why are you here?"

The grin faded. "I couldn't cross," she said, and there was the ache of sorrow in her voice.

Suddenly, it all made sense. Her sister was here, in her true form, to walk among the living on the last night of the year . . . because she hadn't been relinquished. She was uncrossed.

"How much time do we have?"

Her sister looked out the window to the sky. Half the night had passed already.

"Just until dawn."

"Well then," said the girl, snuffing out the candle, "we'd best get going if we're going to reach the cliffs in time."

Her sister beamed at her through the dark.

This time, the girl climbed the sheer rock, even as her legs shook. And though she was terrified, she jumped.

And jumped. And jumped.

Her sister held her hand and laughed the whole way down.

How she missed the sound of that laugh.

The fear didn't lessen with each jump. The girl just didn't care as much about dying as she cared about soaking up her sister's presence. She wanted to spend these last moments doing whatever her sister wanted. Because when the sun came up, that would be it. Her sister would cross, as all souls must.

When the sky turned red, they climbed out of the water, their teeth clattering in the early-morning cold, and collapsed into the grass. The girl clutched her sister's hand, staring deep into her eyes, not daring to look away, even to check the sky.

"Don't go," she whispered. "I don't know who I am without you."

"You're my sister. You'll always be my sister."

Not if you're gone, thought the girl.

The air turned golden. Her sister looked to the sky, watching the sunrise over the cliffs.

The girl couldn't look.

"Don't leave," she begged, watching her flicker and fade. Her vision blurred with hot tears.

When she blinked them away, her sister was gone.

Sixteen

Roa stood in the heart of enemy territory, with Essie perched on her shoulder, watching the dizzying spectacle of Baron Silva's great hall.

In honor of the new dragon queen, Rebekah's guests all wore Relinquishing masks. At least, that's what Roa assumed they were supposed to be. But unlike the masks Roa's people wore on the longest night of the year, these were a gaudy show of wealth. They were golden shimmering things, some inlaid with gems or sewn up with bright ribbons, each one distinct to match the wearer.

A thin, cackling man wore the snout of an elephant. A huge woman with ruby rings wore the face of a hyena. And standing alone, near the wall, a dark-haired young woman with glittering black eyes wore the face and horns of a dragon. It covered one whole side of her face, and half of the other.

Guests laughed as they showed off their masks, casting haughty glances at Roa, Lirabel, and Essie, who stood gaping at the awful mimicry. This was not an attempt to honor Roa and her scrublander heritage. This was little more than a mockery.

"This is supposed to protect us from wandering spirits?" One woman smirked. "I never realized how superstitious they were."

"So backward thinking," agreed the man at her side.

Essie ruffled her feathers in irritation as Roa and Lirabel exchanged furious glances. The masks they'd been given—a cobra and a fox—were buckling in their clenched fists.

Relinquishing masks were simple, rudimentary things for a reason. Fashioned out of wood and painted all in white, they were intended to be plain, each one the same as the next, to confuse and repel the dead—not draw them in with their dazzling beauty.

More than this: the masks were only worn on the longest night of the year—which was still five days away.

"That's right," said Lirabel darkly, eyeing them all. "Keep laughing."

But Roa couldn't afford to let their condescension distract her. She needed to find a way to lose her guards so she could go in search of the knife.

"How humiliating this must be for you."

Rebekah's voice startled Roa. And Essie, too—her claws dug into her sister's shoulder, making her wince. She might not be able to sense her sister's emotions now, but from the way her weight shifted from claw to claw, Roa knew exactly how Essie felt about the newcomer. Roa stroked her wings, trying to soothe her.

"Rebekah," Lirabel answered from Roa's right. Her normally soft jaw was hard and clenched. "What a lovely dinner."

Rebekah stepped up to Roa's left, dressed in gold. Her kaftan was nearly the exact shade as Dax's tunic, and her black hair was done up in an elaborate knot work of braids. Tucked into her sash was a dagger, its blade hidden in an embossed silver sheath.

Roa's own attire was much simpler in style. In an attempt to blend in and more easily evade her guards, she'd donned a kaftan, choosing a shade of pink that seemed to be in style lately and therefore more likely to be worn by other women in attendance. She wore no jewelry. Nothing that would draw the eye.

"Rumor is he's bed every girl in his court," Rebekah said, ignoring Lirabel as she nodded toward the king—who was half-drunk and flirting with Firgaard's wealthiest daughters. Jas stood beside him, watching his cup. "There are bets on how many bastards he's sired."

Roa flinched and tried not to look at Lirabel—who hadn't started showing yet, thank the stars. Essie's grip on Roa's shoulder tightened, piercing the skin. She then flew to Lirabel, as if to reassure her.

"There are even bets on whether or not he's bedded *you*."

The anger emanating from Lirabel was palpable now. Roa, not wanting to give her friend away, stared straight ahead.

Most of Firgaard suspected Roa and Dax's marriage was unconsummated, but there was no proof for or against. Their wedding had happened in a war camp on the eve of a revolt.

"An unconsummated marriage is a precarious position for any king. A weak king especially."

Roa knew this was true. Dax's reign was a frail one, and he needed more than a consummated marriage. He needed an heir.

"Your point?" Roa said as Lirabel reached for her hand, squeezing once.

"He's a man like any other." Rebekah leaned in closer. "He won't wait forever."

Out of the corner of her eye, Roa saw the commandant moving in. But Rebekah would have to be mad to try to harm the queen here, surrounded by so many witnesses.

"One day," Rebekah murmured, "he will grow impatient and *take* what he needs from you."

Roa thought of that day in Amina's stables. Of the unclaimed kiss she owed him.

I'll come to collect when it suits me.

"And if he can't," said Rebekah, at Roa's shoulder now, "he will dispose of you."

Roa glanced up into the girl's dark brown eyes. They studied each other, and just for a heartbeat, Roa wondered if Rebekah had heard about Sirin's attack.

"I'd say she doesn't have to worry quite yet," Lirabel interrupted, watching as the king smiled down at a young woman in a bright yellow kaftan. The girl's ringlets sprang softly outward, haloing her face and shoulders. Dax's gaze fixed on her like she was the sun and he needed to soak up all her warmth. "The king keeps himself well distracted. Wouldn't you say, Roa?"

Roa was surprised at the lack of bitterness in Lirabel's words. Shouldn't she be annoyed Dax had forgotten about her and her baby?

Rebekah didn't seem to hear. She stared at the king, her gaze almost ravenous. Like a lion watching an unsuspecting deer.

Suddenly, the sound of drawn steel came from behind them. All three girls whirled, bracing themselves for a threat. From Lirabel's shoulder, Essie spread her wings in warning.

A draksor with a thick scar running from the corner of his mouth to his cheekbone stood mere steps from Roa . . . with three shining blades pointed at his throat.

Two of them belonged to Safire. The third belonged to Celeste.

"Step away from the queen," Safire said coolly.

"This isn't a battlefield," Rebekah hissed. "Lower your weapons. Garnet is on my staff."

Safire ignored her, keeping her gaze on Garnet. "If he's on your staff, he should know he can't approach the queen, armed as he is. Don't you train them?"

Garnet smiled a tight smile that didn't quite meet his eyes. Lifting his hands, he took a careful step back.

"I won't tolerate this kind of barbarism in my home," Rebekah growled, her attention fixed on the king's cousin— whom she was starting to circle. "Since when are you a house guard, Safire? Who's fulfilling the duties of commandant while you harass my guests?"

Safire let Rebekah circle her, calm as steel, while Roa's other guards moved in to defend her should she need it.

"You've never been very good at this game, have you?" Rebekah's voice lowered to a dangerous purr. "Poor Safire. It's your skral mother's blood in your veins. It's why your place will never be among us."

Roa hesitated, wanting to defend Safire.

But Safire could take care of herself. She stared Rebekah down as she said, "What's the use in being good at a game I have no interest in playing?"

With everyone focused on the storm brewing between the hostess and the commandant, Roa saw her chance and took it. She slipped on her mask. Dressed in an unremarkable kaftan and without a white hawk on her shoulder, the queen went unidentified as she ducked out of the room.

Unrelinquished

It was several days after the Relinquishing when the brokenhearted girl started noticing the bird.

It was a plain desert hawk, with sandy feathers and brown eyes, and it was there in the window every morning when she woke.

It liked to watch the girl and often flew from window to window, depending on which room she was in. It perched on rooftops when she helped in the fields or dueled with her weaponry tutors in the gardens. And if she rode with her parents to one of the other Great Houses, the hawk was there, soaring through the sky above.

Following her.

The girl might have been alarmed if its presence weren't so comforting. Or perhaps that's why she should have been alarmed: because of the hum. It seemed to glow warmest and brightest whenever the hawk was near.

No, she thought. It can't be.

One night, after everyone had gone to sleep, the girl opened the windows and beckoned it in. The bird swooped to her bedside table, perching atop the lantern there. Its claws grappled with the iron handle, trying to keep a steady hold. As if it wasn't used to the weight and shape of its own body.

The girl sank down on the bed beside it, studying the beautiful arch of its throat. The sheen of its feathers. The sharpness of its claws.

It was when their eyes met that a too-familiar voice flooded her mind:

Hello, sister.

The girl reeled from the shock of her sister's voice in her head.

"You didn't cross," said the girl, studying the bird's feathers.

And leave you all alone? *Her sister's voice rang through her mind.* How could I?

The girl thought she might be going mad.

But it wasn't madness. It was true: her sister's soul had come back to her.

Seventeen

Just like in the dining hall, the corridor ceilings were high, rivaling those of the palace. Tall arched windows let the evening breeze blow through, making Roa shiver.

The mosaicked tiles clicked beneath her feet as Roa ripped off her mask, tossing it to the floor. Stuffed animal heads lined the hall here; some Roa recognized—a lion, a deer—while others she didn't—a striped horse, a huge fish with a spiraled horn protruding from its head.

Someone in this household obviously liked to hunt.

Her gaze quickly scanned the doors. A message from Theo had arrived that morning. The knife was in Silva's private collection, he'd written, behind a scarlet door.

Just as Roa turned the corner, Lirabel's voice called out. "Where are you going?"

Roa squeezed her eyes shut, then turned to face her friend, who was already advancing.

Essie rode on her shoulder, cocking her elegant white head as if to say *Don't look at me. This was her idea.*

"Couldn't you stay with Dax?" Roa pressed her palms to her eyes. "Like you usually do?"

Lirabel halted, her forehead pinching. "What is that supposed to mean?"

Roa continued on, turning the corner. "Please go back."

Essie launched herself from Lirabel's shoulder and soared toward Roa.

Lirabel ran after her.

But this might be Roa's only chance. If Lirabel wouldn't do as she said, she would have to let her come along.

The moment she turned the corner, Roa halted.

There was the scarlet door.

It wasn't a Firgaardian door. The patterns were less geometric, more playful. Roa reached out to touch the looping, arching vines painted on the wood, then grabbed the handle.

Locked.

Roa swallowed a growl. She'd forgotten that draksors loved to lock things.

"Maybe I'd spend less time with Dax," said Lirabel, coming around the corner now, "if you didn't shut me out all the time."

"I shut *you* out?"

"Yes," said Lirabel, thrusting out her chin. "Ever since you became queen, it's as if I don't exist. As if you have a thousand better things to do than spend time with me!"

Wasn't it the opposite?

Roa hushed her, glancing down the hall. "What are you saying? That I think I'm better than you . . . because I'm queen?"

Lirabel shook her head, her gaze fiery. "You've always thought you were better than me."

Roa stared at her. That wasn't true at all.

Her shock quickly dissolved into anger.

At least I never slept with a boy you loved, she nearly said, stopping herself just in time. Because it was petty. And nonsensical— Roa didn't love Dax.

"If anyone is shutting anyone out, it's you," said Roa, thinking of the pregnancy Lirabel hadn't told her about. Thinking about whose bed she'd been sharing as of late. "If anyone thinks you're *less than*, Lirabel, it's you. It always has been."

Lirabel opened her mouth to argue, but Roa wasn't finished.

"Ever since my parents took you in, you've seen yourself the way you *think* other people see you: as someone to be pitied. That's not what you are. And even if others see you that way, they're wrong. Don't believe them."

Before Lirabel could respond, a shadow fell across them.

Both friends looked up. Right into the blue eyes of the commandant. She was dressed in dark purple tonight, the color of the midnight sky.

"Safire." Panic spiked through Roa. "What are you doing here?"

Safire wrinkled her nose, as if she smelled something rotten. "Evading Bekah and her ghastly party." Her eyes narrowed slightly as she looked from Roa to Lirabel. "And whatever it is you're doing seems a lot more interesting." She crossed her arms. "What *are* you doing?"

Roa looked to Lirabel. As if Lirabel could save her.

"Trying to pick this lock?" Lirabel guessed, catching Roa's eye.

Safire tilted her head.

"Can you help us?"

Safire opened her mouth to ask another question, when sudden footsteps echoed from down the corridor. Roa and Lirabel straightened. Safire glanced around the corner. "Two servants, heading this way."

Roa motioned to the lock in the door, following Lirabel's lead. "All the more reason to act quickly. Can you pick it?"

Saf studied her, as if trying to decide whether she should help or not.

The footsteps—and voices now—drew closer.

Maybe it was the idea of scorning Rebekah. Or maybe Safire really did trust Roa. Whatever her reason, Safire slipped something from her boot. Crouching down in front of the door, she slid a pick into the lock, the look on her face one of pure concentration.

The voices grew louder as Saf's pick ground furiously against the wards.

Hurry! thought Roa.

Suddenly, there was a soft *click!*

The door swung in.

A dark stairwell yawned upward before them. Safire grabbed Roa and yanked her inside. Lirabel followed, silently shutting the door just as the servants turned the corner.

Roa, Lirabel, and Saf stood shoulder to shoulder, their backs pressed up against the door, holding their collective breath as the servants' conversation drifted through the wood.

"That's a lie," came a girl's voice.

"I saw them," came a boy's lower voice. "A girl with a scarred face riding a one-eyed black dragon."

The girl scoffed. "It was your imagination."

"Listen, I know what I saw," the boy went on. "And if I were the baron, I'd invite her in for tea. I hear the sight of her scar can strike a person dead. I'd like to know if that's true."

"She's a criminal, you halfwit. There's a fancy price on her head. I bet the only reason *he's* here is to lure her in. Bait the trap, so to speak."

Roa's hands started to sweat. She wiped them on her kaftan. Beside her, Safire—normally a portrait of calm restraint—looked like her heart had fallen out of her chest.

They were speaking about Asha, Safire's cousin, as well as Kozu—the First Dragon.

If Asha were captured, she'd be sent straight to finish out the death sentence she'd only narrowly escaped.

"What is she thinking?" murmured Saf. "She shouldn't be anywhere near here."

Roa thought of Asha's letter, still lying beneath Dax's bed in the dragon queen's abode. Roa had meant to tell him. She *would* have told him, if she hadn't overheard his conversation with Lirabel that day. Between her fury at Dax and Essie's second disappearance, and then her own guard attacking her . . .

Guilt pricked Roa. She'd been so preoccupied, she hadn't given much thought to Torwin or why he hadn't returned to Asha.

Now she did think of him. Or more specifically, of the price on his head. A price only marginally less than the one on

Asha's. It was the reason the pair were supposed to stay far away from Firgaard. Because if either of them fell into the wrong hands . . .

Roa shook off the thought. She was here now. She needed to get the knife. Once she had it, she would make sure Torwin and Asha were safe.

"Come on," said Roa, starting up the steps. "Before someone notices we're missing."

Together, they climbed. The red light of dusk slashed across the stone steps, piercing through the window slats. At the top of the staircase stood a simple doorway with a strange symbol carved into the lintel.

The door was ajar, letting dusty-rose light out into the stairwell. Safire pushed it open and Essie flew to perch at the top of the door, a silver-eyed sentinel keeping watch as the three girls stepped inside.

The windows were flung wide, letting in a fresh breeze, and the sweet scent of cedar and roses wafted in from the gardens. Glass cases lined the walls and continued on into the next room and the next. Inside each case were jewels and fabrics, figurines and weapons. Artifacts taken from the four corners of the world.

"What are we looking for?"

"A knife," said Roa. "The Skyweaver's knife."

Lirabel shot her a skeptical look.

Roa couldn't blame her. She'd been skeptical, too.

They searched the cases. Lirabel stood across from Roa now, on the other side of a gods and monsters board, preserved beneath glass. The playing pieces differed from her father's, but Roa could still identify the caged queen and the frail king, the skyweaver and the dragon and the corrupted spirit. All of the pieces were carved out of acacia wood, and a slate of brass was fixed to the side of the case, engraved with the rules of the game.

Suddenly, from the next room over, Safire said, "I think I found something."

Both friends followed the commandant's voice until they saw her, shoulders hunched and eyes squinting as she leaned in toward a case whose corners were decorated with gold filigree.

The case was small, maybe the size of two handbreadths on all sides, and its glass unmarked by dust or fingerprints. On the wooden pedestal that held it up to chest height, a gold plate was fastened.

Engraved into the plate wasn't a description, though. It was a story.

One about the Skyweaver.

Roa's heart pounded in her chest. This was it. The place for the knife that could save her sister.

There was just one problem.

The case was empty.

Skyweaver

Once there was a god who traded her name for a loom, her heart for a spindle, and her face for a knife.

They call her Skyweaver, but that isn't her true name. They say she dwells in the seam between worlds, where only the death marked can find her.

Skyweaver used to be good at many things, but now she's good at only one: all day and all night, she spins souls into stars and weaves them into the sky.

"What are souls," she whispers, "but stars waiting to be born?"

Her loom answers: rattle-clack. Shhhhh. Rattle-clack.

"What are souls," she says again, "but worms inside a chrysalis, waiting to become?"

Sometimes that's how Skyweaver feels—like she's waiting to become. Sometimes she looks around her weaving room and thinks, This isn't enough.

Her shuttle falls silent then. Her loom goes still. She looks down at the blade in her hand, glowing like the moon. In its silver reflection, a faceless girl stares back at her. A faceless girl whose true name she can't remember.

"No matter," she whispers.

Lifting the knife, Skyweaver cuts the old threads and begins her work anew.

Eighteen

Roa stared through the glass.

Why would the case be empty?

She undid the clasp and swung the lid open. She put her hand inside the case, touching the velvet cloth on the bottom, then pulled it out. There was nothing but more glass underneath, and the wood of the pedestal beneath that.

Maybe Torwin did intercept it, she thought.

Or maybe Baron Silva was showing off his new possession to his guests. Perhaps it was being cleaned. Or sharpened. Or possibly it had been decided this room wasn't safe enough. After all, Safire had just picked the lock.

There were a multitude of possibilities. Roa needed to find out which it was.

"We've been gone too long," said Safire, looking to the door. "If this is what you came for, it isn't here. We need to get back."

Knowing she was right, Roa shut the case.

As the three of them returned to the stairs, the story of Skyweaver flooded her thoughts.

Roa thought of the person who'd eluded death eight years ago. The person whose place her sister took. The person whose soul she needed to exchange for Essie's.

For the first time since she'd made her decision, Roa faltered.

Could she really do such a thing—take his soul?

She thought of him in the hall below, loud and drunk and flirting. Thought of him sitting in that council meeting, breaking every one of his treaty promises without hesitation. Thought of his seal in Sirin's pocket.

Yes, she told herself, fists tightening. *I can. I can do it for my sister.*

They were almost to the dining hall when they nearly strode straight into Rebekah. Their hostess looked proud and elegant in the dimming light of day, her golden kaftan gleaming in the torchlight.

Garnet and another burly draksor flanked her. They weren't soldats, but from the way they stood with their bulging arms crossed, they seemed something akin to house guards.

And at Rebekah's side walked . . .

"Theo?" Roa and Lirabel said in unison.

Theo smiled sheepishly back at them. His dark brown hair was pulled back into its usual bun and he wore a silk tunic, in the Firgaardian style, that came just above the knee, with trousers underneath. Roa could see the delicate silver stitching from where she stood.

"What are you wearing?" she asked, looking him up and down. She'd nearly mistook him for a draksor.

Where had he gotten such a fine thing? And how in all the skies did he get invited to this dinner?

"My queen," Rebekah interrupted. "What a coincidence. Your friend and I were just speaking about you." The silver sheath in her sash winked in the torchlight. "What are you doing out here in the hall?"

Roa stared at the dagger, a sudden thought striking her.

"We got lost," Lirabel answered quickly for her. "Safire found us."

Rebekah's dark brown eyes narrowed ever so slightly.

"Safire, Lirabel—you'll excuse us, won't you? There are things I'd like to discuss with the queen."

"I wish I could, Bekah, but—"

Garnet and the other draksor stepped forward, their blades half-drawn.

"It won't take long," Rebekah said, smiling sweetly.

Lirabel's gaze met Roa's as the commandant reached for her hilt.

"No," said Roa, touching Saf's arm. She kept her eyes on the dagger at their hostess's hip. "It's fine. Go back to the dining hall."

"You know I can't do that," said Safire staring down the scarred guard.

"I'm ordering you to."

Safire glanced at her, and for a moment Roa thought she would continue to refuse. But then her hand fell to her side and she bowed her head a little stiffly. "Of course, my queen."

Roa didn't like the way Rebekah studied Safire and Lirabel, as if they were insects under glass in an observatory. She especially didn't like the way Rebekah studied Essie. Like she was less of a bird and more of a . . . meal.

"Go with them," Roa told her sister, pushing her from her shoulder.

Startled, Essie didn't have time to dig her claws in. Before she fell, she spread her wings and swooped toward Lirabel.

With Theo at her side, Roa glanced back once to see Essie, Lirabel, and Saf all watching her with worried eyes.

Rebekah led them to a room full of birds.

Ospreys, owls, sparrows, crows. And worst of all: a desert hawk. All of them unnaturally still. All of them watching Roa from the walls. Their eyes lifeless. Their souls gone.

Roa and Theo exchanged glances.

The room smelled like death and fear.

Thank the stars Essie isn't here.

Rebekah sat in an armchair that was too big for her, staring at Roa from across the desk. "As I said, my father loves birds. This is his second favorite room."

Roa swallowed. What did his first favorite look like?

"Why are we here?" she asked.

Rebekah leaned back, gripping the arms of her father's chair, studying the new queen.

"Theo came seeking my help," she said. "He's very worried about you."

Roa looked to Theo, who sat in the chair beside her. *What?*

"He says you didn't realize what you were doing," Rebekah continued. "He says Dax convinced you to march an army to his side, fight his war, break off your betrothal . . . all in the hope of protecting your people."

Roa lifted her chin. That wasn't how it happened. Dax *asked* for her help, and in exchange, Roa asked for a marriage. She knew exactly what she was doing.

She was not the victim here.

"You realized too late he wasn't the man you thought he was."

Roa leaned back against her chair. This, at least, was true.

"And," Rebekah continued, "now you want to undo the choices you've made."

Roa looked to Theo, wanting clarification.

Theo looked back at her.

And the pieces clicked together.

Why he was dressed like a wealthy draksor. Why he'd been personally invited to a dinner party by Rebekah—a girl who barely tolerated scrublanders.

This was the contact he'd mentioned to Roa last night.

Roa stared at her friend. "Tell me you didn't," she whispered.

"Theo told me everything. I know all about your plot against the king."

Roa's mouth went dry. She looked away from Theo to Rebekah, lying through her teeth. Lying with everything in her. "There is no plot."

"Then why did you sneak out of the palace last night to meet him?" Her lips curled into a smile.

Roa gripped the arms of her chair. Theo couldn't possibly have told Rebekah that. It put them in so much danger.

"You were plotting with the boy you love to remove your husband from his throne."

It felt like her heart had stopped beating.

What have you done? she thought, staring at Theo.

He reached to touch her.

Roa flinched away.

"Her father is the most influential man in Firgaard," he said. "She can help us, Roa. She's offered to give us everything we want."

"Help us?" Roa's heart started to beat again—wildly now. *"Her?"*

Roa started to rise. She couldn't sit here and listen to this. She wanted out of this room.

Theo grabbed her shoulder, stopping her. She looked to his hand, gripping her hard, keeping her down. His golden eyes pleaded. "Roa, please. Just listen."

Roa turned to face Rebekah, her body coiled. The stuffed hawk peered down from the walls, its lifeless eyes staring into Roa. Making her hair stand on end.

"If you're going to do this, you'll need protection," said Rebekah. "My father and I have powerful friends in the court, on the council, and in the army. All I have to do is say the word, and every one of them will support you."

"The army is loyal to Safire," said Roa.

Rebekah smiled. "Not as loyal as she thinks."

Roa thought of Sirin, then. Of how easily her guard had nearly disposed of her.

"I can give you what you want *most*," said Rebekah.

Roa scowled. "And what's that?"

"This." Rebekah reached for the dagger in her sash. Her slender hands slid the weapon from its sheath and held it aloft. The blade glowed faintly. Like silver-white moonlight. Roa could feel the strange hum of it from where she sat across the desk.

"I believe your people call it the . . . Skyweaver's knife?"

Roa swallowed, staring as Rebekah sheathed the blade that could save Essie, tucking it back into her sash.

Exactly how much had Theo told her?

"You and I are more alike than you think, Roa. We see further than those around us. We understand what needs to be done—that sometimes sacrifices must be made in the pursuit of a greater good."

Roa's whole being cried out against this. She didn't want to be anything like this cold and calculating creature.

"Dax is a fickle, incompetent king. He betrayed me, too. And he's as much a danger to Firgaard as he is useless to the plight of your people. I may not like the idea of a scrublander sitting on the throne, but if I must choose, I prefer *you* to him."

Me as a puppet queen, Roa knew.

"If you want to remove him, you need more than a few scrublanders with pointy sticks to do it." Rebekah laughed.

Roa bristled. If she needed any reason not to enter into a bargain with Rebekah, it was this. Rebekah would never see Roa or her people as equals.

"I can help you. I *want* to help you. All I ask in return for the knife is that you involve me in the planning."

Why? thought Roa, glancing at the dagger, then up to Rebekah's face. *What did Dax do to make you hate him this much?*

She could still deny any plot against Dax. It was Theo's word against hers. But the moment Roa let this girl in, Rebekah would have what she needed to accuse the queen of treason.

If she accepted Rebekah's terms, if she let her in on their plans, Roa would be completely at her mercy.

"I can't involve you in a plot I'm not a part of any more than I can give you information I don't have," said Roa. "Now if you'll excuse me, my husband will be wondering where I am."

Roa knew where the Skyweaver's knife was now. She would find another way to obtain it.

She moved to leave. Rebekah's guards stepped in front of the door, blocking her way.

"Let her pass," said Rebekah. "She's heard our offer. We'll give her a chance to consider it."

I will never consider it, she thought.

As soon as they stepped aside, Roa pressed her palms to the door. She was pushing it open when something caught her eye.

Standing in the corner of the room was a bow and quiver full of arrows. They'd been hidden from her view as she sat facing Rebekah, but now she saw them plainly: the bow was fashioned out of blackwood, the arrows fletched with glossy crow feathers.

A little over two months ago, in the ruined House of Shade, she and Lirabel had crouched over a map while Torwin taught Dax how to shoot. The freckle-faced skral used a blackwood bow and arrows tipped with crow feathers to teach him. Roa remembered, because Lirabel couldn't stop staring at them. She told Roa it was the most beautiful bow she'd ever seen.

This bow, these arrows . . .

No, thought Roa.

But who else could they belong to?

Nineteen

Fear coiled in Roa's belly as she stepped back into the dining hall.

Night had fallen and the dining hall buzzed with laughter and conversation. Along the walls, brass sconces now held burning flames, and the masks of the dinner guests sparkled and shone, making Roa dizzy.

She scanned the crowd. She saw Dax first, exactly where she left him. A group of young women surrounded him. They gazed up at their king through long eyelashes, flashing him smiles, laughing loudly at his jokes.

Dax smiled and laughed back. But as he went to gulp down the rest of his wine, his gaze met Roa's over the lip of his goblet. His smile faded at the sight of her.

Roa surged toward him, pushing through the masked guests—who were all half-drunk now. Dax lowered his goblet and watched her for a moment, then set it down and excused himself. His guards followed as he made his way toward her.

When they met in the middle of the room, his gaze flickered over her.

"What's wrong?" He lifted a hand, as if to touch her. "Are you all right?"

Roa shook her head. "I'm fine. It's not me. It's—"

"You're not fine." This time, he reached for both her hands. "Roa, you're trembling."

He held them up to show her. They shook like leaves. Roa pulled free.

"I think something terrible has happened," she said.

A bell chimed from across the room, breaking their gaze. The chatter dimmed to silence. Together, Dax and Roa looked where everyone else was looking: to a tall, thin man standing in the center of the room. He wore crimson and his fingers were littered with rings.

"Baron Silva," Dax said for her benefit.

At the man's side stood Rebekah.

"Honored guests!" Silva's face beamed as he looked out over his dinner party. "The meal is about to be served. But before you take your seats, my daughter has an announcement to make."

He nodded at Rebekah, who smiled prettily back at him.

Suddenly Safire, Lirabel, and Jas were there at Roa's side. Essie hopped from Lirabel's shoulder to Roa's, moving in close, sensing her distress.

"Where were you?" Lirabel asked at the same time Safire said, "What happened?"

But Rebekah's voice cut them off, echoing through the dining hall as she looped her arm through Silva's.

"Several days ago, my father returned from a hunt with some fascinating quarry. He would like to present it now as a gift to the new wife of his good friend King Dax."

Rebekah nodded to Garnet, who disappeared through a set of doors and returned not with a stuffed and mounted animal, but a person. A person whose hands were tied behind his back and whose head was hooded.

Garnet pulled off the tan hood to reveal a young man with freckled skin and cool gray eyes.

A chill like ice swept through Roa.

Dax's hands balled so hard into fists that his knuckles paled. In a heartbeat all trace of the feckless king was gone, replaced by something much more dangerous.

Recognizing the young man across the room, Essie shrieked with rage, her wings spreading, her eyes flashing. Hearing it, Torwin looked up, his eyes alighting on his friends.

"Well, my queen?" Rebekah's voice chimed like glass as she stared down Roa from across the room. "My father caught for you a fugitive and a traitor to the throne. Aren't you going to come and thank him?"

Dax's fingers curled, as if itching to coil around Rebekah's throat. He started to move.

Lirabel grabbed him, her fingers sinking into his arm. "Don't let her bait you," she murmured, holding him back. "Reckless-ness won't get him out of this."

No, thought Roa. *It won't.*

And if she had told someone about the letter from Asha, this might have been prevented.

"I'll deal with this," she said.

Dax leveled a look at her. But Roa was already cutting across the room. Essie's claws dug hard into her shoulder, her hawk eyes glaring at Rebekah.

Halfway there, Torwin's voice rang out.

"Do you know who I belong to?" His gray eyes glinted like firelight on a sword.

A hush fell over the room. Roa paused, as Rebekah turned to him, her thin, black brows drawn into a vicious V.

"Do you know what she does to her enemies?"

For a moment, Roa caught a glimpse of the boy who'd fought hard for Asha's heart. A boy made of sharpened steel. A boy who'd survived monsters and tyrants.

A boy with no sense of self-preservation.

"Have you forgotten that she was Iskari? The *death bringer*?" The firelight caught in his hair, making it flame like the setting sun. "She's sister to a king. Guardian of a dragon so fierce, he'll incinerate an entire city." He stared down Rebekah like she was beneath him. Like he'd stared down far more terrifying things in his life. "To me, she is *beloved*." His voice softened. "And the ones who keep me from her come to unfortunate ends."

What are you doing? thought Roa. He'd just threatened the most cruel and cunning person in the room. The person who could most easily hurt him.

Rebekah came to stand before her father's trophy, her cold eyes looking him up and down. "Perfect. The sooner she comes for you, the sooner I can carry out the sentence our king should have executed weeks ago."

Everyone in the room knew what that sentence was.

Death.

It was clear on Rebekah's face that she didn't want to punish Asha because she believed in justice. No. She wanted to punish Asha because it would hurt Dax.

Roa stared at the regal girl before her, swathed in gold, her hair done up in braids. How had she become this? Someone who reveled in the pain of others?

"I accept your generous gift," said Roa, trying to draw Rebekah's venomous gaze away from Torwin. "We'll transport him to—"

"No," said Rebekah, her voice clipped. "My father and I will hold on to him, for safekeeping." She looked across the room to Dax. "Tell me, my king: what is the punishment for aiding a criminal guilty of regicide?"

Dax glared back at her, silent as a stone.

"We'll put it to the council then. Tomorrow."

Roa's heart sank. This was a game Rebekah was playing. And there was one last move—a move only Roa could make.

"Or perhaps," said Roa, "you and I can discuss more favorable terms?"

That smile returned—sharper and colder than ever. Like a knife blade.

"That would be agreeable," said Rebekah, who looked to Essie, glaring back at her from Roa's fist.

Essie spread her wings in a show of fearless anger. But Roa felt as if invisible bars were already clanging shut around them. She knew what the terms would be. Before she turned away,

Roa looked to Garnet, who held the rope binding Torwin's hands.

"Harm him," she said so only Garnet and his captive could hear, "and you'll be the second guard I leave in an alley with his throat slit open."

And then, in spite of everything, Torwin grinned at her. It was so reckless, so brave, that Roa couldn't help but borrow strength from it.

Twenty

At dinner, the table groaned with food piled high onto platters and silver pitchers full of wine. The sight made Roa ill. For years she'd watched the fields of Song turn from gold to white, watched her parents ration meals, watched her neighbors line up for handouts.

The guests around her gorged themselves, oblivious to her people's hunger.

More than this, they joked and laughed as if Torwin was all but forgotten. As if he hadn't just been hunted down like prey.

Roa didn't touch her food. Her appetite had fled.

Afterward, as the guests left, Roa instructed Dax, Lirabel, Jas, and Safire to go on without her.

"Absolutely not." Safire planted her feet. "Are you out of your mind?"

Dax said nothing, studying Roa. His tunic's golden hue complemented his warm complexion. His curls had been tamed tonight, but his cheeks were still peppered with the beginnings of a beard.

"This is my fault," Roa told him. "I need to fix it."

Safire's blue eyes were wild with worry. "How exactly do you plan on rescuing Torwin alone and unarmed?"

"Just . . . trust me." Roa couldn't quite meet their eyes as she said it. She felt Dax's gaze like a weight pressing down on her.

"I'm coming with you," Safire said at the same time Dax said, "We'll wait for you in the courtyard."

Safire glanced at him, stunned. Something passed between them in a look, and a moment later, Safire relented. "If you take too long, we're coming in to get you."

Rebekah led Roa to a different room this time. One that smelled sterile, like vinegar and cut limes.

The moment she stepped inside, Essie flinched, shuffling across her shoulder, keeping close to Roa. It didn't take long to find the source of her sister's unease.

The longest wall of this room was lined with black cages. Some stood empty, but most were full of birds—some frantically chirping and hopping from one side to the other, others who'd resigned themselves to their fates and sat warily on their perches.

Sharp instruments of all shapes and sizes were laid out on a small table, their blades glinting in the torchlight.

Roa brushed her sister's wings with the backs of her fingers— as much for her own comfort as for Essie's.

Theo entered the room behind her, followed by Garnet

and three other guards. At the sight of her friend, Roa turned sharply away.

"I'm very glad you've changed your mind," Rebekah said as she approached a wide fire basin. "What kind of terms would you like to discuss?"

Roa stepped up to the basin, touching the iron rim. In the scrublands, every basin was engraved with prayers to the Old One. This one was prayerless.

"Hand over Torwin and the Skyweaver's knife to me tonight," said Roa, "and I'll give you what you want."

"Done." Taking up the steel and flint, Rebekah struck it until the kindling in the basin lit. Gently, she blew on the sparks until the twigs caught. "Tell me your plans, and you can walk out of this house with both things."

Roa shook her head. "Torwin is not a thing." And she was not taking any chances. "I need assurance that you'll hand him over to me alive and unhurt."

Rebekah glanced up. "A relationship can't work without trust, Roa."

If her sense of danger wasn't so heightened, Roa might have rolled her eyes. She'd sooner trust a cobra.

Rebekah must have realized this. Because she looked wordlessly to Garnet, who left the room. Heartbeats later, when smoke began to curl up toward the hole in the roof, Rebekah stepped toward the wide window overlooking the grounds.

"Come and see."

Roa joined her, peering out through the glass. In the courtyard below, the door of the house opened and out stepped

Torwin, rubbing his wrists, which were no longer bound. At the far end of the brightly lit court, Lirabel, Safire, and Dax stood deep in conversation, surrounded by the king and queen's guards. The moment they spotted Torwin, their conversation halted and they broke apart, staring at their friend.

Safire ran for Torwin first, nearly barreling him over, squeezing him in a hug. Behind her, Dax's lips moved. As Safire let go, Torwin shook his head, answering Dax's question. Dax looked to the house briefly, his brow furrowed.

"You see?" said Rebekah, returning to the basin, stacking logs onto the flames. "He's safe."

Roa felt trapped, suddenly. As if Torwin going free was the key turning, locking her into the cage.

On her shoulder, Essie ruffled her feathers and shifted nervously from claw to claw.

Garnet returned a heartbeat later, shutting the door behind him.

Rebekah looked up from the fire, to the white hawk perched on Roa's shoulder. "So. You need to kill the king in order to save your sister."

Roa went rigid.

Rebekah knew the hawk was her sister? Was there anything Theo hadn't told her?

Roa pressed her palms to the window glass, letting it bear her up. Essie's claws dug into her shoulder, steadying her.

"How, exactly, is that going to work?" Rebekah pressed.

Roa swallowed. Steeling herself, she turned to face the girl at the fire basin.

"It must be done on the Relinquishing, with the Skyweaver's knife." The same day Essie would resume her true form. "On that night, with that blade"—she nodded to the weapon tucked into Rebekah's sash—"the Skyweaver will accept the exchange of Dax's soul for Essie's, because she died when he should have."

Rebekah studied her. From the look in her eyes, she didn't believe in things like souls or the Skyweaver. But she kept this to herself. "By taking his life, yours will be forfeit."

"That's what we need your help with," said Theo from behind Roa, who hardened at the sound of his voice.

Rebekah nodded. "As I said, my father and I have a great deal of influence in Firgaard. The court was unhappy with Dax's revolt. They are even less happy now that he sits on the throne. If my father and I support the queen, they will too."

The words chafed Roa. She didn't trust Rebekah or the court. But there was nothing she could do: she was in league with this creature now, no matter how much she hated it. This was the cost of Torwin's freedom.

"There will be twice as many people in the city for the Relinquishing," Roa said. "Most of them will be masked. It will be chaos, which means Safire's attention will be divided. You and Theo will need to use the chaos to your advantage while I . . ."

When she couldn't finish the sentence, Rebekah finished for her, watching Roa carefully. "While you kill Dax with the knife."

Roa looked away, thinking of Dax in the dining hall. Of the

way he reached for her trembling hands. Of his pure rage at the sight of Torwin in the clutches of the enemy.

And yet, just last night, she'd found his seal in the pocket of a man who'd tried to kill her.

She pushed the confusion out of her mind, thinking instead of what she must do: cut Dax's soul free with the Skyweaver's knife in order to save her sister.

Theo spoke up then. "I have fifty men on their way here. But in order to take the palace—which we'll have to do if we stand any chance against Safire and her army—we need a way in. The front gate will be too heavily defended."

Rebekah's eyes lit up. "Has Dax shown you any of the secret passageways?"

Roa glanced up. *Secret passageways?* "No."

Rebekah tilted her head, as if this were an interesting fact she was tucking away for later. "He used to tell my father about them. There's at least one that leads out into the city." She lifted her hands to the fire, warming herself. "And since you're the only one of us with unrestricted access within the palace, you'll need to be the one to find it."

Roa's grip on the iron edge of the basin tightened.

"Fifty scrublanders isn't enough to take it," said Rebekah. "But I can triple your numbers."

"How?" asked Roa.

"A great many soldiers were demoted or dismissed when Safire was made commandant. Among them are several formerly high-ranking soldats. All of them are in my father's debt, since it was he who found them new employment; therefore every one of them will be at our disposal." She smiled that chillingly beautiful smile. "While you find that passage, Theo and I will figure out how best to take the palace from the inside."

Roa looked to Theo. His face was in shadow, but the flames seemed to dance in his eyes as she spoke.

"And if I can't find it?" Roa asked. "If no such passage exists?"

"It exists," said Rebekah. "And if anyone can find it, it's the girl who tricked her way onto the throne."

Roa looked to the window, realizing this plan of hers didn't only affect Dax. It would put others in danger too: Lirabel, Safire, everyone in the palace.

What am I doing?

She stepped back from the basin. She wanted out of this room. Out of this house.

"If that's all, then I should be going. The king and his commandant are already suspicious." She held out her hand. "You promised me the knife."

"There's just one more thing," said Rebekah.

Something in her voice sent a chill through Roa. Essie moved closer, brushing Roa's cheek with her wing.

"I, too, like assurances. And since I gave you one tonight, it's only fair you give me one in return."

Roa frowned, wondering what kind of assurance she needed. She felt Rebekah's guards slip into the shadows behind her, keeping themselves between Roa and the door.

"Now that I'm in this, I can't have you playing both sides," Rebekah went on. "I need to ensure you're loyal to *me*."

Suddenly, Essie shrieked and dug her talons in deep. A heartbeat later, they were ripped away, tearing Roa's skin.

She cried out, spinning to find Garnet gripping Essie's body with both hands, squeezing her wings to her sides as she fought and squirmed and tried to bite.

Roa reached for Essie's knife at her calf.

"Take your hands off her!"

When he didn't, she lunged.

One of the other guards held out his arm, hand fisted. Roa ran straight into it, the force of it hitting her in the chest, stealing her breath and temporarily stunning her. He hauled her back, away from her sister. Roa recovered and cracked her elbow hard against his face. The man cursed and dropped her to the floor.

She heard Theo shout. Heard weapons drawn.

Roa spotted Garnet, heading toward one of the cages. Essie shrieked and struggled, trying desperately to get her wings free. The door to an empty cage hung open.

No . . .

Roa sprang to her feet.

Four crisscrossed swords were immediately at her throat as guards stepped in, surrounding her and blocking her path.

Roa felt the sharp bite of steel. She halted, staring helplessly at Essie—who'd gone half-wild at the sight of her sister under threat.

Garnet shoved Essie inside the cage. Slamming the door closed, he twisted the key in the lock.

"No . . . ," Roa cried as Essie threw herself against her cage. Shrieking and flying, again and again, into the bars. Roa moved to go to her, and the blades constricted against her throat. Her empty hands clenched and unclenched as she watched her sister hurt herself, then exhaust herself.

Finally, Essie fell to the bottom of the cage and didn't get up. Her white chest rose and fell quickly with the terrified beat of her tiny heart.

Theo was pinned to the wall, the exposed edge of a saber at his neck. "This was never part of the deal!" he shouted, and even Roa heard the grief in his voice.

Roa reached out with her mind, desperate to brush against her sister's. But there was no response. Essie only stared at her.

"I hear there are worse things than uncrossed spirits."

Roa tore her gaze from her sister to find Rebekah approaching the cage now, the Skyweaver's knife unsheathed at her side. Essie glared up at her through the bars.

"My father doesn't just collect artifacts," she went on. "He also collects stories. When Theo told me about your predicament, that you needed the knife, I searched his library. I found the account of something called a *corrupted spirit*."

Essie isn't corrupted, thought Roa, shivering despite herself. Corrupted spirits were deadly; her sister's spirit was just uncrossed.

"The story said that if the soul of the deceased is trapped here for too long, unable to cross, it eventually becomes a horror." Rebekah gripped one of the cage bars with her free hand, peering inside, as if she wanted to see such a thing. As if hoping Essie would turn into a monster right before her eyes.

Roa's chest tightened, making it difficult to breathe. "Please. Give her back."

Rebekah sheathed the Skyweaver's knife, turning away from the cage. "Not until I'm absolutely certain of your loyalty."

"I'll do whatever you want. I swear it," Roa said. "Just let her go."

"Enough." Rebekah's voice sharpened and her eyes narrowed. "Begging doesn't become a queen. Do as you've promised, and your sister will go free."

When the blades withdrew, Roa sank to the floor, staring at Essie. Caged. Trapped. Taken from her again.

"The Relinquishing is five days away." Rebekah moved slowly toward Roa. "If you deliver the location of the passage to me in three days, I'll give your sister back." She held out the sheathed Skyweaver's knife in both hands. The embossed steel glinted in the firelight. "Do we have a deal?"

Roa's gaze locked with Essie's.

Everyone had a weakness, and Rebekah had found hers.

"Yes," Roa whispered.

"Three days," said Rebekah, passing her the knife. "Deliver it to me by midnight."

Roa's fingers curled tightly around the sheath. It was colder than any steel she'd ever held.

Death cold.

The Last Relinquishing

Every Relinquishing, when the night descended and her household gathered around the heart-fire, the girl crept into the parlor, set a candle burning in the window, and waited for her sister to come.

She always came.

But every time, she seemed a little less like herself.

On the last Relinquishing, as the dawn crept in, the girl sat by the calm waters of the quarry, plaiting her sister's curls in the dark.

"I think I'm disappearing," said her sister.

The girl stopped braiding. "What?"

"I don't know what I am anymore. A hawk? A girl? Or something else?"

She shivered. The girl told herself it was just the cold air.

"I don't know where I belong."

"You belong with me," said the girl, reaching for her hands, linking them hard in her own. "You're my sister. And a daughter of the House of Song."

"Am I?" She smiled sadly down at their hands. "I'll never live in that house again. Or feel the calluses on my palms after a summer in the fields. I'll never fall in love. Never hold my own child in my arms. But you . . . you have a whole life before you. You will grow and change while I stay the same. Forever."

The sun was coming up. The girls could feel the air changing. It was gold tinged and dewy now.

"Sometimes I feel like I'm trapped in a cage," she whispered. "One that gets smaller and smaller every day."

Tears shone in her eyes. The girl gripped her sister's hands harder.

"I don't want to be trapped anymore," she whispered, her face pleading. "I want to be free."

The next morning, when the hawk returned, three of its feathers had turned white. And when its gaze lifted, its eyes were ringed in silver.

Twenty-One

Every step away from that room, away from her sister, broke Roa a little bit more. She'd adjusted the buckled leather straps around her calf to accommodate two sheaths: one for Essie's knife and one for the Skyweaver's. The Skyweaver's knife was there now, hidden beneath her kaftan. But the cold weight of it only made her sicker.

It had come at too high a cost.

Now she had only three days to find a way into the palace for Silva's men. Three days to betray Dax. And after that . . . kill him.

With Essie in Rebekah's clutches, there was no other choice.

Saving her sister was all that mattered now.

"Roa!" Theo's voice rang out from behind her. She quickened her pace, heading for Baron Silva's courtyard, unable to face him.

"Roa . . . please wait."

Theo reached for her arm. Roa spun away from him.

"Don't touch me." Her voice wavered. "Don't ever touch me without my permission again."

Theo's mouth was set in a grim line. "Roa, I'm sorry."

"It's too late for that." The damage was done. He'd given away everything.

It was raining when she stepped into the courtyard. Behind her, Roa heard the doors open and shut as Theo followed her out.

His footsteps halted.

Roa looked up and found the reason. At the end of the lantern-lit path stood Lirabel, cloaked in a now-wet mantle, waiting with her horse. Roa's guards loomed behind her. Celeste, Tati, and Saba were all mounted and ready to ride. Safire, Dax, Torwin, and Jas were missing.

Roa walked toward her friend.

"Where are the others?"

"Getting Torwin to safety." Lirabel pulled Roa's mantle out of her saddlebag. "He needed your horse." She flung the warm, dry cloak over Roa's shoulders. After tying the tassels at her throat, Lirabel flipped up the hood to keep Roa's face shielded from the rain. "You'll have to ride with me."

Roa mounted up behind Lirabel and slid her arms around her friend's waist. Roa didn't look back to where Theo stood, watching in the rain. Instead, she pressed her cheek to Lirabel's shoulder as they rode away from Baron Silva's stronghold, the hooves of the other horses clip-clopping ahead and behind them.

Leaving Essie behind.

◆◆◆

Back in the palace stables, Roa told Lirabel to go on ahead of her. The stable girl tried to take the horse, but Roa insisted on untacking it herself. She wasn't ready to face whatever was waiting for her inside the palace.

Alone with her tumultuous thoughts, Roa took her time undoing the buckles of the horse's halter, listening to the swish of tails and the whuff of horse sighs, when suddenly the stall door swung open.

"What have you done?"

Startled, Roa looked up to find Dax stepping inside the stall. His gold tunic, soaked with rain, clung to his chest and shoulders, and his damp curls stuck to his forehead. As if he'd raced through the storm to get here.

Roa stepped away from the scowling king, deeper into the stall.

"What did you give her?" Dax's voice was thunderous.

She shook her head. "I didn't give her anything."

"That's a lie." His cheeks were wet and his eyelashes clustered together like dark stars. "Under no circumstances would Bekah just let Torwin go."

Roa tried to hold his furious gaze and failed.

"You've been bought," he said as he stepped in closer, trapping her in the corner of the stall. "Haven't you?"

It was strange, but in his voice Roa thought she heard a quavering fear.

"Torwin's free, isn't he? You have what you want. Who cares how you got it?"

His gaze on her face was a dark, hard thing.

What right did he have to be angry? Roa had marched an army across the desert for this boy. Captured Darmoor for him. Helped throw a revolt with him. Broke off her betrothal and caused a rift between Song and Sky . . . all for him.

And how had he repaid her?

First he'd broken Lirabel's heart. Then he broke every one of his treaty promises without a care. And tonight, while she saved Torwin, while Essie was forced into a cage, he'd been openly flirting with Rebekah's dinner guests and drinking with abandon.

"Things could be worse," she said bitterly. "You could be the one married to a drunken whore."

Dax blinked at her, as if surprised.

"Me?" he finally said. "*I'm* the whore?"

Roa lifted her chin, glaring up at him, thinking of the woman in the yellow kaftan tonight. The way Dax drank in the sight of her.

Oh, how she hated him.

"Tonight?" he said, as if seeing the thoughts in her head. "Tonight was just business."

She locked her gaze with his, thinking of Lirabel. *"Just business?"* How many other girls had he left pregnant, terrified, and crying all alone? "Is it *just business* when you warm every other bed in Firgaard but your wife's?"

She regretted the words the moment they were out of her mouth.

That wasn't what she meant to say. She didn't want him warming her bed.

Dax stepped in closer, taking up all her air. "*Are* you my wife?" Soaked as he was, she could see all of him. The hard knot of his shoulders, the smooth curve of his chest. "Do you sleep in my bed or my enemy's?"

She remembered the last time they were alone in a stable— the day she'd lost a race to him. She still owed him something from that race.

"It's true," she whispered, holding his gaze. "I prefer less crowded beds than yours."

They stood for several heartbeats glaring at each other, their chests rising and falling with their synchronized breaths.

"I never should have married you," he said.

"I don't remember you having a choice."

His fists clenched as he scowled at her.

"It's too bad you're such a terrible swordsman," she went on, gaze locked with his. "Otherwise, you could rid yourself of me right here." Well and truly angry now, she thought of the seal she'd found in Sirin's pocket. "You could finish the job you paid someone else to do!"

At those words, the thunder went out of his eyes. "What?"

She motioned to the empty stable. "We're alone. No one would hear. You could do it now and be through with me."

Dax stared at her. "What are you talking about?"

Maybe it was her grief over Essie. Or maybe it was more than that. But something was burning in Roa, and she couldn't stop until it was all burned out.

"I found your seal in Sirin's pocket. Right after he tried to kill me."

Dax's mouth flattened into a hard line and his eyes went black. *"What?"*

Roa had never seen him look like that. The edge in his voice made whatever was burning in her flicker.

She stepped back.

Dax came toward her, closing the gap, tense with fury. "Speak plainly. What are you telling me?"

"Sirin cornered me in an alley," she said. "He told me he'd been paid to rid the king of his problem." She shook now from the memory of it. "I found your seal in his pocket."

For a moment, Dax was silent, remembering the night previous. When she'd run straight into him, alone, without her guards.

"And so," he said, voice bitter, gaze never leaving her face, "you think I'm the one who gave the order."

Roa's voice came out like a whisper. "What else am I to think?"

"That seal was a fake." Dax's jaw hardened. "Someone forged it."

Roa wanted to laugh. "Easy to say."

He didn't move away. Just stood there, studying her.

"I made you a promise, Roa." His voice softened. "The night I married you."

The memory of it glimmered in his eyes: the two of them lying side by side in his tent, in the middle of the war camp.

He lifted his hand and, to Roa's surprise, gently brushed his thumb across her jaw. "I would never hurt you."

Roa stared up at him, immobilized.

But you hurt me every day.

She hadn't meant to say it aloud.

Dax looked stricken, his hand immediately retreating as he stepped back. Roa felt the world rush in, separating them.

"Do I?" he whispered. When Roa didn't answer, he said, "Then I won't impose on you any longer."

Without another word, he turned and walked out of the stall.

The moment he was gone, Roa fell back against the wall. Whatever had been burning in her vanished. She slid down into the hay and pressed her palms against her eyes, trying to numb herself to the storm of confusion within her. Trying to will away the fear.

In the dark and the silence, it was Torwin she saw. His hands bound behind his back as he stared down Rebekah. Love burned out all his fear. As if he'd stared death in the face so many times, Rebekah was nothing more than a mere annoyance.

Roa knew what it felt like to love someone like that.

Reaching for the Skyweaver's knife, she slid the blade from its sheath hidden beneath her hem. It glowed in the darkness, and Roa felt its strange chill sink into her bones. As she studied its sharp edge and the unknown symbols in its hilt, she thought of a white hawk trapped in a cage.

She loved her sister more than anything or anyone. She would do whatever it took to free her.

Even if it meant killing a king.

A Corrupted Spirit

Once there was a dog who loved her master very much. When the master worked late, the dog waited for him at the front door. When the master went to bed, the dog lay at his feet. When the master grew very sick, the dog never left his side. Until one day the master fell asleep and didn't wake up.

The dog whimpered as the family gathered round the pyre. The dog howled as they said good-bye.

For years afterward, the dog would sit staring at the front door. Her ears perking at every noise, listening for her master's footsteps. Certain he was coming home.

For seven long years, the family shook their heads sadly and ignored her. They knew how to let go; the dog did not.

And every year on the Relinquishing, it would get worse.

Just after sundown, the dog would start to bark.

And bark. And bark.

Every year, the family stopped eating dinner and looked to the windows. But the night was ink black and they couldn't see out.

When the dog started to howl and scratch at the door, they lit a candle, illuminating the path to the house. But there was no one there.

Finally, on the night of the eighth Relinquishing, when the dog was old and nearing death, the son of the master took pity on her. "Let her out," he said. So the children opened the door.

The dog ran out, wagging her tail.

Something else slipped in, wearing her master's face.

The next morning, when a neighbor came by, the door hung open, beckoning her inside.

She smelled the blood before she saw it. Felt the chill of death before she even stepped across the threshold.

The family was dead. The man's corrupted spirit had slaughtered them all, leaving only his dog alive.

This was the cost of unrelinquishing.

Twenty-Two

Roa paced her rooms. Her slippers hushed gently against the floor tiles, a sharp contrast to her clenched jaw and furrowed brow.

She needed to find the passageway. Yet she remained heavily guarded. And losing her guards when they'd been assigned to her by none other than Safire was a near-impossible task.

The only time eyes weren't trained on her like arrows was when she was alone in her rooms. And she couldn't exactly search for a way out while confined there.

It was already midafternoon. Roa walked to the archway of her terrace, letting out a frustrated growl.

And then she stopped pacing.

Directly across the garden, opposite her balcony, were the king's quarters. Dax was supposed to be in a meeting now—or so he'd told Roa at lunch—but there was movement inside his room.

Her curtains billowed in the breeze, obscuring her view, and Roa grabbed them, pushing them back so she could see.

The king had just entered the bedroom across the garden. Roa watched him loosen the laces of his tunic.

Had he lied to her about the meeting?

Suddenly, Dax walked out onto his balcony. Roa's heart hammered as she withdrew behind her curtains, trying to keep out of sight. When she dared a glance back, she found Dax leaning over his balustrade, studying the gardens that separated Roa's quarters from his.

The palms rustled in the breeze. The bees hummed in the lavender. And still, Dax stared below. As if he were waiting for something.

Or someone, Roa thought.

If this was the case, she didn't want to watch. She was about to retreat into her room when Dax hoisted himself up and over his balcony, hung from the balustrade for several heartbeats, then dropped to the earth below.

Roa stopped breathing. She waited a moment, then stepped out onto her own balcony to see him striding off toward the north end of the gardens.

Where are you going?

Intending to find out, she kicked off her slippers and climbed over her own balcony. Like Dax, she let herself hang for a moment, closed her eyes, and let go.

The ground rushed up to meet her. Pain spiked in her ankles, making her wince. Quickly, Roa glanced up to the balcony level, but there was no one to see her. Her guards would still be in the hall, watching the doors to her room.

Hiking up the hem of her dress, Roa ran after the king.

These were the former dragon queen's gardens and they

smelled like the scrublands. Roa breathed in the scent of jacaranda and date palms as she followed from a safe distance.

But Dax, clearly confident no one was following him, didn't
look back. After all, it was only him and Roa in the royal quarters, and therefore, its gardens.

When he stepped off the path and waded into a patch of tall
esparto grass, Roa darted after him, stopping behind a eucalyp-
tus tree when he paused in front of the garden wall. From her
hiding place, Roa watched him press both hands to the cracked,
yellowing plaster.

He pushed.

The wall moved.

Roa's mouth fell open.

It wasn't a wall, but a door. In the widening crack beyond,
Roa saw only darkness. When Dax disappeared inside, the wall
moved back, shutting him in and Roa out.

She dropped the hem of her dress. Roa walked through the
hibiscus bushes, their leaves gently brushing against her skin.
She touched the wall, tracing the very fine line she never would
have seen if she'd been walking by.

A hidden door.

A hopeful feeling flooded her.

To ensure Dax wouldn't hear her, Roa waited several heartbeats, then several more. Finally, she pushed the door open.

It was damp and dark inside and Roa had to keep one hand
on the wall to know where she was going. She'd lost all sight
of Dax, but it didn't matter. She cared less about where he was
headed and more about where this passage led.

But instead of heading *out* of the palace, it seemed to go

deeper in, and then up. She climbed two sets of stairs, then ran right into a door.

She sucked in a breath. Fearing it might be locked, she reached for the knob. But when she turned it, the door clicked open. Roa swung it in toward her.

Instead of opening into sunlight, it opened onto . . . fabric.

Roa touched the tangled, colored threads of the back of a tapestry. Stepping closer, she listened. But no sound came from the other side. So, holding her breath, Roa pushed the tapestry aside and stepped into the room beyond.

Bright sunlight splashed across the mosaicked floor and lit up the motes of dust floating through the air.

It was a library.

The room was musty and warm and the shelves were full of scrolls and old tomes, some recently bound, others fraying with age. When the shelf space ran out, chests were filled and stacked on top.

The shelves twisted and coiled, like a complicated labyrinth, drawing Roa in.

But if someone was here . . .

When she stopped to listen, she heard nothing but silence.

Roa looked back to the tapestry she'd emerged from. It was a woven image of the mythical goddess Iskari and her twin, Namsara. Iskari was rendered in dark blues with a moon on her chest; Namsara was woven in gold with a sun. There were other tapestries too, full of the imagery of the old stories. Of Kozu and the sacred flame. Of healing flowers and heroes that took their name from Namsara.

Roa walked along the curving wall. But as far as she could see, there were just more tapestries. The sunlight came from a glass dome in the roof above. And when she finally found a door that *wasn't* hidden, it was locked.

A secret library?

She didn't need a secret library. She needed a secret way *out*.

Still, she'd found a passageway. Now that she knew what to look for, she could find others.

Roa stepped between the shelves, wanting to cut across to the passage she'd come through. But the shelves really *were* labyrinthine. They kept turning her about. She hit two dead ends before finding herself in the very middle of the room.

A circular ebony table was set with eleven chairs and stacked with books, inkwells, and quills. Roa looked past it, turning in circles, studying the twisting shelves.

Which way was out? They all looked the same.

Just pick one.

Stepping into the rows and rows of tomes, she turned the corner and stopped sharp.

There, leaning with his back to the shelf, was the king.

His knee was bent, his arms were crossed, and the back of his head rested against the spines, as if deep in thought.

At the sight of her, Dax's arms fell to his sides and his foot lowered to the floor. His gaze flickered over her, eyes wide with surprise. "What in all the skies are you doing here?"

"Me?" she squeaked. "Aren't *you* supposed to be in a meeting?"

A sudden sound made them both freeze: the soft *snick* of

a door latch, followed by voices. Dax pushed away from the shelves. Roa's heart clanged in her chest.

"He replaced *all* of them?" someone said in the distance. "Can he do that?"

"He made a scrublander queen against our advice. He's the dragon king. He can do what he wants."

She recognized those voices. They belonged to the council.

"But how did he find out?"

"Obviously she told him."

Dax reached for her wrist.

Roa panicked, twisted away, and fled back through the shelves, trying to find her way out before the voices found their way in, trapping her here. But the farther she went, the closer they came, until there was only a single shelf between her and one of the men.

"Who do you think cut his throat and left him to die? Her? Or the king?"

Roa ducked down. Between the top of the tomes and the bottom of the shelf ledge, she could see the silks of their clothes.

Suddenly, from behind her, Dax grabbed Roa hard around the waist, clamping a hand over her mouth and hauling her back with him.

Stunned by his strength, Roa didn't fight. Dax held on, carrying her now as he doubled back to that ebony table, then down another twisting aisle that culminated in a dead end.

That's where he dropped her, running frustrated fingers through his curls as he stared at the shelf blocking his way. As if he'd expected something else.

Roa was about to run, when a voice came down the aisle connecting their dead end to the center of this maze.

"Her new guards are loyal. I doubt they can be bought."

She heard the slow scrape of chairs. Heard them all sit down at the table.

Trapped. She was trapped.

Fear twisted in her belly. Roa backed up, straight into Dax. He reached for her wrist—gently this time—and tapped the bone with his thumb. Twice.

And in that moment, Roa remembered: Essie's code.

She'd taught it to Dax when they were children playing gods and monsters.

Pay attention, it meant.

He was trying to warn her.

Her mind flashed back to the day of the Assembly and how afterward, as she spoke with Rebekah, he'd done the same thing: reached for her wrist and tapped the bone twice.

Was he warning her then, too?

"We have no idea the ways in which she's compromised him," said a man's gruff voice. "I have sources saying scrublander rebels are on their way to the city. That she uses that bird of hers to send messages to their leader—her lover."

Roa's thoughts spun. The council was meeting about *her.*

But why wouldn't they be? Roa was a threat to the throne.

"She has no love for him. It only makes sense she'll try to dispose of him—and that will put Firgaard in a very dangerous position. If we don't act again soon, it might be too late. Our *home* will be overrun."

Roa stepped closer, wanting to know who was speaking. Wanting to know who these sources were, so she could warn Theo.

Before she could, Dax's arm came around her, drawing her away from the danger.

It made her wonder, *What is he doing here?*

Clearly this was the meeting he'd told her about. But why was he hiding instead of joining them? Why was he *spying* on his own council?

If he's clever enough to spy on his council, he's far more dangerous than I thought.

She needed to keep her head. She needed to calm her pulse. And yet, it was impossible not to be aware of him. Of his heart beating through his shirt. Of his fingers curled firmly around her hip. Of the warmth of his forearms wrapped around her midriff.

She could feel him becoming aware of her, too. Of her weight, leaning into him. Of her breathing, so traitorously aligned with his own.

Roa went rigid at the thought.

Sensing it, Dax loosened his hold and stepped back.

His boot hit one of the scrolls on the shelves, and its heavy wooden handle fell to the floor with a soft *thud*.

The voices stopped.

Roa turned to face Dax, her gaze a mixture of terror and accusation.

"Did you hear that?"

There came the sound of wood scraping wood as multiple chairs were pushed back at once.

Caught. In less than twenty heartbeats, the king and queen were going to be caught.

Roa's first instinct was to run. But there was nowhere to go. And if she ran, the council would know she'd heard everything. They would know their lives were forfeit—because the price of treason was death.

The realization would likely make them desperate. If, in their desperation, they tried to dispose of her, right here, it would be easy. Roa was cornered and outnumbered, not to mention undefended.

She thought of her father's gods and monster's board. Of what he always told her about getting trapped.

Confuse and disarm.

Roa looked to Dax.

If getting caught was inevitable, Roa needed to be caught on her own terms. If she could give these councillors a reason to believe the king and queen hadn't heard them, that they hadn't even been listening, it might give her a chance to get out of here alive.

"That kiss I owe you?" She grabbed a fistful of Dax's shirt, peering up at him. "It's time to collect it."

His brows knit in confusion. "Right *now*?"

Roa nodded. She intended to make it look like the king was here doing what he did best: seducing a girl.

The voices were splitting up. Searching the aisles. Getting closer.

They were out of time.

Before Dax's hesitation could ruin everything, Roa dug her fingers into his hair and captured his mouth with hers.

He tasted like peppermint tea. Roa kissed him harder, forcing his mouth open. The warmth of him flooded her.

And then the voices were in their aisle.

Finally understanding the game, Dax stopped hesitating.

He kissed her back, his teeth scraping her lip. His warm hands cupped her thighs, lifting her up. Roa looped her arms behind his neck, wrapping her legs around him.

As their hips connected, they both drew in a breath. Their eyes opened. Their gazes caught.

Roa's heart pounded like a drum as his palms slid slowly up under the linen of her dress. A startling heat coursed through her. Her legs tightened around him, pulling him closer.

Pressing his forehead to her cheek, Dax bit her throat gently. Roa made a soft sound of surprise. He bit her again, and Roa closed her eyes, trying not to forget this was a role she was playing.

Trying not to drown in him.

But the harder he kissed her, the deeper he pulled her under. His hands moved fervently over her skin, flooding her senses, until she couldn't think.

She only remembered the councillors when one of them called out in surprise.

Dax froze, his grip on her tightening.

Their eyes flew open at the same time.

Roa quickly unhooked herself, flushing with heat. Not even needing to pretend.

"Well"—Dax stepped in front of his wife, blocking her from view—"*this* is embarrassing."

His voice was light as he ran both hands through his curls.

"My king . . ." came that gruff voice.

Roa pressed her cheek between Dax's shoulder blades, her body warm in all the places he'd touched her. Her hands fisted in his tunic as she listened to his racing heart, trying desperately to quiet the hunger prowling through her.

The man who spoke cleared his throat and tried again. "My king, what are you doing here?"

A pause.

"What am *I* doing here?" Roa felt something shift in Dax. If he'd truly been nervous a moment ago, he wasn't any longer. "What does it look like I'm doing?"

"One would think . . ."

"Is this not my private library?"

"Yes, but . . ."

"And was not the council to alert me to their meetings here? Was that not the deal we made?"

Roa's fingers unclenched in his shirt. *Interesting,* she thought. *What kind of deal did he make?*

"Yes, my king, but . . ."

Roa felt the speaker's gaze dart over Dax's shoulder, searching for her.

"Don't you and the queen have . . ."

He was clearly struggling to put a voice to his thoughts.

"Don't we have . . . what?" The king sounded amused. "Private quarters?" He pulled Roa out from behind him then. Looping his arms around her waist, he rested his chin on top of her head. "Today we wanted something a little more . . . illicit."

Roa flushed with heat.

Since when is he so good at lying?

The seven council members before her fell silent.

This was their chance.

Looking up at him, Roa put all of her focus into playing the part of a flirtatious wife. "Should we finish this elsewhere?"

His smile widened, and Roa realized with some annoyance that it was the smile she hated most. The one he used to charm and seduce.

Leaning in, Dax kissed her neck, just behind the ear. "Would that please you, my star?"

That name again. Roa wanted to roll her eyes, but quenched the urge. She nodded instead.

Taking her hand in his, Dax marched her straight through the council, who parted like butter at the mercy of a knife.

Twenty-Three

Dax stormed through the corridor, dropping her hand like it burned him. That smile was gone. The charming husband vanished like the act it was.

He'd convinced the seven council members. And—if she were honest with herself—he'd convinced her, too.

But now as she watched him, his footsteps thunderous, his face masked, she wondered: *What was he really doing in that library?*

And from the way he looked at Roa, he was thinking the same about her.

She cleared her throat.

"If you weren't invited to that meeting, how did you know it was happening?"

He studied her, as if trying to decide how much to tell her.

"The girl you were so jealous of last night?"

Roa bristled at the accusation, even as she knew exactly who he was talking about: the draksor in the yellow kaftan who'd been hanging off his arm all evening.

"She's the daughter of Councillor Barek. She alerted me to the meeting."

Roa went quiet, considering this.

"I told you," he said. "It was just business."

Dax turned a corner. Roa followed, trying to keep up with his long strides.

Just business, she thought. Was what they'd done back there just business, too?

He halted in front of a door, guarded by two soldats. He halted so fast, Roa almost ran into him.

"My king," they said in unison. Then to Roa, "My queen."

She nodded to them.

Dax walked straight in.

Safire sat at a desk, her quill moving furiously across a piece of parchment. At the presence of the king, she didn't look up.

"There are seven council members heading for the front gate at this very moment. They'll have taken the most direct route from the atrium, which means by now they'll be in the hall of fonts. I need you to arrest them all for treason."

Safire's quill stopped.

"But, please. Take your time."

The commandant looked up, staring at her king for several silent heartbeats while something wordless passed between them.

Saf rose from the desk. "I'll expect a full report from you when I return."

Dax nodded. "Of course."

Her boots clicked against the tiles as she strode out into the hall. To the soldats standing guard, she said, "With me."

"Once they're subdued and imprisoned," said Dax, going to the window with a view of the Great Assembly's copper dome, "I'll call an emergency council meeting. Tomorrow morning, I think. We'll need to act quickly."

Roa stayed where she was, near the door.

"Act quickly for what purpose?"

He turned around to face her.

"I have reason to believe Rebekah is plotting a coup." Dax watched her carefully as he added: "And that she has allies in the House of Sky."

A chill crept through Roa.

How could he possibly know that? She forced herself to look him in the eye as an even more frightening thought took hold: *If he suspects Theo, does he also suspect me?*

She thought of the accusation the councillors made in the library.

"Do you believe them?" she asked, needing to know. "Do you think I'm using Essie to send messages to Theo?"

Dax's mouth twisted as if he'd just bitten into something sour.

"Of course not," he said. And then, more softly: "Essie would never betray me like that."

Roa studied him.

Dax studied her back.

"You're several moves behind," he said as he turned away, moving for the door. "Try to keep up."

As he stepped through it and disappeared down the hall, Roa remained where she was, her feet frozen to the floor. She needed to warn Theo. But how? It was impossible to do without raising Dax's suspicions, or worse: proving them true.

More than this, Roa needed to find out what, exactly, the king knew.

Just after dawn the next morning, the king and queen made their way to the Great Assembly. The streets were quiet and calm as Dax's guards marched ahead and Roa's marched behind.

Once again, Roa had refused to wear any of the royal kaftans sewn for her after the coronation, nor did she wear the gold jewelry inherited from the former dragon queen. Instead, she wore a long linen dress dyed with saffron and her wrists were adorned with bronze bracelets, hammered by scrublander coppersmiths. Her earned scythe was sheathed at her hip.

Dax eyed her attire before they set out, saying nothing.

Despite the rising sun, it was still cold and Roa pulled her sandskarf tighter around her shoulders, trying to keep warm.

She'd been up all night, worrying about Theo and Rebekah's plan. Worrying about what would happen to Essie if it all went wrong.

So, as the circular building rose before them—its copper dome shining in the sunlight, its white walls as high as the palace's—she spoke her thoughts aloud.

"What reasons would Rebekah have to plot against you?" she asked him.

Dax, who'd been quiet and withdrawn all morning, glanced her way sharply, as if he'd forgotten she was there.

"None that are honorable," he said.

That was not an answer. Roa tried again. "What evidence do you have?"

"Enough to suspect those involved." Her heart hammered at the way he studied her. "But not enough to accuse them."

Roa held his gaze. Again, this answer was too vague to be of any use to her. She needed to be careful if she pressed him further, though. If he suspected Roa's involvement with Theo and Rebekah, then he would already be on high alert. And if he didn't suspect, she didn't want to give him reason to.

So all she said was: "So if you can't accuse her, then what's the point of this?"

They'd arrived at the marble steps of the Great Assembly. Double doors loomed at the top, guarded on either side by two dragon statues. The dragons stared down at Roa, their mouths open, their teeth bared, as if about to roar at her.

Dax stopped at the first step and turned around. Roa studied him in the post-dawn light. He wore a white tunic and embroidered silver dragons chased each other around the collar.

"You told me once that the moment I know my opponent's favorite piece, I know her weakness."

Roa thought of those long-ago lessons trying to teach him how to play gods and monsters. *"Never reveal yourself,"* she murmured, nodding. It was one of the rules of the game.

He looked up to the domed marble building that cast them in its shadow. "The *council* is Bekah's favorite piece. Her power is on full display here."

His guards had reached the top of the steps, waiting for the king and queen, while Roa's guards scanned the empty street at the bottom.

"So what will you do?" she said to his back as he started up the steps.

"Undermine her. Provoke her."

Roa hitched up her dress and followed him. "And then?"

He paused at the top, waiting as two of his guards opened the doors. "And then *wait*. When she retaliates—and Bekah always retaliates—I'll be ready. And I'll have my evidence."

He held out his arm, motioning Roa inside. She stepped into the massive hall, her footsteps echoing as sunlight spilled in long, thin bars across the tiled floor. Again, she wondered at the history between Dax and Rebekah.

"What did you do," she asked softly, so their guards wouldn't hear, "to make her hate you so much?"

Dax stiffened beside her. Their footsteps fell out of sync. He didn't answer for a long while.

"Bekah and I were friends, once." He didn't look at Roa while he said this. "Before the revolt."

Roa waited for more.

"It was only ever a friendship. At least, for me it was."

He looked back over his shoulder, as if checking to see if anyone watched them. But only Roa's guards followed.

"In order to bring down my father's regime, I had to make a choice. I could have gone to Bekah and asked for her help. With her father funding me, it would have been easy. The baron would have given me whatever I needed . . . as long as I made his daughter queen." He shook his head. "But I didn't go to Bekah."

Roa thought of that night in New Haven, the war camp.

How exhausted she was from taking Darmoor, from riding all night. How determined she was to force Dax's hand, and in doing so, ensure her people's protection.

She thought of him in the tent, staring down at the map. As if he were waiting for her. And when she gave him her proposition, he'd been so calm. As if he already knew that she'd ask, and he'd spent the whole night pondering his answer.

"You knew what I'd do before I did it," she realized now.

"I know how to read you." His mouth turned down, as if this were a burden. "I grew up playing gods and monsters with you. You *taught* me how to read you."

"Why?" she demanded, feeling suddenly angry. "Why choose me instead of Rebekah if you knew I'd give you the same proposition she would?"

He looked up at the dais, where twin gilt thrones stood side by side.

"Why do you think?" he said softly.

Roa thought of Rebekah circling Dax like prey at dinner. Of Rebekah hunting down Torwin—Dax's best friend—and keeping him captive. Of Rebekah putting Essie in a cage and using her as leverage.

I'm the lesser of two evils, she realized.

Roa shivered at the thought.

Twenty-Four

The council meeting did not go as Dax hoped.

It was late afternoon and despite the fact that the meeting had ended long ago, Roa and her guards were still within the Great Assembly. They stood at the window, watching the mob gather on the front steps, packing the street.

When Dax announced that seven council members were being held in the dungeons for treason, the initial response was disbelief. When he introduced their temporary replacements— four skral and three scrublanders—the unease set in. And when he called for a vote to lift the sanctions on the scrublands, the vote passed seven to five.

In the midst of her shock, Roa couldn't help but be impressed.

Rebekah was furious.

The city was in an uproar.

They hurled insults and rotten food at the assembly building. They accused Roa of framing the council. They accused Dax of being manipulated by his scrublander wife.

Safire had to send double the guards to retrieve the king and queen. With so many travelers here for the Relinquishing, the streets were crowded and had become nearly impassable.

The king left first. Safire hoped he would draw away most of the crowd, but it hadn't worked. And as the midafternoon sun pulsed above the city, Roa started to pace the hall. She was running out of time. The people of Firgaard had her trapped, and the longer she stayed here, the less time she had to find a secret way into the palace. She needed to report back to Rebekah by tomorrow night.

"Don't worry," said Celeste, watching Roa pace. "It will be all right."

Roa stopped. She glanced at her scrublander guard to find the girl studying her linen dress and sandskarf.

"I have an idea," said Celeste.

Safire, who'd been at the window, fingering the hilts of her throwing knives as she stared down the crowd, snapped out of her brooding. "What idea?"

"The queen and I are roughly the same height and build," Celeste explained, stepping up beside Roa to demonstrate.

It was true. And while Celeste normally wore her curls loose and free—unlike Roa, who kept hers cropped close to her head—today the girl had plaited her hair.

Roa took in Celeste's shirt, which bore the emblem of the dragon king on its sleeve, then her belt, then her polished boots. When she glanced to her face, the guard's eyes were gleaming.

"How do you feel about wearing trousers, my queen?"

✦ ✦ ✦

267

The citizens of Firgaard fell for the bait. Dressed in the queen's saffron gown, with the queen's sandskarf hooding her face and the royal guard surrounding her, Celeste had passed for Roa. The only difficult part had been convincing Safire to let Roa return to the palace alone, dressed as a soldat, without her guard.

Roa waited until the last of the mob disappeared down the street, unbolted the assembly doors, and slipped out.

On her way back to the palace, she thought it strange how quickly Dax acted. As if the new candidates for the council had been determined long before now and not decided overnight when he caught his council members meeting without him.

As if . . . as if he hadn't forgotten his treaty promises but had simply been waiting for the right opportunity to set them in motion.

Roa stepped up to the palace gates. The soldats standing guard stopped her.

"My queen?" The young man's eyes widened at the sight of Roa, dressed in the same uniform as him. "But you . . . I swear you just passed this way."

"That was Celeste," she said, explaining what happened.

His eyes widened further. "Well, she caused quite a stir. She had to be carried inside."

"What? Why?"

"They started throwing rocks, my queen. One hit her in the head."

Guilt flooded Roa. She was the reason Celeste was in disguise. If they hadn't changed clothes . . .

"Where is she?"

"We can take you to her."

Roa looked up to find four soldats approaching. Three men and a woman, ranging in ages. The one who spoke looked twice her age. He had a wide face and kind eyes partially shadowed by the brim of his morion.

"I know where they took Celeste."

"Show me."

He turned and led her into the palace while the other three soldats flanked her. They stood too close though. More than once, their shoulders brushed Roa's, making her wonder how new they were to their posts.

They took her down corridors she'd never been before, then led her out onto an unpolished marble terrace, down an old mosaicked staircase, and into one of the palace's inner orange groves. It was less well kept than any of the palace gardens or orchards.

As the trees swayed around her, Roa realized she had no idea where she was.

"This is far enough, I think," said the soldat to Roa's right, glancing back over her shoulder. She had a slender, wolfish face and blue-gray eyes.

Far enough?

A sudden unease spread through Roa. She looked around them. Except for the sound of birdsong and the wind hushing through the leaves, this part of the palace seemed deserted.

"Where are we?"

"Somewhere no one can hear you." The man with the eyes Roa once thought kind drew both of her sabers—or rather,

Celeste's sabers—and pointed them at her chest. To two of the others, he said, "Go keep watch."

It wasn't fear that swept through Roa as the soldats nodded, jogging back through the grove. It was ire, sharp and honed. She'd had quite enough of being cornered and caged in. Before they could come any closer, she slid her hand into Celeste's boot, where Essie's knife was hidden, and drew it out.

The soldat behind her—the wolfish young woman—moved toward her.

Roa turned quickly, lifting her sister's knife. "Take one step closer and it will be the last step you ever take."

"Such bravado!" said the first soldat—the older man—from behind her. "Unfortunately, there is only one of you and many of us." The way he said it made Roa think he didn't just mean the soldats in this grove, but those beyond it.

"This is for the safety of the kingdom," said the woman before Roa with all the confidence of someone convinced their cause was just. "You're a danger to us—the king most of all."

The man behind her took another step. Too close. Roa lifted the knife once more, her grip tightening on the hilt, trying to keep her eyes on both soldats at once.

"You're a traitor and a spy," the woman continued, stepping closer from the other side. "Everyone knows you're planning to kill the king and take the throne for yourself."

Roa kept her knife on the first while looking over her shoulder at the second. It was all she could do against both armed guards.

"King Dax is just too smitten with you to see it."

Smitten? If she wasn't so terrified, Roa might have laughed.

"Is that so?" said a familiar voice.

Roa froze. Both soldats looked up.

Trying to keep them in her peripheral vision, Roa turned slightly, looking to the owner of the voice.

The dragon king leaned casually against an orange tree, a full cup of wine in his hand.

Surprised, the woman said, "King Dax . . ."

"I'm curious." Dax sloshed the red wine in his cup, and Roa smelled the sharp tang of it even from here. "What gives you the impression I'm smitten with the queen?"

Suddenly, strong hands came down on Roa's arms, pulling her back and trapping her against a solid chest. She struggled, heart pounding, trying to cut and slash with Essie's knife. But the soldat was stronger. He pinned her to him with one arm. Grabbing her wrist, he twisted hard until a sharp jolt of pain made her let go of the hilt. As soon as the knife fell, he caught it and pressed its cold edge to her throat.

Roa went immediately still.

Dax's brow darkened.

"Let her go," he said, pushing away from the tree.

The wolfish soldat stepped between him and Roa. "I'm afraid we can't do that. She's dangerous, my lord."

Roa stared in shock. Disobeying her was one thing. But disobeying the *king*?

"Dangerous?" Dax growled. "She's half your size."

And then, it happened so fast, Roa almost missed it: Dax threw his wine in the woman's face and drew her weapon.

271

The soldat spluttered.

Dax lifted the blade, the look in his eyes pure fury. "Move aside."

The soldat stared at him. Dax lifted the blade higher, pressing the tip against the woman's throat. The soldat raised her hands, backing away from the armed king.

But even from here, Roa could see Dax's grip was all wrong.

For the first time, it struck her as strange. Strange that a boy of twenty-one—a boy who'd been *trained* with weapons even if he was lousy at using them—didn't know how to properly hold a saber.

It was *too* strange.

"My wife is a great many things." Dax made slow steps forward. The blade glimmered as he pointed it at the first soldat while staring down the second. "Cold, calculating, unkind . . . but dangerous? Look at her. She's somehow managed to walk her throat into her own knife."

As he said this, a third soldat melted out of the trees, his hilt raised, ready to knock the king unconscious.

"Dax!" Roa cried out. "Behind you!"

As he turned, Roa rammed the back of her head into her captor's teeth. Pain burst behind her eyes. The guard swore, dropping Essie's knife, and Roa twisted free, snatching it up. The king and queen spun at the same time: Dax toward the two other soldats, Roa toward her captor.

Their spines hit. Dax's back was solid and warm against hers and his peppermint smell enveloped her. He raised his stolen sword, staring down his opponents while Roa stared down hers.

His voice rumbled through her. "As soon as I say the word, I want you to run. Understood?"

Before she could answer, something glinted to her right. She looked to find a fourth soldat stepping onto the path, gripping a small throwing knife in his hand.

From the size of it, Roa knew how fast it would fly, how far in the blade would sink, how deadly it could be if it hit her in just the right spot. She might be able to duck out of the way. But Dax stood directly behind her. If she ducked, if that knife buried itself in Dax's heart, Roa would never set her sister free.

Before she could make a choice, the knife flew, hissing through the air—a sharp, gleaming thing aimed straight at Roa's chest.

Except it never hit.

Or rather: it never hit Roa.

The back of Dax's blue shirt blurred before her. She heard the sound of the blade sinking into flesh, then the harsh grunt of pain.

He staggered back into Roa. The knife in her own hand fell to the earth as she reached to steady him.

"Dax?"

Her heart beat too loud in her ears.

Slowly, she turned him to her. Warm brown eyes looked down into hers. Roa's gaze flickered from his face to the hilt embedded in his left shoulder. The blood was already soaking through his shirt.

"No . . ." she whispered, her voice shaking. "What have you done?"

And then, an angry snarl trembled on the air as Safire burst through the circle of soldats, her eyes blazing, defending the king and queen with her slashing, shining blades.

Roa should have picked up a weapon and joined her.

But there was so much blood . . .

So much of *Dax's* blood.

"Go," said a familiar voice. Roa looked to find Lirabel suddenly beside them: her bow slung, her feet planted, an arrow drawn and nocked. "Get Roa out of here."

Me? thought Roa, staring at the knife in the king's chest. *He's the injured one.*

But Dax's hand was already sliding into hers, gripping it tight. He tugged Roa through the unkempt grove, away from the clash of metal on metal.

And then she was running, hand in hand with the wounded king.

Twenty-Five

Dax led her back through the palace's inner courtyards, through its galleries and arcades, down its shadowy corridors. He didn't stop until halfway down a hall awash in candlelight where he pushed aside a floor-to-ceiling tapestry.

Roa stood motionless, staring at the dark passageway beyond. "In," he said.

Roa stepped into the cold passage and a moment later, the tapestry fell back in place, plunging them into darkness.

Dax didn't need a lantern. He knew the way by heart, guiding Roa through dust and stone, then up. They climbed a narrow staircase, then stumbled down another pitch-dark corridor. Dax halted, fumbling in the darkness. Roa was just about to ask him what was wrong when there was a soft *snick*.

Dax pushed. The wall swung out. Dusky sunlight spilled in.

When Roa stepped through, she found herself in the king's chambers.

The canopied bed, the ornate brass lamps on the walls, the

balcony facing the garden . . . they were all a mirror image of hers.

She spun back to stare at the false wall. Stucco, sea blue, just like the rest of the room, it blended in perfectly.

There was no time to marvel. Because just then, Dax let out a growl of pain. Roa spun. He was trying to pull out the knife.

"No. Stop." She pried his fingers from the hilt, then helped him down to the floor, leaning him against the plaster.

The blade of the knife was embedded on the left side, in the soft spot just below the edge of his collarbone, missing both his heart and his lung. Lucky, that. But his shirt was soaked with blood, and it was difficult for Roa to tell how much, exactly. That knife needed to come out, but once it did, he would lose even more.

As if hearing her thoughts, Dax tipped his chin in a direction over her shoulder. "The chest at the foot of the bed."

Roa went and opened the lid. Inside she found a needle, thread, and a brown bottle of liquid. When she unstopped it and sniffed, she wrinkled her nose at the bitter-strong smell. Spirits.

She came back to Dax and knelt.

After lighting one of the candles, she sterilized the needle in the flame and threaded it.

"This is what we're going to do." Roa looked up into eyes clouded with pain. "I'm going to pull out the knife, and then we're going to take that shirt off as fast as we can."

"Maybe we should wait for—"

Roa wrapped her fingers against the gilt handle and pulled out the knife.

Dax sucked in a pained breath. Blood gushed from the wound.

"Agh! Stars, Roa!"

She tossed the knife aside and grabbed the hem of his shirt, pulling it quickly up over his head. His chest glistened with blood now. Roa bunched up the shirt and pressed it to the wound.

"Hold this," she said. "Press hard."

He did.

That black, rusted key still hung from his neck. Roa tugged it off and tossed it on the floor.

Now for the difficult part . . .

Once she started sewing up the gash, the pain would make him squirm and buck and pull away. So Roa climbed onto his lap, her knees on either side of his hips, pinning him firmly in place.

"Don't fight me," she warned him.

He closed his eyes and leaned his head back against the wall. "I would never."

Roa reached for the brown bottle. Pressing it to her lips, she tipped it back and took a long swig. The spirits burned as they slid down her throat, warming her. Making her bolder than she felt.

"Are you ready?" she said, wiping her wrist across her mouth.

She didn't wait for him to answer. Just pulled away the shirt and poured the contents of the bottle onto his gaping wound, washing the blood away.

Dax's eyes shot open. He cursed her name.

Roa held him steady.

His back arched, but instead of fighting her, he grabbed her thighs, using her as an anchor against the onslaught of pain.

Roa let him. She half emptied the bottle, set it down, and reached for the needle.

"Almost done," she said. This was a lie. There was more pain to come. Though not too much. She could see now that the wound was deep but not wide. It would require only a few stitches.

She met his gaze, silently letting him know what she was about to do. He nodded stiffly.

Roa pushed the needle in, forcing it through.

With nothing to bite down on, his grip on her tightened and his fingers dug into her thighs.

Roa winced. "You're hurting me."

"Yes, well." He gritted his teeth, throat arching as she pulled the needle free and tugged. "You're hurting me more."

She could feel him begin to fade, his eyes closing. Stronger men than him had fainted at this kind of pain.

"I've never seen a grown man protest so much at such a tiny needle," she said, trying to provoke him. To keep him conscious.

His eyes flickered open. "Is that so?" His jaw clenched as she pushed the needle through again. His blood coated her fingers now. "And how many other men have you sewn up?"

As his eyes clouded over, Roa tied off the last stitch.

Stay with me.

She set down the needle and cut a thick strip of silk from his shirt.

"Dax?"

He closed his eyes, unresponsive. Roa's heart thudded pain-fully.

She suddenly thought of him in the Assembly. Lifting the sanctions on the scrublands. Being the king they needed.

"Dax, look at me."

When his eyes didn't open, Roa got desperate. Leaning in, she kissed him hard on the mouth.

Nothing happened.

Roa tried again. Pulling his lower lip between her teeth, she bit down as hard as she could.

Dax's eyes fluttered open. He stared at her, confused. And then his eyes cleared.

"Ouch," he murmured.

Relieved, Roa relaxed and started to wrap the strip of silk tight around his stitches. Dax flinched, then watched in silence as she tied off the makeshift bandage. When she finished, Roa leaned back. She was suddenly very aware of his hands still holding her thighs, pinning her to him.

She knew he didn't mean to hurt her. His grip was merely proportionate to his own pain.

"Dax," she whispered. "You're still hurting me."

Dax looked to his hands and immediately let go.

Roa pushed herself off his lap and rose to her feet. The cool air hit, sucking the warmth from her.

He watched her from the floor, leaning his head against the wall. Sweat shone on his brow, and his hair was damp at the hairline.

"Are you all right?" he asked softly.

Roa stared at the blood on her hands. "Am *I* all right?" She held her hands out for him to see. "This is your blood."

He shrugged—or tried to. It came out like more of a wince. "I can't imagine it's a nice feeling, being cornered like that in your own home."

Roa looked away from his too-soft gaze. It wasn't nice; it was terrifying. But she didn't want him to see that. So she said, "This isn't my home."

A look of hurt flashed across his face. And even though the words were true, Roa regretted speaking them.

Dax took a deadly blow meant for her. And here she was, throwing it in his face.

Here she was, plotting against him, planning to *kill* him, so she could save her sister.

A war raged within her.

Finally, Roa stepped toward him. "Come on." Crouching down, she looped his arm around her shoulders. "Let's get you off the floor."

Dax winced as he pushed himself up. Roa wrapped her arm around his waist, helping him. She guided him to the bed, where he sat down heavily on the edge.

"I'll run a bath . . ."

He grabbed her wrist to stop her. "There are servants to do that."

"I want to."

He stared up at her in silence. "Why are you doing this?"

"Doing what?"

"Being . . . kind to me."

Roa swallowed, looking away. *Because you're hurt, and I'm the reason.*

But no, that wasn't it.

"Because I'm grateful," she said, holding his gaze. "For what you did in the Assembly today."

But this too was partially a lie.

The truth—the whole truth—lay somewhere far deeper. Somewhere Roa was afraid to look.

Twenty-Six

After running a bath and fetching the physician, Roa went to make sure Celeste was all right. She found her guard in perfect form, along with Lirabel in the dungeon. The soldats who'd lied to Roa, who'd attacked her and the king, were locked in cells, being questioned by Safire. It was Lirabel who informed her that an emergency meeting had been called for the next day.

That night, Roa couldn't sleep. She kept thinking of Dax stepping in front of the knife. Putting himself in harm's way to protect *her*.

It was so at odds with the Dax she thought she knew.

Roa pushed off the covers and slid from the bed. Her thoughts were so tangled, she didn't notice how cold the tiles were beneath her bare feet.

In the grove earlier, Dax's grip on that saber had been all wrong. And mere months ago, when he came to the scrublands asking for help, Theo beat him easily in a fight.

She'd gotten used to thinking of him as a clumsy, useless fool.

But Dax was the son of the king. He'd been learning how to wield a blade for as long as Roa had. He might be clumsy. He might be inept. But something like proper grip—after years of lessons—should be second nature.

Dax had spied on his own council. He'd somehow figured out Rebekah was plotting against him and, instead of accusing her without proof, he chose to provoke her. To wait for her to make a mistake.

These were not the acts of a clumsy, useless fool. They were the acts of a careful thinker. A tactician.

Roa stepped out onto her balcony. The stars glittered coldly above her. The night pressed in around her as a thought formed in her mind.

What if Dax wasn't as useless with a blade as everyone thought?

What if he was just pretending to be?

She needed to know for sure. Because when Rebekah's forces flooded the palace, there could be no surprises. Not while she held Essie captive. More importantly, when Roa traded Dax's soul for Essie's on the Relinquishing, there could be nothing standing in her way.

Roa headed for her husband's rooms, needing to find out if Dax was as terrible a swordsman as she'd always believed, or if he was concealing yet another truth from her.

A hundred heartbeats later, Dax's guards opened his bedroom doors for the queen, shooting each other suggestive looks. Roa ignored them, closing the doors behind her.

The light of her lantern flooded the room, coming to stop on a canopied bed where she could see Dax's dark curls against the cotton pillows.

She set down the lamp and drew Essie's knife, sheathed at her calf. Taking a deep breath, she moved for the bed, her bare feet padding softly against the marble floor.

Standing over her husband, Roa pressed the flat of the blade to his throat.

Dax's eyes flew open.

"You're dead," she whispered.

He went rigid, squinting in the dim glow of the lantern, then relaxed at the sight of her. "I didn't expect Death to be quite so beautiful."

Roa slid the knife away.

"Out," she said, drawing back the covers. He wore only cotton sleeping trousers.

Dax sat up, his curly hair mussed. "What is this?"

The night I find out the truth.

But she said, "The first of your nightly lessons."

"Nightly lessons?" He cocked a quizzical brow. A sleepy smile spread across his lips. "Don't those happen *in* the bed?"

Heat rushed through Roa. Standing over him, she pressed the sharpened tip of her sister's blade to the hollow of his throat.

"Out."

Dax was unmoved. "Have you forgotten that I took a knife in the shoulder? For you, I might add."

Of course Roa hadn't forgotten. But she needed to know, for certain, whether he was deceiving her. The success of their plan depended on it. So she shrugged and said, "Once my father traveled to the House of Sky and two bandits attacked him on the road. They broke his arm, and he *still* fought them off."

"And that's why your father will always be a better man than I," Dax said, turning over and lying back down. As if he intended to fall asleep with an armed girl standing over him.

Roa tried again. "Last year, when Theo was out hunting, a wild boar gored him in the leg. Do you know what we had for dinner that night?"

Dax went very still, listening.

"Wild boar."

Dax sat up. The look on his face was stormy as he ducked beneath her blade.

"Let's get this over with," he said, standing barefoot before her. His chest was bare and his shoulder still bruised, the stitches in his skin ghastly. The sight of them made her feel horribly guilty, but she needed to *know*. As soon as she was certain he wasn't deceiving her, they would stop.

Roa sheathed Essie's knife and looked to the wall above Dax's canopy, where two decorative swords crossed each other in an X. Both were straight as needles, their gilt pommels inlaid with jewels. Because they were decorative, the edges were unsharpened.

She needed him to believe this was nothing more than her teaching him how to spar. And these were as close as she was going to get to practice weapons. Roa climbed up onto the bed and took them down, tossing one to Dax. His fingers fumbled the hilt. The blade hit the floor, clattering as it did.

Immediately, a knock came on the door. "My king? Is everything all right?"

"Thank you, Cyrus, everything is fine!" Dax called to his guard as he turned his back to Roa, picking up the fallen weapon.

"Dead again," she said, smacking the flat of her own blade against his lower back.

He winced, then turned to face her.

She stared at his grip on the hilt, shaking her head.

Dax barely had time to lift the blade before hers came down, knocking the weapon straight out of his hands. It went clattering back to the floor.

Roa narrowed her eyes. Maybe he wasn't pretending.

"What are we doing?" he asked.

Picking up the blade, she handed it back to him. "You're learning how to defend yourself."

Something shifted in him.

"You think no one's tried this before?" he asked.

Roa tucked her own blade beneath her arm as she reached for his hand—the one gripping the hilt. "I'm sure they tried," she said, prying his fingers loose from the pommel, then rearranging them in a more secure hold. "Either they gave up too soon, or they were the wrong teachers."

He fell silent, letting her push and prod—not just his fingers, but his elbows, arms, hips, knees—into position. She stepped back to observe him.

"How does that feel?"

"Uncomfortable."

"Memorize it."

His chest heaved. He lowered his arms and all of Roa's work came undone.

"Trust me," he said, setting the sword down. The golden light of the lamps sifted through his curls and caught in his eyelashes. "This is a waste of time."

Annoyance sparked inside Roa, but she held her stance, not ready to give up yet.

"You're a weak king, Dax," she taunted, trying to provoke him. "Everyone knows it. Pick up your sword and defend yourself."

His eyes flashed at that.

Fight back. She glared at him. *Spar with me.*

He didn't even raise his weapon. "What's my incentive?"

"Incentive?"

"For giving up sleep in order to indulge you. While I'm injured, no less."

Roa's grip tightened. *Does he suspect me?*

"I teach you how to defend yourself so you *don't die*," she said. "That's your incentive."

Dax shrugged, his fingers sliding back into the arrangement Roa had just corrected. Holding the blade up to the firelight, he examined it.

"I've spent twenty-one years *not dying*." He caught her eye over the edge of the steel. "Without you."

"Luck," she said, knocking the blade aside.

"Carefully deliberated scheming," he said.

She nodded for him to raise the sword. When he didn't, she

thrust, forcing him backward. Dax raised to block her, leaving his whole left side exposed.

Roa frowned harder. *Is it really possible for him to be this terrible?*

"When you grow up bullied and beaten," he said, "forced to watch the ones you love beaten, too . . ."

She pinned him to the wall with her hip, grabbing the wrist that held his sword and pressing the flat of her own to his throat.

Dead again, her eyes gleamed up at him.

He brought up his knee, not hard enough to hurt, just hard enough to startle, then shoved her back. "You learn that swords don't do much good." His grip tightened on the hilt. "The person doing the abusing will always have a sharper weapon. He'll always know how to wield it better." His eyes looked through her, like he no longer saw her. Like he saw something far away instead.

Roa lowered her blade.

What is he remembering?

"You learn it's better to be weak. Better to be a fool." Dax looked to the blade in his hand as if coming out of the memory now. He set down the sword.

"And when they see through your deliberate scheming?" Roa challenged. "What happens then?"

He came toward her, unarmed. "Why is this so important to you?"

Roa raised the blade, pressing it just below the key hanging from a cord against his chest. Dax took another step. He stood so close now, she could feel his breath on her cheek.

"You saved my life today, when my guards weren't there to protect me." She lowered her gaze, so he couldn't see the lie in her eyes. "One day, your guards might not be there to protect you."

His fingers slid over hers. "And why is that?"

She swallowed as his fingers moved between hers, taking the sword from her.

"Where else would my guards be, Roa?"

Her gaze shot to his, her grip tightening, but it was too late. He had the hilt in his hand, had the blade to her throat. Roa tilted her chin, baring the warm skin of her neck to the cold steel.

"How do I know you haven't come here to find out all my weaknesses, in order to use them against me?"

Roa kept silent, holding his gaze. Because of course that was what she'd come here to do.

"I have an idea," he said softly. "You like deals. How about every time I give you something you want, you give me something I want. For example, a kiss."

Roa remembered the way he'd kissed her in the library and sudden heat flared through her.

She tamped down on it. Didn't he have enough girls to kiss? "You get a kiss *every time* you do something I teach you—like proper grip? Or stance? Or thrust?"

He gave a single, solemn nod.

She made a face. But if this was what it took to find out the truth, Roa would do it. "That's not incentive," she said, playing this game with him now. "That's coddling. If you're rewarded for every little thing, it'll take you years to learn."

And we have only three days until I offer up your soul in exchange for my sister's.

Dax opened his mouth to interrupt, but Roa wasn't finished.

"How about this," she said. "You get a kiss for every time you *beat* me."

With the steel still at her throat, his gaze darted back and forth between her eyes.

"Beat you?" he said, applying pressure. "You mean like *this*?"

Roa smiled a slow smile. *Oh, Dax.*

The steel flashed as she brought her knee up—just like he'd done to her, only harder. He grunted, loosing his hold, and Roa ducked out from under the blade. Her elbow met his ribs and the air whooshed out of him. Before he could recover, Roa grabbed his blade from the floor and now held both swords— one in each hand—crisscrossed over his chest. She pushed, and he stumbled back, wincing.

"Maybe you're right," he said, his hands on his knees, recovering from her blow. "Maybe I had the wrong teachers."

Roa flipped the sword, catching the steel, and handed it back to him hilt first.

Dax studied it for a long moment, as if studying a piece on the gods and monsters board, contemplating the consequences of taking it.

Finally, he reached out, wrapped his fingers around the hilt, and raised it against her.

"All right," he said. "I agree to your terms."

Roa smiled.

And then attacked.

She beat him three times. Each time she grew a little surer her suspicion was misplaced: he wasn't hiding something, he was just a terrible swordsman. And each time she played her role, showing him what he did wrong, and how he might have blocked her.

When she noticed him tiring, Roa lowered her sword to stop.

The moment she did, he parried the way she taught him, forcing her toward the bed. The rush of energy took Roa by surprise and the clang of their blades echoed through the room. But before he could trap her against the bed frame, Roa darted left and swung around to his back.

Dax turned. Roa thrust, catching him off guard, but he parried just in time. She kicked him in the shin and the force of it sent him backward. His legs hit the wooden frame and he lost his balance, falling into the bedsheets and wincing hard.

Roa pounced, pinning the hand that held his sword immobilized above his head while she pressed the steel of her blade to his throat.

Trapped on his back, Dax relaxed beneath her.

It was a good effort, but the effort of a beginner.

So Roa relaxed, too.

Nice try, she was about to say, except the words never came. Because the sight of him now, completely at her mercy, made Roa's stomach flutter.

"Let's do this every night," he whispered, staring up at her.

Roa stared back. She had a startling urge to trace his unshaven jaw, run her fingers through his wild curls, feel the scrape of his teeth on her lip . . .

"My king?" A knock came at the door. "Are you quite sure everything's all right?"

Roa straightened.

"Everything's fine, Cyrus," Dax called from beneath her. "I'm just in the middle of"—his gaze was soft on Roa's face; his voice went even softer—"being obliterated."

Her heart skipped. She immediately withdrew, climbing off him and getting down from the bed.

Dax led her back through a hidden passageway out of his room. He kept the flame of his lamp turned down so low, if he hadn't stopped, Roa would have missed the door entirely.

Passing her the lamp, Dax reached for the latch in the wall. Roa heard that same soft *snick* and then the wall swung out. Dax held it open as Roa stepped through and into her own room.

The dim glow of the lantern flooded the floor, coming to stop on her canopied bed.

"You step here to open it from inside the room," he said, shutting the hidden door and pulling Roa out of the way so when he knelt down and pressed the leaf of a mosaic on the floor, it didn't hit her when it swung out again.

Roa's heart beat wildly.

She shut the door and tried it herself, memorizing the flower—seven down from the corner; yellow with white leaves. Again, the door swung out of the wall.

Dax shut her into the passageway, to ensure she could open it using the latch on the other side. It took a few tries, and for a heartbeat she thought she might be trapped, but Dax shouted detailed instructions through the door, and this time when it swung out, it hit him straight in the face.

Roa winced when she realized it, pulling his palms away from his forehead to assess the damage.

"Sorry . . ."

"You say that, but you're smiling like a child who's just been given a kitten."

Roa smiled harder. Because a passage that led straight to and from her rooms? It would make eluding her guards so much easier. It would make *everything* easier.

Without thinking, she pushed herself up on her toes and kissed his cheek. "Thank you."

Dax's hands moved to her waist, holding her lightly. Almost nervously. As if a single, sudden kiss from Roa could unravel all his charm and confidence.

At that thought, she withdrew. Dax's hands fell away from her.

"If you ever need me in the night"—he rubbed the back of his neck, staring down at the blue and green floor tiles—"take a right."

The silence crept in as both of them thought of the things she might need him for.

"Right. Well. See you tomorrow, then."

Dax picked up his lamp and stepped back into the passage. It was only after the wall closed and the darkness descended that Roa wondered . . . What would happen if she took a left?

Twenty-Seven

That night, Roa had a nightmare.

She dreamed she was locked in a dark and hollow place. There were no walls, and yet no matter where she turned, she couldn't escape. The loneliness crushed her. The smell of blood and rot made her gag.

But she wasn't entirely alone. Somewhere in the shadows, something was searching for her.

Where are you? it called.

Roa knew that voice. Hope bloomed within her. *Essie!*

Where are you? Where are you?

I . . . I don't know!

Roa felt her sister pause. Felt her turn. Hunting for her.

I'm trapped, said Roa. *In the dark.*

I'm coming. Her sister's voice seemed to sharpen. *I'll find you. I always find you.*

But Essie's voice never came any closer. And as Roa tried desperately to close the distance between them, Essie only ever seemed to get farther and farther away.

Soon, Roa could no longer hear her. Just as she was about to give up, the dying echo of Essie's voice reached her ears: *This time when I find you, sister, nothing will ever break us again.*

Roa woke with a start, shivering and covered in a sheen of cold sweat. She tried to shake off the nightmare, but it clung like a shadow.

She'd thought it was about Essie. But then, at the end, that echo . . . it seemed like something *else.*

Someone banged on her door, scattering her thoughts. "My queen?"

Roa looked to find the sun high in the sky. She sat up . . . and groaned. Her whole body ached and it took her several heartbeats to remember why: she'd spent half the night dueling with Dax.

Roa fell back into the pillows, thinking of last night. Of a wounded Dax, gleaming with sweat.

The wound slowed him down, she knew. But even taking it into account, Dax was a worse swordsman than she'd thought. *He favors his left and leaves both sides exposed when he lunges.* He hadn't even come close to beating her.

If it was true that people tried to train him with a sword, either they hadn't tried very hard, or *he* hadn't. It was pathetic how terrible he was—especially since his enemies would be crawling through the palace in two nights' time.

Once that happened, Roa needed to be careful. She didn't trust Rebekah. And she could no longer afford to trust Theo. It was up to her to keep Dax safe from their men long enough to make the exchange.

KRISTEN CICCARELLI

Before any of that could happen, though, Roa needed to find the way out and report to Rebekah before midnight tonight—in exchange for Essie's freedom.

Roa chafed at that. She was at Rebekah's mercy. But soon this would be over.

"My queen." Celeste's voice came again from the other side of the door. "You're late for the security meeting!"

Roa got up. She was tired and sore—out of practice and out of shape. Putting her hands on her hips, she stretched her back, shoulders, and neck. As she dressed, donning a scrublander dress of finely spun pink linen, she glanced quickly at the hidden door Dax had shown her last night.

She was tempted to feign illness and skip the meeting to explore the hidden passage. But if security measures were being discussed, Roa needed to be privy to them in case they interfered with her plans.

Opening her doors, Roa found Celeste, Tati, and Saba looking expectantly back at her from the other side.

"Please, Queen Roa, if you could hurry . . . we're already quite late."

They took her to Dax's rooms. His four guards stood outside the door, chins up, morions gleaming. They nodded to Roa's guards as Celeste led the queen inside, and then to the door of Dax's salon. "We'll be right outside this door. Call for us if you need anything."

Roa nodded, stepping inside.

Safire sprawled out on a low-lying sofa, tossing an elegant throwing knife in the air and catching it, over and over while she talked. Jas sat across from platters full of food, pouring tea for everyone. He would be here for just a few more days, helping Dax plan for the Relinquishing. Lirabel stood near the window, her eyes clouded as she gripped one of her arrows in both hands, bending it as if she intended to break it in half. Roa waited for the *snap*, but it never came.

As Roa sat down next to Dax, her shoulder bumped his bad one and he winced. Roa withdrew, thinking of his knife wound. She shouldn't have pushed him so hard last night.

When she looked up to ask him how he was feeling, the words halted on her tongue.

He looked . . . different.

His hair had been cut. His curls were no longer so wild or tangled. And no hint of any stubble remained on his cheeks.

He shaved, she thought.

The sight of it made her realize she'd been getting used to his disheveled state.

Dax's gaze flickered across her face.

"What is it?" he said, looking down at himself and straightening.

Roa frowned at his smooth cheeks. "Nothing."

Dax reached one hand to rub his jaw.

"You don't like it."

Roa looked immediately away. "Don't be ridiculous."

Dax smiled a little, then leaned back, planting his hand behind her. Leaning in, he whispered against her shoulder, "Good to know."

At the brush of his lips, Roa felt something inside her start to unravel.

What am I doing?

She couldn't let herself unravel. She had a task to perform.

But the more she tried to focus on her purpose, the more her thoughts trailed back to Dax. To the memory of him lying beneath her last night, content to be at her mercy.

By finding Rebekah the way in, Roa was betraying not only him but all of Firgaard—proving they were right to mistrust her. And by plotting to take his life . . .

Roa wrapped her arms around herself, suddenly cold.

Who will I be when all of this is over?

No. She couldn't afford to think like that. She needed to think of Essie. Of the ache growing inside her ever since she turned her back on Baron Silva's home, leaving her sister behind. Alone. Imprisoned in that cage. Surrounded by enemies.

Who will I be when this is over? I'll be the girl who sets my sister free.

"Roa?" interrupted Jas, lifting the teapot. "Tea?"

Roa jerked forward, away from Dax, nodding. Jas filled a cup and passed it to her.

"It's decided, then." Safire sat up and stretched her neck. "We're closing the gates to the city. Beginning today, no one is allowed in or out of Firgaard."

Roa almost spit out her tea. *"What?"*

Everyone turned to stare at her.

Roa forced herself to be calm. "Isn't that a little . . . drastic? For a single breach of security?"

"Yesterday wasn't a breach of security," said Safire. She put both boots down on the floor now, leaning over her knees. "It was a mutiny."

Roa's stomach tightened like a fist.

This would ruin everything. The men and women from Sky were still on their way here. If Firgaard's gates were shut, they'd all be turned away. And if the Relinquishing was canceled . . .

Essie was at Rebekah's mercy. Roa couldn't afford to let that happen. Not until her sister was saved.

"You can't do this," she said.

"This is the third plot against you in less than a week," said Safire. Her glittering blue eyes were cold. "We can't sit back and do nothing."

The third? Do they all know about Sirin, then?

Roa shook off the question and glanced at Dax. "If you shut the city gates and cancel the Relinquishing, it will be yet another broken promise."

"Roa." Lirabel's voice was sharp with warning. She'd turned away from the window to stare down at the queen, her arrow clenched in one hand. "It's for your own safety."

Roa ignored her friend and fixed her gaze on Dax. "If you shut the city's gates, you'll *prove* you're a weak king."

"Isn't a broken promise better than taking another knife for you?!" Lirabel shouted.

Both Roa and Dax looked up at her.

"I never asked him to take the first one," said Roa softly.

Lirabel trembled with anger. "You," she said, glaring at Dax, "are an irresponsible king if you don't do as Safire suggests. And you . . ." Her forehead pinched as she looked to Roa. "I hardly recognize you anymore."

Roa felt herself wilt beneath those words.

"I'll consider it. I promise," Dax said. "Secure the palace, question every soldat and member of the staff, and lock the palace gates for now. As for shutting the gates to the city and canceling the Relinquishing . . . let me think on it. I'll give Safire my answer in the morning."

Lirabel didn't look at the king. "Are we done?" she asked the commandant.

Safire nodded.

Picking up her earned bow and quiver full of arrows, Lirabel stormed toward the door and slammed it on her way. A taut silence loomed in her wake. Rising, Jas followed her out, taking his cup of steaming tea with him.

Safire rose, stretching, then sheathed her knife. "I'm questioning all the palace guards today. If I get so much as a bad *feeling*—about any of them—they'll be dismissed. We can't afford to make any mistakes."

A heartbeat later, she, too, was gone, leaving Dax and Roa alone.

In the silence, Dax plucked a mango from one of the gleaming golden bowls in front of them.

"I can't afford to pretend I'm not losing control," he said as his hands started to slice, peeling back chunks of yellow flesh, cutting them into cubes. "I don't like knowing that you're constantly in danger."

"So you'd rather keep me caged."

He looked up from slicing. "No. That's—"

"Isn't that what you're doing—locking me in? It isn't outsiders who hate me, Dax. It's *Firgaardians*. Canceling the Relinquishing won't make the problem go away."

"I can't just disregard Safire's advice."

"You're king," she said. "You can do as you wish."

His gaze traced her in the sunlight coming through the windows, considering her words. Roa let her own gaze run over the planes of his face, studying those long black lashes, his once dark and stubbled jaw, the crooked bridge of his nose.

"Safire has good instincts," he said. "I trust her implicitly."

And me not at all, thought Roa. But of course, she couldn't blame him.

There was only one thing to do: find the way out and use it to warn Theo.

Before tonight.

Alone

This was what losing her sister felt like . . .

    It was reaching out her hand in the night, only to find the blankets flat and cold and empty.

    It was the story she would never tell and the secret she would never whisper under the covers.

    It was the laugh she no longer heard.

    And the ache that never ceased. .

    And the void that could never be filled.

    It was seeing what she'd lost in the eyes of everyone who looked at her.

    It was pretending not to hear her father weeping in the night when he thought no one could hear.

    It was going to the cliffs to see if she could find a trace of her . . . and finding only the chill of the wind and the silence of the still water.

    It was waking from a nightmare and turning to the one who always sang her back to sleep, only to find she was alone in the dark.

    Alone, forever, in the dark.

    That's what losing her sister felt like.

Twenty-Eight

Roa told her guards not to disturb her for the rest of the day.

And then, lighting a candle, she took it into the passage with her.

If there *was* a secret escape route in the palace, it seemed only logical it would be connected to the king and queen's rooms.

"It has to be this one," she murmured, holding her candle flame close to the walls, looking for latches.

It got cold. And then damp. When her candle nearly burned down to the base, Roa still hadn't come across any doors other than the ones leading to her and Dax's rooms.

And then, just like that, the passageway ended.

Roa set down her candle and ran her hands across the wall, searching for a thin crack like the one in her room. The plaster was cold and damp against Roa's palms, but there was no trace of any door.

No, she thought, wanting to kick it. Why go to the trouble of making a tunnel go this far, and no farther?

Unless it went somewhere once, thought Roa. *And they closed it off.* But why?

And if it *was* the way out she'd been searching for, and it had been filled in, she had nothing to tell Theo.

Panic squeezed her heart.

But the longer she stayed, the more her candle burned down, and if she didn't turn back, she'd be finding her way in utter darkness.

This time, Roa did kick the door.

Pain shot through her foot at the same time something *click*ed. Musty air rushed into her face, following by a soft *creeeeeeaaaak.* She hissed in pain, grabbing her toe, just as the wall in front of her swung open. Roa slowly lowered her foot, staring into the passage beyond, illuminated by her candle.

She ignored her throbbing foot and crouched down, examining where she'd kicked the wall. There was a circle impressed into the plaster, close to the floor. She could tell the circle normally sat flush with the wall, but when she'd kicked it, it sank in. And inside the circle was a familiar pattern, though Roa couldn't remember where she'd seen it before.

Two knotted dragons.

Roa ran her fingers over it. Then pushed.

The door swung closed.

She pushed again; the door swung open.

Grabbing her diminished candle, Roa rose, her heart thumping.

She followed the new passage for a hundred-hundred heartbeats, until she came to a set of steps. These led up to a wrought iron gate. The filigree twisted and coiled in that same knotted dragon pattern. From somewhere beyond it, she heard the rumble of carts and the chatter of voices.

Roa touched the cold iron. Through the space in the twisting dragons, she could see a wall opposite, maybe five steps away. It wasn't the reddish gold hue as most sections of the city. This one was washed in green.

The new quarter. It had been rebuilt and painted after Kozu burned it to the ground.

She saw no stalls, no passersby. This alley seemed barren. But from somewhere nearby, Roa could hear the clang of a hammer on steel. A blacksmith's forge.

She might not know where, exactly, it came out. But she had a rough idea.

And it was a way out.

When Roa reached for the tarnished knob, though, it didn't budge. She tried to turn it, tried to tug, but the gate held firm.

What is it with draksors and their damn locks?

Bending down, she looked through the keyhole, trying to memorize the shape of it.

Roa needed that key.

Who would hold the key to a door leading straight to the royal quarters?

Roa paused then, remembering the key Dax kept on a cord around his neck. A key as black and rusted as this door lock.

Of course he would have it, she thought.

But the key wasn't her most pressing concern. Looking through the gate, she caught sight of the late-afternoon sunlight creeping in.

Roa promised to find Rebekah the way out in three days.

Here it was, the third day. And here Roa stood, staring at the way out. Only it was locked. And Theo was halfway across the city. And the palace was impenetrable.

Roa gripped the iron and pressed her forehead against it, trying to think.

As she did, her candle flickered out.

Roa decided to find Theo and Rebekah, tell them she'd found the way out, then ask for more time to obtain the key.

She made her way to the palace gate and stared up at the four massive bolts—each of them thick as a horse and twice as long—keeping the huge doors buckled tight. The soldats along the gate had been tripled and all of them stood straight as arrows, staring warily at Roa.

She demanded that they open it for her.

One of them took pity on her. "The commandant now has authority over the palace gate in states of emergency."

"What?" Roa frowned. "What does that mean?"

"It means we can't take orders from the king or queen. Only the commandant."

Had Dax done this? Handed over complete control to Safire? *Fool.*

Turning on her heel, she marched straight to the king's quarters.

Before

Roa's opponent slid his carved ivory skyweaver across the checkered board. He'd only just lifted his fingers from the piece when Roa took it with her corrupted spirit, sighing roughly.

"Do you have to be so obvious?"

The eleven-year-old son of the king looked up.

"How am I being obvious?"

"You bring out your skyweaver first. You use her to do all your capturing. You obviously favor her."

"And that's a bad thing?"

"Yes."

"Can you explain?"

Roa breathed in through her nose, then out again. How she was going to get through two whole months with this fool of a boy, she had no idea. But her father had instilled in her the importance of teaching a weaker opponent how to improve. Because a better opponent made for a greater challenge.

Never settle for easy, *he would say.* Always choose the challenge.

So Roa said to the boy across from her: "The moment I realize what your favorite piece is, she becomes your weakness."

Dax stared at her for a moment, considering this, then looked down to his ivory skyweaver.

"So, what should I do?"

"Create decoys." She touched hers to show him: the corrupted spirit, then the dragon. "Try not to favor any one piece. But if you must, don't let your opponent know which one it is."

"Because as soon as she knows my weakness, she knows how to beat me?"

Finally, thought Roa. Progress.

"Never reveal yourself." She slid her dragon across the chiseled stone board. Carved of polished ebony, it gleamed like a starless night. "It's the second rule of gods and monsters." She looked up at him. "Do you remember the first?"

He moved his piece across the board. When he planted it, he leaned back and said, "Pay attention."

"Yes!" Roa smiled. "Very good."

"No," said Dax, tapping her wrist twice. "I mean: pay attention, I'm about to win the game."

Roa frowned.

That couldn't be right.

But when she looked, she found her caged queen wide open and undefended. She'd let herself get distracted. And now, if she couldn't find a way to block him, she would lose her queen and with it, the game.

Roa looked up from the board, stunned.

"Want to know the third rule of gods and monsters?" he asked, grinning. "I just made it up."

Roa crossed her arms as Dax leaned across the board.

"Never underestimate a fool."

Twenty-Nine

Roa banged her fist on the door twice before it swung in. Dax stood in the frame, hastily lacing up his shirt, his lips parting with whatever order he intended to use to send the knocker away.

When he saw her, though, his fingers paused at his throat and the order never came.

"Roa."

Pressing her hand to the half-open door, she gently pushed it open farther, peering into the room.

Except for the warm glow of a lamp spilling across his canopied bed, it was cloaked in shadow. But all Roa needed to see was the bed.

Which was empty.

She let out a breath.

"I need to speak with you," she said, stepping inside.

Dax let the laces come undone again. As if there was no point. As if the effort of looking his best would be entirely lost on his wife. He shut the door behind her.

Roa turned back to find him running a hand through his brown curls.

"The palace gate is locked."

Dax nodded. "Remember the meeting? What part of *we're locking the palace gate* didn't you understand?"

"They refused to open it for me."

"Yes," he said. "Because no one's allowed in or out until Safire is certain it's safe."

"Not even the queen?"

Dax studied her, his brow furrowing. "Why is this suddenly so urgent?"

"Because I need . . ." Roa paused. But it was too late. Dax saw what she was going to say before she said it.

His face darkened. "You need to see Theo."

Roa didn't deny it.

"And the nature of this need?"

Roa burned beneath the question.

Not that, she thought.

But what else could she tell him? She couldn't tell the truth, that she was complicit in the plot against him. That she needed to tell Theo about the secret way into the palace—which Dax himself had shown her.

So she lied.

"If you think I don't have the same needs as you, you're mistaken."

Dax's lips parted in surprise. And then his jaw went rigid.

"All right," he said. "I'll convince Safire to open the gate . . . on one condition."

Roa crossed her arms. "And what condition is that?"

He nodded to the wall above his bed, where the two cere-monial swords they'd fought with last night hung. "You'll have to beat me first."

He wants to spar?

"Right now?" she asked, looking to the windows, where the sun was beginning to set behind the city walls. She needed to report to Rebekah by midnight.

"Why wait?" growled Dax, rolling his shirtsleeves up to his elbows and sliding off his boots.

From the look on his face, Roa could see she had wounded his pride. He wasn't going to open that gate, no matter how she begged.

She would have to beat him quickly.

"Hurry, then."

Dax fetched both swords and tossed her one. Roa caught it, then kicked off her sandals.

He raised the blade. "I've been dying to know: what's so special about the heir of Sky?"

Roa raised her own blade in response and fell into her fight-ing stance, ready to finish him. "Theo doesn't flirt with half the kingdom," she said. "Nor does he sleep with my friends."

Dax lowered the sword to his side. "Those are low standards, I must say."

Roa lunged. Dax barely blocked her, falling back as she thrust again.

"Is it a joke to you?"

"Is what a joke?" he asked as their swords clashed.

"Sleeping with my friends."

Dax threw her off, his brow furrowing. "Are you accusing *me* of such a thing?"

Roa lowered her sword, remembering their last night in the House of Song. The sound of Dax and someone else outside the door.

"I heard you," she said, her anger pulsing through her. "*In my father's house*. You were in the corridor, bringing her back to our room."

"Bringing who?"

"Lirabel!"

His eyes widened then. "You think"—his voice sounded strange—"you think I slept with *Lirabel*?"

Roa gripped her sword hard, glaring at him. "The entire kingdom thinks it."

"I don't care what the entire kingdom thinks," he said, his gaze boring into her. "I care what *you* think."

"It *is* what I think."

He stared at her like the words gutted him. "I wasn't with Lirabel. I wasn't even in the house that night."

Roa narrowed her eyes, thinking of all the time Dax and Lirabel spent in private together. Lirabel didn't spend that kind of time with anyone else.

"And in the sand sea, when Theo came to our aid . . . you weren't in her tent?"

He ran a hand roughly over his eyes. "Stars, Roa. Is this really how you think of me?"

"You retired before everyone else did that night," she said. "And when I came, you weren't there."

"No, *you* weren't there." His grip tightened on his hilt. "You didn't come to bed, so I went to see if you were all right." He looked away from her, jaw clenched. "I shouldn't have bothered. You were with Theo. You were *more* than all right, weren't you?"

Hurt flickered in his eyes, as if Roa wasn't a girl but a knife that wounds.

Roa thought back to that night, to the moments before she'd gone to bed. How Theo asked her to stay. How he'd wrapped his arms around her waist and planted kisses down her throat.

How she'd let him.

If Dax wasn't in Lirabel's tent, nor in his own . . .

He saw, she thought. She could see it plain on his face. He was remembering the two of them—Roa and Theo—alone in Theo's tent. *He saw all of it.*

Roa looked down to her bare feet. "If you weren't in our room the night before we left Song . . . who was?"

"Jas and Lirabel."

Roa glanced back up, startled. "What?"

"I knew you wouldn't be sleeping with me. And they needed . . . somewhere to go. So I let them stay in our room." He shook his head. "I was sleeping on the roof of the garden shed that night. *Alone.*"

Roa stared at him.

Jas . . . and Lirabel? That can't be.

"Lirabel can't stand my brother. Whenever they're in the same room, she flees his presence."

He shook his head incredulously. As if he couldn't believe he had to explain this to her. "Her three younger siblings are wards in your house, Roa. She's at the mercy of your father's generosity. What is she supposed to do?"

Roa frowned. "What are you saying? That my parents would disapprove of them?"

Silence was his answer.

Roa fell back, out of her fighting stance.

"Are you saying," she said, "that all this time, Lirabel has been secretly in love with my brother?"

You gave us a place here so easily, Lirabel told her once. *You could take it away with just as little effort.*

Roa had dismissed her friend's fear as nonsensical at the time. What reason would her parents ever have for sending Lirabel and her siblings out to starve?

This was Lirabel's reason. The one she was afraid to tell Roa.

Lirabel, who had nothing to offer Jas—the heir to a Great House—was in love with him. She had no wealth, no connections, no family except her younger sisters. Nothing to convince Roa's parents she was more than just a destitute girl trying to secure a higher social standing for herself and her sisters.

Is this why she always spurned and ignored him? Roa wondered. *Because she thought if it came to the attention of our parents, they would do exactly as she feared?*

Roa's parents would disapprove—that was certain. But only at first. Her parents would come around because they taught Roa and her siblings to think for themselves and make their own decisions. They would respect Jas for making this one.

And if they didn't . . . well. Roa would change their minds.

Another thought struck her. She looked to Dax.

"Does this mean the baby is *his*?"

That's exactly what it means, said the look in his eyes.

Roa stood motionless, trying to absorb it.

"This is why she never told me," she realized aloud, remembering the argument they'd had in Baron Silva's home. "She thought I'd consider her unworthy to one day be mistress of Song. She thought I would side with my parents."

That her friend could think such a thing, that she would keep such a secret from Roa because she was frightened . . . it hurt. And it made Roa angry—but only at herself.

How could I fail her so utterly?

"You haven't been paying attention," said Dax.

And then he lunged.

Dax beat her, moving fluidly through the steps she'd shown him and finishing with the flat of his sword smacked hard across her shoulder bones.

She winced and reached for the bedpost.

"Roa . . . ." He set down his weapon and took her shoulders gently in his hands. "Did I hurt you?"

"No," she lied, gritting her teeth at the sting and turning to face him. She narrowed her eyes. "That was well executed."

Dax stared down at her, his gaze searching her for a trace of the pain he knew he'd caused.

"It took me a week to learn that move," she said.

A small smile tugged at his mouth. "I have a better teacher than you did."

The compliment loosened something in her, and when he saw it, Dax leaned in and kissed her.

Focus, she told herself, pulling away to look at the sky. The sun had slipped below the garden wall. But she still had time. She didn't need to report to Rebekah until midnight.

Dax pulled off his shirt and tossed it aside. The bruised skin around his stitches looked hideous, but was starting to heal. And the key . . .

The key.

Roa stared at the pattern at the end of the shaft: two intertwined dragons. The same as on the gate that led out of the palace.

Dax wiped his sweat-soaked curls across his forehead and then stretched, rolling his shoulders.

She needed that key.

But first, she needed to beat him so she could report her findings to Rebekah.

Roa thrust and nearly had him, but he parried quickly and escaped out from under her. He grinned and dropped back into the stance he'd now memorized. How had he learned so quickly? Just last night, he carried a sword like it was a foreign object. And now Roa couldn't even beat him *once*?

It was too strange.

Smiling at her, he flicked his wrist, spinning the blade in a way Roa had seen somewhere before. But where? It wasn't a trick she'd taught him.

Because he isn't as helpless as he pretends to be.

It was still just suspicion, though. Roa needed to prove it. So she used a move she knew wasn't fair. One her father would frown at, if he saw. One that would render Dax beaten.

She rushed him, thrusting. When he blocked her, she

thrust again, and as he parried, she hooked her ankle behind his knee and sent him stumbling. Miraculously, he caught himself. But before he could recover completely, Roa quickly disarmed him.

His blade clattered to the floor at their feet. Roa was about to deal the finishing blow, except Dax slammed his heel down on the tip of the sword, and when the hilt bounced up, he caught it and came back swinging in a move Roa *certainly* hadn't taught him.

Just as his blade came down, Roa caught the flat of it against her palm.

"Who showed you that?"

Dax blinked at her. "What?"

"What you just did. Who taught you that move?"

Dax lowered the sword, staring at her. "You . . . did?"

Roa pressed her palm to his chest and shoved. The backs of his knees hit the bed and he sank into it.

"You're a liar."

His eyes flashed at that. "I never lied to you."

"You're lying to me right now!"

"I told you it was a waste of time. It's not my fault you were too busy looking at me the way everyone else does."

Roa stared at him. "What do you mean?"

"My cousin is the commandant, Roa. My sister was once the fiercest dragon hunter in the kingdom. I grew up with both of them. Do you think they would have let me become a helpless king?"

Roa opened her mouth, but no words came out.

He'd played her. He'd been playing *her*, a daughter of the House of Song, like a common fool.

"If you already know how to wave a sword around, then what have we been doing? Why pretend to let me teach you?"

"Why do you think?" he said softly, looking away from her.

"I don't know!" she cried. "That's why I'm asking!"

Softly, he said, "I hate watching you go to him, Roa."

The howling anger inside her died. "To . . . Theo?"

That's what this is about? Theo?

Anger sparked in Roa. "Well, *I* hate watching you court every pretty girl who walks your way. Charming them. Basking in their smiles. Taking them to bed with you."

His eyes darkened. "That's not what I do." He shook his head. "You *love* him."

Those words seemed to take all of his strength.

Roa opened her mouth. And then shut it.

I don't. The thought surprised her.

She had loved Theo once. Or she thought she had. But . . . those feelings were gone.

Roa whispered, "You flirted with nearly every girl in my household while we were home."

Dax covered his face with one hand. "That was . . . unkind." He set down his sword. "My only defense is that I was angry with you. Stars, I feel like I'm always angry with you." He rose from the bed and moved to the fireplace, staring into the embers. "You rode off to Theo *every night*." His fists clenched. "You only married me because you didn't trust me. Because you thought I couldn't protect the scrublands."

Roa stared at him. Those things were true.

"You only married me because you needed an army," she pointed out.

"Roa." His hands uncurled. "That isn't why I married you."

She was about to ask him *why*, then. But something stopped her.

The hum flared up, bright and stark. The bond she shared with her sister reverberated through her.

Essie's white-hot fear flooded Roa as she looked to the terrace.

The sun was gone. The moon was rising.

I still have time. . . .

And then: pain burst inside her, like a sword slicing through her shoulder. Like a fire blazing down her arm.

Essie's pain.

Roa screamed with it. Startled, Dax came toward her. Roa staggered back, away from him, and tripped over the hem of her dress. She plummeted hard to the stone floor, cracking her elbows. But the pain of it was nothing compared to that of her sister's.

It split Roa in two.

She heard Dax's guards call out. Heard them burst into the room, their frantic footsteps thundering across the floor. Heard Dax's voice murmuring. But just like Essie, they seemed a world away.

Essie. Something's happened to her.

What had Rebekah done?

Roa tried to rise and fell again.

This time, instead of cold stone against her cheek, two strong arms caught her. A voice spoke her name. The sound of it brought Roa back.

As Dax's concerned face came into view, she realized she was sobbing.

"What is it?" Dax peered down at her, eyes wide with fear, the crease between his eyebrows deeper than ever. "Are you hurt?"

Not me, she thought. *My sister.*

"Please, Dax. Open the gate."

Thirty

The next morning, Dax told Safire to open the gates. Safire advised against this. Dax insisted. So Safire refused.

What followed was an argument that spanned nearly three halls of the palace and took up the entire morning.

Finally, at midday, Safire gave in and reluctantly ordered the palace gate opened for the queen. Roa and her guards rode straight to the guesthouse where Theo was staying—a trip that took twice as long as usual. Due to the crowds gathering for the Relinquishing, the main streets of Firgaard were packed from wall to wall. And when Roa got to the guesthouse, she found no trace of Theo.

Her shoulder still burned like fire, and the ache of it drove her on. She needed to find out what happened to her sister. Desperate to get to Essie, she climbed back into Poppy's saddle and set out for the only other place he could be. This, too, took far longer than it should have. At one point, Roa screamed at the teeming crowd of visitors to get out of her way—to no avail. There was nowhere to move.

Safire could have made them, Roa was sure. But Safire was back at the palace, overseeing security measures.

Finally, they arrived at Baron Silva's stronghold. Roa left her guards in the courtyard and ran inside.

Two servants led Roa to a room on the second floor. When she knocked on the door, Theo opened it. Dark hollows were carved beneath his eyes and he clutched a brass box in his arms.

He stepped back, letting her in. Two house guards stepped in after her, shutting the door and taking up position against the wall beside it.

"What's happened?" She pushed her sandskarf back from her head. "Where's Essie?"

Theo swallowed, his arms tightening around the brass box.

Roa looked to the thing he was holding.

"It's for you," he said, but he didn't relinquish it.

Roa touched the box. It was made of copper, engraved with a repeating feather pattern.

Very gently, she said, "Let me see."

His jaw tightened, but he didn't prevent her. Just held on to that box as if his own heart lay beating inside it.

Roa clicked open the clasps, then very slowly swung up the lid.

On the velvet bottom lay a single white wing.

Essie's wing.

The pure white feathers, the bloody stump where it had been ripped from her body, the bone sticking out of the flesh . . . Roa couldn't look away, even as the sick horror of it rolled like a wave inside her.

Roa pressed her fist to her mouth.

No . . .

Theo had gone stony. "This is my fault."

No, thought Roa. *It's mine.*

"You let yourself get distracted," said a voice from behind her.

Roa spun. Rebekah stood before her, dressed in swaths of scarlet, her hair falling loose down her back.

"What have you *done*?" Roa snarled, wanting to lunge at her. Wanting to curl her fingers around that elegant throat and *squeeze.*

Behind her, Theo shut the box but didn't put it down.

Rebekah clasped her hands in front of her. "I told you: I can't afford to have you playing both sides."

Roa glared at her. "What are you talking about?"

Rebekah calmly made her way toward a small, ornate table set with a glass decanter and three silver cups. "Yesterday my scouts brought me confusing news." Lifting the decanter, she began to pour. "There are rumors going around the palace. They say the king is more in love than he lets on. They say he's finally winning over his queen." Rebekah stopped pouring and looked up, holding Roa's gaze. "They say the two of you are closer than you seem."

Roa stared, lips parting. "And you believed these . . . rumors?" Her fingers curled into her palms. "*That's* why you took my sister's wing?"

"To remind you of the stakes, yes."

Roa suddenly remembered the night Dax cornered her in the

stable, accusing her of making a deal with Rebekah. Remembered the trace of fear she heard in his voice.

Now she knew the reason for it.

Roa tried to breathe as she watched Rebekah steadily pour the rich, dark wine into the last silver cup. She poured it so smoothly, so calmly. As if she hadn't just done the cruelest thing imaginable to Essie.

"You're a monster."

"Come, now. Once you make the exchange, the wing won't matter. None of this will matter. You'll have your sister restored to her true form."

Rebekah lifted one of the cups and held it out to Roa.

Roa wanted to take the wine and throw it in her face. Instead, she refused it with a solemn shake of her head.

"Besides," Rebekah said as she handed the wine to Garnet, "you didn't report last night. So you might say I preemptively came through on my promise." She turned to face Roa, her eyes dark. "Where were you?"

Roa's fists shook. "The palace gates were locked. I had no way to reach you. I was trying to—"

"Locked?" Rebekah arched an eyebrow. "What do you mean?"

Roa explained about the attack, the locking of the palace gates, and how Safire wanted to shut the city gates, too, and cancel the Relinquishing, but Dax prevented it. He'd made the decision this morning.

As she explained, her gaze scanned the room, searching for any sign of her sister.

"None of that matters," Rebekah said, waving it away. "The plan is to go in through the passage. We can bring a small group inside, take control of the palace, then open the gates for the rest of our men."

"There's just one problem," said Roa. "The passage is locked."

The attention of both Theo and Rebekah snapped to her. "What?"

Roa looked away from them, her fists still clenched, thinking of that fragile white wing. She'd allied herself to a monster, and there was nothing she could do about it. So long as Essie was a prisoner, she had to keep playing this game. "But I know where the key is," she whispered, thinking of Dax, shirtless and gleaming with sweat as they sparred in his bedroom two nights past. Of the key hanging around his throat.

It hurt to think of what she must do. But Roa couldn't afford to be conflicted. Not after what Rebekah had done to Essie. She knew now just how unpredictable Rebekah was. Next time, she would do something far worse.

Rebekah wanted to know everything. So Roa told her about the passage she found connecting her and the king's rooms and how it led out into the city.

"Which part of the city?"

"Near the blacksmith's forge in the new quarter."

"We need that key."

But Roa needed to know her sister was still alive. "Show me Essie first."

Rebekah looked to her house guards. "Garnet? Fetch the queen her bird."

Garnet left and returned with a swinging iron cage, setting it down on the desk before Roa. She leaned in, gripping the bars, staring at the white hawk trembling at the bottom.

Essie . . .

The left side of her body was bandaged and she kept stretching her wing, as if forgetting she only had one, then falling off balance. Hurting herself more.

"My father cauterized the wound to stop her from bleeding to death."

How kind, thought Roa bitterly.

Those silver eyes moved from Roa to Theo to Rebekah. As if she no longer recognized her sister among the room full of threats.

"Essie?" Roa suddenly wished she could go back. Wished she'd never come to Firgaard or agreed to help Dax. Wished she'd stayed in the scrublands.

Essie trembled harder. But this time, that silver gaze turned on Roa and stayed there.

I'm going to get you out of there, she thought. *I'm going to set you free.*

Her sister's mind remained cold and dark.

"I'm sorry it's come to this, Roa. But you're not the only one risking everything. I won't let you compromise the rest of us. If you want my help saving your sister, you must do *exactly* as you're told. Do you understand?"

Roa understood perfectly. She understood that the scales had tipped. So long as Rebekah had Essie, she could make Roa do whatever she wished.

"You need to get that key tonight."

Roa glanced up. *Tonight?* "The Relinquishing doesn't start until tomorrow."

"We can't risk you failing again," said Rebekah. "Get the key and deliver it to me by midnight."

She didn't say what would happen if Roa didn't comply.

The answer was sitting inside a brass box.

Roa returned to the palace feeling numb. The crowds packing the streets made it nearly impossible to pass back through the city, so Roa and her guards took the long way around, using streets farther from the center and therefore less crowded.

The whole excursion took most of the day, and now it was nearly sunset again. The halls of the royal quarters were quieter than usual, with hardly a soldat in sight. She walked, flanked by her guards, thinking of the key hanging around Dax's neck. Thinking of the things he'd admitted last night. Of how wrong she'd been about him.

She thought of stealing that key and giving it to his enemy.

What am I becoming?

She shook the question away, thinking instead of Essie, wingless and cowering in a cage. What was this one small betrayal in light of what she must do in the end? Before the Relinquishing was over, Roa would be guilty of the worst crime: killing the king.

When she opened the doors to her rooms, Roa halted at the threshold.

It smelled like flowers here. Like home.

Jacarandas, she thought, breathing in the sweet scent.

Jacarandas *everywhere.*

They were scattered all across the floor like a pale purple carpet, the smell of them filling the room. Roa took a step inside, letting the doors swing shut behind her.

Someone should let him know you prefer jacarandas, Dax had told her, nights ago now.

She should have hardened herself against the sight of them. But everything hard in her had broken at the sight of Essie's wing.

Roa picked up one of the flowers. She lifted its soft petals to her face and breathed in the soothing scent. Sinking to the floor, she reached for more, gathering them into the linen of her dress.

Her pulse beat loud and hot in her veins as she rose, walking through the spilled jacarandas, trying not to crush their petals, and stepped out onto the balcony.

The sky was a smear of orange and pink as she looked across to the king's quarters, where Dax sat on the flat marble surface of his balcony's semicircular balustrade, his shoulders pressed against the wall, facing her rooms. As Roa's gaze met his, he raised the goblet in his hand in greeting.

But he didn't smile. And his brow was furrowed. She'd left the palace earlier without any explanation for last night. He thought she'd gone to Theo. He'd been worrying about both things there on that balcony, she could tell.

The king and queen watched each other for a stretched-out moment as the sun sank lower in the sky. Like two opponents across a gods and monsters board, both awaiting the other's move.

Dax went first. Tipping back his goblet, he drank deeply before pushing himself down from the marble ledge. Even from this far away, Roa could see the key hanging around his neck. Holding her gaze, he fisted his hand over his heart in a scrublander salute, then disappeared into the orange glow of his rooms.

Roa took a deep breath.

She knew what she had to do. Knew that if she didn't do it, there would be a second wing in a second copper box—or worse. Knew that before this night was over, her heart was going to be broken no matter what choice she made.

It was just a question of what heartbreak she could live with.

Thirty-One

Roa didn't bring a lamp with her. She knew the way to Dax's room by heart now. But this time, as she walked through the dark passage, her fingers trembled as they trailed along the walls. Her stomach felt full of knots.

She stood before the hidden door, pressed the latch, and pushed it open.

The dragon king was alone, stretched out on his bed. His elbows were crooked and his hands were cupped behind his head. His mouth curved down and his forehead pinched into a delicate frown as he stared up at the ceiling.

At her presence, Dax didn't sit up. Merely turned to look.

His gaze swept over her. She wore a kaftan this evening. He himself had given her this one. It was dark purple—the color of bruised storm clouds—and the silk was so sheer as to be almost translucent. It matched the jacaranda tucked behind her ear.

The way he was looking at her now was all tenderness. His face was wide open, letting her read him. Letting her know everything he was thinking and hoping and wanting.

"I assumed we were done with lessons," he said, sitting up, his hands gripping the wooden bed frame beneath him.

"I'm not here for lessons," she said.

Dax's feet were bare. His shirtsleeves were rolled up to his elbows again and the laces at his collar were loose. As if he found his clothes confining.

"Then what are you here for?"

Roa looked to his throat. As her gaze fell upon the shape of the key hanging there, she had a strange and sudden urge to tell him everything.

That, of course, was a terrible idea. It was the fastest way to seal Essie's fate—not to mention her own.

The cost of treason was death, and Roa was certainly committing treason.

But the cost of not going through with the plan was Essie.

When she didn't answer his question, he asked another one. "How is our friend Theo?" He looked down at the floor as he said it, avoiding her gaze. But she knew what he thought. She'd given him every reason to think it.

"Dax," she whispered. "I don't want Theo."

When his face tilted up again, she saw the question in his eyes: *Then what do you want?*

Deep below the surface, something thrummed within her. Something she hadn't let herself desire before. Because he was the enemy. Because he preferred Lirabel. Because Roa needed to save her sister.

Except . . . only one of those things was true now.

She hugged herself, suddenly afraid of her own conflicted heart.

Gathering up her courage, Roa moved toward the bed.

"I'm not interested in being one of many," she said as she slowly stepped between his legs, which were bent at the knees. Dax's hands tightened around the edge of the wooden bed frame. As if he didn't trust himself to let go.

"Say you're mine," she whispered, staring down at him. "Or I won't have you."

He tilted his head back, raising his eyes to hers. "Who else's would I be?"

She thought of his reputation. Of all the girls he gave his smile to and took into his bed.

"You're the one who taught me to never reveal myself." He let go of the bed frame, his gaze tracing her. "You taught me that once my enemy knows my weakness, he knows how to beat me." His hands slid to her hips, bringing her closer. "So I hid my true weakness behind rumors and flirtations and decoys. Because if my enemies knew just how much she meant to me, they would take her from me."

Roa frowned, her lips parting as she suddenly saw the game from his side of the board. Saw it clearly.

With his face turned up to hers, Dax said: "The only girl I've ever wanted is the one sleeping across the garden."

Me? she thought. *I'm his weakness?*

The realization came with a rush of tender feelings.

Roa pressed him back against the bed. Dax let her. His breath hitched as she lowered herself over him, planting her hands on either side of his head, sinking down onto his hips.

Roa tried to separate out her purpose from her desire, but they were all snarled up together.

Knotting her fingers in his curls, she kissed him. He made a soft sound and reached for her, crushing her to him. He rolled her onto her back, then lowered himself down until their bodies aligned.

"Why are you really here?" he whispered, his eyes a storm of emotion.

She traced his cheeks—which were rough again. "Because I want to be."

It was both the truth and a lie.

He pulled off his shirt and threw it aside. The key hung free now, dangling between them. Roa reached up to touch it, tracing the knotted dragons, until Dax lifted the cord over his head and dropped it on the floor.

His fingers slipped hooks out of eyes. Her breath sped up as his hands skimmed down her stomach and hips, then slid beneath the silk of her kaftan, setting her nerves on fire. When his palms glided up her bare thighs, though, Roa tensed and sucked in a breath.

Dax went very still, watching her.

"You're afraid," he realized, pushing himself up onto his hands. Cold air rushed between them as he stared down at her.

"It's just that . . . I know what to expect." Her cheeks burned. "I know there will be pain."

His face softened, then. "Oh, Roa, no. It doesn't have to hurt." He pressed his forehead to hers. "I told you I would never hurt you."

She thought of the night she gave herself to Theo.

"You might not know," she whispered.

He frowned hard, his gaze flickering over her. "Of course I will."

She should have stopped him then. Should have told him everything.

But if she did, she would never save her sister. She needed to play this game through to the end, or Essie wouldn't just be punished, she'd be lost forever. And despite the war waging in Roa's heart, she loved her sister more than anything or anyone.

It should have been Dax who died that night eight years ago, not Essie.

Roa needed to make it right.

She needed her sister back.

But deeper than all of these things was a much simpler truth: now that it was far too late, now that it was entirely out of reach, Roa wanted this. Wanted *him*. Wanted to be loved by the king.

And so she was.

Afterward, Roa listened to the sound of his breathing, trying not to memorize it. Trying not to need the beat of his heart against her spine or the weight of his arm curled securely around her, even in sleep.

As she listened to him breathe, she tried to push this bright new wanting back down from where it had come.

Roa shut her eyes tight, trying to remember her purpose. Trying to sharpen it inside her like a knife.

Essie.

The key.

Midnight.

Untucking herself from Dax, she pushed herself to the edge of the bed. Casting her gaze over the floor, she found his shirt. And then the key.

Her eyes burned as she picked it up and slipped its cord over her head.

Outside in the night sky, the moon had almost reached its zenith.

Roa quickly dressed. But just before stepping into the passage, she looked back to the bed, where Dax slept, oblivious to her treachery. Her gaze traced the gentle curls of his hair, the ears that stood out a little too far from his head, the solid line of his shoulders.

She turned away from the sight, then took the passage. When she finally came to the locked iron gate, she lifted the cord over her head. Her hand trembled as it slid the key in. Her stomach twisted as she turned it.

There was sharp *click*—like the sound of Roa's heart breaking—and the gate swung open.

She should have felt triumphant.

Instead, she wept.

Thirty-Two

Roa stepped out into the darkened alley and swung the gate closed. In the distance, Roa heard the noise of Firgaard. The music and shouting of its night market. With so many travelers visiting the capital for the Relinquishing, most of Firgaard was bursting at the seams. But this stretch of road was barren. Silent.

She couldn't get the taste of Dax out of her mouth. Couldn't banish the memory of him lying next to her in the bed, his heart hammering against hers, their legs tangled up together.

Who would she be when this was all over?

A monster, realized Roa.

But to stop now was to lose Essie forever.

Suddenly, silhouettes emerged from the shadows. Rebekah's men. By Roa's loose count, there were at least four dozen. Possibly more hidden in the shadows.

Why were there so many? The plan was to infiltrate the palace during the Relinquishing. *Tomorrow*, not tonight.

The face of the one who led them was hooded, but Roa

recognized the height of her. The line of her shoulders. Her proud gait.

Rebekah stopped before the queen and held out her hand, palm up. "Give me the key."

Roa peered over Rebekah's shoulder. "Where's Theo?"

"Your friend proved to be . . . disloyal."

Roa's mouth went dry as cotton. "What?"

"My men are searching for him now," Rebekah said. "There's been a change of plan. Give me the key, Roa."

Roa touched the key at her throat but didn't hand it over. "Give me Essie first."

"How do I know there aren't a legion of soldats waiting for us the moment we step inside?"

Roa stared into the deep shadows of her hood. "How do I know Essie's safe? Or that you won't kill her the moment you get what you want?"

Rebekah motioned to one of the men behind her. He stepped forward and lifted a familiar cage. Inside a one-winged hawk cowered, her silver eyes flashing in the night.

"I've been betrayed once tonight. I'm not risking a second time."

"And I've risked everything tonight," Roa countered. "So you need to trust me with this one small thing."

Rebekah was silent. After a long moment, she growled: "Fine. Keep it. Just take us in."

Roa's heart felt heavy as a stone as she led them toward the gate. She swung it open and went in first. Rebekah stared into the darkness ahead, breathing deep.

"I've been waiting a very long time for this day," she said.

The men at her back followed them in.

This is wrong. The thought beat through Roa's mind like a pulse. *All wrong.*

She shook her head. She couldn't afford to think like that. She'd always known what the consequences were.

There was no going back.

When they arrived at her rooms, Roa pushed open the hidden door and stepped inside. Rebekah stepped in after her. The night was blue-black beyond the windows. The lamps burned low. Wilting jacaranda flowers still littered the floor.

"How many guards stand outside your door?" asked Rebekah.

Roa told her.

A dozen men took up position along the wall next to Roa's bedroom door.

They needed to do this quietly and covertly. They couldn't draw any attention from the commandant or her army, who would be fully occupied with Firgaard's security on the eve before the Relinquishing. They needed to take the palace one step at a time.

Rebekah drew her dagger and pressed it to Roa's throat. "Call them," she said.

Roa hesitated, wondering what Rebekah would do once Celeste and the others entered.

Rebekah pressed harder and Roa felt the sharp steel prick her flesh.

So she called.

But nothing happened.

Several heartbeats passed and . . . silence.

"Again," Rebekah commanded.

Reluctantly, Roa called for Celeste, and then Saba, and then Tati. Wishing there was a way to warn them.

Again, silence answered her.

Rebekah motioned for someone to go look. One man opened the door and stepped out, then came back in.

"There's no one out there."

The hair on the back of Roa's neck rose. Her guards never left their posts. Safire would dismiss them in a heartbeat if they did.

Something was wrong.

But even as she thought it, a tiny spark of hope flared to life inside Roa. If her guards weren't here, Rebekah's men couldn't hurt them.

Rebekah lowered the blade from Roa's throat and went to look. The moment she came back, her gaze fixed on Roa, and for maybe the first time, there was something like fear in her eyes.

"Where are they?"

The palace was empty. No soldats stood on watch. No servants walked the halls. Rebekah had opened the unguarded gate and let in her men without any resistance. They searched every shadowed corner and garden and hall, but there was no sign of the king—or anyone else.

Meanwhile, Roa searched Dax's room.

All was quiet and still, the bed loomed large and empty. The faces in the tapestries hanging from the walls seemed to watch her, making her skin prickle with wariness.

The Skyweaver's knife was sheathed at Roa's calf beneath her dress, right next to Essie's earned knife. Gripped hard in her hand was the hilt of her scythe. She was sufficiently armed. And yet Roa trembled as she called Dax's name into the darkness.

No answer came.

She trod softly to the terrace. But there were only the stars, winking above her. The sky was lightening. It would be dawn soon. The day of the Relinquishing.

Once the sun set, Roa could make the exchange. She could save her sister for good.

She just needed to find Dax.

A sudden sound issued from below, like the thud of a punch being thrown. Roa heard the loud snickers of multiple men and looked down, scanning the garden.

Near the wall of the arcade, she saw their silhouettes.

Two of them had weapons drawn. They stood in a ring around a young man on his knees. The one who'd been punched.

Roa leaned over the balustrade, looking harder. She saw the tallest one start to undo the buckle of his belt. Then the buttons of his pants.

The sight of it made her frown. From here, it looked like they were . . . like they were going to urinate on him.

Or worse.

Suddenly, she knew exactly who knelt in the middle of the circle.

Dax.

Roa didn't think about how they outnumbered her four to one. Just bit down on the steel of her scythe, keeping it securely between her teeth.

Hoisting herself over the balcony, she dropped to the earth below.

Thirty-Three

Rage thundered through Roa as she moved quickly down the garden's dirt path toward the voices. With her hilt gripped hard in her hand again, she advanced on the men.

"If you value your lives," she growled when they came into view, "you'll walk away. *Now*."

The men looked up, their laughter dying. The smiles falling from their faces at the sight of the scrublander queen.

Dax looked up, too, staring at his wife from where he knelt on the ground. A bruise was forming on his jaw. His curls were a mess. And his eyes were dark with betrayal as he stared at the key hanging from Roa's throat.

"Go back inside, scrublander." In the light of the few torches lining the garden walls, she saw it was Garnet. The scar through his lip giving him away. "You don't want to watch this. We'll bring him to you and Rebekah when we're done."

"Did you not hear what I said?" She glared at Garnet even as her heart pounded an erratic tattoo, her body coiled to spring if he challenged her again.

The other three stepped in closer, their hands going to their hilts.

Roa's senses flared with warning.

She couldn't fight them all. Nor could she leave Dax at their mercy.

"Drop your weapon, scrublander. Or you'll join him."

Roa looked to her husband, who was rising to his feet behind her. Their gazes caught and held. In a heartbeat, something swift and silent passed between them. Dax nodded—the motion so slight, it was almost imperceptible.

"I said," Garnet growled, "drop your weapon."

Roa threw down her sword. The tip landed near Dax's left foot.

"Good girl."

Before the words were even out of his mouth, Dax slammed his boot down onto the steel. The hilt of her sword bounced against the dirt path and swung upward.

Dax caught it. Roa drew her sister's knife.

The two men directly before them stared in disbelief. Like everyone else, they'd been completely taken in by Dax's charade of a useless swordsman.

As they hesitated, Roa and Dax lunged. With a fierce cry, her knife plunged into Garnet's heart while Dax opened the chest of the one beside him using Roa's scythe.

That's for my sister, thought Roa as Garnet's eyes widened in shock.

The smell of hot, coppery blood filled the air. Both men went down.

Roa drew Garnet's saber. She and Dax turned to face the

second set of Rebekah's men, who were only now recovering from their confusion and drawing their weapons.

"Where is everyone?" she asked Dax quickly. "Why is the palace empty?"

"We knew an attack was coming," he said, keeping his eyes on the enemy. "Safire evacuated the palace."

Roa frowned. The whole palace? That wasn't possible. Rebekah had eyes everywhere. She would know if an entire palace's worth of soldats and staff had left through the front gate in the middle of the night.

Unless they didn't leave through the front gate . . .

"On the count of three," Dax murmured, snapping Roa's attention back to the danger at hand.

As one, they thrust. Roa's opponent was twice her size but also twice as slow. She slashed and lunged, again and again. A heartbeat later, the man was disarmed and backed against the wall beneath the arcade, his eyes pleading, his hands raised in surrender.

Roa heard the thump of a body hit the earth behind her.

"I'll finish him," said Dax, stepping up to her side.

"You think I can't?"

"No . . . " Dax said, taking the saber from her and giving the man a quick death. Roa watched the dark red blood streak down the plaster wall as his body slid to the ground. " . . . I just didn't want you armed when I did *this*."

Raising both blades, Dax turned on her.

It was Roa whose back hit the wall now, two bloodied blades turned against her.

Dax's thoughts were diamond clear on his face. He was

remembering the way she'd stepped into his room earlier tonight. The way she'd come into his bed.

He was seeing her wait for him to fall asleep, then pick up the key from the floor.

Seeing her unlock the gate.

I've ruined us, she thought. *I've ruined everything.*

Or maybe they were ruined long before now.

Maybe they were ruined the day her sister died in his place.

"A message arrived tonight," he said, his voice low, "telling of a threat *inside* the palace." He gripped both weapons properly now and held himself like an expert swordsman. "I prayed to every god it wasn't you."

Roa lifted her chin, even as her heart quailed.

"But the proof is right there, hanging around your throat."

He was looking at her like she wasn't the girl he'd made love to earlier. Like that girl no longer existed for him.

She doesn't exist, Roa realized. *I can never be that girl again after what I've done tonight.*

Dax stepped closer. "Did you plan it all out with her? How to best seduce me?"

She could hear the sound of his broken heart in his words.

Roa knew what a broken heart felt like. She'd felt hers shatter into a million pieces the day Essie died.

She felt it shattering now.

Roa tried to harden herself against it. *You've come this far. There's only a little bit farther to go.*

She thought of Essie locked in that cage. Essie fading away. Essie gone forever . . .

"What have you done with the girl I love?" Dax came closer.

Their gazes locked. "I want her back." He dropped one blade— Roa's scythe—in the grass and gently touched her cheek. "Give her back to me."

Roa wasn't sure which was more dangerous: his steel or his touch or his words.

"That girl is gone," Roa said, thinking of everything she'd done and still had yet to do. "Don't waste your love on her."

He lowered his sword. "You think love is as fragile as that? Like a stalk of wheat, easily broken in a storm? That's not what love is."

Dax stepped in closer.

"Real love is the strongest kind of steel. It's a blade that can be melted down, its form changed with every bang of the hammer, but to break it is a task no one is capable of. Not even Death."

Roa stared at him. What was he saying? That he loved her— even now?

"You're a fool," she whispered, the words stinging her throat.

And then, with his sword lowered, she shoved him hard enough to send him stumbling.

Roa found her scythe lying in the grass. In a heartbeat, she had her alabaster hilt in her hand, the curved blade raised and ready to strike.

But Dax struck first. Roa barely caught the flash of steel coming at her.

Their swords clashed. Dax forced her back, relentlessly thrusting. Roa ducked, forever moving so he couldn't back her into another wall.

It was then that she realized just how much he'd been holding back.

She could barely fend him off.

His furious blade came down on hers, knocking it out of her hand. He shoved her, just as she'd shoved him. Roa tripped and went down hard. Pain shot through her elbows.

A heartbeat later, he had her pinned beneath him. One hand kept her wrists trapped above her head while the other held his blade across her collarbone.

Shocked at the quick defeat, Roa stared up at him. They were nose to nose now, breathing hard.

"You're not the kind of girl who grasps at power for its own sake," he said, the heat of him rolling over her. "Why have you done this?"

Here, the light of the garden torches made his skin glow gold. Just for a moment, he seemed almost godlike above her. As if Namsara himself, the golden god of day, had come down to this pit of darkness just to interrogate her.

Roa gave in to him.

"You weren't who I thought you were," she whispered, her gaze tracing his face. *And then, suddenly, you were.* "I thought you'd broken all your promises. I thought you didn't *care*. I thought you were a dangerous king."

The pressure on her throat let up—just a little.

"And even when I realized the truth . . . I still needed to save my sister."

He went rigid at those words. "What?"

"Essie never crossed." She held his gaze, daring him to

disbelieve her. But Dax knew the stories of her people. Knew about the Skyweaver and uncrossed souls and the reason for the Relinquishing. "She's trapped. I have to set her free."

There was a fierce crease in his brow now. With his blade still pressed to her throat, he said, "Go on."

She looked beyond him, to the lightening sky, thinking of the Skyweaver's knife sheathed beneath her dress. Of what she must do once the sun set tonight.

"When someone dies in another's place, an . . . exchange can be made. But it must happen on the Relinquishing."

She could see him trying to recall everything he knew about the Relinquishing. Everything her tutors had taught him, all those years ago.

"It was supposed to be you," she whispered, looking up into his eyes. "Not her. You were the one who was supposed to die."

"Like Sunder," he said. It surprised Roa. She hadn't expected him to remember that story. "The man who eluded Death. So Death took someone else in his stead."

Before Roa could answer him, a sound broke the moment. Footsteps rang out through the arcade, and with them came voices. One voice made both Dax and Roa stiffen.

Rebekah.

But before she came within view, darkness drenched them. A black shadow flew overhead. Roa felt the rush of wind on her face, felt the earth shudder beneath a great weight. A familiar sound echoed through the garden: several loud clicks in rapid succession.

She knew of only one creature that clicked to communicate.

Dax looked back over his shoulder. Whatever he saw made him rise to his feet.

As soon as the weight of him lifted off her, Roa rose too, grabbing her scythe.

A dragon loomed over her, his scales dark as polished ebony. One eye was blind; the other slitted and staring her down.

"Kozu." Roa stepped back.

A second dragon stood behind the first. Half the size of Kozu, its golden scales gleamed in the blue twilight and its two ash-gray horns twisted toward the sky.

Two riders dismounted. The first was Safire, who immediately made for the king, seeing everything—the bloodied blade in his hand, the bruise forming on his jaw, the way he put too much space between himself and the queen. When Roa's gaze fell upon the second rider, her breath hitched.

The young woman had dark hair braided over one shoulder and a burn scar took up half her face and neck. Two twin slayers were sheathed across her back.

Asha.

"Get on," the former Iskari told her brother while her black eyes gleamed at Roa.

Dax obliged—heading past Safire and toward the golden dragon, lifting himself easily up onto its back. As if he'd done it a hundred times before.

Roa should have tried to stop him. Should have called for help. She should have done something—anything—to detain him.

But as desperate as she was to save Essie, Roa knew now exactly what it would cost her.

She loved this boy—this *king*—who wasn't at all what she'd feared, but rather, everything their people needed.

In order to save her sister, Roa would destroy far more than just Dax. She would destroy her own self.

"I know what Essie is," said Asha, her voice urgent. "I know what she's becoming."

Becoming? Roa turned to face Dax's sister. What could Asha possibly know about any of it? She was a draksor.

As if sensing her thoughts, Asha said, "I know something of bonds. And loyalty."

Loyalty. That was something Roa once knew. And now? Was there even a single person she hadn't betrayed?

My sister, she thought. Staring down at the scythe in her hand, Roa whispered, "I have to save her."

Asha shook her head. "You have to *relinquish* her, Roa. It's your bond that's keeping her captive."

Roa hardened at those words. She thought of that night on the roof. Of Essie's curls slipping through her fingers as she lunged to save the son of the king. Of Essie falling instead of Dax.

Roa clenched her fists so tight, her knuckles hurt.

Dax was the reason Essie fell from the roof. If her sister's entrapment was anyone's doing, it was his.

The footsteps in the arcade came closer. Asha glanced in the direction of the sound as Kozu spread his wings wide, telling his rider it was time to go. Safire, who was already mounting the First Dragon, called her cousin's name. But Asha remained where she was, eyeing the scythe in Roa's hand, as if afraid to turn her back on it.

And in that moment, more than the burning fire of anger or the piercing blade of grief, Roa felt the shadow of shame. In Asha's eyes, she saw what she'd become.

Roa threw down her weapon. "Go," she whispered. "Hurry."

Asha went to Kozu, hoisting herself up behind Safire, then looping her arms securely around her cousin's waist. As she did, Rebekah's men flooded into the garden.

Kozu hissed, crouching low. The moment they advanced, the massive black dragon leaped over their heads and onto the roof.

Roa looked at the golden dragon Kozu left behind. Sensing danger, it spread its elegant wings wide. Yet it waited, perfectly still, for its rider's command. As Rebekah shouted and her men swarmed, Dax hesitated from atop its back, looking to one person only. As if it broke his heart to leave her behind.

The sound of drawn steel made him tear his gaze from Roa. Dax bent low to the creature's shoulder, clicking softly.

The dragon vaulted them into the sky.

Thirty-Four

"First you kill my men, then you let Dax *get away*?"

While Rebekah circled her, Roa stood in the middle of the carnage, exhausted and heartbroken and wanting her sister.

Rebekah's fists were tight and trembling. Her hair hung limp along her face. And there were deep hollows carved beneath her eyes.

Unfortunately for Roa, one of the men had survived her attack and told Rebekah everything.

"What are you playing at?"

Roa hardly heard Rebekah. She was thinking of how she'd let Dax walk away. In letting him go, had she doomed Essie?

What have I done?

"I want to see my sister," she said, turning to leave the garden.

Four armed men immediately blocked her way out.

"Seize her," said Rebekah.

Roa drew the Skyweaver's knife—her last remaining blade. When they grabbed her arms, Roa tried to fight them off.

She used her elbows and knees. She slammed her heels into their shins. But there were so many more of them, and they held her firm, prying the Skyweaver's knife from her fingers. It fell to the earth with a thud.

"Let me go," she hissed.

Rebekah picked up the knife, tucking it into her sash.

Just then, a pair of frantic footsteps sounded in the arcade. Hands went to hilts. All eyes turned to the sound, ready for a fight.

But it was just one of Rebekah's men: a young man with light brown hair cropped close to his head. "Mistress." He was out of breath and doubled over. "It's gone."

"What's gone?" Rebekah's voice was razor-sharp.

"I think . . . I think you should come and see."

They dragged Roa back through the empty royal quarters. She didn't fight this time. There was no point. Rebekah had the Skyweaver's knife, and Roa was surrounded and overpowered. She would have to wait for the right moment to escape and find Essie.

Torches burned in their sconces while the early-morning sunlight crept in, chasing the shadows out of the corridors. They passed the throne room and stopped when they came to the hall of fonts.

Seven fountains flowed throughout this roofless court. Between them grew geometrical gardens, full of trees and shrubs and flowers of all kinds. They stopped at the largest fountain, surrounded by a circle of bright yellow hibiscus in full bloom and half-shrouded by tall cedars.

As the gentle sound of falling water echoed through the hall, Rebekah stopped sharp.

Roa peered around her.

Essie's cage lay before them. Only something was wrong.

It was mangled, the black bars twisted back, gaping open like the splayed rib cage of an animal.

Empty.

But it wasn't the only thing wrong. Two bodies lay half-hidden behind the hibiscus bushes. Roa recognized the first one as the man who'd been carrying Essie's cage into the palace. He and his comrade lay on the floor tiles, their necks snapped, just beyond the hibiscus.

There was no blood. No sign of a struggle. Whatever had done this had done it very quickly.

An ice-cold feeling spread through Roa.

"What happened here?" Rebekah demanded.

No one answered her.

It's begun, thought Roa, looking to the rising sun. The Relinquishing was upon them. Today, uncrossed souls resumed their true forms and walked among the living.

Essie? Roa scanned the trees, the pools. *Where are you?*

She reached for the hum and found it gone.

That can't be . . .

Roa reached again. But there was nothing there this time.

The hum was dead within her.

Rebekah looked from the broken cage to Roa. "Do you know what did this?"

Roa knew.

"A corrupted spirit," she whispered.

◆ ◆ ◆

They threw her into a room with no windows or bars.

Roa had never seen the inside of a cell. Scrublanders didn't have things like cells or dungeons. This one was chilled and damp and dark. It smelled like rot and the only bit of light came through a sliver in the bottom of the door.

It was like a tomb of stone. Suffocating her.

Is this how Essie feels, every single day?

But it was the Relinquishing. And Roa had seen that empty cage.

Wherever she is, Essie is free of her bird form.

She banged on the door. When they ignored her, she banged louder, demanding to be let out. She had only today and tonight to find Dax. And in this windowless room, she couldn't tell how much time was passing.

When her banging proved futile, Roa began to pace the grimy floor.

Essie, where are you?

She wanted her sister—the only one who could soothe the lonely ache in her. The one she belonged to.

But her sister wasn't here. And Asha's words had claws.

It's your bond that's keeping her captive.

When the door swung open, the red-gold glow from the dungeon bays flooded in. Rebekah stood in the frame, blocking the light and staring down at Roa. The Skyweaver's knife was tucked into her sash.

She wasn't alone. Behind her stood the seven councillors who'd been plotting against Roa in the library. The very same councillors Dax had locked up for treason.

Rebekah must have found their cells and let them out.

For what purpose?

"Time to go," Rebekah said as four men entered the cell, grabbing Roa.

This time, she didn't put up a fight, just let them drag her out.

"How much time has passed?"

Rebekah, who walked ahead of her, didn't answer.

"Where are you taking me?"

"To the city square."

Roa went rigid. The city square was where Asha's sentencing would have been carried out. It's where the chopping block sat.

"Why?" she whispered.

"We're going to offer the king something he can't resist."

Suddenly, Roa could see Rebekah's next move. Could see just how she would manipulate the pieces on the board to ensure she got the outcome she wanted.

But Dax had proven himself equally good at manipulating pieces on a board. At games of strategy.

"He'll know it's a trap," Roa whispered.

Rebekah smiled back at her so confidently, dread curled within Roa.

Thirty-Five

It was well past midnight when Rebekah and the king's former councillors dragged Roa through the crowded streets, bound and gagged. All around her, she heard the shocked murmurs, the confused questions.

Where are they taking the queen?

Where is King Dax?

Everyone in the crowd wore Relinquishing masks. Carved of wood. Painted white. Hiding their identities and making it impossible to tell who was who.

Still, Roa searched them, looking for her sister.

You should all be in your homes, locking the doors, she thought as her gaze scanned the masked crowd. It was how she knew the faces behind the masks didn't belong to scrublanders. Scrublanders would already be gathered around their heart-fires by now, their doors bolted, their lights snuffed.

As they dragged her, Roa heard Rebekah shouting up ahead, leveling her charges against the outlander queen, telling all of Firgaard what she deserved.

Roa didn't need to hear the charges; she knew what she'd done.

Plotted to kill the king.

Let his enemies into the palace.

Utterly betrayed him and their friends and their *people*.

Roa knew what she deserved.

Essie, where are you?

From somewhere in the crowd, she thought she heard someone call her name. But when she looked, Roa saw only blank masks, the firelight flickering over them.

"Roa, here!"

She looked again, trying to see. But the masks made everyone look the same.

Finally, Roa saw her.

Lirabel.

She'd pulled her Relinquishing mask down, just for a moment, allowing Roa to identify her.

Lirabel was fighting to get to her. Roa could have dug in her heels. Could have made it difficult for them to keep dragging her—at least until Lirabel caught up.

But then Rebekah would take Lirabel, too. Roa couldn't let that happen. She'd promised to keep her friend safe.

Suddenly, the crush of the crowd overwhelmed them, and Roa lost sight of Lirabel. Her handlers dragged her onward, bruising her as their fingers drove into her arms. The moment they entered the public square, Roa saw the chopping block, its surface hacked with the sentences it had carried out. The wood was stained brown with blood.

Her stomach twisted at the sight of it.

Rebekah wouldn't . . .

She couldn't . . .

Beside it stood the broad-shouldered and brawny execu-tioner. Both his hands gripped the hilt of the biggest, heaviest sword Roa had ever seen.

Her blood ran cold.

Rebekah's men formed a ring around the chopping block, keeping the crowd at bay. One of her men grabbed Roa's shoul-ders, forcing her to her knees so hard, the pain made her gasp.

The rope tying her wrists bit into her skin. Her gag cut into the corners of her mouth. Roa cast her gaze over the sea of masked faces, looking for one face more than any other . . .

Where are you, Essie? I need you.

"Tonight we put a traitor on trial!" Rebekah called to the crowd, her face glowing in the firelight.

Roa—who was losing feeling in her bound hands—looked up over the buildings and the city walls. A pale waxing moon hung over the Rift mountains beyond the temple walls, and the sky was lightening in the east.

"For sabotaging the safety of our city . . ."

Roa looked away from the sky, to the torches burning in the hands of the perplexed crowd. Like beacons of light.

"For plotting the death of the king . . ."

A movement in the square caught her eye. One person shoved forward, fighting their way through a crowd that didn't know who to side with—their outlander queen, or the king's councillors.

"We find Roa of the House of Song—"

"Let her go, Rebekah."

Roa straightened, trying to see.

Just beyond the ring of men, the king himself pulled off his mask and dropped it at his feet. A storm of murmurs rose up from the crowd.

Dax, she thought, her heart twisting. *You've played right into her hands.*

The murmurs were getting louder and angrier now. At first it seemed to Roa that Dax had lost them completely by coming to his traitorous queen's defense. Except . . . no.

More and more people stepped up to the king, in order to stand *with* him. The fury of Firgaard was turned not on Dax or even Roa, but on the woman who'd dragged their queen through the square and declared her a traitor, when the king was clearly safe.

The people of Firgaard were on Dax and Roa's side.

The king was here. The tide was turning. Rebekah had lost. And yet, she didn't seem concerned.

"As you wish." Rebekah bowed her head slightly to Dax, then made her way to where Roa knelt. Roa felt the cold steel of a blade slide between her wrists as Rebekah sawed through the ropes.

Her hands came free.

Rebekah pulled Roa to her feet, then grabbed her wrist tightly, pressing the hilt of the Skyweaver's knife into her palm and wrapping Roa's fingers around it.

Roa looked up to find the girl's eyes dark and glittering and full of vengeance.

"Now's your chance to save your sister," she said. And then, to Dax: "If you want her, come and fetch her."

As the guards parted and Dax stepped through, Rebekah turned Roa toward the king and gave her a small shove. Roa stumbled, then looked up—right into the eyes of the boy she loved.

This was her plan all along, Roa realized. *For me to kill him with all of Firgaard watching.*

By ensuring there were witnesses to Roa's murder of the king, Rebekah would get everything she wanted: Dax dead and Roa dethroned.

Rebekah had won.

Because soon the sun would be up and the Relinquishing would be over. Once it was, Roa's chance to save Essie would be gone.

If Roa wanted to set her sister free, she needed to act, now, before the night was over.

Dax stepped in close, loosening her gag and pulling it down.

"I told you what I would do," she whispered, staring up at him. "Why would you come for me? Why would you walk straight into a trap?"

"Because if it wasn't for me, Essie wouldn't be gone," he said, brushing his thumb across her jaw. "And because this is destroying you." He cupped her face in his warm, strong hands. "And because I love you."

For a heartbeat, Roa saw that little boy sitting across the gods and monsters board. This was the end of their game. Roa had to make this move, and he was going to let her.

Roa's eyes burned with tears as she looked to the lightening sky, then down to the white humming blade in her hands.

"I'm ready," he said, as if seeing the thoughts in her eyes.

Roa lifted the knife.

And then a voice cut through the night.

"Where is my sister?"

Roa paused. Her heart began to hammer fast and loud in her ears.

She knew that voice.

Turning, she saw a girl step out of the crowd. She wore a sky-blue dress that came to her knees. Except for her hair—which was plaited—she seemed a mirror image of the queen.

"Essie," Dax and Roa said at the same time.

But the hum was still silent. And as Roa reached desperately for their bond, she found it gone.

Instead, there was a gaping wound. An empty void.

As if this wasn't her sister at all.

From behind the circle of Rebekah's men, Essie saw Roa. Their gazes caught. And Roa saw that her eyes were no longer dark brown, but silver.

"There you are." Essie smiled, but it wasn't her usual smile. This was something colder and hungrier. "I've been searching all night for you." Essie looked to the men separating her from Roa. "Let me pass."

They didn't. Instead, they drew their blades.

Essie's smile twisted into a snarl. She raised her hand and when she brought it down, their necks snapped like twigs. The light in their eyes went dark. They crumpled to the ground.

Corrupted.

The word bled through Roa's mind, even as she fought it.

No . . .

More men replaced them. These too went down, dropping to their knees. Their eyes went wide and their fingers clawed at their throats while Essie choked them to death without ever touching them.

When their bodies hit the ground, the silence in the square was thunderous.

Roa stared at her sister while the screams rose up, like a wave crashing from one wall to the other. The crowd pushed at one another, trying to get away from the horror standing at its center.

But this was still her sister, Roa knew. Still *Essie.* Only twisted. Poisoned. Changed.

Her spirit was corrupted.

Roa thought of the dead men beside that broken cage. Thought of what brought the House of Shade to ruin. Thought of the corrupted spirit that left no one in his family alive but his dog—a creature that didn't know how to let go.

More than all of these things, Roa thought of the last Relinquishing.

I don't want to be trapped anymore, her sister told her that night. *I want to be free.*

What if Roa had misunderstood?

What if, by not relinquishing Essie, Roa had kept her trapped, caged, unable to cross?

Now, when Essie tried to get to Roa, no one stopped her. "Did they hurt you?" That silver gaze was tender on her face.

Roa shook her head, reaching to touch her sister. Essie's cheek was warm and soft and so familiar beneath her hand, it made Roa want to weep. She pulled her sister close, holding her tight.

With the hum silent, with their bond gone, Roa couldn't sense her sister's thoughts or feelings. Which meant Essie couldn't sense hers either.

"I thought you wouldn't find me," Roa whispered, their cheeks pressed together.

"I'll always find you," Essie said.

"I thought you were gone."

Essie shook her head and pulled away, looking into Roa's eyes. "I'm here. And I won't let anything separate us again."

Roa turned to Dax. But her hand reached for her sister's, gripping it tight. With their fingers woven, Roa memorized the warmth of Essie's palm. The pulse beating in time with her own.

"I'm sorry," she said, keeping her gaze locked with the king's. "I never meant to hurt you."

Dax halted, glancing from Roa's hand—entwined with her sister's—to her face.

"I never meant to break us," she said, squeezing Essie's hand, never wanting to let go.

As the unearthly knife hummed against her skin, she thought of her sister's loud laugh and the sight of her bright smile and the comforting warmth of her spirit.

"Everything I know about love I learned from you," she whispered, her vision blurring. "You taught me that sometimes love means holding on so tight."

Her fingers tightened around the knife. A knife that loosed souls from their moorings.

With her sister at her side, Roa lifted the blade.

"And sometimes . . ."

The tears slid down her cheeks.

"Sometimes it means letting go."

Turning away from the king, Roa plunged the knife into her sister's corrupted heart.

Thirty-Six

The breath hushed out of Essie's lungs. She looked down to the hilt of the Skyweaver's knife, embedded in her chest. Her silver eyes widened. Her legs weakened.

Roa caught her before she fell, sinking down to the ground, pulling her into her arms.

The hum flared up, loud and fierce between them. The silver bled out of Essie's eyes, leaving those ebony irises. Essie held Roa's gaze, unwavering.

"I'm sorry," Roa whispered.

Essie reached to touch her sister's face. "No," she whispered back. *"Thank you."* She smiled faintly, as grateful tears shone on her cheeks. "Thank you for setting me free."

There was a sound like a sigh as Essie closed her eyes . . . and dissolved into silver-bright mist.

The mist swarmed Roa, kissing her hands, her face, her hair. And in it Roa heard her sister's laugh, light and happy and *free.*

Just for a moment, the mist fastened itself into the shape of a hawk, soaring high, circling Roa once.

And then it was gone.

Forever.

Grief clawed its way through Roa. A soul-splitting sound erupted out of her. Dax stared, not quite understanding what just happened, only hearing that it had broken Roa's heart.

He fell to his knees before her.

Dax was so concerned about Roa, he forgot the men at their backs. Forgot who'd brought them here.

Steel flashed behind him.

Roa looked up to see Rebekah gripping the executioner's sword in both hands, raising it above the king, about to deal a killing blow.

Roa let out a warning cry, but it was too late.

The sword came down.

Roa pushed Dax out of the way, putting herself in its path instead.

But someone stepped between. Steel clashed against steel. Roa looked up to find . . . Theo. Intercepting the blow.

The heir to the House of Sky drew his second blade, defending Roa and Dax.

Beyond him, more members of Sky came out of the crowd, drawing their weapons against Rebekah's men. With them came Safire, her crest of a namsara flower blazing bright, and at her back were a myriad of soldats.

A roar rumbled from above—like thunder from the sky—as a huge black dragon with wings spread wide descended. The earth shook under the weight of him, and Rebekah's men cowered beneath the gaze of his one slitted eye.

Kozu.

On the First Dragon's back sat Asha, with Torwin behind her. As one, they dismounted. The former Iskari drew her twin slayers from their sheaths at her back, her gaze deadly as Kozu snapped his needle-sharp teeth and slammed the closest of Rebekah's men into the trees with his tail. Armed with a bow, Torwin nocked an arrow just as Lirabel stepped up to his side, drawing her own. Together, they kept their aim trained on Rebekah.

As the First Dragon prowled, they all formed a protective circle around the king and queen. Beyond them, Safire's soldats and the House of Sky kept Rebekah's men at bay.

The next time Roa looked, Theo had Rebekah disarmed and was forcing her to her knees.

The commandant sheathed her weapons and came forward to where Rebekah knelt with Theo's steel at her throat. Safire crouched low, forcing the baron's daughter to meet her gaze, and though she spoke quietly, Roa heard the words she said.

"You were right, Bekah. My place will never be among you." Safire looked up to Torwin on one side, to Asha on the other, then behind her to Dax. She turned her gaze on Roa last. "My place is right here—defending the ones I love."

As Safire rose to her feet, Asha stepped up to her side, snaking a comforting arm across her cousin's shoulders.

"Take her away."

Thirty-Seven

In the weeks following Essie's passing, Roa felt like a soldier who'd come home from battle without a limb, convinced she could still sense it.

But it wasn't a limb she sensed. It was her sister. The hum had been glowing faintly inside Roa ever since she drove the Skyweaver's knife into Essie's heart. It wasn't as bright or as warm as it once was, but it was *there*. As if Roa's bond with Essie—now gone forever from this world—was still, somehow, unbroken.

She told this to Lirabel in the letters she wrote almost daily.

Her friend had returned to the scrublands weeks ago to prepare for her wedding. A celebration would take place tomorrow in the gardens of the House of Song.

Roa pushed the thought of it out of her mind, trying to focus instead on the Assembly meeting before her. Because when she thought about it, the sorrow welled up like blood from a cut. She wanted to be there, watching her brother and her oldest

friend bind themselves to each other beneath the mighty jacarandas of Song. Roa wanted to be the one braiding flowers
into Lirabel's hair and dabbing rosewater behind her ears and
helping her into her dress.

But Roa needed to be *here*, in Firgaard. Because today the
new council—one representative of the kingdom instead of
purchased by the wealthy—had gathered to vote on the ancient
law against regicide. They were here to decide whether it should
be allowed to stand or if it was time to strike it down.

The king and queen needed to be present for the vote.

The sunlight streaming through the windows turned
golden in the encroaching dusk and the round Assembly room
brimmed with spectators, making the air hot and stuffy. Roa
counted a dozen people falling asleep in their chairs or leaning
against walls. It had been a long day of arguing and debating,
and with one council member absent due to illness, the vote
kept ending in a draw.

In order to break it, the council decided to give the king a
vote.

Which was when the snoring started.

Horrified, every person in the room looked in the direction
of the sound. Roa sighed, looking too.

Dax sat hunched in his pale marble chair, the image of a
crown chiseled into the headrest. His cheek sat propped on his
fist, his brown curls tumbled into his eyes, and his chest rose
and fell with his snores.

Roa had spent enough nights in his bed now to know the
sound of his snoring by heart.

These were fake.

Dax had been a bundle of coiled energy all day. His knee hadn't stopped bouncing from the moment he sat down in that chair to the moment the vote came back a draw for the third time. In fact, if Roa looked close enough, she could see his knee bouncing now.

Something had him excited. And an excited Dax was not a sleepy Dax.

He was feigning sleep. And Roa knew why.

This new council deferred to their king, always. It was Dax's opinion they sought both in and out of Assembly meetings, never Roa's. And here they were again, looking to Dax.

But if he was asleep, he couldn't cast his vote.

"My queen?" The eldest councillor looked to Roa. She was a skral woman with long gray hair that fell loose down her back.

The queen glanced away from her snoring husband, fixing her attention on the ten men and women now awaiting her decision.

"What is your vote?"

A memory bloomed within Roa. She thought of the day of her earning. Of standing in the mist at her sister's side, gripping her blade as her sister refused her own.

"The old stories say we belong to each other." Roa spoke Essie's words from that day to the room. "If that's true, then our enemies are not our enemies, but our brothers and sisters."

She paused, looking over the crowd of skral, draksors, and

scrublanders. All of them enemies at some point, gathered together under one domed roof. There was so much work still to be done.

"Unless we treat all lives as sacred," Roa continued, thinking of Rebekah and the others, guilty of treason, awaiting their sentences in dreary dungeon cells, "even those who've done unspeakable harm . . . we will never have peace." She scanned the faces of Firgaard, all of them looking to *her*. Their queen. "So I vote to strike the law down."

The room fell into silence. For a moment, Roa braced herself for dissent. For the room to erupt in outrage.

Instead, the silence turned to whispers. The whispers to murmurs. The murmurs to quiet conversation. No one shouted. No one accused her of trying to sabotage Firgaard or the king or the throne.

The elderly councillor nodded. "Then it's done."

Roa loosened, falling back against her own marble chair as the council members turned to each other, speaking quietly together as they wrote the declaration down and signed it. Beyond them, the audience rose and began to leave. The room hummed with conversation.

When Roa noticed the snoring beside her had ceased, she turned to find Dax sitting upright, watching her.

"You are incorrigible," she said.

He smiled that charming smile of his.

Roa felt herself weaken, falling prey to him. She narrowed her eyes. "Don't look at me like that."

He leaned over her chair, propping his elbow on her

armrest. "You mean, like this?" His gaze softened, hooking into hers.

"Yes," she murmured, leaning into his warmth.

"I'm merely admiring my queen." He kissed her brow, where a gold circlet rested. "Truly, she has no equal."

That night, just before snuffing the lights, Roa walked out onto the balcony. Her nightdress brushed her knees and her bare feet padded on the cool tiles. It had rained all evening and though a fog had turned everything silver, Roa could just make out the balcony directly across the garden.

Though it was her room, she hadn't slept there since the night she saved her sister. Now, when the ache of loneliness threatened to swallow her whole, she pressed her back to Dax's and fell asleep to the beat of his heart. When she dreamed of Essie only to wake and find her gone, Dax held her while she wept.

He held her every time.

The sudden smell of peppermint engulfed Roa, bringing her out of her thoughts. She turned her head and listened.

Silence.

Roa waited, a smile creeping across her lips.

More silence.

When she could feel the warmth of him against her back, she said, "I know you're there."

The air rushed out of him in an exasperated sigh. "How do you always *know*?"

His warm arms came around her waist. Roa leaned back against him.

"I wanted to surprise you," he whispered into her neck. "My star."

Roa was about to tell him he'd have to try a lot harder, but those words stopped her.

My star.

"Why do you call me that?" She leaned back against him, touching her cheek to his stubbled one.

His arms tightened around her.

"Before the revolt, I knew what I wanted: to protect my sister, and Safire, and our people. I knew what it would take: that I would have to pit myself against my father. But every time I thought of what I must do, I doubted myself. I convinced myself I would never be strong enough or smart enough or brave enough to steal the throne from one of the most powerful dragon kings in history."

He turned his face into hers, brushing his forehead against her temple.

"It was in those times—when I felt the most lost, when I felt like giving up and letting the dream of a better world die—that I thought of you, all the way across the sand sea. I would imagine us sitting down at a gods and monsters board, and as we played, I would ask what *you* would do—and what you would want me to do—and whenever I did that, I wasn't lost anymore. I could see the path clearly." He nuzzled the spot just behind her ear, then looked to the sky again. "Like a sailor who needs the heavens to find his way home, you were my own star, burning in the night. Helping me find my way."

Roa went very still. No one had ever told her anything as beautiful as that.

She turned, reaching for him. But the moment she faced Dax, her hands paused. She frowned at the dark blue sandskarf wrapped around his throat, then reached to touch the fitted leather jacket buttoned up tight.

"Why are you dressed like this?" she asked, when she found his hands too were covered in dark leather gloves.

His gloved fingers twined through hers. "I told you," he said, pulling her through the curtains and back inside the room. "I have a surprise. Come and get dressed."

She let him pull her but glanced over her shoulder to the night sky now blocked by the curtains.

Now? She'd just changed into her nightgown.

"Why? What are—"

A loud *thud* came from above, shaking the room and interrupting her question.

Roa glanced to the ceiling. "What was that?"

Dax shrugged, grinning a little.

Someone jumped from the roof to the balcony, their boots echoing loudly on the terrace tiles. Roa eyed Dax warily, then started in the direction of the sound.

Pushing back the curtains, she found Safire leaning against the balustrade, her legs crossed, her hands gripping the marble edge. The commandant wore a black jacket and gloves and her dark hair was pulled back.

"Roa," Safire looked her nightgown up and down, clearly disappointed by something. "You're not dressed."

A cool shadow slid over Roa. She looked up to find Kozu's onyx head staring down at her, jaws closed tight, one slitted yellow eye fixed on both of hers. Beside the First Dragon, at the roof's edge, crouched Asha—her hair bound in its usual braid and her face half hidden by a sandskarf. Her black eyes peered down at Roa.

"Seriously, Dax?" Asha called at the sight of Roa's night-gown. "We gave you one task!"

"What's going on?" Roa asked them.

"I was supposed to make sure you were dressed when they got here," said Dax stepping out, holding clothes all folded neatly in a pile: jacket, gloves, wool leggings, boots, and one of Roa's sandskarves. A faded yellow one. "If you put these on, we'll tell you everything."

Roa stuck out her chin in defiance. "Tell me everything and I'll *think about* getting dressed."

Suddenly, a second serpentine face looked down over the roof, startling Roa. It was the golden dragon Dax had escaped on, the morning of the Relinquishing. Smaller and more elegant than Kozu, its scales rippled in the misty starlight.

It clicked at Roa.

Roa stepped carefully back. Right into Dax.

"Don't be scared," he said, his arm hooking around her waist.

"Don't be scared?" she whispered. "Of the dragon staring at me like I'm its next meal?"

He shook his head. "She's gentle. And I'll be flying with you."

Roa tensed. *Flying with me?*

She stepped away from the king, looking from him to Safire to Asha above.

"*This* was your surprise?"

Dax, who was pulling his sandskarf up over his nose and mouth, stopped and tugged it down. "Don't you want to see Lirabel get married?"

Roa's mouth opened. Then shut.

"*That*," said Safire, "was the surprise."

"Oh," Roa whispered. As the realization sank in, a slow smile spread across her lips. Her heart glowed within her. She looked to Dax, who was watching her with a tender expression. Flinging her arms around him, she kissed him hard on the mouth.

"There's no time for that!" cried Asha from the roof.

"Thank you," Roa whispered, kissing Dax once more before grabbing the clothes, ducking inside, and getting dressed.

By the time she reemerged, Asha and Saf were both seated atop Kozu on the roof. Dax and the golden dragon stood waiting on the terrace.

"This is Spark," he said.

Spark stared at Roa with pale slitted eyes. She smelled like smoke and sand. Stepping closer, Roa realized she had no idea how to mount a dragon.

Seeing it, Dax got down on one knee and cupped his hands for her to step into. The moment she did, he pushed her up, telling her where to step—on the back of Spark's knee. And where to grab hold—the bump of his shoulder bone. It took several tries, but Spark remained stoically still and eventually Roa pulled herself up.

Dax lifted himself easily behind her. As if all those days he'd gone missing in the afternoons, this was what he'd really been doing. When his arm came around her, he looked up to Asha and Safire, mounted atop Kozu.

"Ready?"

Before Roa could respond, Spark crouched low, spread her golden wings, and leaped into the sky.

They flew through the night. Roa fell asleep curled up inside Dax's jacket, and when she woke, the highlands were rising out of the horizon. Roa could just make out the lights of Song in the distance. Lanterns and candles and heart-fires were being lit. The day was breaking. And though the sky was lightening in the east, the stars were still bright in the sky.

Roa looked up. Shining directly above them was a star she'd never seen before. One that burned a little more brightly than the rest.

Roa tipped her head back against Dax's shoulder, watching it.

Kozu flew beside them. Roa could hear the muffled sound of Asha laughing at something Safire said. And at some point in the night, they'd been joined by another dragon. The rider's sandskarf masked his face, but from his tall thin form, Roa knew it was Torwin.

Spark propelled them closer and closer to the House of Song. The fields rolled beneath them. And all the while, the hum glowed warmly within Roa. Telling her Essie was near. That the bond they shared would always be there, whether Essie was physically present or not. Whether Essie was alive or not.

Because it was just like Dax said. Love withstands all things. Even death.

Especially death.

Acknowledgments

So much love and gratitude to:

Heather Flaherty, for always having my back.

Kristen Pettit, for taking the flailing mess that was this book and corralling it into something *better*.

Rachel Winterbottom, for loving this story even when it was a hot mess and helping me fix it at the eleventh hour (or rather, multiple eleventh hours!).

Everyone at HarperTeen, especially Elizabeth Lynch, Renée Cafiero, Allison Brown, Michelle Taormina, Audrey Diestelkamp, Bess Braswell, Olivia Russo, Martha Schwartz, and Vincent Cusenza.

Gemma Cooper, without whom I never would have found my way to Gollancz.

Everyone at Gollancz, for your enthusiastic support and making me feel so at home across the pond. Most especially: Stevie Finegan, the most delightful bookshop crawl buddy; Paul Stark, for making an audiobook that (as my mother likes to say) is "even better than the book-book"; Cait Davies, for marketing my books like whoa (and being my go-to guide for all things London!); and Gillian Redfearn, for being a generous, brilliant badass.

The team at HarperCollins Canada for all the work you do this side of the border, especially Ashley Posluns, Shamin Alli, and Maeve O'Regan!

Myrthe Spiteri, for your wisdom and support.

My foreign agents, publishers, translators: I'm so grateful for all of you. Seeing my stories in languages other than my own is real-world magic.

Jenny Bent and the Bent Agency team, for the tremendous work you do on my behalf so I can focus on what I love most: getting the words written.

The librarians and booksellers I've met along the way, for your kindness, enthusiasm, and support.

Anna Priemaza, Faith Boughan, Gareth Wronski: for debut year (Canuck) solidarity. Isabel Ibanez Davis, for keeping me accountable when I needed to just get the darn thing written. Tomi Adeyemi, for your spot-on feedback and grounding voice of reason. Chris Cabena, for telling me the book was broken so I could make it better. Boyce Roberts, Cheryl McCarron, and Wayne Bartlett: for taking in a lost author and helping her find her joy again.

Every single one of my family and friends: for filling two hundred seats at my book launch. For dressing up as my characters on Halloween (Aunt Mary, I love you). For buying my books, pushing them on your acquaintances, and turning them face out on the shelves (my apologies to booksellers every-where). I wouldn't want to do this without you all!

Mum, for your selfless love and shining example. Dad and Jolene, for your constant support.

Joe, for being there through all of it—my good, happy, hopeful days and my bad, crazy, sad days—and for being my coadventurer in this wild and beautiful life.

Pa, for showing me there's a time to hold on and a time to let go, and that letting go doesn't mean love ends. Your life and death taught me that love always triumphs.

My readers and fans, for your overwhelming support, stunning bookstagram photos, kind and encouraging messages, reviews, fan art, all of it. Thank you from the depths of my heart.

And for those of you who need to hear it: Real love isn't just stronger than death. Real love transforms the living; it transforms the world. Never forget who you are and the kind of love you're capable of—death-defying, world-altering love.

Turn the page for a sneak peek

at the final novel in the Iskari series

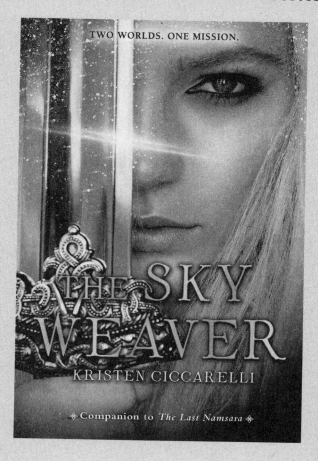

TWO WORLDS. ONE MISSION.

THE SKY WEAVER

KRISTEN CICCARELLI

◆ Companion to *The Last Namsara* ◆

Eighteen Years Previous

Skye was only a child the first time she watched them put a traitor on trial. She saw them take the man's hands. Saw the blood run swift and dark over the stone altar as the soldier wiped his blade clean, like a storm sweeping over a sapphire sea.

Skye remembers the way the severed hands twitched like crushed spiders dying on their backs, thin legs curling inward. Remembers the way the enemy stared at the stumps of his arms as the blood ran down to his elbows.

Remembers how he screamed.

That was a lifetime ago. Tonight, they'll put another traitor on trial. Skye is waiting in her cell. Because it won't be an enemy's hands they take this time—it will be Skye's hands. And she has only herself to blame.

Be a good girl. Keep your head down. Remember your place.

These were the words she lived by once. The lessons instilled in her since birth.

That was before she met Crow. A boy from the shadows undid all her lessons. He undid everything.

Crow. Like a swallowed thorn, the name stings her lips and tongue and throat.

How could she be so naïve?

Skye will tell you how. She will weave you a tapestry while there's still time. It will be her last weaving. Because once the moon rises and they come for her, Skye will weave no more.

You can't weave without hands.

One

Eris had never met a lock she couldn't pick.

Lifting the oil lamp, she peered into the keyhole, her wheat-gold hair hidden beneath a stolen morion. Its steel brim kept slipping forward, impeding her vision, and Eris had to shove it back in order to see what she was doing.

The wards inside the lock were old, and from the look of them, made by a locksmith who had cut all possible corners. Any other night, Eris would have craved the challenge of a more complicated lock. Tonight, though, she thanked the stars. Any heartbeat now, a soldat would round the corner. When they did, Eris needed to be on the *other* side of this door.

The lock clicked open. Eris didn't let out her breath. Just slid her pin back into her hair, rose to her feet, and wrapped her slender fingers around the brass knob, turning slowly so as not to make a sound.

She glanced back over her shoulder. The hall lay empty. So Eris pushed open the door and stepped inside.

Holding up the lamp, its orange glow alighted on a simple desk made of dark, scuffed wood. An inkwell, a stack of white parchment, and a knife for breaking wax seals were neatly arranged on top.

Eris shut the door gently behind her. Her gaze lifted from the desk to the object hanging on the wall: a tapestry woven of blue and purple threads. The very thing she'd come for.

Eris knew this tapestry by heart. It depicted a faceless woman sitting at her loom. In one hand, she held a silver knife curved like the moon. In the other, she held a spindle. And on her head sat a crown of stars.

Skyweaver.

The god of souls.

But it wasn't just the image that was familiar. It was the threads themselves—the particular shade of blue. The thickness of the wool and how tightly it was spun. The signature way it was woven.

The moment Eris glimpsed it from the hall two days ago, she nearly stumbled. Every morning for years, this tapestry stared down at her from stone walls flanked on either side by the sacred looms of the scrin—a temple devoted to the Skyweaver.

What was it doing here, in the dragon king's palace, all the way across the sea?

Someone must have stolen it, she thought.

So Eris decided to steal it back.

She had the time, after all. Her captain—a heartless man named Jemsin—was currently meeting with the empress of the Star Isles. It was why he sent Eris here, to steal a jewel from the dragon king's treasury. Not because he needed the money. No. He needed Eris out of sight while the empress and her Hounds came aboard his ship—for his sake as much as hers. If it was ever found out that Jemsin harbored the very criminal the empress had been hunting these seven long years, it would mean death for both Eris and her captain.

But Eris had already stolen the king's jewel. And since Jemsin hadn't summoned her back, she had time to waste.

So here she was, wasting it.

Eris pushed herself away from the closed door and set the oil lamp down on the dark wood of the desk. The moment her gaze lifted to Skyweaver, there was that sharp shock she'd felt two days ago. Memories of warmth, friendship, and belonging flooded her . . . quickly followed by feelings of terror, grief, and betrayal.

She narrowed her eyes.

"I'm not doing this for you," she told the god as she reached to untie the tapestry from where it hung on the wall. "As far as I'm concerned, you're a traitor and a fraud." She kept her voice low, knowing the security had been doubled since the king's jewel went missing two nights ago. "I'm doing this for the ones you betrayed."

Eris no longer believed in Skyweaver, god of souls. But the one who'd woven this tapestry believed in her—and he'd died for that belief. So, lifting it down from the wall, Eris rolled it up tight, then tucked it carefully under her arm. As she did, she plucked the gray, spiny scarp thistle from the pocket of her stolen uniform. Careful not to prick herself on its thorns—which were poisonous—she set it down on the desk.

In some ways, the signature was more for Eris than the ones she stole from. A way of proving to herself that she did, in fact, exist. She might live an invisible life, but she was still *here*.

Still alive.

The scarp thistle was proof.

With the tapestry still under her arm, and her signature there on the commandant's desk, Eris reached for her spindle. It was time to go. She would take this tapestry and put it with the rest of her loot. Then she'd head for the *Sea Mistress* and wait for her summons.

But before she could pull the spindle free of its pouch, a voice behind her broke the quiet.

"Who let you in here?"

The voice was low and gruff and it made Eris freeze—except for her right hand. Her fingers tightened around the smooth, worn wood of her spindle, slowly drawing it out.

"I asked a simple question, soldier."

Soldier.

Eris had forgotten she was in disguise tonight. With the heightened security, it was easier moving through the palace dressed like a guard.

So Eris turned. A soldat stood in the doorway. He hadn't quite stepped into the room, clearly startled by the sight of her, but he wore the same uniform she did: a steel morion on his head and the dragon king's crest across his shirt. The only difference was that a saber hung from his hip, while a woven pouch hung from hers.

Eris hated soldiers.

"I was sent to remove this ratty old thing," she lied, nodding her chin toward the tapestry of the god of souls, rolled up beneath her arm. She winked as she said, "Apparently our commandant isn't exactly the pious type."

Her wink had the desired effect. The soldat relaxed. He smiled then, leaning against the door, seemingly about to remark on the commandant's piety or lack thereof, when something on the desk caught his eye.

Eris's watched his face go blank, then alight with realization. Looking where he looked, she silently cursed herself.

The scarp thistle.

"You . . . you're the Death Dancer."

He didn't wait for her to confirm it. Just drew his weapon.

Eris gripped the spindle hard in her hand as she crouched down. As the soldat stumbled into the room, she pressed the spindle's edge to the mosaicked floor and drew a straight line.

The line glowed silver. The mist rose.

The soldat lurched toward her, calling for help and alerting the other soldats nearby.

But by the time he rounded the desk, Eris was already stepping into the mist, and beyond it.

By the time he reached for her, Eris was already gone.

When the mists receded heartbeats later, Eris was not where she should be.

Instead of being *Across*—surrounded by stars and darkness— she was surrounded by walls. A dark hallway spread before her, lit every few paces by flickering torchlight. Beneath her feet lay that same mosaicked pattern as the room she'd just left. And it smelled like mint and lime.

She was still in the palace.

Eris gritted her teeth in annoyance.

It happened sometimes. If she was concentrating harder on the place she was trying to leave rather than the place she was trying to get to, the spindle would get confused and blunder up the crossing.

Eris was just about to curse the godsforsaken splinter of wood when something slammed into her from behind, hurtling her forward and causing her to drop the spindle altogether.

"Kozu's balls!" She spun, watching the spindle roll toward two black leather boots with silver buckles polished to a shine. A hand reached down, picking it up, and as the newcomer rose, so did Eris's gaze.

The young woman before her was dressed like a palace guard. Only instead of the king's crest, a flame-like flower blazed across her shirt. She wore no morion, and tucked into her belt were five throwing knives.

"Apologies, soldier." The young woman's voice was hard and commanding. The voice of someone used to giving orders—and used to her orders being obeyed. "I didn't see you there."

Eris's gaze snapped to eyes as cold and blue as sapphires. The torchlight made it impossible not to notice the girl's strong cheekbones or ink-black hair braided away from her face.

Eris knew who this was.

The commandant.

This young woman before her was not only cousin to the king—and therefore royalty—she held that same king's army in her fist.

A dark memory flickered in Eris's mind, of another cold commander. Fear pooled in her belly. She shook the memory off, stepping back. But the sharp sliver of it lodged in her chest, reminding Eris of who she was. That she needed to leave this place.

Now.

Except her spindle was currently in the commandant's hand.

The young woman's gaze moved over Eris quickly and dismissively. It made Eris stiffen. She should have been glad the commandant found nothing of interest in the girl standing before her. Eris wanted—no, *needed*—to be invisible.

For some reason, though, that indifferent glance rankled Eris.

The commandant's lips parted, as if she were about to say something, when a shout echoed from down the hall, interrupting. Making them both turn.

More and more voices joined the first. The soldat Eris had just left was alerting the entire palace to the thief in their midst.

It was an alarm.

Eris waited for the truth to dawn on the commandant's face the way it had with the soldat. But the commandant was no longer looking at Eris, only frowning in the direction of the alarm.

"That Death Dancer." Her eyes were sharp with ire. "If he thinks he can steal from the king without consequence, he has no idea who he's dealing with."

Eris should have kept her mouth shut. This commandant had her spindle, after all. Her only escape.

But Eris couldn't help herself.

"How do you know it's a *he*?"

The commandant looked straight at her then. Eris shivered under that cold gaze. *Stupid,* she thought, even as she stared into the girl's eyes. *What a stupid thing to say.*

The commandant studied her as the alarm grew louder in the distance. On her face Eris could clearly see the need to respond to the alarm warring with . . . what? Wariness? Suspicion?

Any moment now, she's going to figure it out, draw her weapon, and arrest me.

But the commandant did none of those things. Instead, she held out the spindle, her eyes seeing Eris now, taking all of her in. "You dropped this," she said.

Eris swallowed, staring at the elegantly carved spindle lying on that callused palm.

Is this a trick?

When Eris reached to take it, though, the commandant's hand fell away. She turned on her heel, as if Eris was already forgotten. "Now let's see what that cocky bastard has done this time. . . ."

Eris crouched down to draw a silver line across the floor.

Cocky? she thought.

It felt like a challenge.

She shook her head. She couldn't let herself get distracted

this time. She needed to pour all of her focus into her destination.

As Eris finished drawing the line, the air grew thick and damp. The mist billowed up. But the sound of those diminishing footsteps drew her attention back. Eris paused, watching the commandant turn the corner. Watching her disappear from view.

Eris rose to her feet. Before putting Firgaard and the palace and that girl out of her mind, she thought: *I'll show her just how cocky I can be.*

And then she stepped across.

Two

Ever since the door to the king's treasury was found open and a bright red ruby missing, Safire hadn't been able to sleep.

Someone had walked the halls of *her* palace, slipped past every single one of *her* guards, entered a locked door, and stolen the very ruby King Dax intended to give the scrublands tomorrow. One that would be sold and the profits divided to help remedy the starvation caused by the blight—one known as the White Harvest. Years ago, it had spread like wildfire through the scrublands, destroying all their crops, cutting off their main sources of food. Every season, farmers would try again, but the blight would only infect the new harvests, driving them further and further to the brink of starvation.

Safire knew things were getting worse, but it wasn't until Queen Roa returned from her last visit home that Safire realized how dire the situation really was. Roa's father was now bedridden. Unbeknownst to her family, he'd been going without food for some time now, so that those less fortunate than him could eat. But it wasn't only Roa's father who was at risk of starvation—her best friend, Lirabel, was also chronically malnourished due to her pregnancy. The physician told Roa if they couldn't get access to substantially more food, and quickly, Lirabel would lose the baby.

When Roa returned to Firgaard, even Safire had seen the change in her. She looked exhausted and frail. At meals, Dax cast worried glances her way whenever she refused to eat— because how could she, when her loved ones were starving to death?

They needed a permanent solution, and quickly.

Dax planned to sell the ruby in the royal treasury—a jewel that once belonged to their great-grandmother—and use the profits to buy meat and vegetables and grain to supplement the weekly rations Firgaard was already sending, in hopes of keeping starvation at bay.

The fact that someone had stolen the jewel without a second thought? It was intolerable. Unforgivable.

It made Safire tremble with fury.

There was one clue left behind: an ugly gray thistle.

Safire had never seen anything like it, with its stem littered with thorns, some as long as her smallest finger and nearly half as thick. So she showed it to the palace physician.

A scarp thistle, he told her. *It grows on the scarps of the Star Isles. A single thorn carries enough poison to make a person sleep for days.*

More than both of these things, though, it was the mark of a criminal. A thief known as the Death Dancer because he walked through walls, was uncatchable, and constantly eluded death. He'd been haunting the halls (and treasuries) of barons and kings for years.

Well, thought Safire that day, *he won't elude me.*

So she'd doubled the guards and started patrolling the palace herself.

Now, two days later, she stood staring down at a *second* scarp thistle. Only this one lay on her own desk, behind her own locked door.

As the soldats in the room around her whispered to themselves, all of them watching their commandant, Safire's eyes lifted to the wall beyond it.

This morning, a tapestry hung on that wall. It had been a gift from Asha, her cousin. The tapestry was gone now. The plaster wall stripped bare.

The thistle on her desk told her the thief had taken it.

Why?

Safire's eyes narrowed. She understood the king's ruby. It was worth more money than most people saw in a lifetime. But a ratty old tapestry? What could possibly be the value in that?

Unless, thought Safire, *he's trying to taunt me.*

And then, suddenly, that young soldat's lilting voice rang through her mind.

How do you know it's a he?

Safire's stomach twisted.

She'd been in such a hurry, she'd thought nothing of the girl's morion—which, now that she was thinking about it, was far too big for her and shielded half her face.

But there were other things, too.

The soldat carried no weapon, and she spoke with an unfamiliar accent. Safire had never heard a lilting voice quite like hers. It was almost . . . lyrical.

Not to mention that rolled-up bundle tucked beneath her arm.

Safire froze, thinking back to that bundle. The old, fraying threads. The considerable size.

It was a tapestry.

Her tapestry.

The one Asha had given her.

Safire sank down in her chair. "That thieving bastard."

Safire tripled the guards. She stopped leaving the palace and remained on patrol through the night. The next day, despite her vigilance, the king's seal went missing from Safire's drawer. The day after that, Safire left her rooms only to return and find every single one of her uniforms gone. And in their place? Scarp thistles.

It was enough to make a person lose her mind.

Safire now had a small collection of the gray thistles sitting in a glass jar on the windowsill of her bedroom. When she was feeling particularly broody, she would lock herself in and glare at them for hours, trying to think of a solution to this infuriating problem.

"I don't think she's a threat," said Asha as she picked out a rock lodged in Kozu's claw. The First Dragon stood over her like a shadow while Safire lay in the warm grass beside them, staring up at the indigo sky.

Where they sat, the former hunting paths ended in a scrubby field surrounded by forest. To the north, a huge round tent was pitched, and between them and the tent several dragons prowled, all of them being trained by hopeful riders. Safire could hear he clicked commands from where she stood.

These were the dragon fields. Asha hoped to build a school here—one that would simultaneously preserve the old stories while repairing the damaged relationship between draksors and dragons.

"A thief who can walk through the palace halls completely undetected doesn't sound like a threat to you?" Safire asked, her hands cradling her head.

Asha set Kozu's foot down, thought about it, then shook her head. "This one doesn't."

Safire sat up and crossed her legs. "Please explain."

Kozu—an enormous black dragon with a scar through one eye—nudged Asha's hip with his snout, as if to tell her something. But whatever passed between them was a mystery to Safire.

"She sounds . . . bored," said Asha, rubbing the First Dragon's scaly neck. "Like she's tired of being the cleverest person in the room. What if she's *provoking* you—because she needs a challenge?"

Safire frowned at this. "Do you think I should give her one?"

Asha left Kozu and came to sit in the grass. Her black gaze held Safire's. "*Can* you? Right now she seems three steps ahead of you."

Safire bristled at this.

Seeing it, Asha leaned forward. "All you need is to get *one* step ahead."

Propping her elbow on her knee, Safire rested her chin on her fist. "And how do you propose I do that?"

In the rising heat, Asha began undoing the brass buttons of her scarlet flight jacket. Dax had it sewn especially for Asha, to mark her as his Namsara. As Asha shrugged it off, the buttons flashed in the sun and Safire leaned in, squinting, to find that each brass orb was impressed with the image of a flame-like seven-petaled flower—the namsara, Asha's namesake.

"These are the things you know about her," Asha said, laying her new jacket down beside her, then ticking fingers off her burned hand as she spoke. "She's brash—there's no room in the palace she won't break into. She steals things that have monetary value—the ruby, Dax's seal. And she steals things that are valuable only to *you*—like the tapestry I gave you and your uniforms."

Asha leaned back, planting her palms on the red-brown earth beneath her. "So," she said thoughtfully, looking out over the dragon fields, "what is the brashest, most valuable thing she could possibly steal from the king's commandant?"

They both fell silent, thinking.

Safire didn't have any valuables—other than maybe her throwing knives, which were a gift from Asha. She might have royal blood running through her veins, but there had been nothing royal about her upbringing. Safire didn't like to think about the time before the revolt, when she was kept out of sight, forbidden to touch or even stand near her cousins, taunted and abused while the palace staff looked the other way.

Just as she was shaking off the memories, a sound issued from across the field.

It was a series of quiet, nervous clicks familiar to both Safire and Asha, who looked up. Across the grassy plain, away from the commotion of the dragons and their riders, a tall, thin boy with coppery hair and freckled skin made his way toward them. *Torwin.*

Several paces behind Torwin walked an ivory-scaled dragon with one broken horn. He stepped warily, casting his gaze ahead and behind, looking like he would bolt at the slightest irregular movement. Safire knew this dragon. His name was Sorrow.

Several weeks ago, while Asha and Torwin were collecting old stories in Firefall—a city west of Darmoor—they'd found this half-starved creature chained in the courtyard of a wealthy home, with an iron muzzle locked around his jaws. He'd been severely abused by the children of the house, who were keeping him as a pet.

As a result, Sorrow let very few people get close. He stayed deep in the Rift mountains and never came near the city. Asha didn't think he'd ever pair with a rider, because he was so mistrustful of humans. A few had tried, but the bond that normally formed in first flight never took.

As Torwin stepped toward the two cousins, then sat down in the dirt next to them, Sorrow crept toward Kozu, whose hulking black form was curled in the sun, soaking up the warmth. Sorrow's ivory scales were a sharp contrast to Kozu's obsidian.

"Everything's packed," said Torwin. He held a large knife in his hands, its silver sheath embossed with intricate star patterns. "If we leave at dawn, we should arrive before sundown."

Despite having just returned from Firefall, Asha and Torwin were flying to the Star Isles tomorrow. The reason for their trip was currently gripped in Torwin's hands: the Skyweaver's knife.

The weapon had saved Roa's sister a few weeks previous, and Roa now wanted it returned to where it came from. She believed it was too dangerous an artifact to keep here in Firgaard. So Asha and Torwin had gone through the accounts of the last man who'd bought it—one of Firgaard's wealthiest barons—and tracked down its history to a place called the scrin.

"If Roa wasn't so insistent, I'd drop this thing to the bottom of the sea and be done with it," said Torwin, sliding the blade out of the sheath just enough to reveal the silver-blue blade concealed within. He shivered. Looking up, he squinted through the sunlight. "Are you sure you don't want to come with us, Safire?"

"Come? To an archipelago known for its monsters, tempests, and ship wreckers?" Safire wrinkled her nose, thinking of the treacherous waters of the Silver Sea. "I think I'll pass. Besides, Roa and Dax will be joining you in a few days."

The empress of the Isles—a fearsome woman named Leandra who was rumored to be deathless—wanted to present the new dragon king and queen with a gift. One that Leandra hoped would help the dire situation in the scrublands. As Dax's Namsara, Asha had been invited to the empress's citadel, too, but she'd turned down the invitation.

I don't have the time or the interest in rubbing shoulders with foreign monarchs, Asha told Safire when the invite came. *That's Dax's role.*

"Someone has to be the responsible one," Safire said. "Someone has to stay behind to ensure this city doesn't fall apart."

Those were her official reasons for remaining in the capital. But as she spoke them, she thought of the criminal prowling through the palace like it was her own personal playground.

Safire would never leave Firgaard at the Death Dancer's mercy.

Torwin, as if sensing her thoughts, said, "Caught that thief of yours yet?"

Sighing, Safire fell back into the grass. "No."

That was why she was here on the dragon fields. The king's commandant was running from her own failure. She'd hoped to have the Death Dancer locked in a cell by now. Instead, the criminal continued to elude her.

Sometimes she felt a . . . presence. In the middle of the day or the night. In the palace or in the street. Watching her. Trailing her. But when she turned, knife in hand, all she found was shadows. Sometimes, when she entered a room, she couldn't shake the sense that her thief had been there just a heartbeat before. It felt as though they were playing a game of cat and mouse.

Only Safire wasn't sure who was the cat and who was the mouse.

She needed to catch this Death Dancer. She wanted to see the look in her eyes when Safire locked her up for good.